INTERNATIONAL
ACCLAIM

ONE PIANO—EIGHT HANDS

|——————•|

A NOVEL IN FIVE MOVEMENTS

MICHAEL LAWSON

Also by Michael Lawson

Books

Sex & That (Lion)
Facing Anxiety & Stress (Hodder & Stoughton)
Facing Depression (Hodder & Stoughton)
Facing Conflict (Hodder & Stoughton)
Cautionary Tales (Marshall Pickering)
The Unfolding Kingdom (Kingsway)
Living by God's Masterplan (Christian Focus)
Reforming the Denomination (Orthos)
D is for Depression (Christian Focus)
Conflict (Christian Focus)
Dealing with Conflict (23rd Publications, USA)
Healing Life's Hurts (23rd Publications, USA)
Grandpa Goes to Pixie Land (Amazon)
The Relationship Guide (Amazon)

Documentary films

Mozambique's AIDS Orphans (ALMA)
India's Broken People (PVT)
India's Hidden Slavery (PVT)
India's New Beginnings (PVT)
India's Forgotten Women (PVT)
The Other India (PVT)
I Forgotten Children (Amazon Prime)
India's Untouchables (Vision Video)

Documentaries from Pipe Village Trust (PVT) Vision Video and
ALMA are available on DVD, YouTube, Vimeo, and at
www.michaellawson.info

International Acclaim

Copyright © Michael Lawson 2021

Published by Amazon (fifth edition) 2022

TABLE OF CONTENTS

1ST MOVEMENT

2ND MOVEMENT

3RD MOVEMENT

4TH MOVEMENT

5TH MOVEMENT

1ˢᵀ MOVEMENT

1

DANIYAL STEINFELD waited impatiently at passport control. Repeatedly checking his watch, his neck craned like a periscope, he scanned the hall for anyone who might listen to his complaint. Pacing back and forth as a caged animal protests its captivity, with furrowed brow and shifty eyes, Daniyal muttered his frustrated protest.

No-one heard.

Suddenly, the six-foot-two lumbering juggernaut screeches to a halt. Standing fast, Daniyal looks back and contemptuously inspects the queue. Nothing to report. Periscope down; he snorts—loudly.

The cycle repeats.

The man's irritation is evident, even from a distance. Two little children point their fingers in his direction; the parents tell them to shush.

"I've told you, pointing's rude. It's past your bedtime, so calm down." But as the pacing continues, others waiting in line also begin to stare.

Before landing, Daniyal had enjoyed a few drinks, which as alcohol often did for him, raised his irritation threshold. But when the children pointed, Daniyal welcomed the attention. "No problem!"

The theatrics were, of course, a tactic. Daniyal wasn't captive. But he was increasingly annoyed with the passport official and the man's reluctance to stamp his passport "to permit the bearer to pass freely, without let or hindrance."

No doubt, the official was tired. As the hour was late, everyone was. Nonetheless, Daniyal, being Daniyal, had hoped for a more admiring greeting after his long flight. The polite but toffish way in which he had doffed his hat and offered his posh "Good evening" had not impressed anyone. The official eyed Daniyal up and down (he'd seen his sort before) and quickly returned to his papers.

Daniyal should have known better. Class may impress the Brits. But Yanks, especially border officials, aren't as easily influenced.

Yet despite the cold formality, Daniyal had not expected any delay for his passport to be stamped. The frustration was genuine.

"It will soon be midnight," Daniyal complained to no one in particular. "You'd think they'd try and move us on." But of more concern was how the official was treating the pages of his passport like his favourite novel. He appeared to savour every detail, checking the arrival and departure stamps, scrutinising the end page, and comparing the photo with whatever was on his green screen.

Daniyal tried snorting again. After all, he had been first off the plane. America was supposed to be in the vanguard for processing arrivals. All those computers, wired for speed!

Daniyal could, of course, manage without the official's deference. Even without VIP treatment, he would at least have expected a swift and cheery wave through. "Welcome to the United States, Mr. Steinfeld. Have a nice day."

"Well, thank you, sir," he'd reply. But now with all this, would it be that nice? Great chance! Not just because he hadn't left him much of the day. More to the point, the issue wasn't even personal. (Even though following the cabin incident, Daniyal was still grumpy.) The main frustration was protocol. Since the war, especially with the new culture of suspicion fostered by the infamous Senator from Wisconsin, times had changed. Unfortunately, at the border, apart from the privileges accorded to the diplomatic corps, fast-track immigration was a fading memory and certainly well beyond the scope of the "special relationship."

The world had changed. Wherever Daniyal travelled, he found this hard to accept. Neither leapfrogging, tipping, nor even special pleading cut it anymore. If you happened to be from an upper caste, the occasional baksheesh may still work in Bombay or Delhi. But anywhere else? It's unlikely, especially in any cities with concert halls large enough to accommodate Daniyal's adoring crowds.

Coming to the US, where the major halls were as prestigious as London, Berlin and Vienna, Daniyal loved the people, their accents, their expansive ways, their food and of course, their orchestras. But as he was discovering again, however posh-sounding and well turned out; however famous and deserving of deference; these days, like any world travellers, the days of privilege are long gone. Arriving Brits are bundled together in a pen, funnelled through roped off tributaries, and drip by drip fed into line.

"Like cattle, awaiting slaughter," Daniyal mused.

After the pampered comfort of first-class, the shock did bear some resemblance to a chilly shower. Daniyal's feelings, though inflated, were understandable. As the climax to their journey, I have not met anyone with a passport and landing card in hand who enjoys the ubiquitous, slow-moving line. But a few hours later, as Daniyal urbanely told his wife in his usual, "arrived safely darling" transatlantic call: "One recognises the necessity, doesn't one? I mean, my dear, who would have it otherwise? What would happen if they weren't vigilant? Think of it. Every cold war spy, every criminal and communist, every underworld Tom, Dick or Harry, they'd be welcomed by the drove—as though they were the special relationship incarnate! No wonder McCarthy made all that fuss."

Sweet reason. Or was it? I will mention the obvious. Daniyal Steinfeld wasn't a spy, criminal or communist. Neither could he be described as a generic Tom, Dick or Harry. Far from it. But in practice, his reason wasn't quite as sweet as he expressed in those calls home to Mariah, his wife. Daniyal believed, perhaps not that secretly, that he deserved special treatment, and not just from Immigration Control. Since childhood and his early years of astonishing international artistic success, the adulation that came with it bequeathed him an unquenchable desire for attention and entitlement.

In certain respects, the approbation was well justified. You will remember, I'm sure, that as a child, Daniyal Steinfeld had been what the Germans call a *wunderkind*, the Chinese, 神童-*Shéntóng*, and most of the world, in some recognisably similar etymology, calls a *prodigy*.

Daniyal had indeed been a child prodigy of astonishing virtuosity and musicianship. Like his older contemporary, Rachmaninoff, he had large hands with long fingers. By his mid-teens, he could span an octave and a half—from middle C to high G.

Daniyal's unusual hand stretch certainly attracted medical speculation. As with Rachmaninoff, some suggested Marfan's Syndrome (which was possible) and even Acromegaly (which was less plausible as among other things it usually occurs later in life.) Conjecture aside, what can be said with certainty is both pianists simply had large hands! That in whatever way they became such, for both virtuosos, the long stretch, the chordal spread, and the speed with which they could change position in complex passagework at least contributed to their legendary technical wizardry.

2

Everyone loves a prodigy. Or at least many do. When a child is found to have exceptional gifts—say, in mental arithmetic, dance, song, sport, an instrument, or any expertise generally reserved for high functioning adults, the fascination of the freak show, laced with superstition, mystery and magic still intrigues. Such children become objects of amazement. We point our fingers, catch each other's eye, and stare with wonder.

When a precocious, yet fully formed, boy pianist such as Daniyal touches our hearts with the beauty of his art; when the intensity of his passion releases our emotions and reveals meaning and truth beyond the normal reach of this world—isn't something akin to worship kindled deep within us? Do we not feel like crying out, "Behold! Mystery and marvel!"

By the time he had reached his teenage years, Daniyal had trawled a huge worldwide catch of adoring fans. Like a drunken crowd, intoxicated with wonder, they lifted him high above all others and, on their shoulders, carried him to their pantheon. There, they placed him on the pedestal of fame and crowned him with the kind of adoration uniquely reserved for their greatest and most adored.

Not that Daniyal consciously sought attention. Not at first. There's a photo of him, a graceful yet shy thirteen-year-old, blushing with modesty as an audience garlanded him with flowers and other expressions of enthusiasm. Even those critics who were more accustomed to venom than to celebration succeeded in penning their praise, and for many seasons continued to spread the love.

Daniyal described the longer-term effect. "No carefree years for me. They placed me firmly in the fast lane and crowned me king before I could ever be Prince Charming. All because I had learnt to run before I could walk."

As I wrote in an article for The New Psychological Review: *"Can a child ever receive too much love? It has long been observed that in early life, emotional deprivation contributes to later life instability. But what of the reverse, where there is too much love rather than too little? We are now discovering that when the growing ego is exposed to sustained exaggerations of esteem from parents or any circle of admiring approval, the effect long-term can inhibit the growth of a healthy and robust, self-critical super-ego. In popular language, the over-loved 'spoilt child' takes his addiction to esteem unchallenged into adult life. There he continues his quest for the holy grail: the 'love' which recognises his ego superiority, the magnetic allure of inauthentic entitlement."*

Not until several years later did I broach with Daniyal the question of whether the wunderkind does or indeed can ever grow up into mature and unneurotic adulthood. For now, let me say in my long career, in their later lives, I have known (and treated) many prodigies, including Daniyal. We had been friends for a good long time before we ever discussed his depression—which was only partly linked to his prodigious early beginnings. Nonetheless, as I have observed in the mature years of some "grown-up" prodigies, especially those exposed to the greatest early life adulation, the acquisition of humility has felt like squeezing into clothes that don't quite fit.

3

⊢————⊣

"To be *liked* for one's charm is not the same as being *admired* for one's humility," Daniyal said, announcing our subject for discussion. It was for one of our regular walks in New York when we were both in town. He had an especial affection for Gramercy Park, a private gated paradise of two serene acres set in the middle of Manhattan. Like Fitzroy Square in London, regular access to the Park is restricted to residents and admission is jealously guarded. But the first time Daniyal had played in New York (when, by the way, the concert had been a sensation), a grateful, wealthy resident and Park trustee honoured Daniyal with the coveted gift of a Gramercy key. Daniyal has enjoyed the kindness ever since.

Gramercy is one of New York's most marvellous gems and a perfect place to walk and talk. Over the years, we had probably spent a dozen or more memorable days there. Daniyal was a thinker. If he hadn't been a pianist, he might have occupied a chair in philosophy somewhere prestigious. Our chats were always stimulating.

We'd find a coffee, or in Winter, bring a thermos, then walk a while. Finally, we'd settle on a park bench. We'd admire the luscious foliage, identify the birds and their song, and continue setting the world to rights.

We had undoubtedly become creatures of habit. As though an alarm had been set, at 11:30 a.m., one of us would look at his watch and declare, "lunchtime!" It was a four-minute walk for bourbon and chips, usually at Pete's Tavern, NYC's oldest continuous speakeasy bar on East 18th Street.

On this occasion, however, although it was still a warm day, it had begun to rain. Coming out of the Park, we hailed a cab. The car journey cannot have been much more than two minutes, and as we alighted, Daniyal handed the driver a $20 note with a cheery, "Keep the change." Delighted, the driver replied, "Thanks, Mr. Steinfeld." Daniyal looked surprised. The driver added, "Heard you last night at Carnegie. Great show. Have a nice lunch, gentlemen."

Lunch was very nice: Several Bourbons, a healthy burger with triple cooked fries, onion rings and a large dressed salad.

So I pulled Daniyal's leg about the taxi driver. "You love being recognised, don't you?"

"Yes, I do," Daniyal said. "But it has become a problem for me. I don't know why. It is as though I have developed a thirst, a hunger, but coming from somewhere unknown. I crave esteem, much more than I have looked forward to this bowl of fries, and even seeing you, Michael. Sometimes the passion for it consumes me."

We drank and ate some. Daniyal ordered a second bowl of fries, which we shared, and two more bourbons. By this time, we were both feeling a little schicker, and Daniyal's words were slurring slightly.

"You know this story the Hassids tell? A man comes to the Tzaddik, who obviously is the holy guy, and knows all about godliness. The man has a complaint. 'All my life,' he says, 'I have tried to follow the advice of the rabbis. They say the one who runs away from fame will find that fame pursues him. Yet when I run away from fame, fame never pursues me.' The Tzaddik replies: 'The trouble is that when you run, you are always looking over your shoulder to see if fame is chasing after you.'"

"It is one of those paradoxes," I said. "When you know your worth, you come close to being a victim of pride. Yet humility cannot mean that we have to pretend we are of less worth than we really are."

"So how do you resolve that?" said Daniyal. "To be honest, over the years, I've studied Talmud, but I have never found an answer that works for an artist."

I asked him if he remembered the letter Maimonides wrote to his son. He both recalled it and could quote it. Even without the help of bourbon, Daniyal always had a better memory than me. I quoted the part I had in mind.

"I shall explain how you should become accustomed to the practice of humility in your daily life. Let your voice be gentle, and your head bowed. Let your eyes be turned earthwards and your heart heavenwards. When you speak to someone, do not look him in the face. Let every man seem superior to you in your own eyes. If he is wise or rich, you have reason to respect him. If he is poor and you are richer or wiser than he, think to yourself that you are therefore all the more unworthy and he all the less, for if you sin, you do so intentionally, whereas he only sins unintentionally."

"Mmm. I'm not convinced, Michael. Pianists need passion, not humility. Speaking of which, a long time ago, I had a student who I nick-named Uriah Heap, but not to his face. He was humble in the extreme. He always spoke in whispers, and his playing was the same—hushed and passionless.

"Many times I tried to ignite some passion in his playing. And as many times I failed. So one day, to see if any emotions in fact existed in this repressed individual, I worked out a plan. As he began to play, his emotions again on mute, I began to slap him on the back, bellowing, 'Passion! Passion! Give it some Passion!'

"But Uriah didn't react. He looked straight ahead and never turned towards me. Determined to retain his veneer of 'humbleness,' he played on, with no increase in dynamic or feeling. Then suddenly, but not in the music, the emotions surface. Like a churlish mouse whose cheese has been stolen, Uriah lifts his hands, grabs his music, scuttles to the door, careers down the stairs and flies onto the street.

"I never saw him again. He probably tells anyone who'll listen that I am a bully and a tyrant and have no humility." Daniyal paused and grinned. "But I am not sure humility and the piano live well together, Michael."

With that and the bourbon cheering our way, we hailed another cab and returned to the hotel.

4

"How are your Orchids, Daniyal?" I asked as we were going back in the taxi. It was one of his passions, and over the last few years, he had become quite an expert grower. A couple of walks ago, Daniyal had told me of his efforts to obtain The Gold of Kinabalu Orchid. It is extremely rare and only found in Malaysia. One stem can cost over $1000!

"Well, I still haven't landed a Kinabalu. But I hope Mariah is keeping an eye on our collection. It's not their value I worry about. Like many things of beauty, they're so delicate and easy to break."

"I've found that with our Bonsai collection," I said. "Bonsai trees are more robust than orchids, but they're like children that keep on outgrowing their clothes. You have to keep repotting them. At the beginning of the year, I left one for too long, and it keeled over and died."

"Yes," Daniyal said. "The equivalent with orchids is overwatering. It's one thing you mustn't do. Never overwater. If the soil is soggy or wet, that's when you run out of options. In the time it takes to swallow a couple of bourbons, it can be whoops, no orchid!"

Returning to our topic in the Park, I said, "Don't you think humility is a bit like that? To grow strong, it needs regular care and attention. When it comes down to it, humility is quite a delicate plant."

I pointed out that as children, we were taught to check our change, clean our teeth and wash behind our ears. But as a youngster, I cannot remember that ego checks ever figured at all. Except for the occasional rebuke for being stuck up or bossy. It's a strange omission when one considers the importance of ego maintenance to mental health and maturity.

I said to Daniyal, making light of it, "Wouldn't it be good if we had some effective way to teach our babies and our children psychological hygiene! It would have made your life easier, Daniyal. And mine too!"

Daniyal went quiet for a moment. I noticed a hint of moisture in his eyes. It was brushed away in a couple of blinks. "For growing up prodigies," he said, "that really would be a big thing!"

It is only all these years later, I have become aware of the complexity of what lay behind that moment.

5

In the sense of money changing hands, Daniyal was never really a patient. True, he often drew on my insights, as I drew on his. His as an artist, mine as a therapist. Sometimes he would ask me something about himself, though roughly disguised and attributed to an acquaintance, but not in our circle. Our pattern? I would pontificate for a while. In conversation, as with music, Daniyal was a deep listener, and never missed a nuance.

But behind the noise of thunder, Daniyal Steinfeld was a private, reflective personality. In these kinds of conversations, ("You know they're about me, Michael, but let's pretend it's someone else,") his response was to resist being drawn. "Mmm," he'd say. "Mmm. Thank you. Thank you so much." And having drunk his fill, he'd change the subject.

Nonetheless, more generally as friends do, we often talked of joys and sorrows, even disappointments and struggles. But then, occasionally, in less veiled moments, usually after the third glass of bourbon, we also spoke of losses—some of which for Daniyal were current, but also some of the fading memories of early life. The kind wherewith passing years, though remembrance blurs, an ache remains. A silent witness, where scars like a headstone above a grave, keep their memory alive when we stop there and reminisce.

Daniyal once asked me about analysis and what theories I work to, and which best helped me understand what underlies the struggles of those I meet professionally. He quoted a well-known conductor, whose name I should not disclose. But he was really talking about the parallel with himself. "In private he's very gentle, but professionally he's incredibly unforgiving." And he went on, "Imagine if a horn should split, or on a high note an oboe squeaks; we're talking about the best players and a rare occurrence. But when that happens at a rehearsal or a performance, you can see him visibly bristle, and afterwards, everyone knows all hell can be let loose."

"Well," I said, slipping into professorial mode, "Unlike great Dr. Freud, I think it is too deterministic to blame it all on potty training. But there's little doubt that early life is formative, especially from our attachments, most of all from the early bonds we developed with our caregivers."

"You see," I went on, "All trees have roots, and so do people. Children who instinctively know they have a secure bond with their parents tend to grow up emotionally stable and level-headed." I foresaw he would jump on my generalisation.

"Michael, I had great parents. But I wouldn't describe myself as that level-headed. Would you?" He added, smiling, "On a few occasions I have been known to shout at conductors, and the French horn, and the oboist!"

"No, you're not that easy going, for which of course there are reasons, but you're delightful too. Together they shape your quality. What lies underneath your most stretched moments contributes as much to your genius as to your pain. That's another conversation. But just to say the history of humanity illustrates the outcome of parenting and our early years is nowhere near as predictable as this. However good or bad the parenting style, the presence of how much love, or no love, the emerging adult is subject to a myriad of other influences.

"It lends itself to so many metaphors. Trees and roots, buildings and foundations, what it takes to climb a mountain. To put it simply, think of your life as four seasons, one painting for each. Naturally, the first painting is your early life; the rest are still to be painted. This first landscape is the one upon which all the others depend. On this first canvas, the subject is our childhood. It depicts the foundations of so much which will underpin and influence our later adult life. Though the seasons will change, from Spring to Summer, from Autumn to Winter, season one sets the scene for the rest."

Daniyal listened with his customary concentration. Then, suddenly, he looked up and said, I sensed ironically, "That sounds all neat and tidy. Perhaps I am more predictable than I realised!"

"Not really," I said, "If this were paint-by-numbers, like a child's colouring-in set, I agree, everything might look more predictable. The colours would be bright and contrasted, everything would fit neatly within the lines. But when you look at the colours and lines on this first picture, you'll see it's been delivered daubed and splashed, as though an artist blinded by the headlights has randomly thrown his paint and stained the canvas throughout with amorphous blotches.

"Their message becomes clear when the four landscapes are hung alongside each other. Together, they form a single portrait of tremendous complexity. Remember, the effect is cumulative, and the truth behind that portrait depends on that first canvas."

"Mmm. Thank you. Thank you so much."

6

D aniyal had changed the subject. We were to have further discussions on what formed his internal drama, whose passion he knew existed, but in his music-making he drew on mainly unconsciously. However, without him being a patient, I always looked out for his mental health, and broadly, his spiritual well-being. It is true that as the years went by, his need for what I'll call a deeper conversation, and for therapy, increased, especially later on when the expectations of the Steinfeld Commission and his family's multiple traumas began to haunt him. That meant encouraging him to speak reflectively about himself and his family's painful history. Some of these issues I'll explore at a future point in this reminiscence.

Of course, Daniyal loved talking about music, but not to other pianists. He found the attitudes of some to be so competitive, it had put him off. But he was still passionate about all aspects of the subject. And beyond music he was equally passionate about life, people, family, art, philosophy, religion - and his orchids. As I have described, when in town, he liked nothing better than to walk and talk, in the Park, or over a drink or dinner in the evening.

Whatever the subject, sometimes he did most of the talking, sometimes it was me. We were both voluble. On this occasion on a beautiful spring day in March, we were walking in Central Park in New York.

As we sauntered on, we were like a couple of Rabbis walking, talking, debating, at times raising our voices and waving our arms. So our conversation moved to hubris. Hubris being unbending, excessive pride. "I am right, and I will always be right," and "look at me!" It was one of our familiar themes.

Daniyal had read a book about hubris and politicians which had set him thinking.

"But it wasn't so much about politicians that I wanted to talk about." Daniyal regarded most politicians as a race of lost causes. "It was whether hubris can affect the creative arts. What, for instance, have you observed about musicians and hubris?" he asked me innocently.

I didn't think that Daniyal was suffering from hubris at all, but I did ask in my usual oblique way, "Are you afraid of spiders? Arachnophobia?"

"Why?" he asked back.

"Just answer the question."

"Well no, but I am not terribly fond of them. Is that a sufficient answer?"

"So, have you heard about Arachne?" I asked. "You see, through their myths, the Greeks and Romans loved to tell their cautionary tales about hubris. It was one of their big themes. In their picture language, hubris is unmasked when mortals think they can do better than the gods. Psychologically, these myths are so insightful, and show they understood the machinations of the human heart somewhat more urgently than we do today.

"So Arachne. She was a talented young weaver. Unfortunately, having grown too big for her boots, she unwisely challenged Athena, the goddess of wisdom and crafts, to a weaving contest. Arachne proceeded with inflated pride, creating a completely flawless tapestry. Athena saw red, and after a few shenanigans, promptly transformed Arachne into a spider! Watch your arrogance, says the myth.

"Then there's Tantalus, famous for the gruesome offering of his son, Pelops, as a sacrifice. What got him into big trouble was he stole ambrosia and nectar from the table of Zeus. That was bad enough, but it was the motive that caused the real alarm. He intended to reveal the secrets of the gods. For all this, he was made to stand in a pool of water beneath a fruit tree with low branches, with the fruit ever eluding his grasp, and the water always receding before he could take a drink. Tantalising! That's where hubris gets you.

"And then most famous of all, there's Icarus, who flew too close to the sun wearing wings constructed from feathers and wax.

His father, the clever one, warns him not to fly too low or too high. But Icarus thinks he knows best and flies too close to the sun; at which point the wax melts and he tumbles into the sea where he drowns."

This last story about Icarus, ignoring the wise advice of his father, got a reaction that I could hear in Daniyal's voice. For a moment, I thought I saw his hands shake.

7

I should explain that Daniyal was religious, and yet not religious. Or if you prefer, not religious, and yet religious. I am aware that's ambiguous. And yet, when you plot its movement over a lifetime, the avowal or denial of faith is often a winding, even equivocal path. We sometimes speak as though belief or non-belief have a flashbulb moment, defining forever our spiritual status. But in reality, don't convictions vary over time? Their light flickering, sometimes illumined, sometimes darkened according to all kinds of inner and outer circumstances?

So in therapy, we find that something traumatic, long forgotten, may be suddenly reignited brought into the patient's consciousness, and triggers distress. Or some present sorrow, like a poignant loss or some profound disruption to a community like a pandemic, causes re-evaluation of belief or non-belief—even where previously those issues had generated little interest or attention.

Years ago, I was a graduate student at the Boston Institute of Psychoanalysis. Carl Gustav Jung was my professor. And one day, in the Q & A, I asked him if he thought the religious instinct was universal, or if it was like some are born left-handed, others right-handed. I remember how he paused, brought out his pipe, lit it, and puffed for a moment. He replied in his heavily Swiss accented English, "You will note the brain appears to have developed in ways which facilitate spiritual experience."

He inhaled and puffed upwards, and for a few seconds like Moses on Mount Sinai, we were swallowed up in wafting clouds of smoke.

As soon as the miasma cleared, he added, "You will have also noticed, in a crisis, as many are won to religion, are those who are lost to it. That neither confirms nor denies the truth about what some believe and some don't. It does speak of the variation as well as the varieties of religious experience. It tells you, when this happens, that in the heads of these people, many things are going on. You may not be able to find out what they are. But it is evidence of the pressures which influence conclusions and cause them to vary."

A little later, after a few further puffs on his famous pipe, he came back to the subject, and added, "Let me say, I believe the religious instinct is universal, but it is an instinct, not a law. It beckons but does not command."

Since that time and further exploration among the great Greek thinkers, I'm struck that what was boldly deemed the unexamined life is not worth living. But as we have also seen, even the well-examined life may not spell consistency. The vigour of what we affirm and the way we affirm it, like a petrol gauge showing the range of full to empty, depends where and how far we travel, consciously or unconsciously, and the day or the hour we take a reading.

Daniyal's was the examined life, certainly, and for him, these issues were more than just opinions. But to speak at any one moment of faith or no faith, or whatever it was that held his inner world together—the direction of travel was not strictly linear. Like Jung said, the consciousness of deeper awareness and conviction waxes and wanes.

To illustrate this, I'll briefly quote an extract of a Steinfeld interview in the Tel Aviv edition of the Jewish Observer. Daniyal had been asked what he valued most about his Jewish heritage.

"I was raised by wonderful Jewish parents. But my beliefs have been shaped as much by the Holocaust and earlier persecutions of the Jews, especially in Poland. So, no. I am not an observant Jew in practice or belief. But in another way, religion means the world to me—in the sense of appreciating our history, traditions, values, and the deep emphasis we place on the family. You see, I am the third generation of pianists who bear the name, Steinfeld. My father and grandfather were Poles and prominent concert artists. My great grandfather was also a musician and a distinguished Beethoven scholar.

"The tragedy that befell the family in Lwów in 1918 was a pogrom in which my grandparents and father's siblings all perished. At the expense of their lives, they enabled Aleksander, my father, to escape and eventually come to London. It is solely because of their sacrifice I am now the third generation of pianists in our family. But with this privilege comes a responsibility. My father called it 'The Solemn Commission' to live the Steinfeld name for new generations. I have come to realise I am haunted by all that, especially as I was named Abramczyk, after my grandfather. I never knew him. I dearly wish I had. But I think about him and his commission, every day of my life.

"My family's story moves me each time I tell it. It is a mixture of inspiration and pain. But I am so thankful for my wonderful parents, my father, Aleksander and my mother Leah, who in the richest sense gave me life. What an upbringing! At their knees, I learnt my love for family, my faith, my values, my music—and my mission. What better way can I express my tribute to my Jewish heritage?"

8

|————————|

Springtime in Central Park is like a fanfare announcing the cherry trees are about to bloom. The arrival of the cherry blossom is one of New York's most uplifting wonders. In just a few days the Park undergoes an almost magical transformation and becomes immersed in a spectacular carpet of pink: a carnival of flowers, a celebration of spring. It is an attraction that never fails to stimulate the senses and delight the eye.

The blossoms appear between April and May, and the greatest number of cherry blossom trees are found between 72nd Street and 96th Street, which is where we had chosen for our walk.

"Aren't they breath-taking?" Daniyal said. "When I was a child, we had a cherry tree which bloomed right outside my bedroom window. Glorious. I loved it, and every year so looked forward to its flowering. But here, we're treated to a whole forest-full, and it's the best time—just after the first buds open. It stirs you, doesn't it? It awakens joy. For me, it's like the Jupiter symphony and the final fugato. I cannot imagine what was going on in Mozart's head. It is so joyful. So gloriously glorious. There! I've run out of superlatives!"

I shared his enthusiasm, and not with any intention to put a damper on it. "And then it fades," I said, "Such ecstatic beauty, yet a life so fleeting."

"But we still have the music."

We paused for a few moments, as though paying our respects, but in a deeper remembrance.

The crowd was growing. There were visitors from all over, celebrating the carnival with as much noise and enthusiasm as we were. We were beginning to have to duck and dive.

Daniyal craned his neck. At the other side of the path, I could only just catch his words.

"Here's one!" he shouted. He was pointing to an unoccupied bench on the other side of the path. Waving me to join him, we hurriedly pushed through the crowd, found the bench and promptly perched ourselves on either end, filling up the space with our bags. It was our way of declaring, if anyone was unwise enough to attempt to breach our defences, "This space is occupied. Go away!"

We shared a boyish sense of *finder's keeper's*. It was a bit like the disproportionate sense of good fortune when you discover a lost coin on the street. Or, as though we had just found a bargain in the sales and were delighting in our excellent purchase.

With a knowing glance, we congratulated ourselves on our stroke of providence and resumed our conversation.

Daniyal was all fired up about hubris. So from hubris and musicians, he wanted to talk now about hubris and the Mitzvah. In particular the commandment, "You shall have no other gods but me."

Just as Daniyal was about to speak, someone brushed past us, dropping his newspaper from under his arm. Daniyal bent over, picked it up, and returned it to him

"It strikes me that commandment is like a newspaper headline," he said. "All religions and systems of ethics—they tell you what you can and cannot do, and woe betides you if you stray. But none begins with a headline like this. Start here, it says. 'You shall have no other gods but me.' For anyone who knows the inner workings of the heart, that's quite a challenge, especially for a performer!"

"A challenge about what?"

"About the muddle the ego can get us into. The Hebrews understood this even better than the Greeks. The ego can cause us to stray even further into idolatry. The point about idolatry is it steals a glory that belongs to another. For instance, when an audience erupts into rapturous applause, the game begins. 'Look at me!' So if since childhood—week in, week out—you have regularly known acclaim like this, as I have, the esteem and the adrenaline rush it stimulates becomes a drug. Quite honestly, it is so intoxicating I have become dependent on it. And you know how the mind works this out?"

"You're about to tell me."

"The ego has such an appetite for acclaim it will doggedly pursue a glory which should remain out of bounds. But for me at least, my ego is so conditioned it will plough on and grab whatever it can, making an idol of the adoring crowd and its applause."

"You mean performers are not meant to be appreciated?"

"Yes, of course, *appreciated*—but not worshipped. If worship is a divine prerogative, and you know my belief wobbles on that, nonetheless I still think it's clear, artistically, spiritually, and psychologically the worship of performers and performance should be out of bounds. But in practice, it absolutely isn't.

"Michael, believe me, I'm an expert on this. For years I have been like a shoplifter who takes without paying, stealing the limelight wherever I can. In my line of work, when you are good at what you do, especially when you are *very* good, the more you beam and bow, the more you are commended. Audiences love a winner, so they too can worship. And I tell you truly, I'm a sucker for it. But it's a snare, Michael. It can mess your head up, and I suspect your body too. Frankly, I'm a bit worried that one day it may do just that to me." Daniyal looked disturbed at his disclosure. He took a deep breath and exhaled slowly. When he had calmed a little, I reflected on what he had said.

"I'm quoting from memory. But years ago, I heard a talk on the artist's internal struggle. I can't be sure, but I think it was given by Jean-François Lyotard, the French philosopher. But I do remember the title. It was called, 'The Prelude to Nemesis.'

"It was vivid. He compared high achieving artists to fire swallowers on a darkened stage, where vision is limited to the light of the fire they consume and exhale. Semi-blinded, they little realise they have stumbled into a jungle of snares; how beckoning pride and trumpeting supremacy entangles their thoughts; entraps their motives; banishing any hint of blushing humility. And there in the place of folly, the hardened heart, as the fire eater ascends its stairway, an invisible hand etches the calloused inscription, 'Upon this spot, by Destiny, on this pedestal, I am called to stand!'

"The orchestra plays the prelude to the dark music of nemesis. And as the writing on the wall appears, Hubris passes the hemlock, whispering its hissing mendacity, 'You are the best. You are Supreme. You deserve this.'"

9

W e'd returned to our condo on Central Park West, the property Clara and I inherited from her mother five years ago. Since our wives were away, Mariah in London, and Clara visiting our daughter in Kentucky, I fixed supper. Or rather, ordered pizza from Lombardi's on Spring Street.

After some humming and hawing over the menu, Daniyal settled on a Mozzarella, Ricotta and Romano with added pancetta. And I went for my usual Margherita, extra cheese, and some sauteed garlic spinach.

Since Daniyal was due to play at the Lincoln Centre tomorrow evening, the Prokofiev 3rd with the NY Phil, we decided to go easy on the iron dram and stick to Budweiser. One can each.

While I sorted out the order, Daniyal was eyeing our new piano. It's a Steinway Model B, of which we had been the proud owners for only three weeks. It is two feet shorter than a full-size concert grand. But it is still a big beast, and yet a perfect fit in our bay window with a beautiful view of the park.

"Are you pleased with it?" Daniyal asked.

"Very," I nodded.

"Do you mind if I try it?"

I was thrilled at the idea. In my early 20s, before training in psychotherapy, I had a brief and minor career myself as a concert pianist. I'd studied at Julliard and in Paris. In those days, I could certainly play. Years of neglect mean I'm a little rusty now. Actually, very rusty. But with pianos in both our homes, the other is in Boston, I am hoping I'll find an opportunity to practice again.

So there it was, standing in the bay window, our new shining black Steinway—like a great black Doberman on guard duty; ears pointed, obedient, ready for its master's call.

Hushed by the evening light, the view over the Park's unbroken panorama was graced with magic. The cherry blossom was gently falling, settling like snowflakes along the path. From a distance, it resembled a cascading pink chiffon scarf, quietly shifting this way and that in the wafting breeze. It was that time in the evening when the colours are most vivid and intense. Their spectacle crowned nightly over Central Park Reservoir, where billowing waves of deep red and orange signal the sun is returning home, ready to draw the curtains and bring an end to another good day.

A piano sounds rather different when you are playing it yourself. So I had hoped and planned for the piano's delivery to be in time for Daniyal's visit and was looking forward to being the audience and hearing its full richness. And as much, I was looking forward to hearing the sound of a real pianist, I was especially keen to know what the world's greatest living pianist would bring forth from the instrument.

"Be my guest," I said.

Daniyal opened the fallboard, briefly admired the meticulously fashioned, lustrous, ivory keys and the bright burnished Steinway gold insignia. He then lifted the piano's lid onto its full stick. He never liked playing on the short stick, even for singers and chamber music. He said it changed the piano's tone. "To play quietly, you just have to play quietly!"

He sat down. After adjusting the height of the stool, he tried a few chords and a scale pattern.

I had hoped the instrument would be in tune. You see, tuning can slip when a piano is moved. When ours was delivered, it wouldn't go up the stairs, so our bay window had to be temporarily removed. It was quite an operation. Fortunately for us, we chose a dry day in March. From a crane mounted on a lorry, the piano had to be hoisted 110 feet on the outside of the building. Following the steps of a stately but unchoreographed dance, it floated gently back and forth under the New York sky, with me hoping against hope that it would be delivered safely, and repeatedly checking if I had remembered to add the black beast to our insurance.

I can't lie, I was antsy. But then, in a flash, the uncertainty was over. As NASA scientists expertly guide a missile re-entry, the skilful piano removers successfully directed the willing animal safely through the window, bringing it gracefully to rest in its reserved space by our drawing room's bay window. In no time, like a proud statue, it looked as though it had stood there for centuries.

And it was good to go. Steinway suggested letting it settle for a few days, so we hadn't yet had a visit from the tuner. I have perfect pitch, but that is not always a blessing! However, I am glad to say, overall, the tuning did sound pretty good to me.

The scale pattern finished, and lending me a nod of approval, Daniyal launched into the fugato, the final section of Liszt's B minor Piano Sonata. It is music of intense power and poetry. And for any pianist, exceptionally difficult, especially if delivered at the furious speed the composer intended.

Daniyal's playing was perfection. Not a hint of a smudged note. The octaves conveyed with stunning, breath-taking velocity. In my experience, it was as fast as you will ever hear them played. Although much of that last section is climactic, it is not all pyrotechnics; there are moments of exquisite poetic delicacy. My impression of his playing was the sheer musicality, permitting the music to breathe as Liszt intended it. So beautiful, so passionate, so much from the heart. "Strong fingers, strong emotions." The overall effect was electric.

And I have to say, the new Steinway's sound was thunderous. It is a good-sized instrument, even for a substantially designed room! I was pleased we'd spent the extra dollars to have the apartment acoustically insulated, although it was a shame the neighbours missed such a treat.

Daniyal was on his top form. Though, was he ever not? It bodes well for tomorrow's concert.

As he finished, I applauded and he bowed. "You should play the whole thing as an encore tomorrow night," I said, jokingly.

"Don't tempt me!" He replied, saying he had learned something about handling the audience's cries for 'More!'"

It was time for a drink. I took the Budweiser cans from the fridge, now nicely chilled. We pulled the rings and poured two glasses. Job done, we settled ourselves into two easy chairs.

"It's a beautiful piano, Michael. A Steinway grand can sing like a bird, roar like a lion and be as spirited as a puppy!"

I laughed. "You sound like the Louisville Lip."

"I am the greatest!" Daniyal smiled. I'm pretty sure he was joking, but it took us back to Franz Liszt, the world's forever number one piano champion.

"By all accounts, he was incredible," I said, as I rummaged through the cupboard for some pretzels. "Although, as there are no recordings, his reputation could be inflated."

"It is certainly possible, but we do have reliable accounts from pretty impressive sources. Think of Thalberg, Clara Schumann, even Grieg. And a lot more. It appears everyone who heard him was gobsmacked, and there was no one to touch him. Even though we cannot hear him on an Edison cylinder, piano roll or a scratchy old 78, his compositions give us a pretty good idea of how he played. Much of it is not only monstrously innovative, it is designed to show what an unutterably brilliant performer he was. And he wasn't playing a modern Steinway. A lot of those old pianos were much less responsive than today's instruments."

"So are their pieces which illustrate that more than most?" I inquired.

"Yes indeed. For instance, the Grand Galop Chromatique. I am to play it tomorrow night. It is just an entertainment piece for a bit of showing off. But I tell you, it is finger busting. In his heyday, even after glugging most of a bottle of champagne, with the piano standing on its back feet and obeying his every command, Liszt could play it up to speed, note-perfect, and audiences simply roared their approval."

"And you play it at full speed?"

"Yes, of course. But not after a bottle of champagne!" he laughed heartily.

"Do you know if Liszt ever played a Steinway? What do you think he would have made of an instrument like this?"

"Honestly? I think he'd be enthralled. He'd love the sound and the action. In fact, in 1883, three years before he died and long after his playing career, he did try out a new design of Steinway and described it as a glorious masterpiece. But our modern machines are far in advance of those days. Liszt mainly played Bechstein, Blüthner, and Pleyel. Even though they were pretty good for their time, it is kind of a miracle that he was able to perform as astonishingly as he did."

Suddenly our doorbell chimed. The pizza had arrived downstairs. I let the delivery boy in and he kindly brought up the two boxes with the sides. When he arrived, he took one look at Daniyal, and happily surprised, said, "Good evening, Mr. Steinfeld. I am coming to your concert tomorrow night." As Daniyal smiled and said hello, the young man added, "I imagine most of New York is coming too." Daniyal couldn't help feeling flattered, but his reply was gentle and unassuming. "Yes, it will be special. I will do my best to make it a nice evening."

"Thanks, guys. Enjoy your pizzas." And the young man from Lombardi's disappeared into the night.

10

I arranged a couple of plates for us in the kitchen. I took out the salads and the other sides. Daniyal poured some fresh orange juice, and I had a soda. We served ourselves slices of the steaming pizzas. When we had eaten all that we wanted, Daniyal wiped his fingers, sipped the last dregs of his orange juice and said, "You know, there is a good reason to believe that Franz Liszt was probably one of the most conflicted performers of the romantic period."

That was a new thought. "Why?" I asked. "I know he loved the limelight."

"That is putting it mildly," Daniyal said. "Think of it. The mid-19th century was the age of the virtuoso. Mendelssohn, Chopin, Thalberg, Dreyschock, Herz, Clara Schumann—they were all superb. But Liszt outclassed them all. The outstanding Frau Schumann despaired that 'Liszt can play at sight what the rest of us toil over.'

"And what about showmanship, Can you believe this? When I take a taxi to a concert, my wife teases me. 'It's bad for your humility, Daniyal. You should try walking.' And I reply, 'When Franz Liszt played a concert, he'd arrive with six white horses pulling his carriage!'"

"As you say, Michael, he loved the limelight. He'd have three pianos placed on the platform, so on a whim, he could slip from one to the other and back again. Before he had even played a note, he would arrive at the keyboard, feign a swoon, be carried off the stage by uniformed guards, and then, to cheering and stamping of feet he'd bound back onto the stage, like Houdini bursting forth from one of his death-defying escape tricks.

"Was that mere showmanship, or something more pathologically driven?" I asked.

"Who knows? But he must have had virtuoso sex appeal too. When he did get round to playing, posh ladies would be so excited they'd fling their jewellery onto the stage. Afterwards, they'd tear his clothing for souvenirs, fight for locks of his shoulder-length hair and at the sight of him standing in his tight trousers, some would faint and require first aid! There was nothing comparable until Elvis Presley started wowing the fans a hundred years later. Weird, don't you think?"

"So, you never had the girls fall for you like that?" I said, tongue in cheek.

"Well, not at that level," Daniyal said, smiling. "Yes, audiences sometimes go over the top. And occasionally, some of the ladies appear to want more than just arpeggios. I never oblige. But the applause, and the thirst for it, the adulation, the love—without the histrionics—well, over the last few years it has become an increasing problem for me. I seem to need that 'love' more and more. To be honest, I stand there while applause plays, and in my head, I am measuring its intensity, counting every decibel. It is like having a built-in Beaufort scale. If the applause is not gale force, I feel let down and disappointed. Deflated."

He looked distracted and stared quietly at the ceiling. "You're the expert. Am I a head case?"

"No, of course you're not. But esteem is intangible. It's not on sale at Walmart in nice, neat packages. And most of us don't understand what it is, the way it works, and what it does for us. Yet, esteem is as important to our mental health as vitamins are to our bodies. And yet again, for a small minority who are likely to experience a surfeit of it or even an overdose, its presence can be as toxic as its absence."

Daniyal was up for the discussion, but prefaced it by saying, "I don't think I have ever told a soul about this. Promise me, you won't go and sell me to the Washington Post!" He knew of course I would not dream of it. But he needed to say it, and it was important to me to reassure him of our friendship but also the complete privacy of our conversations.

I will mention later how he asked me to tell his story.

So I began to explain.

"We have talked before about attachments. Think about how formative your advanced piano training was for your musical development, your skills and musical sensibility. Like the potter at his wheel, this illustrates the critical value of shaping. We sometimes think shaping is purely progressive—as we move forward, life shapes us. It's not the whole story. Because in important ways, shaping is reflective. Our life responses reflect so much from the past, our earliest, usually forgotten memories. They reflect the emotional bonds developed with our parents or caregivers and our reactions to them. Do you get that?"

"Yes, I get that. But although I had great parents, despite appearances, I don't always feel as secure as I might."

"Okay. Let me ask you, have you ever had an intrusive thought? Something unintentional, maybe alarming. It could be violent, sexual, grandiose or something else. Like when the telephone rings it breaks into your silent world, but you ignore the call and don't pick up. For most people, intrusive thoughts are like that, interrupting, fleeting, but brush them away and they're gone."

"Can I add to that the odd panic?" Daniyal said. "I call them flash thoughts. Like, I panic that I'll be late. Or, what happens if I have a memory lapse? It usually happens when I am tired, and as you say, you can usually brush them away."

"Yes, flash thoughts are very common. But the most interesting, and of course painful, are the thoughts that get stuck and keep on reappearing, usually with anxiety. It crops up a lot in therapy. It is very distressing for the sufferer. Often they are symptoms of OCD or PTSD and can be effectively treated, although underlying health issues can also be the cause.

"But the thing I want to explain, Daniyal, is the circuit switch. You see, given certain emotional conditions, usually inherited from childhood, there is a switch mechanism inside our brains that is activated by a particular thought or emotional need. And like a needle on an old 78 record, it can get stuck. Round and round it goes, same story, same message. The more it goes on, the longer it is left unchallenged, the more difficult it is to shift.

"As you say, you had great parents, and it sounds as though they did very well by you. So your switch response does not necessarily have anything to do with any overt parenting deficiencies, because the human heart with its enormous subtlety and sensitivity is a world of its own. It's wired up with a foreign circuitry that is not easy to unravel. So, unfortunately, no, it is not a straightforward matter to travel within and map our emotional needs, or to identify the events, remembered and unremembered, which have shaped and influenced them."

"But like intrusive thoughts that are connected with actions, we also get intrusive emotions, which are connected with deeper feelings, like insecurity, inferiority, body image issues, and so on. Emotions can get just as stuck as thoughts do. If only we could get a handle on them, we might be able to trace back most of them to early life or formative experiences. But most of us can eventually fight the emotions off. It's like in the middle of the night. You're half-awake and you sense the sound of dripping water. Is it a leak, a flood, perhaps life-threatening? You don't know, you can't tell, and maybe it's just a dream. For most of us we just turn over and ignore it.

"I'm clearly not most of us," Daniyal said. "I do have trouble shifting some of these tap-tap-tapping-at-the-door emotions. I can sometimes turn them off, but it depends how familiar they are. So supposing the drip turns into a puddle, and the puddle a flood? What happens when the emotions force their way in and become more dominant, more intrusive, and create a thirst—an appetite? Or they stoke the fires of existing struggles or bad habits. What can I do about them then?"

Daniyal looked thoughtful and momentarily troubled. I decided to be more specific.

"You remember you said how you crave esteem and count the decibels! For artists and other high achievers, that's probably where you enter the danger zone. It's where the normal appetite for esteem can surge and become toxic. Now clothed in an outer garment of unassailable self-belief, it begins to claim superiority, and demands its entitlement."

Daniyal shifted in his chair. I paused and looked at him, and he looked back at me, but neither of us said anything. So I continued.

"In the danger zone of esteem—of course this particular formulation doesn't only apply to high achievers—I end up telling myself, 'I am good beyond all others. Just look at me. Aren't I fantastic!' Whatever metaphor we choose, be it fire consuming, intoxication or addiction, this endorphin-stimulating power of esteem is one size that fits all. It works the same in everyone, whatever our psycho-developmental profile.

"So the thing to grasp is esteem, whatever its source, in whatever kind of setting, has an unparalleled psychological impact. Like so many human instincts, it is good in itself, but can be easily exploited, risking the path taken by Dr. Faustus.

Of course, esteem is essential, and from the earliest years, in moderate doses, it contributes fundamentally to inner well-being and healthy inner development. What's more, its absence, especially from childhood formation, keeps psychotherapists like me in business. What would we do without developmental neuroses and imperfect attachments!"

Daniyal laughed, but he was weighing everything I said. So I felt I should add a little more about the danger zone.

"Thinking about the right 'dosage' reminds me esteem is also, alas, an unstable drug. Misuse it and over time it will surely bite back, creating disequilibrium, mercilessly unleashing cravings, leaving the soul sore and the heart longing for you don't know what. Nemesis in this realm—I have seen it too often—is when, with inner damage complete, fatally, all balance is lost. From your plinth of glory, like an angrily dislodged statue, you topple unceremoniously to the ground. The once cheering crowds have exchanged their cheers for jeers. All that remains is a pile of broken pieces. It is as dangerous as swallowing fire."

11

All these conversations took place some ten years after Daniyal visited Boston and the frustrations he experienced at passport control. Of course, our discussions over these years covered many continents of thought. But these I have chosen not simply as a reminiscence, but because of the light they shed on Daniyal's inner world; some aspects of which, in a strange and unexpected manner (he is the first to admit it) bubbled to the surface and burst forth huffing and puffing in his reactions that day.

I should tell you more.

Daniyal continued to pace back and forth, periscope up, still scanning the hall for someone to whom he might complain, without success. For the rest of the crowd, still held securely like cattle in the wait-in-lines, the only post-flight entertainment was betting on the armed border guards. The children started the game, and some adults followed. Which of the guards will be the next to shift his weight from one foot to the other? When you're bored and the line's not moving, you have to find some way to get through it.

So in truth, Daniyal wasn't alone in snorting displeasure. However, in the grand scheme of human suffering, there cannot be many for whom this experience could ever be described as any more than a minor inconvenience, and certainly not the cause of an emotional upset.

For Daniyal, his inner chaos was warming towards a boil. At this stage in his distinguished life, his entitlement temporarily unacknowledged and unrecognised, the relatively short time for which he already waited felt more like hours than minutes.

Daniyal stopped his pacing and stood motionless at the immigration desk. It was his turn but nothing was happening. What transpired was partly the effect of the alcohol he had consumed on board. Whilst standing there, his mind began to wander. The 'tick-tock, tick-tock' from his precious handcrafted Girard-Perregaux timepiece was all he heard. The metronomic clicks, back and forth, crescendoed, a little at first, and then increasing, louder and louder—from click to beats to hammer blows, driving him to the scaffold.

When the furious pounding piano octaves joined in, Daniyal realised the music he could hear was Berlioz, the Symphonie Fantastique. For his Boston recitals he had been practising the Liszt piano transcription, and now the music was stuck in his brain, matching his mood but ricocheting through its corridors like a buzzing angry wasp.

The symphony is about a dream. An artist is convinced that his love has been spurned, and despairing, he poisons himself with Opium. He falls into a heavy sleep in which he dreams he has killed his beloved, he is condemned and is now witnessing his execution. Eyes, hands and feet bound, he is marched to the scaffold to face his fate.

It wasn't just the music that was haunting him. In his head, Daniyal was that prisoner, his pleas unheard and facing inevitable execution and oblivion.

Waking dreams, even nightmares, may portray hours, but in real time are usually over in minutes or seconds. When Daniyal came to, he felt he had been away for days. He was hyperventilating, shaken with anxiety and smothered in panic.

He turned to the official, as though he was in the dock before the Lord Chief Justice, and shouted at the top of his voice, "You know I am not guilty. Not guilty, my Lord!" The veins in his neck bulged as he bellowed his innocence. Fortunately, the voice was inside his head and not heard outside. But shout it he did—inwardly, in his overstrained mind.

As his mist cleared, Daniyal had the sensation that those standing behind him were similarly exhausted. It was late. Maybe like him, they had drunk more of the airline's complimentary wine and spirits than was now comfortable for them. He thought of it as a moment of fellowship, standing together in shared dissent, an angry vigil of protest.

The children giggled as a guard shifted his weight from left to right. Of the rest, the line had gone silent.

Before we jump to conclusions about what happened next, (especially, "Could there an explosion imminent?") I note although it was a struggle, Daniyal had at least learnt how to keep the lid on his frustration. It was something we talked about often, how to manage the ladder of steps that lead to an uncontrolled outburst. Where those slippery steps come from and how to stop them going places where they do damage. Sometimes I told him, "It would be good if you could work as hard on yourself as you do on your scores." And many times he did. He saw both as challenges for better all-around performance. Although I guess in the end it was clear which was declared the winner!

Being realistic about his sense of time, if Daniyal hadn't checked his watch (which he had done almost continuously since his arrival), he would have sworn an hour or more had passed since his ordeal began. In reality, it wasn't nearly that long. But the official did look as though he was searching for something, checking and rechecking his passport and documents. Drugs, bugs, something elusive, maybe sinister?

Perhaps something was wrong. Maybe it was the company he kept. If the FBI could seriously suggest that his friend Lenny (Bernstein) was a communist, (which they did, and he wasn't) he hoped such suspicions weren't contagious. Daniyal Steinfeld was a celebrated public figure, self-consciously upright and transparent. No one who actually knew him could ever describe Daniyal Steinfeld as clandestine.

However, something, if not already wrong, was brewing. Attention was drawn away from the game of guards to the paper shuffling at the passport desk. Daniyal Steinfeld's documents were becoming an increasing subject of interest, attracting more than the usual scrutiny. Someone behind him dug his wife in the ribs, whispering, "Remember Viktor Navorski in The Terminal?" Daniyal overheard and did remember. He shivered momentarily, recalling Tom Hanks' protests as he is led away by US Border Protection.

12

The papers were rustling, but not much was happening. While Daniyal's feelings were yo-yoing, it wasn't clear in which direction the drama would unfold. All that can accurately be said about the timing of this opening scene was that everything felt longer than it actually was. It was still just ten minutes since the desk had been opened. Normally, like on a good day when the trains run on time, officials can process a passport at the rate of one per minute. Unless something is wrong.

The queue, however, had not moved for 10 minutes. That's why progress felt so delayed. You could see the frustration on the faces. Everyone was tired and anxious to meet and greet family and friends waiting for them on the other side of the barrier.

Daniyal moved a little closer to the desk. As he did, the border official picked up the phone and muttered something about names. Daniyal just caught the muffled reply, "Ask him if..." but as the official saw Daniyal was eavesdropping, he turned his head and Daniyal didn't hear the rest. One moment later, the call was on hold, with more delay for everyone.

"At least the cogs are turning," thought Daniyal. "Something's bound to happen soon."

But not that soon. As time passed, so multiplied Daniyal's frustration. From the imagined sound of hammer blows, the second hand of his watch now became a slow swinging pendulum; back and forth it went, like a metronome, in dull regular strokes; the gravitas of its *tick-tock* reverberating like an echo through a quiet and peaceful house.

Except to say, that Boston's Logan (or to put it more grandly, General Edward Lawrence Logan International Airport) was anything but quiet or peaceful. Even though the hour was late, with new flights arriving every few minutes, in a slow crescendo, the arrivals hall was becoming progressively noisier. The percussive sounds inside and outside Daniyal's head increased. He felt a headache coming on, and his stomach was complaining too. It had happened before, but his physician had reassured him, "Everyone has a stress organ. Nothing for you to worry about, Daniyal. Keep your hat on and save your energy for Beethoven."

But it was difficult keeping his hat on. Like a barometer on a hot day, Daniyal's mercury was rising. With increased ostentation, he continued to check his watch, strained above the crowd to identify a supervisor, and grunted disapproval even more audibly. But when his palms began to perspire, that was when he heard his inner alarm. Because professionally perspiring hands were a sure index of stress and something he needed to avoid with all his might. It was one of the issues about which he had once sought my help.

"I need a whisky," he said out loud to no one in particular. "A bourbon will do!" But there would be no chance of any liquor until his passport was stamped. So to irritation and frustration, mounting stress, an aching head and complaining stomach, add in prohibition. Unfortified, Daniyal's reserves of patience were on the wane.

Let me pause and describe the broader canvas. Here is the famous Daniyal Steinfeld, recently arrived in Boston from London Heathrow. We have seen him stuck at the US border, held up like a naughty schoolboy who has been sent to the headmaster's study for some paltry misdemeanour. His journey began late last evening from London's South Bank. When his waiting car, a Rolls Royce Silver Shadow, complete with its distinguished cargo pulled out from the lower concourse of the Festival Hall, the journey had been something of a mad dash.

13

Frankly, it was crazy. It should have taken 45 minutes to get to the terminal. But they were running a half-hour behind schedule. Who was responsible? Daniyal Steinfeld (and no one else!) Lesser mortals become delayed by mistakenly settling a bill with an unsigned cheque or getting stuck in a meaningless lover's tiff. No, Daniyal had made himself late. How? By choosing to play too many encores to the adoring capacity crowd of London's brand-new Festival Hall!

The Royal Festival Hall officially opened on Thursday 3 May 1951. It was built on the South Bank of the Thames for £2 million as part of the Festival of Britain—a celebration of all things British and Britain's successful recovery from the war. It remains an icon of modernist architecture, and one of Britain's premier concert centres.

Because of his high international standing, the organisers of the opening event were keen to showcase Britain's leading virtuoso pianist. Daniyal Steinfeld was invited to play a concerto at the

Royal Gala on Thursday, and a solo recital the next day. It was, of course, a significant honour to appear before King George VI and Queen Elizabeth. The thought made Daniyal wistful. If only his father and grandfather could have been present.

The opening concert was to be an all-British programme, and Daniyal was the soloist in the Vaughan Williams piano concerto. Sir Adrian Boult was the perfect advocate for Vaughan Williams' score, and a sympathetic accompanist. The performance went well. At the end, the audience was highly enthusiastic, clapping and shouting wildly; but as Daniyal was told, very politely of course, when he came off the platform, "Only one more bow, sir, and no encores under any circumstances!"

That was not Daniyal's style. He liked to give what he called "full value" and loved to play encores. But in due deference to the King and Queen who liked to retire early—on Thursday night, no encores it was.

Friday night was different. Same hall, same piano, same capacity. But this time he had the whole programme to himself. He played like an angel with wonderful musicianship and eye-watering virtuosity. So at the end, after Liszt, Chopin, Beethoven and Alkan, all stunning performances, there were encores—plural!

After all, what can more encourage a performer than to hear an audience shouting, "more, more!" The encores were not just because Daniyal was a sucker for applause, or that he was a showman, (he had become both of those) but because the audience demanded them.

At almost 30, Daniyal was good looking, smiling, charming and confident. Worldwide, he had been an audience favourite for 20 years. When he was 10, Daniyal's Carnegie Hall debut had awe-struck music critics comparing him to Rachmaninoff, Hofmann and Godowsky. And the next year when he played the Grieg Piano Concerto at the Proms with Sir Henry Wood conducting, the British press positively hooted their joy. "Young Steinfeld's extraordinary promise." "Britain's new world-class player." "On a path to become the best of the best."

From the crowd's point of view, "too many" was not considered excessive. They adored him. Given half a chance they would have kept Daniyal there till midnight! No, too many were because Daniyal was due to travel straight to Boston that evening and he needed to arrive at the airport on time. One encore would have done nicely. But why four? Godowsky, Rachmaninoff, Chopin and Medtner? That little box of fireworks added an extra 30 minutes to the concert and unhappily made him late. The staff too. He had ruffled some feathers.

The opening week was particularly demanding for the hall staff, and despite a successful evening, some had long journeys home, and some walked out cross. The musical extras also meant the hall management was not too pleased. The concert was due to end at 10:10 p.m. timed to include one encore. As it turned out, the stage lights went down at 10:40 p.m. When concerts run over, staff have to be paid overtime. Though Daniyal was responsible, he was not affected—his fee was fixed. Daniyal got the glory while the concert promoter picked up the tab.

Yes, we can blame Daniyal. I know he's wonderful, charismatic and charming. But he's all for one! Rarely one for all. Most of the people who knew him at this time thought that he was unlikely to change. When you first meet him, you encounter his charm first and swiftly realise that Daniyal loves to be adored. For him, adoration is the only drug stronger than whisky. And when the crowd shouts and stamps he can hardly resist.

Those encores were the equivalent of a lover's embrace. Kisses on both cheeks and back again. They loved him, and he gave them as good as he received, even when he knew it would make him late for the plane and the rest of us late for bed.

With their applause still ringing in his ears, ignoring the odd cross faced hall employee, Daniyal clambered into the back of the Rolls. His manager, Georgio, who'd carried his bags, placed them in the boot and waved his kisses and goodbyes. Without a word of greeting to Fred, his longstanding driver, Daniyal, in commander-in-chief mode, bellowed through the glass, "Pull out the stops, Fred. Put your foot down. Take the shortest route, and make sure we get to the flight on time." Which Fred did. Miraculously carving off several full minutes off the normal 45-minute journey. Fred was used to it by now. And relieved, as he disembarked, Daniyal did remember to thank him.

Daniyal was now dangerously late (he said "overdue") and *sans doute*, it would have been a disaster if he'd missed the flight. It was good his manager had called ahead, and Daniyal was glad he'd booked first-class. It was an expensive way to extend the margin. But it had worked before, and you wouldn't normally catch Daniyal arriving on time or travelling cattle class.

Swiftly passing through immigration, Daniyal heard the tannoy, "Will Mr. Steinfeld please go to gate 16," and thought in his entitled way, "They all know me!" And sure enough, there, in a welcoming line, were the boarding staff who, hoping against hope, were awaiting the extra minutes for their distinguished guest to show. Their patience was rewarded. Daniyal doffed his hat, and with no minutes to spare, climbed aboard.

Safely aloft, Daniyal greeted the cabin crew: usual smiles and bon mots, and only the merest hint of an apology—a truncated, "Just a little overdue!" If only minutes before he had heard the chief steward exclaim, "He must think he is the bloody Queen of England!" But he was there now, and in moments champagne was in hand, and with a little bowl of cashew nuts all to himself, he slipped effortlessly into entitlement mode. Deferentially, he greeted the few other passengers in first class with a nod and charmed half-smile, and then settled down for his accustomed large whisky—no water, no ice—which was brought to him immediately.

Once they had taken off and were cruising comfortably, the journey should have been uneventful. He would do some reading, have a meal (the food was acceptable in first-class, as, "it's what you pay for,") and then he'd get some sleep.

The reading items were scores that he had to check for the first concert the next day. There was to be a lecture-recital in the afternoon and a concerto in the evening. There was a new piece he especially needed to look at. It was by an American composer, who, like Daniyal, had been coached by the celebrated French teacher, Nadia Boulanger. He hadn't had a chance to work at it. Not his normal practice, but as the work was new it would justify using the music in the performance. Like his father before him, Daniyal was a brilliant sight-reader.

"Yes," Daniyal thought. "I can do enough work on the plane to get me up to speed. I'll be able to play it in Boston alright." So with a large glass of claret, the Château Bonalgue he had been looking forward to, he settled down to read the score through. He hoped young Mr. Bernstein would be pleased with his performance.

Daniyal was in his element, enjoying the cross-rhythms and clever counterpoints of the new piece when in an instant the glass went flying. Daniyal felt like exploding at the hostess. It was an accident, but when passing his seat she had unintentionally brushed his hand.

At home, there would not have been a problem. But on the plane, having his glass held high, gently waving it in time to the music, was to invite calamity. The wine splashed everywhere, apart from Daniyal, whose suit shirt and tie were unaffected. He was protected by the score, which looked thoroughly battle-scarred.

All credit to the air hostess. She was not just apologetic, she did her very best to clean up the mess efficiently and effectively. Daniyal gave her the score to wipe and restore. As he did, he had the bizarre thought: If he had to choose, what would he care about the most? The wasted claret or Bernstein's now splattered handwritten score? He did not need to choose as the hostess soon returned the cleaned-up score and poured him another glass of wine. Fortunately, she resisted the temptation to say, "Be careful what you do with your hands."

After several more glasses, more than he normally drank, Daniyal realised it was his fault and he needed to take extra care. By now he was getting schicker, which may have explained his later behaviour, but at least it was calming his nerves. The score was fine, he decided, although the red wine had stained the paper, and there was one short section where, for the life of him, he could not read the notes. *Oh, well,* he thought. *I will just have to wing it. If he's had a few, I don't expect Lenny will notice.*

14

Once again, Daniyal stared at the face of the official. Not intentionally, but as one does when distracted. The craggy lines of his face and the louring scowl of his jaw appeared to stifle any apparent signs of warmth or pleasure, even the suggestion of a smile. And then Daniyal noticed his ears. They were large and flappy. It made him think of an African elephant. He suppressed a smile. "I hope they keep him warm in Boston's freezing winters," he teased to himself. Then on a roll, he constructed this mockingly, silly, (you might say intolerant) analysis. "He is probably tone deaf and can't carry a tune in a bucket. That's it, he has cloth ears, what else!"

To be sure, the older man's ears were actually, well, quite elephantine. Though not to be unkind, Macrotia, as I believe it is called, can develop with age. Daniyal continued his intolerance. "With ears like that, he's probably tone deaf. I bet he loves the 1812." (Tchaikovsky's overture, not the actual battle.) "He'll probably think the firing canons are part of the brass section." This dialogue was more tongue-in-cheek than malicious, but it was still good there were no mind readers or reporters present.

In some ways, these reactions are revealing. They were typical of what Daniyal often did. He set great store on first impressions, increasingly in his senior years becoming judgemental and dismissive of anything and anyone less sensitive and artistically passionate than himself. Indeed, in public, on more than one occasion humour gave way to malice, which took many hours of his PR agents' time to resolve.

The man was now off the phone. He looked like a detective, one who has just discovered the clue to unlock the case. The big ears flapping and the brooding scowl suddenly animated, he looked up and stared back at Daniyal, like someone who thinks they have spotted a film star. In this case, the recognition was not stage or screen, and certainly not musical. The question was about the man's youthful sporting hero, or even his father or grandfather's sporting hero, as the champion in question departed this life in 1914.

"Are you by any chance related to Harry Steinfeldt, the baseball star?" the official asked cheerily, chewing his pencil and checking the details of Daniyal's landing card against his passport and visa.

"No," replied Daniyal tersely, without elaboration and trying to sound calm, relaxed and patient. In his overnight flight from Heathrow, even with the faux luxury of first class he had not slept too well. The champagne (the full bottle), a couple of whiskies, and fully reclining seat hadn't really done the trick. This was annoying, as it might jeopardise his plan to be fresh enough to fit in two concerts in the next two days.

Daniyal was feeling grumpy and ill-disposed to run through the Steinfeld family tree. He even denied himself the response, "Alas, despite his clearly stupendous talent and achievement, the great Harry Steinfeldt was not a relation. Not even my third cousin thrice removed!" But why waste words? The irony probably would not have registered.

However, one thing Daniyal had learnt in early life was to avoid antagonising minor officials. "You never know how upset they'll get." To be conflict averse wasn't in Daniyal's genes—it was in the very warp and woof of his family's history.

Daniyal's father had always taught him, "Avoid conflict, and as diligently as you work at your scales, practice staying calm. Practice makes perfect."

But at the moment, Daniyal was neither perfect nor calm. He felt heated and hadn't identified the underlying cause. But whatever the reason, his father's words came to him, and he intended to honour his wisdom.

Daniyal's attention was drawn back to the ticking of his Antique Girard Perregaux Repeater Pocket Watch. It had belonged to his father and was inscribed with his name, Aleksander Steinfeld, with the words in Polish, "Dla naszego syna i spadkobiercy w jego 25. urodziny." "For our son and heir on his 25th birthday."

It took him back to all his parents and grandparents had been through in Poland in the first part of the century. Despite the doors that slammed shut to Jews all over Europe; despite persecution, pogroms and holocaust; despite every effort to extinguish not only his family but his entire race, the Steinfeld name had won through to another generation. Daniyal was the living evidence. It seemed ironic indeed that at the doorstep of the world's greatest democracy, the leader of the free world might not let him through.

All was quiet on the western front. The queue hadn't moved and nothing else changed. Except for the man's enthusiasm, which as quickly as it had come up for air, had slithered back into its shell. His face reset in its concrete crags and scowl.

15

The man continued to stare at him.

"I am a pianist," Daniyal said quietly.

"So you're no baseball fan," drawled the officer sarcastically, his logic imprecise.

"No, I play the piano." Daniyal said again, trying not to be cross, but exploding the sound of the "P." "I am a pianist."

He wasn't in the mood to boast at this hour, but he had actually wanted to say, "I am a *famous* pianist." Or even, "...the world's *greatest* pianist." But it was unlikely that his prowess would impress Cloth Ears. Harry Steinfeldt already occupied that throne.

"Did you say, pianist?" Big ears was now leaning conspiratorially over his desk. In his shabby unpressed suit, he reminded Daniyal of Columbo, the TV detective, as he was poised to unmask the identity of the murderer.

Unguardedly, Daniyal was about to laugh when Big Ears interrupted. Elongating each syllable, the cogs turning slowly.

"Pianist eh?"

A pause.

"Oh, Steinway!" said Big Ears, triumphantly. "I've heard of you." He really did sound like Columbo.

Daniyal couldn't believe what he was hearing. He looked witheringly at the man, taking care not to translate his feelings into words.

"No," said Daniyal. "Steinfeld," he said slowly. "Steinway is a piano. Steinfeld is a pianist."

"Oh." said Detective Columbo. He then added in a stage whisper to someone, maybe himself, Daniyal, or no one in particular, "I thought he may have confused the names."

Daniyal was trying hard to resist getting angry. That would be neither good for his reputation, nor his heart for that matter. He swallowed as much of his pride as his disposition would allow, and continued to stare the official in the eye, willing the man for God's sake to speed up and let him through.

Shambling and relentless Columbo looked up, checked his screen, and said in his drawling New York-ese, "Say Mr. Steinfeld, who knows you in the US?"

Daniyal paused, trying to think of a modest answer.

He couldn't. Instead, he blurted out, "They all know me!" Momentarily, this brought forth a startled though unbelieving reaction. Daniyal had not meant to say anything and he knew this would not help his case. Like an incrimination, the thought had just slipped out. It failed to impress.

By now, as though ready to extract a confession, the detective was staring relentlessly into Daniyal's eyes.

Daniyal did not have a clue as to what was in his mind. As he looked round, he also realised he was the last passenger standing. The others had now been dealt with by other staff brought in especially to deal with this emergency.

Columbo was looking tired and cross, his big ears sagging, feeling he was not being properly supported by his superiors.

"He must know more than he is letting on," Daniyal thought. "Who knows me in the US? Apart from everyone!" And then he had a brainwave.

"My agent will be here. At least, he is bound to have sent a car for me. No, actually, I expect he will come himself. He'll be waiting outside. There can't be many people left in the arrivals hall. Why don't you get someone to see if he or at least a driver has my name on a card? They'll tell you who I am."

The official responded slowly. "Sir, I don't know who you are—but it is important that I know who you are not." And with that, he picked up the phone. He turned again, so Daniyal was not able to eavesdrop on the conversation.

The phone was put down. There was silence. By now, the two protagonists stared at each other like prize-fighters in their final bid for victory.

The phone rang again. A moment's covert conversation. The final round didn't take long, but it felt like a lifetime.

"Herr Steinfeld?"

"It's Maestro."

"Sure," he said with a drawl. "Meister Steinfeld."

It would do.

"Meister Steinfeld, I suppose the name Sachsenhausen-Oranienburg doesn't mean too much to you."

"Of course it does. I'm Jewish. Sachenhausen was a Nazi concentration camp."

"Sir, I know then you will appreciate the continuing efforts of the United States to bring war criminals to justice. But I have made a discovery that you will find emotionally upsetting. I want you to be prepared for that. There's a guard from the camp whose real name is Gunther Felding who so far has evaded justice. Earlier this afternoon, we received intelligence from Mr. Simon Wiesenthal to say that Herr Felding was a passenger on your flight from London to Boston."

Daniyal looked more puzzled than ever.

"You will understand now, sir, why we have been concerned. Herr Felding travels under an assumed name. In fact, a German-Jewish name. Daniyal Steinfeldt. I still don't know who you are. But today, it's who you're *not* that makes the difference."

Pulling his rumpled beige raincoat over his suit and tie, the official offered his hand to Daniyal. "Welcome, Mr. Steinfeld.

Welcome to the United States of America. And I hope for what's left of it, you have a nice day."

As the official stamped the passport, in his head Daniyal heard the full force of an orchestral hit, tutti e fortissimo, echo climatically as though throughout the entire arrivals hall.

16

With a mixture of elation (for obvious reasons) and depression (brought on by alcohol dosed with circumstances) Daniyal pushed his two cases the few yards through to the arrivals hall. He hoped someone would be there to meet him.

As he came through the double doors, an immense cheer went up, flashbulbs popped, and reporters scribbled excitedly on their notebooks. Daniyal needed a moment to realise the welcome was for him. But that is what it said on the placards. "Welcome Daniyal." "Welcome Daniyal Steinfeld to Boston." "The Boston Symphony Orchestra welcomes Maestro Steinfeld." "Daniyal Steinfeld, the world's greatest pianist." There must have been a dozen of them.

Still slightly inebriated, he wasn't focusing too well. But he was sure he saw one that had spelt Steinfeld wrongly—there was an added 't' on the end. "They should know better," he mumbled to himself, and immediately barked the order, "Andy, get that sorted please." (Andy, who had just turned up, was his US agent.) "Or they'll have me standing trial for war crimes before I can play another note!"

Andy hadn't a clue what he was talking about and put the incoherence down to the drink he could smell on Daniyal's breath. But just to be sure, he made a mental note to get the placard fixed.

Daniyal loved the attention. It was all the more sweet after his bruising experience at the hands of Colombo. Once he gathered his composure, he beamed warmly at everyone in the welcome committee, especially the ladies from the Boston Musical Appreciation Society. He signed a few autographs and made a short speech of thanks.

Then Andy said, "That's probably enough, maestro. You have a concert tomorrow afternoon, so we must get you to the hotel and to your bed." Daniyal normally would have resisted. He was enjoying himself. But he had to admit he was tired (the trial had taken it out of him) and with the demands of the next few days he would need all the refreshment good sleep would bring.

Andy took his bags and placed them in the boot of the yellow taxicab. Antonio, the driver, was used to VIP's and had been doing agency pickups for years. "It's all paid for, Daniyal. All you have to remember is to get out at the other end." With a cheery wave, and a "See y'ah tomorrow," that was Andy for the night.

17

The Old Boston Hotel on Dalton Street was around a twelve-minute drive from Logan. Not that much time for a conversation. Maybe Daniyal would shut his eyes.

Not for long!

"Good flight, sir?"

"Yes wonderful thanks. Very comfortable. Great service."

"You were a little later than we had expected. Was there a problem?"

"No, nothing. They were looking for someone I think."

"Yeah, I read it in the evening paper. Some war criminal called Daniyal Steinfeldt."

The words were like shards. It felt like waking up in a mortuary, your every limb encased in ice.

"Well, that's my name," Daniyal stuttered. "But it's spelt differently."

"Sure thing, Mr. Steinfeld."

Then the quiet that Daniyal craved.

Again, short lived.

"Talking of pianists," (Daniyal wasn't.) "Have you heard of Mr. Rakmanov?"

"Er, do you mean Rachmaninoff?"

"Yeah, that's him. Big, tall guy. Six foot six, he told me. I have never had such difficulty fitting a fare into my cab. It was his knees, so I had to clear the front seat for him, while his missus stayed in the back. But it gave us a nice opportunity for a chat. So Mr. Rakmanov..."

"Rachmaninoff."

"Yeah, Rakmanov. It was just before the war and Mr. Rakmanov had the world on his shoulders—pretty gloomy I would say. But when we got speaking together about Mother Russia—I was born there too—he really perked up. Especially when he discovered I had been brought up close to Oneg, near Veliky Novgorod, one of his family's estates. He went from misery to joy in seconds, like I'd just cracked a top one-liner.

"So we arrived at the hotel, and he asked me to wait for a moment while he went inside. When he returned a couple of minutes later, he had two tickets for his concert in his hands. (I noticed how huge they were). I called up my wife, and we went together that evening. Now sir, I don't know anything about music, but he was sensational. They said Mr. Rakmanov was the world's greatest living pianist."

"I thought I was," Daniyal said; fortunately, it was not loud enough for the driver to hear him.

Just before midnight, the taxi stopped outside the Old Boston Hotel. Awaiting his arrival was a distinguished senior looking gentleman resplendent in his red and gold livery. Daniyal nodded with appropriate respect as he walked past him into the reception area. His bags followed him, travelling first class in a trolley so ornate it would not have been out of place in a maharaja's palace.

The manager beams. Daniyal catches his gaze and wonders, "How is he so cheerful at this time of night!"

"Welcome back Mr. Steinfeld. You are our most honoured guest. We have been so looking forward to your return to the Old Boston."

Daniyal smiled. It was nice to be appreciated.

"We have prepared your usual suite, sir. Mathias will take you there."

The visitors book was proffered, which Daniyal signed, taking care not to attach a random 'T' to his surname! (Columbo's nonsense earlier was still whizzing round his head.) However, the thought of his own space, some down time, and a good sleep was alluring.

Matthias opened the door, and as he did so, they were greeted by a salmagundi burst of the sweetest scented fragrances. Crocuses, Hyacinths, Roses, Peonies, Lilac and other freshly cut spring flowers, arranged in a tall Royal Doulton antique crystal vase, gracefully welcomed their distinguished visitor back to his VIP suite.

"Nicer than placards," thought Daniyal.

"Is there anything else you need, sir?"

"Thank you, Mathias. No, I am all set." Mathias offered a modest bow, then turned around. He left, shutting the door behind him.

The hotel room was enormous. It was the old Boston's best suite. They had entered into the main sitting room, which was adorned with two Victorian mahogany wing sofas and four matching armchairs. The sitting room was flanked by two main doors. A door on the right opened onto the bedroom with a super king size bed.

"That could fit a chamber orchestra!" said Daniyal, speaking only to himself.

The bathroom was ensuite and tiled throughout in an original Victorian peacock design. It was fully equipped with a bath, shower and all the accoutrements required for luxury ablutions.

The double door from the sitting room opened into a music room. And there was the Bechstein grand, sitting patiently, like an old friend waiting to greet him.

Daniyal lifted the lid and played a scale and a few arpeggiated chords. The sound was good. The action was perfectly regulated and it had been tuned that day. It took Daniyal back to December three years before. Grappling with freezing temperatures, turning up the central heating had sent the piano right out of tune.

Daniyal had created a fuss. (He often did.)

Now, however, the piano sounded wonderful. He could still smell the scent of the exquisite spring flowers. Daniyal felt comfortable on the inside and was beginning to look forward to sleeping. On returning to the sitting room, he noticed what he had not seen before. Alongside the flowers was a welcome bottle of vintage Dom Pérignon, waiting invitingly on ice. All in all this time, the old Boston had done him proud.

As it was later than his usual retiring hour, Daniyal decided to be strong and give the champagne a miss. He undressed, carefully put away his clothes, showered briefly and climbed into bed. It was now 2:00 p.m. in Boston. Feeling he deserved every minute, Daniyal slept deeply for his normal full six hours.

He would have slept longer had it not been for the gentle knock at the door. Room service.

"Shall I bring your breakfast in now Mr. Steinfeld, or would you prefer it later?"

"Now," Daniyal grunted. The waiter brought in his usual—eggs and bacon (he was neither kosher nor observant) wholemeal toast, and Fortnum and Mason's marmalade, together with fresh orange juice and a pot of steaming coffee.

Daniyal Steinfeld, the world's most celebrated virtuoso pianist had at last arrived safely in Boston and soon would begin his US tour.

2ND MOVEMENT

1

Daniyal's parents, Aleksander and Leah Steinfeld, were Jewish emigrees. His mother was originally from Russia and his father from Poland.

Aleksander was descended from a long line of leading Polish musicians. His father, Abramczyk, a brilliant pianist, had studied with Czerny (who in his turn had been a pupil of Beethoven.) Abramczyk was Aleksander's first teacher until his eleventh birthday. Aleksander then enrolled as the youngest ever student at the Moscow Conservatoire, and took private piano lessons with Alexander Siloti, an outstanding pianist and the favourite pupil of the greatest of all pianists, Franz Liszt.

Under Siloti's expert instruction, the young Aleksander developed into a world class player, noted for his musical sensitivity as well as an astonishing technique. From his professional debut at just 15 years old, he became swiftly recognised as one of the most admired concert pianists of his generation. Musically, as in so many ways, he owed so much to his parents—in particular to his father—for an enlightened musical upbringing and a home which was full of music, where he met and played with many of the world's finest musicians.

One such musician, who was destined to play a pivotal role in Aleksander's later playing career, was the leading Polish virtuoso, Josef Casimir Hofmann. Abramczyk was a man of great friendships, and Hofmann was one of his closest. He was also, for many years, his two-piano colleague. They performed duets. In fact, as a piano duo, Hofmann and Steinfeld senior gave many public recitals and two piano concertos. Some still remember their altogether magical performance of the Mozart Concerto for Two Pianos at the Filharmonia Narodowa. The final rondo brought the house down!

A famous Warsaw violinist who consulted me a few years ago (she was then in her nineties) was in the orchestra and recalled the sheer joy of the music and music-making. Her memory was vivid.

"Technically it was brilliant, with perfect ensemble," she said. "Mozart has written in so much affection in the give and take between the two players. Hofmann and Steinfeld's looks of friendship made me imagine the sight of Mozart and his sister Nannerl playing it for the very first time. The pianos sang, and the music danced. It was like the heavens opened."

As a solo pianist, Hofmann toured and performed extensively over the next 50 years as one of the most celebrated pianists of the era, making the United States his base during World War 1 and becoming a US citizen in 1926. In 1914, when he heard the news that Hofmann was bound for New York, one of Abramczyk's pupils said Abramczyk looked wistful for a moment, then with a warm smile said, "Well done, Yankees. You've caught two birds with one stone." By which he was noting that Hofmann was both a formidable pianist, and an inventor of genius.

And what inventions! Hofmann had over 70 patents. Most famously he invented pneumatic shock absorbers for cars and airplanes. Other creations included a windscreen wiper, a furnace that burned crude oil, and a house that revolved with the sun!

One invention which he would have loved to have brought into being—but someone else thought of it first—was the reproducing piano. This was a machine attached to a grand piano which could record and replay with stunning accuracy every nuance of a great pianist's performance. Hofmann was one of the first pianists to record extensively in this way. Being an inventor, he loved its ingenuity. And being a performer, he loved the opportunity it offered not just for the present, but to preserve his playing for future generations too. It was indeed an invention of considerable significance, not only for some of the greatest pianists of this time, but also, as it would turn out, for the Steinfeld family.

Hitherto, pianolas or player pianos were musically crude devices which used a series of levers via a perforated paper roll to play the keyboard. But the sound was so mechanical, it was more like a fairground organ than anything approaching the subtlety of a live performance.

It was a young German inventor, Edwin Welte, who first developed the reproducing piano. Unlike a pianola or player piano, his machine would play back a recorded performance with perfect fidelity, just as though the original pianist was playing live. The Welte-Mignon was launched in 1904. The invention quickly caught on. Within 10 years, competing companies developed their own hi-tech versions of the reproducing piano, most notably The Duo-Art and Ampico pianos. These were recording machines of astonishing sophistication. They reproduced performances by many distinguished figures, such as Hofmann, Paderewski, Friedman, Josef Lhévinne, Alfred Cortot, Sergei Rachmaninoff, and George Gershwin.

In the end, the reproducing piano disappeared, not because it was inadequate, but, because it was expensive. 78 rpm records took its place. But Welte's invention still stands as one of the most innovative of its kind, and Josef Hofmann, the genius inventor-pianist, knew it. Hofmann, who in 1926 settled in the US, was such an enthusiast he recorded rolls for a number of companies. In the end, he signed an exclusive contract with Aeolian for his Duo-Art recordings, where his friend, W. Creary Woods was the recording producer. In time, that connection would preserve the extraordinary playing of Aleksander Steinfeld for generations to come.

Hofmann failed to interest Abramczyk in Duo-Art recordings. Despite their great friendship, Hofmann and his piano partner had different priorities for their lives and careers. As a concert pianist, Abram was certainly a leading player. Orchestras as far away as New York, Berlin, London and Vienna practically begged him to accept concerto engagements. But Abram did not enjoy touring. It took him away from Anna for too many days. So before they had children, he and Anna decided to move to Warsaw. Abram still played in public but decided to devote the bulk of his time to teaching. With open arms, Warsaw's Institute of Music in Okólnik Street, now the Warsaw Conservatoire, welcomed him as professor of piano.

Abram's friendship with Hofmann continued, by letter and with Josef's occasional visits home. Notably, their last formal partnership was not at the keyboard, but just before the outbreak of war as joint patrons of the Chopin Liszt Warsaw International piano competition. A competition which had launched the careers of many brilliant young pianists and one day would again embrace the piano genius of the Steinfeld family.

2

At the Warsaw Institute, and privately too, Abramczyk had many fine students. Among them, Ignaz Friedman and Alexander Siloti (both of whom later became pupils of Franz Liszt.) Siloti went on to become the teacher of Rachmaninoff and Medtner, and later we will return to his further role in the Steinfeld history.

Abramczyk proved to be a born teacher and many later-to-be leading musical figures flourished under his tutelage. But however much Abramczyk valued his work with these talented young players, when Anna fell pregnant with Aleksander, their firstborn, they both felt it was time to move back from Warsaw to Lwów as a new start for their family.

Shortly after their move, and once settled, Abram became Principal Professor of Piano at the Lwów Conservatoire. It was a leading institution, which had opened in 1854, under the leadership of the pianist and composer Karol Mikuli, a former pupil of Chopin.

Within the Conservatoire Abram founded a centre for gifted young players, to ensure good technique and musicianship were formed early in their playing careers. He used to say, "The teacher is the potter to the clay. And every young player is a work of art in his hands. Good teaching for young players is inestimable."

It used to be said, "if you cannot do it, teach it." However, the saying undermines the stature that the art of teaching is in its own right. It's about imparting skills, sensibility and musicianship. In a village or small town as much as in a Conservatoire, teachers can be found who not only have a special gift, but also a special devotion. They lavish care and time on their students' general life development as much as musical technique. At the most advanced level, the truly great teachers are few rather than many. Names such as Clementi, Czerny, Chopin, Liszt, Leschetizky and Nadia Boulanger make up this distinguished list. But in addition, upon this honoured roll—in technique, musicianship and teaching effectiveness at every level—we can confidently add the name, Abramczyk Steinfeld.

3

One evening in summer, when Aleksander was little, Abramczyk returned home from his work at the Lwów Conservatoire. As he came through the front door he could hear the piano being played in the music room. He entered to find three-year-old Aleksander, fluently picking out tunes with all the fingers of his right hand.

Abramczyk said to Aleksander, "Would you like to play a music game?"

Aleksander nodded. "What game is it?"

"It's called, *Sing me a song.* I sing you a short song, and you play it back to me at the piano. For each song, if you get the notes right, you win a prize."

Abramczyk sang him a nursery rhyme, and Aleksander played it back on the piano with perfect accuracy. Abramczyk sang another, and then another, each time adding extra bars to make the song a little longer. And still the rendition was perfect, every note in place and the rhythm steady. Then, Abramczyk tried changing key, going higher and lower.

"Remember the song you've just played. Now, play it back to me, but starting on this note." He'd then pick out a new starting note and a new key.

Every time the result was faultless. Aleksander loved the game. And as promised, the boy received his prize. A half-sized box of chocolate marshmallows, and a big hug from his father. Aleksander was delighted. So was Abramczyk.

And with that his mother called, "Czas na herbatę!" (Teatime!)

4

The very next day Aleksander began lessons with his father and his progress was lightning charged. No inducements, incentives or prizes were required, (although plenty of hugs were still on offer.) But if practice makes perfect, Aleksander was clearly aiming for the moon and beyond. At every opportunity, he would climb onto the piano stool early in the morning before breakfast and begin his practice for the day. With school and other responsibilities permitting, he would stay there until late at night. At which point he had to be practically unglued from the piano.

Aleksander would carefully practice his scales and arpeggios on the metronome until every note was in its proper place, with even articulation and beauty of sound. He learnt his pieces slowly, left hand and right hands separately, only adding to the speed when he had reached perfection. With any brush or smudge, he would pause, analyse, and correct, returning to the slowest speed where all had previously been well, and continuing from there. This was the method Abram taught his son. Every new day Aleksander would achieve ever greater heights and the boy loved his new achievements won in every practice session.

It was the whole inner world of music that he was discovering—the expression, emotion, and communication—that drew him and held him. Even at his young age, despite the remarkable technical advances he was making, Aleksander was clearly more in love with the music itself rather than just the technique or the physical act of making it happen. Away from the piano, he used to practice his pieces by singing them loudly around the house, uninhibited at the top of his sweet treble voice. Even his father, with all his long experience of teaching the most able and gifted, was amazed and delighted at his son's progress.

Aleksander was so often found at Abram's piano, he was reluctant at bedtime to end his sessions and put down the piano lid. It was as if he had adopted the piano as his special friend, and the two were not to be parted.

For a couple of years, Aleksander continued to progress with extraordinary energy and attainment. However, given the importance of encouragement, and especially for Aleksander in his playing, Abram had not complained at all. Yet he was finding it increasingly difficult to gain access to the piano for himself to practice and to play. He did not wish to at all discourage his son's upward trajectory.

A solution needed to be found.

Abram and Anna put their heads together and consulted the manager of their bank. It didn't take long to come to a decision. The Steinfelds resolved together to buy Aleksander his own instrument and set up one of their two guest rooms as his special place for making music and practice.

They knew this might be risking the wafting sounds of Mozart reaching them in their sleeping state at 6 o'clock in the morning! Though they were sure that they would be able to find, if necessary, one or two inducements to manage that.

As the pages of history turn, this decision would emerge as a key point in the Steinfeld dynasty's remarkable contribution to pianistic excellence.

5

The piano shop, Lew i Sala, was within walking distance, close to the Steinfelds' home. So it was, after school on a beautiful spring day in March, that Aleksander set out with his parents down Zachodnia Avenue to look for a piano.

Aleksander was excited. "My very own piano!" He could hardly believe it.

Abram had made an appointment for 3:45 p.m. for the three of them to visit. The piano showroom was usually busy, as practically every family in their town owned a piano and played it. The owner, Mr. Sala, had suggested the time as it would be quieter then, and he would make sure there were no other appointments.

From a distance, they could see the lofty silhouetted figure of Mr. Lewandowski, the manager of Lew i Sala, waiting for them outside on the street. At 6' 2" he dwarfed most people he met.

"No need to be afraid of him, Aleksander," his father said. "He is very kind." Slightly apprehensive, Aleksander nodded, with a look that said, "It remains to be seen."

As they arrived, Mr. Lewandowski shook hands warmly with Abramczyk and Anna. They were well acquainted through Shul, and close up, Aleksander recognised him and felt less nervous.

Mr. Lewandowski immediately passed on a message he had been asked to convey.

"May I first offer apologies from Mr. Sala. He had especially wanted to greet his old teacher and Mrs. Steinfeld, and of course to meet Aleksander. He is so sorry he has been called away on urgent family business." His regrets were sincere and understood. The message delivered, the gentle giant looked down.

"So this is Aleksander," said Mr. Lewandowski, his face genuinely kind, putting out his hand to exchange greetings with the boy. Aleksander was looking spick and span in his freshly pressed sailor suit. His parents were so proud when Aleksander gave the manager a broad smile, bowed and shook Mr. Lewandowski's hand, not once but twice, up and down, up and down, in a grandiose but respectful gesture.

"Well now, young man," said Mr. Lewandowski, guiding Aleksander by the shoulder into what can best be described as a sparkling sea of black and white keys, "Let's see if you can play the piano as nicely as you shake hands."

Aleksander was overwhelmed with delight. He had never seen as many pianos before—there must have been almost 100 of them. Some uprights, some grands. Some old, some new. Makers from Poland and all over Europe: Budynowicz, Buchholtz, Blüthner, Bosendorfer, Bechstein, Ibach, Pleyel, and quite a few others.

However, one instrument overshadowed them all. In pride of place, right at the centre of the showroom, there was an enormous nine-foot Steinway Model D concert grand.

With the precision of a long-range rifle scope, Aleksander spotted it immediately, and limpet-like fixed his sights on the sleeping black beast. Looking first to Mr. Lewandowski, and then to his father, he ran straight towards it, his eyes and demeanour clearly speaking the same silent request: "pleeeeze!"

"Mr. Sala said I was to grant you every facility, Mr. Steinfeld. The Steinway is a wonderful instrument. It has just arrived from Hamburg this week and had its first tuning this morning. The touch will be a little heavier than Aleksander is used to."

Turning to Aleksander, he said, "Go ahead young sir. I'll put the lid up for you. A grand piano always sounds better with the lid up. I always say to play quietly, you just have to play quietly!"

Aleksander couldn't wait. He also couldn't reach the pedals. But he made up for that by his sheer musical intelligence and keyboard control. At a brisk allegro he began the C minor prelude of the second book of Bach's 48 preludes and fugues, with beautifully even semiquavers, rapid, flowing, and stylishly Baroque.

Aleksander's audience of three stood in complete silence. At the prelude's final chord Abramczyk and Anna exchanged a single glance. Mr. Lewandowski said nothing, though if anyone had noticed his moistened eyes they might have read his emotions.

Aleksander began the fugue, his phrasing noble, his part playing transparent and convincing. Towards the end, and the final recapitulation of the first subject, allowing the sonority of the instrument to build to a tremendous climax, he added octaves in the bass. The Steinway in its turn roared its approval, and Aleksander steered the piece back safely to dry land, holding his young head high and alert as the final chord died away.

The audience burst into applause. His parents were as proud as they were impressed. Mr. Lewandowski was simply moved. For a moment he was almost unable to speak. From the son of one of the world's greatest piano teachers, he had expected a creditable performance. But this was beyond all expectation. Such technical control. Such maturity and musicianship. Such passion and drama. Yet all in proportion to the stylistic requirement of the music.

Aleksander bowed to the three of them, and then turned and bowed deeply and reverentially to the piano.

"If it was mine, I would gladly make a present to you of this fine instrument, Aleksander!" said Mr. Lewandowski. "But I am sure in your lifetime, you will befriend many Steinways in the world's greatest concert halls. I am also sure that playing them you will bring such joy to your parents in the wonderful performances that you will give."

Towards the end of this modest but heartfelt speech, Mr. Lewandowski's voice cracked momentarily.

Sensing his emotion, Abramczyk filled the silence, appreciatively. "I'm sure Aleksander would love nothing more than to wrap the piano in brown paper and take it home immediately. But we'd have to buy a far bigger house—a model D Steinway wouldn't squeeze through our front door!

Everyone laughed, including Aleksander.

6

Since 1828, Bösendorfer has been one of the world's greatest piano manufacturers. For those who know pianos, the Bösendorfer name has evoked the same kind of reverence reserved for Steinway, Blüthner and Bechstein.

Aleksander noticed the Bösendorfer upright as soon as he had entered the Lew i Sala showroom. So now, following his audition of the Steinway, he ran over to the Bösendorfer, and without thinking further, lifted the keyboard cover. Aleksander then remembered his manners and looked longingly at Mr. Lewandowski for permission to try it.

Mr. Lewandowski was about to say something, but Aleksander was so keen he hopped on the stool and began playing it immediately, and what was to have been said would have to wait till later.

This time, by adjusting the stool downwards, Aleksander was just about able to reach the sustaining pedal by twisting himself slightly to the right. He began to play the Chopin C minor nocturne opus 48, transporting his small but discerning audience to a plane of ravishing beauty and expression. His shaping of the slow-moving opening was so magical it caused Mr. Lewandowski to whisper into Abram's ear: "Where does a child gain an experience of life like that? It's miraculous."

The miracle continued unabated till the final sustained C minor chords. Then, smiling sympathetically, Mr. Lewandowski stepped forward. After expressing his appreciation to the young pianist, he said what he had intended to mention before Aleksander had begun the Chopin.

"I think, Aleksander, this Bösendorfer would be the perfect choice for you at this stage of your studies. However, I am sorry to be disappointing, for this one is already promised to another customer." Then he turned to the parents. "Mr. and Mrs. Steinfeld, I expect you know that Bösendorfer uprights are made in comparatively small numbers and their owners tend to hold on to them. So it is rare indeed to find a used model for sale like this one."

Abram nodded.

"But I have an idea. Please bear with me while I fetch my diary."

Returning from the back of the store, diary in hand, "I thought so," he said. "The annual piano auction takes place in Warsaw next week. I hadn't planned to go as our stock is quite full at the moment. But if you would like me to go and look for a similar model to this one for Aleksander, I would count it a privilege. If we can find one, a used model will save a great deal of money, and if any work is needed we can do that in our workshops. For the reasons indicated I cannot promise I will be successful. What I can promise is I will try my best."

So it was a rare opportunity when Mr. Lewandowski was able to bid for a pre-owned "top of the range" upright Bösendorfer in the piano auction in Warsaw the following week. It was the same model as the one Aleksander had played in the Lew i Sala showroom.

Aleksander stayed at home with his mother while Abramczyk and Mr. Lewandowski travelled to Warsaw together. It was a two-day round trip. The auction room hushed to a respectful silence when Abramczyk Steinfeld stepped forward to examine the instrument, casting an expert eye over the keys, strings, hammers, soundboard and pedal action. Then he sat at the Bösendorfer and played Siloti's arrangement of the Tchaikovsky Pas de deux from the Nutcracker ballet.

Abram played with such heartfelt passion that at the conclusion the normally hard-nosed piano buyers completely forgot the commercial reasons for their presence and cheered and stamped their appreciation. Even though it was not in any sense a recital, Abram felt from respect and courtesy he should bow and gratefully acknowledge the enthusiastic reception.

At the end of the auction, the auctioneer, Mr. Maciej Kremblewski, invited Abramczyk and Mr. Lewandowski to join him for a coffee together. Once he had made his formal introduction and again expressed his sincere appreciation for the playing of the Tchaikovsky, Mr. Kremblewski said there were two matters he wished to mention.

"The first," he said, "is that good news travels fast. We heard about your son, Aleksander, through some of your old colleagues at the Warsaw Institute of Music who I understand visited you last month. They spoke about his extraordinary precocity and so his reputation travelled here many weeks before your visit today. Once it became known among the bidders the purpose for which you and Mr. Lewandowski were braving the long journey for this auction, they wanted to ensure this piano was reserved for Aleksander. The seller also wished to help, and this was why, completely voluntarily, they kept the bidding down, and you have been able to obtain it at such a good price."

"Thank you, most sincerely," Abram said, both surprised and pleased. He looked gratefully at Mr. Lewandowski, for this kindness was surely also part of his doing. Then, back to Mr. Kremblewski.

"You said there was a second point?"

"Yes. In a Bösendorfer of this quality and age, its provenance may hold special importance. In this case, I am sure you will be interested to learn that this piano was once the property and practice instrument of none other than Franz Liszt. I am only mentioning it now since the seller did not wish to convey this information publicly or as a selling point. All I am able to say is that it was sold on behalf of Cosima Wagner, the widow of Richard Wagner, who was of course the daughter of Franz Liszt and The Comtesse Marie d'Agoult. When he died in Bayreuth in 1886, it was Marie d'Agoult who initially inherited Liszt's estate. Although this Bösendorfer (along with many other fine instruments) has been kept in the family since that time, it is well known that Liszt owned such a large collection of pianos, that at some point, the collection would need to be slimmed down. Hence the appearance of this Bösendorfer at auction today."

Abramczyk was fascinated to hear the story, and to learn who had originally played the instrument, and the stunning pianism it must have partnered.

"Well!" he exclaimed. "Franz Liszt's piano! If that doesn't inspire Aleksander to practice his scales, nothing will!"

7

After some more coffee and swapping some stories of music and musicians, Abramczyk and Mr. Lewandowski shook hands warmly with Mr. Kremblewski and went off to arrange the delivery of Aleksander's Bösendorfer.

"It will be with you on Friday afternoon," the shipping clerk said. "It will be conveyed to you with the utmost care."

"Are you sure it will fit through our front door, Mr. Lewandowski?" Abramczyk asked, mainly in jest, but with a touch of anxiety at the back of his mind.

"Yes, I assure you. The fit will be perfect."

And come Friday, so it turned out.

The front door was easy to navigate as the delivery men placed the piano on a special piano dolly, practically whisking it in. The stairs, however, were a different issue, and the piano had to be lifted up them. The men were well practiced and not fazed by the weight of an iron frame, although the load was considerable. After a few strained calls of "up a bit" and "down a bit," in no time, the piano was on the top step and rolled comfortably into the newly decorated music practice room. There, at Abramczyk's direction, it was settled in the bay window where also it was a perfect fit. The piano enjoyed a lovely view of the Steinfeld's garden.

Mr. Lewandowski, an experienced and expert piano technician in his own right, came round immediately when he heard the piano had been safely delivered, and spent some time checking it over. When he had finished, he said to Abram, "It needed hardly any work. Just a small adjustment to the tuning and very minor regulation and voicing." With that, he put his coat back on. As he was preparing to leave, he doffed his cap and said, "When he returns from school, give my warm regards to Aleksander, and say I hope he and Mr. Bösendorfer will soon be best friends, and enormously enjoy one another's company in all their playing together."

8

By the end of his first year of tuition Aleksander was five and had already advanced from Haydn to Mozart and Clementi piano sonatas. With the stimulus of his new piano he continued his spectacular progress, learning Bach's two- and three-part inventions. By the time he was six, he graduated to both books of Bach's 48 preludes and fugues and committed all the music to memory.

Every day for an hour before school Aleksander would work on technique. Abramczyk gave him scale patterns in all major and minor keys, exercises in thirds, sixths, and octaves, and for the development of touch and velocity, there were large doses of Czerny. (The scores had Czerny's pencilled-in fingerings and were the actual ones his father had worked on with Czerny when he was Aleksander's age.) The next year, to fully extend his technical capacity, Aleksander graduated to the Chopin studies, which were a revelation to him of ingenuity and expression; by the time he was seven, he had mastered them all.

Friends remark on his large hands, his long tapering fingers and his long thumb. Like having the right tools for the job, there was no doubt that his hands were ideal for a pianist. But on their own, large hands do not automatically produce dexterity. There is something inexplicable, marvellous, and divinely given about such ability in one so young. Who knows why, how, or for how long a marvel like this will endure? But surely where there is no doubt, was that at this age Aleksander was a prodigy and had already achieved an advanced standard of technique and maturity in interpretation that was way beyond his years, well exceeding that of many already established professional artists.

Before the purchase of the Bösendorfer, when three of his old piano teaching colleagues from Okólnik Street (as the Warsaw Institute was referred to) came to visit Abramczyk and Anna, they had no idea of Aleksander's pianistic prowess. All three nodded politely in support when Aleksander asked his father if he could play something for the three nice gentlemen from Warsaw. They weren't expecting fireworks, but they felt the son of Abramczyk Steinfeld would play something simple and well. It was good for him to have an audience, they thought, although just the four of them, and Anna baking in the kitchen.

Abramczyk smiled at Aleksander, and seeing his father's approval, Aleksander immediately skipped across to the large grand piano, lifted the lid, and climbed onto the stool. Like a professional, he adjusted the seat right down so he could reach the pedals. Just. Preparations complete, in a loud voice, Aleksander announced his choice. "Chopin, Winter Wind." And without any hesitation, launched straight in to the first four bars.

The dotted rhythm opening theme was played quietly and with intense concentration. Then, like an exploding volcano, a tumultuous cascade of sixteenth notes erupted from the top of the keyboard; the left-hand leaping in punctuating fury, driving forward the rhythm of the raging wind and sudden lightning flashes. So the storm continued unabated until the coda, and the final statement of the theme, bringing Chopin's death-defying Etude No 11 op 25, to its breathless conclusion.

Having concluded some particularly demanding piece, there are players who love to add some histrionics to their performance. To let us know that they have danced with death and prevailed, and that we should be stunned at their heroics, their shoulders rise and fall with their heavy breathing; their hands run maniacally through their tousled hair; they practically swoon there on stage in front of us.

None other than Franz Liszt was the inventor of this bizarre behaviour. But never in his career would Aleksander be attracted to such melodrama. On the contrary, after a polite little bow in response to the stunned applause, he ran off meekly to the kitchen to help his mother make tea.

"The world must hear him, Abramczyk," the three excited visitors said, practically in unison.

"Thank you," he said. "Anna and I know Aleksander has a very special gift, but we don't consider him ready yet to face the crowds. The time will come, but when it does, we will need to introduce him gently to manage the adulation as there will inevitably be. Too much attention at an early stage in life, as Dr. Freud is teaching us, is not good for the ego or the soul."

That gentle exposure began through his performances in the family's musical soirées. Pianist friends and other musicians would come and play, and Aleksander was allowed to play one piece (usually not as showy as the Chopin.)

Aleksander remembers one of these evenings especially, and over the years spoke of it with particular affection. Guests that night included Rachmaninoff, his cousin and teacher Siloti, and Josef Hofmann. The evening in question was devoted to piano duets.

And what duets! Brahms' 21 Hungarian dances are indisputably the most cheerful music Brahms ever composed. (And it seems, the most profitable!) Abram and Hofmann planned to play the work divided into two sets, which they did with outstanding panache—the first set before supper, and the second planned for after.

Anna was a great hostess and had hired in help for the evening. Dinner was traditional Polish cuisine, including a choice of two soups: duck (czarnina), and red beet (barszcz). There were dumplings (pierogi), smoked salmon and eel; a range of dry pork sausages and sauerkraut; and roasted chicken served with a sweet sauce. If anyone had any room after this (and the men did!) there was Pączki (fruit-filled deep-fried pastries), Polish cheeses, and gooseberries fresh from their Steinfeld garden.

With all this fine food (and vodka) to sustain them, the party made their way back to the drawing-room. Aleksander was allowed to stay up, though, he would have sat listening at the top of the stairs otherwise!

The atmosphere was very cheerful, a combination of the food and music, enlivened by several bottles of Wódka Wyborowa which had been brought (and consumed) by Rachmaninoff and Siloti. The evening was about to become even more cheerful.

Anna was called in to enjoy the rest of the Brahms. Just as Abramczyk and Josef were preparing themselves to play, Rachmaninoff stood up. At 6' 6," by anybody's standard he was a giant. The great Russian bear moved towards Aleksander, and in a fireman's lift transported him across to the piano.

Abram looked on, admittedly a little puzzled. But then, with a grand theatrical gesture, Sergei lifted Aleksander high above his towering mass until Aleksander's head almost touched the ceiling; then brought him into land, setting him gently down upon the piano stool.

Once he got his breath back, Aleksander thought this was hilarious and could hardly stop laughing. Anna too. In fact, everyone in the room laughed till almost exhausted. The noise was so great it alarmed the kitchen staff who came upstairs to check if everything was alright.

Everything was alright. And then "the man with the six-foot scowl" (which is how a newspaper once described Rachmaninoff) who also could not stop laughing, announced in his thickly accented Russian: "It is time for Aleksander and me to entertain you."

Sergei sat down next to Aleksander and opened the music. Then a single word of command: "Play!" Which they did, with Aleksander sight reading Brahms' entire second set.

The music bounced along, con brio. Their audience clapping in time, murmuring their approval throughout. When they finished, and everyone had applauded, congratulated, and said what a good evening it had been, Anna said to Aleksander, "It's past your bedtime, say good night to everyone."

Aleksander received warm hugs and "night-night" kisses from everybody, and last of all from the great Russian bear. Sergei once again lifted Aleksander up, who was momentarily submerged in his great bulk, hugged him and said into his ear, "Well done, young Aleksander. You are a great talent and when the world discovers you, you will make your parents and your country so proud."

10

Despite the attention Aleksander was gaining through his performances in the family's musical soirées, his father would not yet allow him to play in public concerts. Abramczyk considered that artistic development should take account of the well-being of the heart and soul as much as the fingers. In the past, he had discussed this subject on several occasions with his own piano professor, Theodor Leschetizky, who, along with Franz Liszt and Anton Rubenstein, was among the most influential teachers of the 19th century.

Leschetizky was born in Lancut in south-eastern Poland in 1830. He was a virtuoso pianist and a capable composer of small-scale works, but his lasting fame rests upon his outstanding international reputation as a teacher. Although Leschetizky's technical legacy is legendary, his students speak of an even greater inheritance: the development of their aesthetics, interpretation and artistic integrity. As he often said, "No life without art, no art without life!"

In the late 1870s Leschetizky moved to Vienna. There in his villa in the Währing Cottage District on Karl-Ludwig-Straße, he established one of the most eminent private piano schools in the world, a magnet for promising young professional pianists from across Europe. Many now are household names like Ignacy Jan Paderewski, Aleksander Brailowsky, Ignaz Friedman, Ossip Gabrilowitsch, Mark Hambourg, Mabel Lander, Benno Moiseiwitsch, Artur Schnabel—and Abramczyk Steinfeld.

Leschetizky's aim was to develop the individual characteristics of each student. He would invariably leave time at the end of a lesson to discuss deeper understandings of music and ideas, connecting music with the wider meaning of art, philosophy, religion, and the emerging science of psychology.

At such a time, at the end of a lesson, Leschetizky expressed the opinion that an excess of applause at an early age may help create unhealthy performance appetites in later life. Abramczyk asked him to elaborate.

"Delayed gratification tames all kinds of potentially exaggerated appetites, including the thirst for attention, or even showing off. It is natural," said Leschetizky, "to give a child a bonbon to celebrate a deed well done. But if we give him the whole box, he will end up wanting more, and, maybe with screams and tantrums, will not rest until he has secured that to which he feels he is now entitled. As I have found with some of my most famous and most gifted students, especially the prodigies, allowing too much applause early on may over-develop their taste for adulation and become as important as the performance itself."

Abramczyk asked him about showmanship, and how in his early years Franz Liszt would unashamedly squeeze the last drop of adulation from an adoring audience.

Leschetitsky replied admiringly, "Of course, Liszt is one of the greatest pianists of our time. Maybe, the greatest." But he added, "Great music deserves modesty and dignity from its interpreters, not an eye to the adoration of the crowd. But from Liszt's early example, see now how showmanship has developed at the keyboard and in the Concert Hall."

He stood up and shut the piano lid, walking round the piano as though joining the watching crowd.

"Don't we love to create heroes and gods out of our performers! It's a joint enterprise, a kind of conspiracy between the psychological needs of the artist and audience. But recall the composer's motive. Think of Chopin. Unlike some of his contemporaries—Herz, Kalbrenner, Thalberg—his piano writing is clearly fashioned to inspire the spirit, not to draw attention to clever fingering! Even if the music is virtuosic, and its agility is part of its appeal, the performer should always be the servant of the music, not the other way round."

He walked back to the piano, but without sitting, continued, "You ask me about Liszt. These antics the newspapers called "Lisztomania" spread widely. Some performers have little insight. They don't see how their thirst for esteem connects with untamed desires, like instant gratification. Self-indulgence can only undermine the music. That said, there are exceptions. Among the truly greats, Clara Schumann is a remarkable virtuoso, a most sensitive player and composer. She is always the servant of the music. Have you heard her, Abramczyk?"

Abramczyk nodded.

"Then you will have noticed the maturity in her playing and the modest way she responds to applause. Maturity and modesty belong together. So my good friend Franz Liszt? I'm glad to say that now he has taken holy orders, he has at last cured himself of all that nonsense."

11

A bramczyk recalled that discussion when he and Anna discussed the question of young Aleksander's concertizing. They were conscious that short term decisions may not be good for Aleksander's long-term wellbeing. Although by this time, as a prodigy, Aleksander was already in certain respects a mature artist, nonetheless, they both agreed he was not yet what he would one day become.

"We do feel," they explained to a group of their musical friends, "that not only does Aleksander's musical development require wise guidance; most importantly, we have to remind ourselves that Aleksander is a child—a young child at that. We need to ensure, like any normal boy, he has time for friends and fun; time to enjoy his schoolwork and benefit from his studies; time to kick a ball and play; time to discover himself. Aleksander would become all the less of a person if we should deny him that, and eventually all the less of a musician too."

For this reason his parents agreed that he would not take on any public concerts until his 7th birthday, and then following only one or two concerts or recitals in the year. So that very day, the fifteenth April 1898, Aleksander made his public debut in the music room of the Potocki Palace, the grandest residence in the city, located on the street Kopernyka, 15. Alfred Józef Potocki, the owner of the recently constructed palace and former Minister-President of Austria, had agreed to the concert taking place and planned to be present. Although he was sceptical about how well he expected the child would play, he was warm in his welcome both to Aleksander and his family.

Standing before a capacity audience squeezed into the music room, Mr. Potocki said, "Ladies and gentlemen, it is my honour to welcome you this afternoon with three debut appearances. The first is of our new Potocki Palace. Many of you will have watched its construction. My congratulations are in order, as you are now our first and most valued visitors. We hope you enjoy what you have already seen and what you will see of this magnificent building." There were murmurs of approval and appreciation

Mr. Potocki then made a gesture towards the platform. "The second debut is of this majestic nine-foot concert grand Bechstein. The renowned Bechstein company was founded in Prussia in 1853 by Herr Carl Bechstein and is one of the world's leading piano manufacturers. They have made pianos for the Tsars of Russia, Queen Victoria, and many other distinguished houses, including today for the Potocki Palace."

More applause.

"Under the guidance of Herr Bechstein, his craftsmen have lavished eighteen months of expertise to build this combined marvel of art, science, and engineering. Mr. Bechstein is present among you today, and I thank him and his colleagues for their great accomplishment."

Herr Bechstein was asked to stand and was greeted by further applause.

"May I just add that I am but an amateur pianist. So may I also say how grateful I am to Mr. Sala and Mr. Lewandowski, of Lew i Sala, for their recommendation of this fine instrument which will be played for the first time this evening."

He gestured towards the aforementioned gentlemen who were both sitting with Herr Bechstein in the front row. The two gentlemen nodded and smiled at the ensuing applause.

"It is well known that Mr. Lewandowski is especially well informed about the rising stars in the sphere of piano performance. It was he who encouraged us to invite our special guest and soloist for this evening. As I said to him when he made the suggestion, I have never heard a child of seven play the piano in public, let alone play a whole recital of Chopin, Beethoven and Schubert.

"I have studied the piano for years and admit the pieces he will play are way beyond my ability. But I understand Professor Steinfeld, his distinguished father, has taught his son from the very beginning, and we must thank him and Mrs. Steinfeld for their careful nurturing of their son's talent." For which comments, there was a flutter of gentle applause.

"This is the first time our soloist has appeared in public. Today is his seventh birthday. So for the most important of our three debuts tonight," he turned gingerly and whispered to Aleksander, "Aleksander will you come and join us." Turning back to the audience, he continued, "Ladies and gentlemen, will you please welcome to play our new Bechstein at the Potocki Palace, Aleksander Steinfeld."

Aleksander bounced onto the platform, smartly dressed in his favourite sailor's suit. He beamed at everyone. The ladies present were especially delighted to see his confidence and winning smile. He bowed to Mr. Potocki, then to his parents, and then to Herr Bechstein, Mr. Sala and Mr. Lewandowski in turn. Finally, towards the magnificent Bechstein, he bowed low and respectfully, under his breath wishing it, "Happy first birthday. I'm sure we are going to be friends."

12

After Mr. Potocki's splendid speech, following Aleksander's arrival on stage, in anticipation of what was to come, the room became suddenly full of excited chattering and whispering. It was as though everyone had a birthday that day and couldn't wait to open their present. Aleksander used the time to settle himself and adjust his stool to the right height. Once he was ready, he observed his audience. Ladies smiled at him like adoring mothers. Several gentlemen caught his eye and nodded warmly. After a few gentle words of "hush-hush," the audience settled, quiet and attentive.

Between them, Master Steinfeld and his new friend, Mr. Bechstein, the piano, delivered three magnificent and memorable performances.

The recital began with Chopin's Fantaisie-Impromptu in C-Sharp Minor, op 66. Aleksander played with outstanding fluency, tenderly shaping the rising and falling phrases with poetry and seemingly effortless virtuosity.

To this day, no one knows definitively why Chopin did not permit this powerful and expressive piece to be published during his lifetime. Perhaps someone had suggested resemblances between Chopin's opening theme and an Impromptu by the Bohemian pianist, Ignaz Moscheles, or even with Beethoven's rising arpeggios in the last movement of the Moonlight Sonata?

In both cases, the similarities are superficial, and no one then or now could seriously suggest plagiarism. There's a clue on the manuscript. It indicates more than just a dedication: "Composed for the Baroness d'Este by Frédéric Chopin." Chopin had received a paid commission and had therefore sold the Impromptu to Madame la Baronne d'Este. So for that reason, like others of his commissioned works, it could only be published posthumously.

The world had to wait its turn. But when all was revealed, it became obvious the Impromptu was a forgotten Chopin masterpiece.

It was not to remain forgotten for much longer. Soon after the Impromptu's eventual publication, Abramczyk, himself a child prodigy, had learnt and played it. He was one of the first Polish piano virtuosos to popularise the piece and played it often in salons and in recitals. It was also the first major Chopin piece Abramczyk taught Aleksander. They both loved the work. That long term knowledge, that confident familiarity, like the ease of an old friendship, shone through Aleksander's performance. So much so, that several in the audience that day spoke of the pure affection and inspiration of the boy's rendition.

"Inspiration comes, where thought is saturated in emotion, and emotion is imbued with sense." Those words of the composer-pianist Nikolai Medtner exactly describe the emotional strength of the Fantasie-Impromptu, and all the performances that afternoon.

It was not surprising, therefore, at the end of the Chopin and the Beethoven Pathétique Sonata which followed it, that the audience was breathless in its appreciation. During the interval, the buzz of excited conversation was almost as intoxicating as the complimentary champagne that Mr. Potocki had so kindly provided. Laughter and yelps of appreciation ricocheted off the walls of the gilded stucco reception hall. Everyone seemed as taken with the genius of the pianist as they were with the beauty of the music. The bar was set high for the performance of Schubert's Wanderer Fantasy.

For the concert's second part, the audience settled quickly—less chatter, but with appetites whetted, more anticipation. A child prodigy hadn't been heard in Lwów for some 30 years. The last occasion was when crowds had flocked to hear the young Edvard Grieg, who at that time was known as a pianist, though later his lasting fame would be as a composer. In Aleksander's audience there were several who remembered Grieg's excellent musical playing, but also recalled the nasty cough and breathing difficulties from which he was to suffer even more in later life.

A prodigy, by definition, is a rarity. Possibly one in five or ten million people. Most, sadly, do not deliver beyond their early promise. The exceptions are those whose careers, ignited in childhood as by a brilliant firecracker, continue, their light burning ever brighter to the end of their lives. Some like Mozart and Clara Schumann whose highly ambitious fathers pushed their children to the limit; for others like Beethoven, Chopin and Saint Saëns, appear, in this sense, to be self-starters.

So, why were child prodigies so popular? Unusual talent there has to be. But it can be argued, for less than artistic reasons, it is the audience that creates prodigies. For some will flock to see a child perform as they might jostle for the best seat at the circus. After all, the circus was a No. 1 in popular entertainment.

From the late 18th century onwards even the smallest towns in Europe looked forward to a circus visit. Roaring lions, trumpeting elephants in their menageries, and death-defying trapeze acts under the big top became magnetic attractions. But in practice, the attractions of spectacle and dare-devil danger were not just entertainment. They were designed to bring relief to ennui, to the listless dissatisfaction of bored and humdrum lives. And the idea worked. After Philip Astley staged the first modern circus in London in 1768, the idea quickly caught on. Within a hundred years, the circus was crowned king. By the 1870's the railways were enabling huge extravaganzas to tour across Europe and America, often with two or three trainloads of equipment.

The Potocki Palace was no circus of course. Count Potocki would have been mortified at the suggestion! But it may well be true that some in the audience in the Potocki Palace were present for similar reasons; to be wowed as much at the prodigious skills of this child musician and his command of the keyboard, as they would utter "oohs" and "aahs" at the parade of elephants, the roaring of the lions, and dizzying hold-your-breath moments in a circus high wire act.

But what they heard and witnessed that afternoon was something more impressive. The musicality was as astonishing as the technique.

It is possible to imagine a seven-year-old actor playing Hamlet and speaking all Shakespeare's lines from memory. But it is unlikely that a child actor, however brilliant, could attain the depth of feeling and expression that an adult professional would bring to the part.

This is why Aleksander was a quite different prodigy. He was certainly a performer. Technically he was already superb. But as his father had always reminded him: "Performance is about the music, Aleksander. Playing the piano is for the sake of the music alone. It is why God has entrusted you with this gift. That you should be the servant of the music and bring the music to the people."

So in the second half when Aleksander presented Schubert's magisterial Wanderer Fantasy, the performance was as far from a circus act as Dan is to Beersheba. If you shut your eyes, as many did, you could not have possibly realised the pianist was only seven years old! It was an explosion of pianistic and emotional energy, of poetry and sheer musical drama. It certainly banished ennui. Attention was rapt throughout. With hands flying, fingers racing, the brand new Bechstein reaching up to obey its lion tamer's every command; then singing its heart out in pure poetry, at its conclusion the performance drew a huge roar of approval and applause.

Aleksander bowed politely to the audience, and then to Mr. Bechstein the piano, and then to his parents who were beaming with pride and approval. Mr. Potocki stepped forward. Austria's former Minister-President was so transported by the music, he was clearly overcome with emotion. But when the audience had quietened, he calmed too. With glowing praise he first thanked Aleksander and then his parents. After a few further words thanking the guests for coming, he then called on Mrs. Potocki, who stepped on to the stage smiling, carrying a bag of small parcels.

Turning to Aleksander, Mr. Potocki explained. "Following a recital, we normally offer flowers as a thank you to the pianist. But in knowledge that today is your seventh birthday, Aleksander, the entire audience has subscribed to these presents for you. I'll leave you to unwrap them at home. But there is a Dreidel, small spinning top with a Hebrew letter on each side, for Hanukkah. Then some miniature toy soldiers and horses. A wooden train set. And then from myself and Mrs. Potocki, an original 1849 hand carved Staunton chess set, specially imported from London, the box engraved in silver with the words: Aleksander Steinfeld, Potocki Palace, 15th April 1898.

Then Mr. Potocki stretched out his hand to Aleksander. As they shook, he was struck, in comparison to his own, by what a large hand young Aleksander had.

"Happy Birthday, Aleksander!" Everyone applauded. The mood was festive and the applause and the birthday wishes seemed as though they would never end.

13

As you would expect when he returned home there was another birthday party, prepared and ready, waiting for Aleksander to appear. Standing on the front step, looking out for the arrival of his father's car, were five friends from school, including his best friend, Paweł. Paweł was an older boy and had a beautiful, still unbroken treble voice. He and Aleksander loved to sing and play together which they regularly did during the school's lunch break.

Anna's brother Stefan had just arrived. Stefan lived close by in Lychakivskyi District. Anna was grateful he was able to "stand in" for Grandpa and Grandma Rosenwasser, as the journey from Łódź was too far for them to come for the day. Unfortunately, Stefan had missed the concert. He had been delayed by some scuffles and street fighting, which his carriage driver had only managed to avoid by taking a longer route. Nonetheless, Anna was relieved to see him safe and well recovered from his recent illness.

Suddenly, there was a beep-beep as Abramczyk manoeuvred his three-wheel Benz Patent-Motorwagen to a stop outside the house. A big cheer went up as Aleksander climbed down from the splendid three-wheel vehicle. He gave a little bow to his friends, and to the neighbours watching and applauding from their windows. Everyone knew it was Aleksander's debut day as well as his birthday. He was getting used to applause.

As Aleksander went inside there were pats and hugs from friends and family, except from baby Gerda who was already asleep in her bedroom. But the twins, Jakub and Syzmon, had been allowed to stay up. Like searchlights their eyes were fixed on the large bag of presents being brought in by Abramczyk.

The boys were very interested in all Aleksander's presents, especially the wooden farmyard animals. With cows and chickens in hand, they were running around mooing and clucking, utterly absorbed in their new game of Chase the Hen.

An especial joy was that Granny Steinfeld had been able to travel from Warsaw. She had come for the concert and the party afterwards. She also came carrying a big parcel for Aleksander. Likewise, Stefan had brought beautifully wrapped gifts from the Rosenwassers senior, plus one of Grandpa's huge funny cards. Grandpa was famous for his cartoons, and this was a comical drawing of Aleksander, pictured with huge hands and fingers flying in all directions, the piano sitting up and begging like a pet dog. Everyone laughed at it. It said, "To Maestro Aleksander—seven today. What will you achieve next! Much love, Granny and Grandpa." They also added they hoped Aleksander would visit them soon.

So there were many expressions of delight and congratulations on the two fronts, the 7th birthday and Aleksander's public debut as a pianist. As well as Grandpa's cartoon, there was a big pile of cards from the family near and far, from Aleksander's friends and many well-wishers. There were gifts of music, especially the complete Beethoven 32 piano sonatas in the edition edited by his Steinfeld Grandfather, Solomon Ebenezer. Aleksander was very pleased with the gift and wanted to try out the music right away. His father gently said, "No, but why don't you ask Paweł to sing for us, and you can accompany him."

Paweł already had something prepared. He had written it earlier in the week. It was a birthday song, dedicated to Aleksander. Music by himself, Paweł Bohdanowicz—a beautiful, haunting melody. And words by their school friend, Mirtel Grzelak

Któż może przewidzieć przyszłość,
któż może odgadnąć, co nadejdzie.
Tylko Bóg zna drogę, którą pójdę w czasie sztormu,
w czasie walki czy gdy moje życie będzie zagrożone Jutro, jest
w rękach Boga.
Who can see the future
Who can tell what is to come,
In storm or strife, or threat to life
God only knows the path I'll take.
Tomorrow is in his hands
W radości, smutku, żałobie czy bólu
przyjdzie czas, gdy zło się skończy
Na tej myśli skupiam wzrok.

Cokolwiek się stanie,
będę ufał Bogu.
In joy and sadness, grief or pain
The time will come,
When wrong shall end.
This is where I fix my eyes,
What'er befalls, I'll trust in Him.

Paweł sang it beautifully. Aleksander had the melody written out and improvised a delicate, flowing piano accompaniment. There was warm applause from all the partygoers, but especially the adults, who particularly appreciated the pathos of Paweł's words. One or two whispered, "What a remarkable poetic gift in one so young!" Stefan's eye caught Abramczyk's in a brief moment of apprehension.

Then there was food followed by present opening, and finally by speeches.

The final speech was reserved for grandmother Steinfeld.

Aleksander's grandmother, Elsa, a strong woman with a chiselled face, a straight back even in her 80s, and a mass of grey hair tied back in a bun, stood up to speak. Grandma Steinfeld was usually quite reserved and not normally given to either flattery or praise. But she could not contain her enthusiasm. Wagging her finger, as she always did, cross or elated, and for which she was famous in the family, Elsa declared with uncharacteristic enchantment, "Aleksander, your mother and father are so proud of you, and so am I. God's gift to our family is music, Aleksander. And in each generation, it seems a

Steinfeld heir receives the musician's mantle. This was the gift to Solomon, your father's father, a Beethoven scholar; to Abramczyk, your father, a great pianist and teacher, and now to you, a virtuoso pianist in the making.

"Today's concert was an anointing, Aleksander. You are that heir, and now tomorrow belongs to you. It is the most precious gift, my child, and you must cherish it..." She hesitated before her final words, "For even the best gifts don't last forever!" and added the words of the song, "Jutro, jest w rękach Boga." ("Tomorrow is in God's hands.")

During the warm applause, sitting down, Elsa caught Abramczyk's eye on the other side of the room. As with Stefan earlier, the same brief moment of apprehension passed between mother and son.

While there was more chatting and laughter, all the friends played together with Aleksander's new toys. Just before everyone went home, Elsa took Abramczyk to one side.

"It has been a wonderful day Abram. Thank you for so much that you have done, not only for the birthday, but in the way you and Anna are caring for all your children and especially Aleksander. I just wanted to say to you what I know you already know. That is what can happen to the prodigiously gifted if the needs of their young lives are not well understood by their parents. You know what happened to your father. Solomon was in the exactly the same situation as you and Aleksander. But he burnt out, and one of the reasons we think lay behind that was that too much expectation and too much adulation came his way at too early an age." Abram noticed his mother was being careful not to wag her finger.

Abramczyk sighed as he said appreciatively, "I am very well aware of that and thank you for saying it. It is opportune. Although today was a great debut, while he is a boy, with any kind of regularity, we cannot allow Aleksander to be exposed to so much applause and everything that goes with it. For audiences seem to create the very idea of the heroic prodigy. Upon the very gifted, audiences can place far too much expectation and project their own aspirations on the child. They can turn the child into something like a circus attractions or magic trick. In a sense, they create the prodigy.

"Anna and I have discussed ways in which we may nurture Aleksander well and ensure we maintain the growth of a steady, mature child who will grow up into a happy and effective adult. That is far more important at this stage than the number of concerts that he plays, and however much the public demands for more."

Once everyone had gone home, Abramczyk and Aleksander did some tidying up together.

"It has been a great day, Aleksander. We are all so proud of you. I wonder, what was your best bit of all?"

"My presents, Papa."

"And did you have a favourite? The chess set or the Beethoven, perhaps?"

"No Papa, best of all is my wooden soldiers."

14

Aleksander continued to perform at home in the Sunday night salons his parents organised. Now that his older friend's voice was settling into a light and clear high tenor, they joined forces in delightful performances Schubert's Die Winterreise, Schumann's Dichterliebe, and many of the Fauré melodies. Aleksander's favourites being Après un rêve and Claire de lune.

Abram considered the opportunity to accompany a talented young musician like Paweł was invaluable for Aleksander's musical and artistic development. He arranged for Paweł to have vocal coaching. The boy was certainly good enough to have a future career as a singer, but care would be needed to look after his voice and not strain it.

Abramczyk and Anna were exercising similar care. There could be no doubting Aleksander's robust musicality and technique, but they were concerned for the stresses and strains of his inner world. Musically, Aleksander continued to flourish under his father's tuition. Every day, he was rigorous in his practice regime. It was a routine as regular as cleaning his teeth and drinking milk for breakfast. He never missed a practice session. School began at 10:00 each day. So for an hour after breakfast, first he would play his scale pattern in all keys major and minor, and practice exercises from Czerny's *School of Velocity,* and Hanon's *The Virtuoso Pianist.* He would finish the morning hour with some graded sight reading, working up to advanced pieces like Alkan's Symphony for solo piano, which even Aleksander found a challenge. So many notes!

On return from school, with homework and supper done, in his evening session Aleksander would practice new repertoire, play through orchestral scores at the piano, and work at transposition and improvisation. His father gave him two lessons a week, concentrating as much on musicality and musicianship as on technique. If there had been any concern about overstretching the boy, it was clear that Aleksander loved, indeed, *adored* music and the piano. It was his world and he was very much at home in it.

Abramczyk, concerned as always to do the best for his son, discussed with Anna if it would be good for Aleksander to have input from another teacher.

"He is such a quick learner, Anna. So he requires a teacher who is not fazed by such remarkable virtuosity in one so young. Like any player, Aleksander needs ever greater development in the practical disciplines and emotional depth."

As a student, Abramczyk had appreciated the connections Leschetizky had made with the wider meaning of art, philosophy, religion, and psychology. That had certainly increased his own appreciation of music and performance.

"I have made it my aim to guide Aleksander in this way," said Abramczyk. "But given his age it will be difficult to find a teacher with all the necessary technical and musical experience, plus the wisdom of mind to advance Aleksander up to higher level of artistry and understanding."

"Do you know who that person might be?" Anna asked.

Abram shook his head. "We are not short of teachers, even great ones. But to identify one who can shape the artistry of a young boy with prodigious talent like Aleksander—that's difficult!"

Abramczyk and Anna waited two more years before agreeing that Aleksander could play again in public. Aleksander didn't mind. He valued the music more than he craved applause. However, for some years, he had looked forward to playing a concerto and hoped his parents would one day let this be possible. Just as he loved playing with his singer friend, Paweł, he thought that same sense of musical give and take would be even greater playing with a whole orchestra.

He didn't have long to wait. Not long after his 9th birthday, Aleksander made his concerto debut with the Warsaw Philharmonic Orchestra under their founder conductor, Emil Młynarski. Aleksander wasn't aware till afterwards of the presence in the audience of the great piano virtuoso, and future Polish Prime Minister, Ignacy Jan Paderewski.

Greig's Piano Concerto—now a repertoire favourite, but then hardly known—was the major feature for the second half of the programme. Aleksander walked on to the stage with Maestro Młynarski. He still had not had his growth spurt and looked dwarfed by the great conductor, but he was completely at ease before the audience and his platform manners were impeccable. He stood with his back straight, his left arm outstretched, and his hand upon the piano. He bowed deeply. There were muffled comments in the audience.

"Isn't he small!"

"Doesn't he look smart!"

"I hope he'll manage okay."

After a few moments, there was no doubt he'd manage. From the opening A minor flourish, and then from the piano's restatement of the dotted theme onwards, Aleksander looked and sounded perfectly at home, as though he had been playing this concerto for a lifetime. He kept a firm eye on Mr. Młynarski. Everything was beautifully coordinated. Furthermore, nothing seemed to stretch his technique, not even the thundering cadenza. The slow movement was as dreamily expressive as you could hope for. And then in the in the triple time section of the Hallingdansen-like finale, Aleksander's rhythms were so lively and entrancing, the audience waved their heads in time like they might do to a Johann Strauss waltz.

I can only say the roar at the end was deafening. They called him back and back. Before the concert, Abramczyk had said "no encores." But on the fifth call, Aleksander looked at his father in the front row, who smiled and nodded gently. Aleksander sat at the piano, turned to the audience and announced in his high-pitched voice, "Chopin's Fantaisie-Impromptu in C-Sharp Minor, op 66."

15

When the audience left at the end of the evening, they were in high spirits. Chattering pleasure and enchantment at the glorious Grieg and the Chopin encore, the splendid performances by the remarkable young player were deemed in every sense an outstanding artistic success. Many comments were reverential.

"Such fluency!"

"Radiant talent!"

"Dazzling virtuosity!"

"Pure poetry!"

"Inspirational!"

In short, the evening was a triumph.

The audience's reaction was mirrored backstage. Standing around Aleksander and Abramczyk was a group of figures whose excitement was illustrated by waving hands, laughter, and raised voices. Commanding the group's admiration for the young performer, and himself equally the object of admiration, was a man whose shock of long curly golden red hair, moustache, quick, intense gestures and strong orator's voice made him instantly recognisable.

Ignacy Jan Paderewski, now in his forties, had already led an extraordinary life. His outstanding gifts and ability were already celebrated around the world. Pianist, composer, orator, politician, statesman, humanitarian, businessman, patron of music and the arts, he was an astonishing talent. He was also a talent *spotter* par excellence.

Paderewski was what today we would call a self-made man. From an economically modest background, but armed with talent, a relentless work ethic, and a gift for self-promotion, he made it his aim to pursue fame, money, adulation, and powerful friends. This he used as fuel for his passions: Polish independence, music, and philanthropy. By the turn of the century, Paderewski had become an extremely wealthy man. He made large donations to numerous worldwide causes. In particular, Paderewski shared his fortune generously with his fellow countrymen, especially musicians.

Ignacy and Abramczyk had been friends when they had been fellow students of Leschetitzky in Vienna. Abramczyk was an admirer of his Polish friend's playing (which, with three years input, had blossomed under Leschetitzky's direction) and his undoubted talent as a composer.

Paderewski's opera the lyric drama "Manru" received its premiere in Lwów in just a few weeks before Aleksander's

Warsaw concert. It was later to be staged in 13 different cities around the world. Abram had taken Aleksander to the first night in Lwów for the rare opportunity to hear a new opera.

To be frank, the story of the love triangle between the gypsy Manru, Ulana and Asa was not that appealing for Aleksander, although he did like the magic potions, and musically, the use of Wagner-like leitmotivs.

"My father took me to your opera, Maestro." Aleksander said, bowing respectfully.

"Oh good, and what did you think of it?"

"I liked the music very much, although I didn't fully understand the story. But I thought the idea of using special themes for each character was a very clever idea."

Paderewski beamed. After the Grieg and Chopin he was already impressed with the young boy, his precocity, his talent, exemplary manners, and his obvious musicianship and technical command of the keyboard.

While Aleksander and his mother chatted with some of the well-wishers, the conductor and members of the orchestra, Paderewski and Abramczyk moved to a quieter corner.

Ignacy said to Abram, "What do you consider should be Aleksander's next step? I assume you don't wish to parade him around the world like a circus act, as Leopold did to Wolfgang."

"No," said Abram. "It's one thing to have a prodigious gift, quite another to present yourself too early and too regularly to the public. Gifted young people like Aleksander have strong fingers, but we have a responsibility for his soul too. As parents, we want him to develop normally and healthily, and protect him from the constant pressures and adulation that audiences unthinkingly bestow upon their young heroes."

"And what about further study? Would you consider sending him to Leschetitsky? There wouldn't be a language problem. He lives in Vienna, but he hasn't forgotten his Polish!"

"Yes," said Abram. "You and I both owe so much to Leschetitsky. But I wonder what you think about his temperament in relation to teaching a child?"

"Well, we both agree, Abram," said Ignacy with a sigh. "Theodor has huge perception and insight. But you're right, there is a mercurial side to him."

"Yes indeed. It's rare. But when he's oversensitive and sarcastic, when he's stubborn and cross, that's what raises questions for me. To commit our son to Leschetitsky's care at this point in his development, Anna and I have to remember that Aleksander is still a young boy."

The conversation continued, with many positive reminiscences of their time together in Vienna with their great teacher, and their many now distinguished fellow pupils.

When Anna came over to them both and whispered to Abramczyk, "It is getting late," the two old friends embraced and Paderewski kissed Anna on both cheeks.

"Thank you Aleksander," he said, "for a totally magical evening." And then to Abram and Anna. "Whatever you both decide for Aleksander, I am sure it will be for his best. But be assured, if there is a way in which I can help you further your plans for him, I will be so honoured."

It was clear what he was suggesting, and Abram thanked his friend warmly. Then he added, "Actually, Ignacy, we do have a plan."

Paderewski smiled knowingly. "Perhaps Rachmaninoff's teacher?"

"Yes, indeed. When he's eleven, we'd like Aleksander to go to Moscow and study with Sergei Vasilyevich's cousin, Alexander Ilyich Siloti."

16

In the Steinfeld kitchen, the entrance to the pantry was via an arch. This had once been a doorway—the door itself having been removed some years ago. The arch being rather low, and with the danger that implied, Anna had cleverly tied a small partridge feather from the top, a dangling reminder to those who passed through to duck or grouse!

For the young growing family, this provision was proving increasingly useful.

Inside the large pantry area there was a plain wall, upon which in pencil four columns had been drawn. Each column was headed by one of the children's names: Aleksander, Jakub, Syzmon and Gerda. As you may have already worked out, it was a height chart. The initial entry was from 11 years ago, when Aleksander first stood upright, and similarly for his siblings following in their turn. What is it about increasing height that is so important to children? Whatever the answer, the four young Steinfelds were passionate in their request to be measured at least once a month. Anna stood firm and came up with a solution. The chart would show four readings per year, one every three months, with an extra reading on each child's birthday.

Aleksander went first in November 1891. He was seven months old and in that week had stood bolt upright for the very first time. He measured an impressive 2 foot 4 inches. A good, though not excessive height for a well-nourished little chap of his age.

Eleven years later, by the time of the latest entry, like an old-fashioned tote board, the pantry wall was covered in pencil scribblings. Aleksander's column showed the odds increasing with every stroke. It was clearly a race to the finish.

The finishing line was the 15th April 1902, Aleksander's 11th birthday. The entry indicated our front runner had experienced a considerable growth spurt. At five foot eleven and a half inches, Aleksander was now officially "tall for his age." As you might imagine, he would really have liked to add on the extra half inch and bring his height to an impressive round number.

Conscious of this, Aleksander asked his mother twice to check and recheck the measurements. Anna was an expert, of course, and the entry on the pantry wall remained. He'd only missed by a nose.

Still, in practice, he was just shy of six foot. So what was entered on the wall in pencil, as five, eleven and a half, in his mind Aleksander inked-in as 'a full six foot'. He needn't have worried as there was more growth yet to spring from his young bones.

But for the time being, and rounded up, "six foot" would become his standard response to those familiar questions beloved by great aunts and uncles everywhere.

"My, how you have grown, Aleksander!"

"And how old are you now?"

"Only eleven?"

"So tall for your age!"

"How tall are you?

Aleksander was proud of his stature. At the age of eleven, he already felt grown up musically; and although he was honoured to be the youngest student in the Moscow Conservatoire, being tall meant he wouldn't be treated as a baby.

The new chapter in Aleksander's life was drawing near. He would shortly travel to Moscow in time to begin his course of studies on Monday 1st May. Arrangements had been made for his lodgings, and the amount of time to be spent away from home had been negotiated with the Director of the Conservatoire, Vasily Safonov, a friend of the Steinfelds.

Safonov agreed that in consideration of his age and the distance involved, Aleksander would be allowed to return home for nine days every six weeks during term time. He would work from home under the supervision of his father during the time he was away from Moscow. Most important of all was that Safonov agreed Aleksander could study piano privately with the highly revered Alexander Siloti. Siloti had recently retired from the Moscow faculty to pursue his playing and conducting career. In the Conservatoire, Aleksander would follow the advanced curriculum of theory, composition and musicianship, with supervision and individual lessons in counterpoint, and free composition from Sergei Taneyev.

Taneyev taught at the Conservatoire for 30 years. Among his other talents, he had been a child prodigy, and in 1875, while still a teenager, had given the Russian premiere of Brahms's First Piano Concerto. His greatest accomplishment was a substantial and influential two-volume treatise, *Convertible Counterpoint in the Strict Style*. The result of 20 years labour, it is still in print.

All in all, it was the prospect of a superb musical education under the guidance of some of Russia's greatest teachers.

Paderewski had been keen for Aleksander to study under Siloti. "He's a great pianist and a great teacher—one of Russia's jewels." Tchaikovsky himself had great regard for Siloti, and even when he was a student entrusted to him the editing of his first and second piano concertos.

In the generation prior to 1917, Alexander Siloti grew to be one of Russia's most important artists. When he began his own advanced studies with Franz Liszt in 1883, the greatest of all pianists described him as "an honour to his teacher." Among composers who had written or dedicated scores to him include Arensky, Liszt, Rachmaninoff, Stravinsky and Tchaikovsky. He was not only a brilliant virtuoso pianist (his cousin Rachmaninoff, who he also taught, dedicated his first piano concerto to him) Siloti was also a composer and the arranger of over 200 widely performed piano transcriptions of significant works.

It is hardly possible to overestimate Siloti's artistic legacy as a pianist, as a conductor and through the numerous internationally acclaimed artists that he taught and mentored, in Moscow, St. Petersburg, and later at the Julliard School in New York. Among them Marc Blitzstein, Eugene Istomin, Konstantin Igumnov, Bernhard Stavenhagen, Alexei Haieff, Marc Blitzstein and Sergei Rachmaninoff.

The year Aleksander began his lessons with him, Siloti also became conductor of the Moscow Philharmonic Orchestra, and two years later, in 1903, he founded his own orchestra in St. Petersburg. In his now famous Siloti concerts, he introduced works by dozens of composers new to the Russian public, including Albeniz, Debussy, de Falla, Delius, Elgar, Enesco, Mahler, Schoenberg and of course, Rachmaninoff. Being brought into the Siloti circle at such a young age was of inestimable benefit to Aleksander for his development and his future.

In years to come, Aleksander would often speak, as did others, of Siloti's prowess as a giant of the keyboard. Like many of the Liszt pupils, Siloti had an enormous piano technique. He was a performer in the grand style and his performances reflected the legendary splendour and dignity of his teacher: energy and fire, a beautiful tone, always supremely musical and refined.

In his teaching and conducting Siloti was also known for his sympathetic communication. The rapport he had with his players and pupils that he took an especial care to cultivate. Over the years, many among his artist-colleagues, friends and former pupils have commented on Siloti's wisdom, kindness and compassion towards all he met. He was a man of stupendous gifts, yet of genuine self-effacement, who placed the needs of others and their future careers at the forefront of his energies. He was clearly the ideal choice to teach and mentor one as promising as Aleksander.

But as promising and prodigiously gifted as Aleksander was, he was not immune to being overwhelmed at the thought of working with someone so distinguished and accomplished. He had never experienced another piano teacher. Would Mr. Siloti be strict and demanding, or perish the thought, dull and boring?

Even though he was now six-foot(!) and preparing to be away from his family, Aleksander began to feel anxious about what the future might hold. His fear was mainly to do with the high level of achievement of his future teachers, and how he, being young, and they, being old, would get on with one another.

From a conversation between Abramczyk and Alexander Ilyich, young Aleksander had learnt that Russian Maestros had a reputation for being stuffy and unapproachable. Aleksander picked this up from comments about the famous Anton Rubinstein who had died in 1895. In his time, he had a massive reputation as Russia's greatest pianist.

Siloti, who clearly admired his other former teacher, told Abramczyk. "Brilliant though he was in all aspects of music—

as a teacher he was often cold and aloof, and certainly did not know how to encourage me or anyone else for that matter."

It is difficult to say whether this dry aloofness was part of the Russian character, or whether it was simply, though disappointingly, the received teaching style of the era. In more modern times we have come to prize the idea of the teacher-pupil relationship, that encouragement helps the disciplines of application, rigour and precision to flourish.

On the occasion that Siloti and Abramczyk had spoken about Rubinstein, it was part of a wider conversation. Abramczyk had anticipated his son's concerns.

Aleksander was to be possibly the youngest student ever admitted to the Conservatoire, and Abramczyk (like Aleksander) was concerned how his teachers would react to his youth.

"He may be outstandingly gifted, a prodigy indeed, but he's still a boy," Abram said to Siloti. "How do you think Taneyev will get on with him? Will he inspire him?"

"Well, frankly Taneyev is a dry old stick. As you know, some of us find his compositions devastatingly dull. Hardly any tunes and not one bar of colourful orchestration! He's not great fun either. His only leisure activity seems to be log-cutting at his country dacha. Sometimes he invites senior students over to help him. I went once.

"You have to picture this rather portly academic looking gentleman with his very long beard chopping the firewood. He has a famous two-handled saw. And with a student on one end,

Sergei Ivanovich on the other—back and forth, back and forth—he chops firewood all weekend with all the energy he would pour into the performance of a concerto. You wouldn't want to go there twice, but I have to admit the sight of it was quite entertaining."

"Yes," said Abramczyk, amused by the description. "But Taneyev does have a reputation as a brilliant teacher of counterpoint."

"I agree, but he is insufferably boring, pedantic, and famous for a waspish element to his personality."

It appears that Taneyev had more than once upset his own teacher Tchaikovsky with his damning remarks, verbally trashing several of his scores. In particular sections of Tchaikovsky's 4th symphony, he came in for a despicably venomous attack. "It's trivial, nothing more than ballet music!" he wrote to the Master. To which Tchaikovsky, more than a little irritated, apparently replied, "What on earth's wrong with that?"

Fortunately, history has had no hesitation in siding with Tchaikovsky. And neither has Taneyev's tarnished reputation faded with time.

What he had heard about the Dry Old Stick began to alarm the young Aleksander.

Then what about Siloti himself? Aleksander knew he too was a great Maestro. So did that mean Siloti would also be superior and humourless? At the very least, being only 11, Aleksander did wonder how he was going to get on with all these crusty old gentlemen.

Aleksander decided to ask his father for his opinion, in particular about Siloti.

"Papa, may I ask you," said Aleksander, feeling a little nervous about being so direct. "Is Mr. Siloti rather grand like other professors? Does he like children? Does he know any jokes? Has he ever played with toy soldiers?"

"In answer to your question about children," his father said, "I can tell you he and Vera have a delightful little girl called Kyriena who has just turned six. But for the rest, you can ask him yourself. He's coming to see you on Thursday!"

17

Before the Thursday meeting, the only time Aleksander had met Siloti was at his parents soirée. That was the time when Rachmaninoff had "stolen" the piano from Abramczyk and Hofmann, for Rachmaninoff and the six-year-old Aleksander to duo the Brahms Hungarian dances. It was easy stuff for Rachmaninoff as he had played the Brahms many times before. Aleksander had drawn the short straw, having to read the music at sight and he couldn't afford to look anywhere but straight ahead.

Nonetheless, as they were playing, out of the corner of his eye, Aleksander noticed something odd. It caused a rapid double take, and he almost lost his place in the music. But again he swiftly turned to check what he thought he had seen. He was right. It was very unusual and he had never seen anything like this in any other pianist. It was the colossal size of Rachmaninoff's hands! By anybody's standards, not just a six-year-old's, they were gigantic.

He looked again. Of course, Aleksander should have been concentrating on the music, but he was good at reading ahead, and this was too fascinating not to watch. Just looking at them. Those huge hands, so agile, so commanding, tumbling up and down the keyboard like a couple of monsters at play time.

Simultaneously sightreading Brahms' most tricky configurations and contemplating this freak of nature—two names came to him, one for each ginormous hand. He had not meant to, but said out loud, "Big hands, I name you Behemoth and Leviathan!"

Rachmaninoff looked at him, but all he heard, above the cascading torrent of sound, was Aleksander's muffled chuckle. Behemoth and Leviathan kept Aleksander smiling all evening.

18

When Thursday came, Aleksander was ready to meet his new teacher. He didn't think it was possible that anyone could be as kind and teach as effectively as his father. He had never had another teacher, so his nervousness was understandable. The idea of being tied up with another Dry Old Stick for three years would not be too appealing. In fact, he had not slept too well the night before as he had been continually turning over his anxieties in his mind.

This would be only the second time that Aleksander had met Siloti. The great man arrived at coffee time, and it was clear that Abramczyk wanted to make the most of the visit for he immediately suggested, "Alexander Ilyich, why don't you take coffee with Aleksander in the music room? Then you can get talking right away."

So upstairs they went, Aleksander keeping an awestruck but respectful silence. The door to the music room was open, and Alexander Ilyich, seeing the piano, said, "Is this where we go?"

"Yes," said Aleksander, stifling a yawn and with it, his trembling voice.

"I've heard about your Bösendorfer from Mr. Lewandowski. These Bösendorfers are one of the world's finest instruments, and he said this one will have been very well looked after by my own teacher, Franz Liszt, before it was delivered into your care. Do you mind if I try it?"

"Please do," said Aleksander, as he opened the piano cover.

Aleksander thought Siloti would want to demonstrate what a clever pianist he was by playing something shockingly fast and difficult; something more pianistically demanding than anything he might assume that Aleksander could manage. Just to show him who is boss!

He was wrong. Siloti began the Chopin prelude in E minor op 28 No 4, with its slow-moving quaver chords in the left hand, and its expressive melody in the right. It is a piece many identify with loss and mourning; indeed, Chopin had requested it to be played at his own funeral. It is one of Chopin's easiest pieces to play, and yet one of the very hardest. Or to put it another way, one of the easiest to play badly and exceptionally hard to play well.

The notes themselves are straightforward. But to play the left hand so smoothly that the right hand can sing with a quiet and heartfelt passion—that's where true artistry is required. This exquisitely beautiful yet mournful song requires not only the fingers of a master pianist but also the ears of a poet. In addition to Siloti's tone, the actual sound he coaxed from the Bösendorfer was so exquisite, so even and controlled, that when he finished, Aleksander realised his eyes were moist. He was truly moved.

"Bravo maestro," Aleksander said, clapping his hands with great sincerity.

Siloti smiled warmly, and said, "Mr. Lewandowski was right, wasn't he? It is a lovely instrument."

"It is," said Aleksander, slightly distractedly. He had noticed something but didn't say anything—at least for the present.

"You must play for me in a minute, Aleksander. But first, let's have a getting to know you session. I'll tell you about myself, and you can tell me about yourself. Would that be okay with you?"

Aleksander nodded.

"Why don't we start with the funniest things that have ever happened to us?" said Siloti.

That was a surprise. "Maybe he does like toy soldiers after all," thought Aleksander.

"So you go first, Aleksander."

Aleksander thought for a moment. There were times in school when he and Paweł had played practical jokes on their friends and even once on their science teacher; that one had backfired on them, and they ended up with a hundred lines each. They still laughed their heads off. But Mr. Siloti probably wouldn't see the joke. So while it was fresh in his memory, Aleksander thought he would tell him what happened that night with Behemoth and Leviathan. He started to giggle even before he had started the story! Calling himself to order, he recounted the tale in every detail.

Alexander Ilyich certainly did get the joke. In fact, he was so taken with it, he guffawed and positively bellowed with mirth! So much so that downstairs Abram and Anna wondered what was happening. But everything was fine, except that rehearsing the story from every point of view, upstairs they were in paroxysms of laughter. Alexander Ilyich living the action through Aleksander's eyes, and Aleksander re-living the fun of it a second time over; this time without having to muffle his amusement. It took them several minutes to regain their calm.

They sat there for a moment. And then, in complete silence, Alexander Ilyich looked Aleksander straight in the eye. Holding his gaze, and with an amused look on his face—Aleksander wondered what on earth was to happen next—like a surrender, in slow motion Siloti raised both of his enormous hands in the air, high above his head, and held them there.

Aleksander could not believe his eyes. Behemoth and Leviathan! Oh my! Siloti had matching hands to the Giant Rachmaninoff!

They both started laughing again.

"I hope I have not been offensive," said Aleksander anxiously after a minute or two.

"Not in the slightest," said Siloti. "Although I taught Rachmaninoff, we are in fact cousins. I am ten years his senior. So it is no surprise that we should share some family characteristics. I am not quite as tall as he is, although I am six foot four, but our hands are very similar." With that, he went back to the piano, and briefly illustrated how he could finger the left-hand octaves in the Chopin A flat polonaise, using the massive stretch between his left-hand thumb and second finger.

"You have much bigger hands than I have," commented Aleksander, stating the obvious, but wondering if his hands were still not large enough to develop a full technique.

"Yes, but for your age, your hands are capable of managing any kind of music. And your technique is already well in advance of many outstanding professional players. Don't worry, Aleksander, you will soon be a Maestro in your own right. But clearly not of the boring variety!"

The boy and his master got on extremely well. They talked and played for each other for at least another hour until Jakub, Syzmon, and Gerda, who were curious to know what all the laughter was about, came in to announce it was lunch time.

Later, when it was time for Siloti to return home, he warmly thanked Abramczyk and Anna for their hospitality. He then added prophetically, "I think we're all becoming aware in these coming times it is going to be increasingly difficult for the Jews. I hope you'll take strength from the psalm, 'But though he slay me, yet will I trust in him.'"

Then, finally as the coach arrived, there were hugs all round.

Aleksander went out to the coach with him.

"Well Aleksander," said Siloti with an impish look on his face. "We will see each other very soon. You know my friend, not many people have played piano duets with Rachmaninoff and survived!"

"You mean because of the monsters?"

"Precisely. Behemoth and Leviathan. I must tell Rachmaninoff your story. It will make his day!"

19

The next day was Friday. The tickets were booked for that afternoon. Abramczyk and Aleksander would travel together—a long journey they were to share on a six-weekly cycle for the duration of Aleksander's studies.

After their overnight expedition, they were due to arrive at Moscow Passazhirskaya station on Komsomolskaya Square late on Saturday. Abramczyk's sister, Alicja, would be waiting to meet them. Alicja was married to Pyotr Yermolov, a Russian army officer. As soon as they had heard about Aleksander's studies, they had offered to look after Aleksander and for him to stay with them throughout his time in Moscow.

Alicja was beside herself at the thought of seeing her brother, Abramczyk and her nephew, the now not-so-little Aleksander. The distance from Lwów being what it is, she hadn't seen either of them for almost two years. Although she assumed Aleksander had grown, she had no idea by how much.

In the last hour before they were due to leave, an envelope was delivered addressed to Aleksander. He didn't receive many letters, and so he opened it eagerly. It was from his mentor.

"My dear Aleksander. I want you to know you are very much in my thoughts as you travel to Moscow. I know this is a big undertaking for you, and I'm sure you'll feel somewhat nervous about it. But permit me, if I may, to try and put your mind at rest, at least in some small way.

"You are going to study with one of the world's greatest pianists and teachers. He will give you everything you need to develop your musicianship and technique. But I thought I also should mention that you will soon discover Mr. Siloti has a great sense of fun and good humour. I feel sure you will get on, and you will have many opportunities to laugh and smile together.

"There's one last thing, Aleksander. I am confident that in time your career in music will be very successful and will take you to the ends of the earth. Even when you achieve all that success, I implore you, never forget your roots: your country, your wonderful family and the way the gift of outstanding pianism has been passed to you across the generations. You are the heir to this great tradition, Aleksander. Steward it well, then one day hand it on to future generations as yet unborn.

"Who knows what days of joy and fulfilment lie ahead for you! I am so delighted, humbly and with devotion to our art and country, to be able to assist you in this immense adventure. Yours with respect, Ignacy Jan Paderewski."

Generously, thinking of his every need, Paderewski had offered to cover all of Aleksander's costs while in Moscow: his tuition, his lodging and travel, and an allowance for music and pocket money. When Abramczyk informed Paderewski that Aleksander's lodgings were already met by the generosity of his sister and brother-in-law, Paderewski had said to keep what was left over in a savings account as an emergency fund or for any special needs that might arise.

The time came for them to depart for the station. Aleksander was carrying his large holdall packed and ready, his music bag stuffed with scores, and his chess set (to keep them amused on the long journey) tucked under his arm. You'd think Aleksander was leaving for life! Everyone was in tears, although they were reassured that they would all see each other in six weeks' time. After such a good meeting with his new teacher, Aleksander was looking forward to his musical adventure. He felt tearful too, though he could not exactly work out why. After all, he wasn't leaving his family behind forever!

20

In fact, in one sense, Aleksander's family had increased, not contracted. His aunt and uncle in Moscow, who up till now he had hardly known, were a delightful discovery. Alicja and Pyotr did not have children of their own, and for them it was a happy novelty to have a young person around the house, especially one so well brought up and talented as Aleksander. In every way they were kind, generous and encouraging, taking seriously and joyfully their new role *in loco parentis*.

Then, of course, the other addition to Aleksander's family was Sasha, Aleksander's canine namesake, a white Caucasian Shepherd Dog. Sasha was a characteristic choice for an army officer: big, heavy and strong; a guard dog, but once trained, loyal and delightful. On their first meeting, Sasha had given Aleksander a good overall sniff. They quickly became inseperable.

Just as every adult has their child within, so every grown dog has a puppy. Tough dog though he was, Sasha loved to play, especially with Aleksander. He liked to fetch and catch, and when Aleksander jogged around the park, he enjoyed nothing more than to run alongside his newfound friend, barking and tail wagging. Sasha also liked to relax and curl up with a good book—the one on Aleksander's lap, of course—for extra cuddles on the sofa. But most of all, when Aleksander played the piano, Sasha would sit on his haunches in rapt concentration, apparently taking in every note—like that famous picture of Nipper, the fox terrier, devotedly listening to his master's voice.

Aleksander quickly settled in his new Moscow home. At the Conservatoire, and in his private tuition with Siloti, both his teachers noted his substantial early progress. This was especially encouraging as there had been some doubts expressed as to how Sergei Ivanovich Taneyev would relate to someone so young, and how the two of them would get on.

Early in his time at the Conservatoire, Abram had written to Aleksander to see how he was faring under Taneyev's direction. In his reply, Aleksander mentioned this about his new theory teacher.

They say here that Professor Taneyev has a brain the size of a Russian hockey pitch, and everyone agrees he is just as dry and crusty as I was promised he would be. But no one faults him as a musician. He is a brilliant pianist and music theorist. It's rumoured that to send himself off to sleep at night, he composes four-part fugues in his head! (That would keep me awake till the early hours!!)

The Professor is very cultured and aristocratic and maybe that's why he appears to look down his nose at everyone. True to what I was warned, at first he was very superior towards me. However, something amusing happened—I beat him. I beat Sergei Ivanovich at chess!

This is what happened. In one of my lessons, Professor Taneyev had likened the beauty of contrapuntal lines to a game of chess in the hands of a grand master. I won't bore you with the details of how he expanded on it, except to say after the lesson I told him that I have a special chess set and that I had brought it with me to Moscow for Papa and I to play on our train journeys. So, would he like to see it?

He was a bit huffy at first, (after all, I am only a child!) but then he said yes, he would.

So I brought the set in the next day, hoping in some way it might kindle a non-counterpoint conversation and sweeten our relationship—and perhaps persuade him just because I'm the youngest doesn't mean I'm stupid! I wasn't optimistic. But at the end of the session, where again he had been picking on me, I took the chess set to the front of the class to show him.

When Dry Old Stick saw it, to my great surprise, he was enthralled. He took a very close look at the board, the pieces and the wooden box. "Do you realise, boy, what this is? This is an original 1849 John Jacques Staunton chess set! It's hand carved, you know. The best of its kind."

I did know—but didn't say anything. I smiled innocently.

The knowledgeable professor, who by the way knows most things about everything, had an admiring look at all the antique Staunton pieces. He turned them this way and that and holding them up to the light admired the detail of the workmanship. And then—when Dry Old Stick saw the Potocki inscription—he didn't just smile. His face began to sparkle. He beamed so brightly; it was as if the clever Professor had invented sunshine itself and was suddenly determined to turn it up to full brightness.

"Aleksander, this is one of the loveliest sets I have seen."

It was like a grand contrapuntal climax! He was clearly impressed. And then out of the blue he said, "Let's play!"

He meant there and then. I was a bit startled, and a bit worried he might beat me, and I would need to slink back to the status of a stupid eleven-year-old. I realise now he was testing me.

So we set up the pieces. While we were doing that, I tried to recall what you had taught me on the train coming here. I think you called it the Danish Gambit. So that's what I opened with. Good choice, Papa! It was checkmate in 20 moves! The King was dead! Long live the humble eleven-year-old pawn!

Since that match, Dry Old Stick has been so much nicer to me—and what's more, he's explaining things more on my level. My counterpoint skills are well on the up!

21

As much as Aleksander was glad to be surviving his demanding theory lessons (and his teacher!) he was positively ecstatic in his enthusiasm for his new piano professor. Siloti well understood the needs of young players and recognised that Aleksander's virtuoso technique was already effectively formed by a mix of sheer talent and skilful teaching, love and encouragement from his father.

In a conversation with Abramczyk, Siloti was adamant that gifted children should neither be exploited or pressurised by ambitious parents.

"This was brought home to me, Abram, when a father brought his gifted child to our home for an audition. He was hoping I would teach her and was asking me when I thought she would be ready for public performances. He wanted me to write commendations for her and seemed very ambitious. His eye appeared to be more on his chequebook than the child and her need."

"And how was her playing?" Abram asked.

"Oh, the girl played beautifully. But when her finger slipped and she struck a wrong note, the whole atmosphere changed. Her father jumped to his feet. She visibly froze, as though she knew what would happen next. Then immediately he slapped her around the face. I have to say I was furious. Poor child! And without further ado showed the 'misguided' father and the unfortunate talented young girl to the door. Afterwards I wrote both to the girl, sympathetically, and to the father, rather firmly."

Abramczyk said, "I am encouraged to learn from your insight, especially given your new responsibility for Aleksander. He thinks now that he is six foot, he is a man already. He is certainly mature for his age, but he has still only just turned eleven. Anna and I have always tried to ensure there is plenty of fun and non-musical stimulus in Aleksander's young life. One element in Aleksander's happy and stable outlook, is I think because we have avoided pressure, particularly in relation to practice. He takes criticism positively, because when occasionally he struggled or did not do well he was secure in our love, and there was never any sense of us withdrawing our approval."

"Yes," Siloti replied. "For me, I see it is essential that a child is allowed to enjoy their childhood to the full. Whatever their gifts, or absence of them, undue pressure and fear of unreasonable discipline usually does damage. And certainly, however wondrously musically gifted, no one should allow a prodigy to perform pianistic stunts to order or be exploited like a dancing bear. Audiences, like misguided fathers, can be as cruel as they can be kind. We have to protect the child, for our children are always more precious in themselves than their gifts. But respect the child's inner world with love and care, and we will create the ideal conditions for the gift to flourish. That's what I said, at slightly greater length to the father. He never replied!"

So as advanced as Aleksander's playing had become and though there was still technical work to be done, most of all Siloti wanted Aleksander to engage with the music and be delighted by it. He took great pains to help Aleksander avoid falling into the virtuoso's trap and exploit technical wizardry for its own sake. He once told Aleksander, "'Look at me, and see how high I can jump' is not only infantile, it's bad for the music and bad for the ego."

The child in Siloti came to the fore when he worked and played with children. Later in life, Aleksander would recall a lesson for which he had practiced especially hard. The music he was working on was a left-hand-alone version of Chopin's famous revolutionary study. Arranged by Leopold Godowsky, it was hugely demanding and Aleksander had given it his all.

"Very slow practice, increasing the speed by one metronome notch at a time at each play through. Any mistakes—practice that passage in isolation, then go back a notch and start again." That's how Siloti had taught him, as he had taught the same to Rachmaninoff.

In this lesson, Aleksander had played the Godowsky version particularly well—note perfect, up to speed, and with real drama too. At the end of the piece, his teacher sat quietly, smiling quizzically, though with his head down.

"Play it again!" he commanded. So Aleksander began the furious C minor piece a second time over. While he was playing, out of the corner of his eye, he noticed Siloti stand up and walk out of the room, calling out, "Carry on. Carry on." Which he did.

Moments later Siloti returned. He was so thrilled with his pupil's progress, he'd donned a one-piece clown suit, a red nose and a clown's hat, just like he'd do when his own children achieved something special. He danced to the music, contorted his face and stuck out his tongue. When Aleksander finished, he smiled the biggest smile imaginable, and with a "Well done Aleksander, great achievement!" broke into wild applause.

Aleksander loved to tell stories about his teacher. How, at his very first lesson, Siloti had invited Aleksander to come and play duets with "the two cousins."

"Who are they?" asked the mystified Aleksander.

Siloti held up his hands triumphantly. "Behemoth and Leviathan of course, Mr. Aleksander!"

There was a lot of laughter in Aleksander's lessons. Siloti was convinced a child, however gifted, should remain a child and not ape adulthood. So he would use childlike humour, even hilarity, to connect with Aleksander's world. He'd invent numerous games, put on funny voices, as well as on the never to be forgotten occasion, dress up in that clown's costume.

One of the first serious questions Aleksander had for Siloti was to seek his advice about practice.

"I've heard that Mr. Hofmann plays so many concerts, he has been known to walk onto the platform with the concert programme in his hand to discover what he has to play. Can a pianist get to a point where he just plays and practice is no longer required?"

"The short answer, Aleksander, is the better you get, some technical things get easier. But to do the music justice, a real artist can never shirk practice. Like a Shakespeare play, there's poetry in every line waiting to be discovered. A casual read through will inevitably miss the richness. Beauty is discovered in the practice studio.

"The story about Josef Hofmann? Of course you know him from his duo performances with your father. I have heard that story, although it may be exaggerated. If only a little. I do know when he was 10, his father booked him to play 52 concerts in 10 weeks! Apparently he was playing concertos and solo pieces brilliantly, but the New York Society for the Prevention of Cruelty to Children were so alarmed they tried to stop his father's exploitation. Fortunately, a New York philanthropist stepped in with a large donation on the condition that Josef withdraw from the concert stage until he was 18.

"I expect you have heard from Abram, there are many intriguing stories about Hofmann, and most of them are true! Did you know, for instance, that his hands are so small, certainly in comparison with mine, that Steinway have designed a piano with slightly narrower keys to make playing more comfortable for him? Josef was an early starter, and just like you at the Potocki Palace, at the age of six he astonished audiences with his musicianship and virtuosity. Everyone says he did not play like a clever child. The music was everything for him, and I have heard no one except Franz Liszt who can make the piano sing like he does.

"And you asked about practice. For myself, I practice slowly, as I know you have learnt too. Fast practice is the undoing of many a young student. So slow practice—and also medium power, not full power. These days I do not practice scales and finger exercises like I did when I studied with Nikolai Zverev. But in his turn, he had learnt the best ways to practice from his teacher, Adolf von Henselt, who Liszt had greatly admired, especially for his unrivalled cantabile and legato. 'He could make the piano sing like a bird,' he once told his students.

"In fact, these days, I prefer to follow von Henselt's pattern and work on passages from difficult places from the whole piano literature, or perhaps I should say, from my repertoire.

I also regularly play through Bach's 48 preludes and fugues and then parts of the Chopin Études, octaves from Tchaikovsky, or anything that exercises the various muscles or requires constant repetition. The Schumann Symphonic Studies also have much technical value, aside from being great music. So yes, Aleksander, one must always practice; an artist can never get away from that!"

Overall, Aleksander Ilyich impressed upon Aleksander, "Like your father taught you, it is your duty to develop strong fingers and strong emotions." Aleksander was always passionate about his practice. He loved the music and the piano too much to do otherwise. Every day, he was spurred on by his music loving aunt Alicja who would sit and listen for hours as Aleksander played and rehearsed Beethoven sonatas, Chopin studies, and many works by Schumann, Brahms and Medtner. When his Uncle Pyotr returned at night, he'd ask Aleksander what he had been practising. Aleksander would immediately reply, "Can I play it for you?"

Aleksander's aunt and uncle gave him every encouragement and arranged regular soirées in which he would play their beautiful Érard grand piano to the cream of Moscow's artistic and musical fraternity. These unique opportunities to learn and perform so much of the best and most demanding of the classical repertoire (like Clara Schumann, he always played from memory) continued weekly for three years.

Almost to the day, following Aleksander's first lesson with Siloti four years previously, Siloti said to him at the end of his lesson, "Aleksander, I have something important to say to you. I'll put it simply. You have proved yourself to have strong fingers and strong emotions. For that reason, I believe you're ready to make your debut No. 3!"

Aleksander was 15 years old. In four years, he had grown to a strapping 6 foot 2, and from a prodigy to a mature, exciting, and outstandingly gifted young artist. He would take the musical world by storm.

22

After his now famous (third!) debut concerto appearances in Moscow and St. Petersburg, Aleksander found himself in constant demand, with concerts booked throughout Russia, Poland and across Europe.

For three years, his father had accompanied him on these travels. It had been agreed between them, that by the time he was eighteen, he would, in Abram's words, begin to make his own way in the world. So shortly after his eighteenth birthday, Aleksander made arrangements to move out of his aunt and uncle's Moscow home. Although, he wasn't averse to popping back for supper when he was in the city! He found his own apartment nearby and began to travel alone.

By this time, Siloti had moved to Saint Petersburg. The relationship between Aleksander and Siloti was close; a friendship which extended to the whole Siloti family: his wife, Vera, and the children. They all loved Aleksander. The children especially enjoyed his sense of fun, how he would dress up in their father's clown's outfit and show them magic tricks. With his big hands he could easily conceal all kinds of little objects, and then produce them from behind the ear of one of his young audience members. "Do it again," they'd cry. "Do it again!"

But he never did. "Don't risk undoing a child's sense of mystery and wonder," he told the Siloti's eldest daughter, Kyriena. "They'll need it later in life." Although four years his junior, Kyriena was tremendously good company and like another sister to him. Even at that age, Kyriena was a very accomplished pianist, and they played Mozart, Schubert and Brahms duets together. Aleksander missed her.

Nonetheless, even without the on-hand mentoring of his father or Siloti, Aleksander continued to work ever as hard on technique as he had always done, letting the music possess his emotions and speak through them. "Strong fingers and strong emotions." That passionate advocacy for the music and dazzling keyboard facility that accompanied it were hallmarks of this extraordinary and celebrated young artist and were cherished by audiences wherever he played across Russia and Eastern Europe.

In 1911, his first international tour began in London. At the Proms, in the Queen's Hall, his performance of Rachmaninoff's second piano concerto caused a sensation. Ernest Newman, for 50 years the doyen of English music critics described him as "the most outstanding virtuoso of his generation—bar none!" Aleksander received similarly enthusiastic notices from his concerto and recital appearances in St. Petersburg, Vienna, Berlin, and Paris. Wherever Aleksander played, he was feted not just as a spectacular virtuoso (which audiences loved) but as a true poet of the keyboard. His reputation was growing.

23

Aleksander Steinfeld had become the talk of the international music world. His strong, stylish playing delighted audiences, and critics were fulsome in their praise. "A pianist of distinction" and "a name to be reckoned with." Good news travels fast, and such positive critical recognition stimulated many invitations for concertos and solo recitals.

In his article following Aleksander's London Prom Debut, Ernest Newman had favourably compared Aleksander to Godowsky, Hofmann, Rachmaninoff and Medtner—leading pianists of the time. This was the age of the virtuoso, and to speak of him in the same breath as these dazzlingly accomplished figures was to accord Aleksander the highest status and acclaim. Newman also knew his comments would invite international attention.

At the time, Newman himself was building what became a towering reputation as a musicologist and critic. He was insightful and erudite, but not immune to controversy. In all his writing, Newman's hallmark was intellectual objectivity.

Newman's career began on the Manchester Guardian, where his reviews were invariably accurate and well informed, but also trenchant and sometimes cutting. The paper had been used to notices couched in a more urbane style, and initially his editor did not thoroughly warm to Newman's frank tell-it-as-it-is approach. Editorial discussions about his brittle remarks came to a head over a series of derogatory reviews concerning an especially valued and venerable local institution. The assault on its reputation became a cause célèbre.

Like all orchestras do from time to time, Manchester's normally excellent Hallé orchestra, founded by Sir Charles Hallé in 1858, was going through a bad patch. Performance standards had slipped, and Newman was not shy in pointing this out to the great Mancunian public. Newman castigated the orchestra, their famous conductor, Hans Richter, and even their complacent audiences.

"Dull performances, under-rehearsed, shoddy ensemble, and poor instrumental playing. It really won't do." And "not only the reputation of the orchestra, but the reputation of British music-making is at stake." With such sharply-chosen phrases, Newman pointed out the present inadequacies of the Hallé.

Of course, a local fuss ensued. Such a brouhaha! The paper's board met in emergency session. These remarks, and they claimed, all Newman's reviews, were forthwith deemed as "deleterious to the paper's reputation." In other words, not good for business! Newman's editor found it difficult to defend his young staff writer, since even valuing objectivity, he was not used to such sharp-edged criticism either in his columns or from his readership. The controversy continued for a while, but so did a mounting campaign from the locals. So, reluctantly, the beleaguered editor decided to rescue the ailing column inches, and Ernest Newman was asked politely to take his undoubted talents elsewhere. The Manchester Guardian had just sacked the man who was to become the greatest music critic of his time!

Fortunately for the music world, Newman's talents were quickly snapped up by the Birmingham Post, where he stayed just a short time before his move to London for the Observer and then to the Sunday Times, where he remained as music critic for forty years. But Newman did not change. As the British say, he called a spade a spade, and he continued to write with the same commitment to objectivity—though possibly without quite so much savagery.

Newman was valued. Newman knew what he was talking about. And Newman's opinions were noticed, read and respected on both sides of the Atlantic. This is how Newman's assessment of Aleksander Steinfeld had reached the ears of the New York Philharmonic Orchestra, and its Czech conductor, Josef Stránský.

Newman's piece on Aleksander had been brought to Stránský's notice by Henry Theophilus Finck, the music editor of the New York Evening Post. He knew that the NYPO were keen to bring in younger talent, especially from Eastern Europe. In particular, in recent years, Russia, Hungary and Poland had produced performers of such excellence. Brilliant new talent might be an exciting addition to the coming season's programme.

On the 21st May 1912 Stránský wrote to Finck, "If Steinfeld is even half as good as Newman says he is, he will be a great catch for the orchestra. We had Godowsky playing with us at the beginning of the month. Apparently, Godowsky knows the whole family. He says there's no chance we will be disappointed. He said, 'If you really want to know, why not contact Siloti?' So when I saw him and asked his opinion, like a big brother, Siloti put his arm round my shoulder and said, 'Don't worry, Josef. The boy's a wizard!'

"So thank you for the suggestion, Henry. We've discussed it here and the management are all in agreement. We will write to Aleksander's Moscow address, with a copy to his father. We'll invite him to play two concertos in the next season, plus a couple of recitals. For the solo items we agreed to ask him to be sure to include some Chopin, as Aleksander being Polish it will be a good selling point and go down well with the public."

24

Tired from his journey, Aleksander had returned from Paris late on Tuesday night. Although it had been a welcome change not to have to set his alarm, the following morning he had woken later than he had expected—possibly an indication of how drained he was feeling. At about 11:30 a.m., the bright Moscow sunshine seeping through the blinds, there was Aleksander, still in his pyjamas and silk dressing gown, enjoying a late breakfast of black bread, butter, and sliced sausage, just about to pour some coffee.

Inconveniently, there was a rat-a-tat-tat on the front door. "O Kurczę!" he said to himself—his first quiet breakfast in weeks interrupted. Aleksander put down the new French silver coffee pot—one of the many gifts he had received on his tour—went over to the window and peered through the blinds. The lady had her back to him, but he immediately recognised the red coat and the stylish tan mink and wool fur hat. It was his aunt Alicja, the one person in Moscow he was delighted to see at any time, even in his dressing gown!

Alicja sat herself down and with coffee in hand heard all about the tour including Aleksander's stories. In Berlin, there had been the conductor who dropped and lost his baton. In Paris, the lady who gave a solo standing ovation—during a pause, the piece hadn't yet finished. And then, in Vienna, there was the Blüthner piano lid which came crashing down at the first forte chord of the Chopin B flat minor scherzo.

Alicja could see from his skills as a raconteur how much Aleksander had grown since in confidence since he had first stayed with them. "You've advanced in so many ways," she said.

"Yes," agreed Aleksander, "and I cannot thank you enough for the anchor you have been and still are to me. When I am away, I so look forward to returning home to my parents, and then coming back to Moscow and seeing you and Pyotr."

"We always love seeing you too, Aleksander," Alicja responded. "But tell me, what is it like to do a long tour like you have just done? Not so much the events themselves, which I know are very exciting, but what about personally—what's it been like for you?"

"Well Aunt Alicja, I'll tell you—touring is a lonely existence. Without friends or family, it is difficult to relax and unwind. But it is also difficult because concert promotors never let us artists rest. There are always interviews and new people to meet. They like us to be on show, on our best behaviour and presentable at all times. And despite what some of us may think, with all of our cultural advances, many in Europe still do not do 'informal'. You certainly can't welcome guests in your pyjamas! I have actually heard it said that only the US knows how to loosen up and enjoy real leisure time. We should be made to take lessons from them!"

"And what about the concerts themselves? When your father wrote he said the reports were excellent."

"Yes, of course. The tour was a great success. The orchestras were fine ensembles. The conductors were first class. It was Felix Weingartner in Vienna who sent his baton flying into the brass section. I'm not sure anyone noticed apart from the tuba player who caught it in the bell of his instrument. But what a conductor! He made Brahms 1st piano concerto sound as though it was Brahms' 5th symphony. I have never heard the drama and tension in the music so viscerally portrayed. The Vienna Philharmonic lived up to its reputation. It was such a privilege to play with them."

Alicja then asked about the practicalities. "How was it getting from place to place—the trains and hotels and managing everyday needs of your own?"

"As I say, I am really grateful for the opportunity and the honour of it. But behind the glitter and attraction, and all the practising and performing, what the public does not see is the pressure. For me, the main anxieties come from administration. Even working out travel arrangements is a stress in its own right. Railway timetables have the same effect on my brain as logarithms. They tie me in knots!"

This conversation continued until it was time for lunch. Aleksander declined Aunt Alicja's kind invitation to come over to their house but did politely invite himself for supper so he could run a specific question past Pyotr. She had planned to make sure he would come in any case.

When Aleksander arrived for dinner, the table was laid, and the food was already served and waiting. His aunt and uncle were so generous; there was much more than enough for three people! Greeting Aleksander like a victorious returning General, Pyotr thrust a very large glass of vodka into his hands and proposed a toast. "To our family, to music and to welcome you home, Aleksander." Everyone, including the victorious army man, drank to that.

Then, as if on cue, from behind him a voice that Aleksander knew like his own said, "We'll drink to that too!" Aleksander turned round, and there to his total and joyful amazement were Abramczyk and Anna, who had been hiding upstairs since Aleksander had arrived ten minutes or so before. Alicja and Pyotr loved springing surprises as much as Abram and Anna did. Pyotr had prepared the plan like a military exercise and timed it down to the last second. As surprises go, this one was extra special. Because of his tours, Aleksander hadn't seen his mother and father for at least six months. And because of the home from home distances involved, Alicja hadn't see her brother, Abram or Anna for years rather than months.

All round, the hugs were as rich and comforting as deep velvet; for Aleksander, the mixture of vodka, journeying tiredness and the emotional atmosphere quickly switched on the tears. They ignited the whole room. Even the normally stiff-upper-lipped General Yermolov had to get his hankie out. But they were tears of joy, not sadness. There was much happiness from that well planned surprise. Truly, an evening to remember.

25

"What are you doing here?" Aleksander had thought of asking the question of his parents, but in the excitement he had not got round to it. Now, while they were still drinking vodka, Abramczyk volunteered how he and Anna had been able to make the long journey from Lwów to Moscow together.

Aleksander was well aware that throughout Eastern Europe his father was held in high esteem both as a pianist and music educator. So, although he had been specially invited by the Moscow Conservatoire twice before and had regretfully declined, this year they had tried a third time.

"The invitation is to chair the examining committee for the Great Gold Medal," he explained. "It's intended as an honour, and I feel I should now accept the invitation before I am too old to do so!" He added, "I do welcome the opportunity to express our family's gratitude for all that they did for you, Aleksander."

Then he said with an unmistakeable twinkle, "Especially for all his good efforts on your behalf, to thank Sergei Ivanovich!"

Aleksander hadn't thought about Dry Old Stick for ages. "How is the wise Professor Taneyev?" Aleksander asked, feeling the benefit of the vodka warming his attitude.

"He is still there,'" Abram replied. "Still composing, still writing his counterpoint book, and he still hasn't forgiven you for the Danish Gambit!"

"Time for us to eat," said Alicja. "Or all this alcohol will go to our heads!" So, glasses refilled, Alicja brought in even more dishes as they all sat down at the burgeoning table and relaxed further together.

There are sometimes moments in company, when it is as though the ambient sound is suddenly muted, and you find yourself alone, preoccupied in discussion with your own thoughts. In just that way while others talked, Aleksander was reflecting just how grateful he was for his family, and how good it was to be in their company. He would have loved his two brothers and his sister to be present. But the pleasantly unexpected prospect of spending a whole week in his parents' company soon banished any sadness.

In the same reflective moment, it was as if a dark cloud passed over. It was when he unexpectedly thought, "I could never bear it if for some reason we were parted altogether, never to see each other again." It was sharp and painful—one of those intrusive contemplations upon which deeper anxieties sometimes fasten.

He batted it away without further consideration. There was no basis for such a fear.

"Wake up dreamer," his mother said. "Which masterpiece were you playing?"

"You're the masterpiece, Mother—and Papa's sister for making this amazing meal. Two masterpieces in one room, aren't we men privileged?"

Alicja must have spent the whole afternoon in the kitchen for the meal was sumptuous. Appreciative words, joking and laughter accompanied each choice, as she explained it. What a menu!

There was Borscht; Crispy fried chicken; Kotleti patties served with buckwheat kasha; Pelmeni stuffed with lamb, pork and beef, served with sour cream; Salted herring, rye bread and sliced onion; Pickled vegetables; Pan fried Pirozhki pies with sweet cottage cheese and home-made strawberry jam; and traditional Medovik honey cake.

As they ate, they talked about the plans Abram and Anna had for retirement. With their ideas for travel, playing, teaching and a new edition of Bach's 48 preludes and fugues, it didn't at all sound like retirement to anyone else! They spoke about Gerda, Jakub and Syzmon; the conductors Aleksander had recently worked with; the interest Paderewski, Hofmann and Siloti were still showing in Aleksander's career. And of course, the endless funny stories.

When the time came for coffee, brandy and cigars, all but Pyotr passed on the brandy. As was the custom, the three men retired to the smoking room. Alicja was quite happy. It gave her a chance to catch up with Anna, and both of them would help Yelena, their maid, with the dishes.

As the boys went up the stairs, Anna laughed and said to Alicja, "I think the boys are a little shickher!"

"Only a little?" replied Alicja.

As she spoke, there was a gentle knock at the front door. And then a second knock.

"I'll get it," shouted Aleksander, careering down the stairs to see who it was. When he opened the door, standing before him was a distinguished looking man in a splendid black uniform, the jacket edged in blue with six silver buttons on either side. With his peaked cap and finely coiffured handlebar moustache, its extremities carefully twirled with wax, he had a definite air of dignified authority.

Aleksander thought the official must be a General, and a colleague of his uncle's. He was just about to call up the stairs to General Yermolov, when the smartly moustached official dug down in his bag and produced an envelope.

"For you I believe, Mr. Steinfeld. I brought it to your apartment at nine this morning but could get no reply. It needs to be signed for, and as I know your aunt and uncle, I thought I would try and deliver it here on my way home."

With that, the postal official handed Aleksander an envelope sent from the US with a stamp depicting George Washington, addressed to Aleksander Steinfeld, Apartment 5, No 26 Arbat Street, Moscow.

Aleksander received it gratefully, signed the confirmation of receipt, and thanked the gentleman for his evident kindness. Aleksander politely watched him depart down the drive and shut the door.

26

"Who was that?" asked Uncle Pyotr, when Aleksander came into the smoking room.

"A man with a handlebar moustache and an envelope," Aleksander replied.

"Oh, you mean Viktor Bogdanovich. He's our postman. Such a kindly man. He's served this district for years. What did he want?"

"He brought this envelope."

"Is it for me?"

"No, for me."

"Have you opened it?"

"No."

"Are you planning to?"

"Er, yes."

"Well get a move on," his father interjected.

Aleksander was feeling a little nervous. But with a paper knife from his uncle's desk, he opened the envelope, taking care not to tear its contents or spoil the postage stamp.

He read the first part of the letter silently, then looked up. "Would you like to hear what it says?" Abram and Pyotr both nodded. Aleksander continued, "Do you mind if the ladies join us?"

They nodded again, and Abram said, "I'll get them."

Two minutes later, Anna and Alicja came up the stairs. As they approached, the room seemed wrapped in an air of mystery. Or was it the cigar smoke? Alicja didn't normally venture up there, but Abram said he thought Aleksander had received important news, though he didn't know what it was about. So Anna and Alicja bravely entered the smoking room, looked around for a moment, and then perched themselves on the Duchesse brisée.

"The letter has been sent from the United States of America," said Aleksander solemnly. "It is from the New York Philharmonic Society." He looked up to check they were listening, and then read it to them.

Dear Mr. Steinfeld.

I write to offer you an engagement with the New York Philharmonic Orchestra for our next season.

Your growing reputation has reached these shores, and we have read of your triumph in London at the Queen's Hall, especially through the comments of Mr. Ernest Newman, whose opinions are respected throughout the English-speaking world. In addition, your esteemed colleagues, Messrs Siloti, Hofmann and Godowsky have all spoken of your remarkable virtuosity and musicianship. So even though we have never met, or even for myself, I have never heard you play, I feel confident to ask if you would kindly accept this invitation to travel to New York to be our soloist in the first week of the New York Philharmonic Season. For this we would like to offer you two orchestral concerts and two recitals.

For the opening concert of the 1913 season on Saturday the 8th February, may I suggest the Tchaikovsky Piano Concerto No. 1 in B♭ minor, op 23, and then on the following Saturday, the 15th February, we would love to have you play the Moszkowski Piano Concerto No 3 in E major, op 59. For the two recitals on the intervening Tuesday and Thursday (the 11th and 13th of February) we are happy for you to choose your own programme. Though if you felt minded, may I suggest the Schubert Wanderer Fantasy, the Liszt B minor Sonata, and the Schumann Études Symphoniques would all be appreciated by our audiences here. You might also consider including some Chopin in your programme. The idea of a Polish pianist playing music of Poland's greatest composer always holds a special magic for New Yorkers.

We heard of the unfortunate Blüthner piano lid in Vienna and can assure you of a better experience in New York! As you know, we are proud of our association with Steinway who have been manufacturing the finest pianos here since 1853. Needless to say, we are well served in all our venues with the best concert instruments available.

Finally, we will pay all your travel, accommodation and out of pocket expenses, in recognition of the time you are away from home and other employment, and of course a generous fee for all four concerts which we can negotiate once we hear of your acceptance of this invitation.

Do not hesitate to contact me with any questions you may have. In addition, the aforementioned gentlemen have all played as soloists with our orchestra and have intimate knowledge not only of the NYPO but also of the city itself.

I send you my respectful good wishes.

Sincerely yours,

Josef Stránský
Conductor
New York Philharmonic Orchestra

When Aleksander had finished reading the room broke into applause. Mildly embarrassed but evidently pleased, Aleksander said, "With all that talk about 'your triumph in London' I was wondering if Mr. Stranksy thinks I am a prize-fighter!" Everyone laughed. But Abram, his faced flushed with pride said, "You don't need to be modest, Aleksander. You deserve the acclaim. Joking aside, to be invited to be a soloist with the NYPO is a tremendous honour and one you thoroughly deserve—at your age or any age!"

"More vodka!" cried Pyotr. And all five of them tumbled downstairs to the drawing room where toasts were proposed, again and again.

Sensing the atmosphere, before Yelena could bring in the tray of coffee she had prepared, and sounding at first in every way like an Orthodox cantor, in his clear tenor voice, Pyotr broke into the Russian folk song, *Kalinka, Kalinka*.

Pyotr started Lentissimo—slow and steady: "Калинка, калинка, калинка моя!" Step by step, with a lumbering accelerando, he increased the tempo—deliberately, then dramatically—and everyone joined in the lively chorus. Pyotr continued to waive his arms. Faster and faster they went. Until at giddying speed, gesticulating wildly and singing at the top of their voices, Sasha woke to hear the noise and bounded upstairs to bark his contribution.

Kalinka, Kalinka. They linked arms, and in flamboyant celebration, sang and danced *Kalinka* all the way round the Yermolov drawing room, Sasha running and jumping with them. Around they went, many times over. Then, feigning exhaustion, one by one they fell on the sofas with tears of laughter—happy for Aleksander and happy for the family.

It was the best of times.

Yelena brought in the coffee.

27

Next morning, after another late breakfast, Aleksander, who had stayed the night in his old room, had a headache. It wasn't too serious, but when he came downstairs, everyone was already at the breakfast table. As they had feasted the night before, Alicja had asked Yelena to prepare simple dishes of porridge and fresh blinis with strawberry jam and bowls of mixed fruits and berries.

"You're quiet this morning, Aleksander," said his father, helping himself to another blini.

"Sorry Papa. I was lost in my thoughts. I was awake some of the night thinking about New York, and of course I am thrilled. But there is a problem I was planning to ask you and Uncle Pyotr about yesterday and didn't get a chance."

"Do you want to discuss it now?"

"Yes please, if you don't mind."

Pyotr left the room for a moment to ask Yelena to make some more coffee.

Aleksander began to explain his concern to the others, and especially to his father. "It's just with all these concerts the demands are increasing. I am thinking of organisation. A pianist cannot be good at everything. Give me a Chopin study and I will play it blindfolded for you. But give me an administration task like deciphering a train timetable or planning an itinerary, then I will fumble and worry till my brow perspires, and in the end nothing is achieved. That's why I wonder if I would benefit from some kind of artist management. Then, I could concentrate on the music and leave the administration to someone who could manage it for me."

Pyotr was back in the room by now, but Abram was the first to respond. "I can well see the need, Aleksander, but frankly for musicians I have never heard of the idea. The only real Artist Managers I have heard of are the Nikitin brothers, Dmitri, Akim and Piotr. I know they work with the best artists from all over Russia, but they only manage circus acts. And as we've always said, you're not one of those!"

Aleksander's headache beat a little more uncomfortably, and he didn't laugh, though he tried a smile. Well-meaning as the comments were, he didn't think he was going to get that far towards a solution this morning.

Then Pyotr joined the conversation. "Aleksander, I know exactly what you mean. What you need is an Adjutant! I have one myself. His name is Mikhail Batorsky." Pyotr went on to explain with some relish the good order of the Imperial Russian Army.

"In the Infantry, we have two manager ranks, one called the Quartermaster general, who's responsible for the army's supply needs, and the Adjutant general, an assistant who attends the Tsar, a Field Marshall or a General like me. So under my command, Captain Batorsky is my right-hand man and responsible for all my correspondence, my travel arrangements within Russia, and anything to do with the organisational side of my role in army life."

Aleksander appreciated the insight, and thought, but didn't say, "I am neither a clown nor a soldier, so where can I find help like this?"

Abram, reading his face if not his thoughts, said, "Pyotr has given me an idea."

28

At the turn of the century, artist management for classical musicians was only beginning to emerge. For the time being it was restricted mainly to the US, and only for those few leading figures whose worldwide engagements justified the employment of such expertise and expense. Abram had been correct. Representation of this kind was as yet unheard of in Russia or Poland.

Yet, when Pyotr had explained his Captain's role, Abram had seen the point. He suggested to Aleksander that he would ask some of the senior staff at the Warsaw Conservatoire if they had any suggestions. In fact, he already had someone in mind.

In Warsaw, the director of the Warsaw Conservatoire, Abram's friend, Stanisław Barcewicz, welcomed Abram warmly. "It's not every day that I get to spend some time with a distinguished Lwów Professor!"

Stanisław immediately asked Abram about Aleksander. "How is your young son faring with so many concert engagements and other demands? It must be very satisfying to hear how well everyone speaks of him. If I may say so, Abram, you and Anna have managed his early promise so well. You must be very proud of him."

"Thank you. As indeed we are, Stanisław. We are proud of all four of them. Anna and I both find the older we get, our love for all our children grows even stronger. When they were babies, we had no idea what their future would hold. Now that they are adults, we simply long for their well-being, especially in these unstable times."

"Yes, I feel the same." Stanisław replied. "As you know, we just have Krystyna. She is studying violin here at the Conservatoire, and she'll turn out to be a good orchestral player. That I think will be her limit, but she is the loveliest person, and the young man to whom she is betrothed is surely the luckiest boy in Poland!"

Abram returned to the subject of Aleksander and the need as he had outlined it a few days earlier. As he spoke, Stanisław listened and nodded without interruption.

"I think your Aleksander is right," Stanisław said. "In the future, with the impact of advanced conservatoire teaching, a greater number of brilliant students, and increasing demand from orchestras and promotors, young virtuosos will have to travel to many far away destinations; managing their practical needs will be a big challenge. Even within a single country, negotiating contracts, fees for rehearsals and performances, and terms and conditions are all becoming an increasing challenge to artists. Though I know of no such agent or agency, as you were telling me about Aleksander, I did have a kernel of an idea."

The idea was a name—Michał Arct, a leading Polish bookseller, and a distinguished authority on music publishing throughout Eastern Europe. In his professional career, he had considerably developed the retailing of scores, as well as introducing a system of lending music for the students of the Warsaw Conservatoire. Abram had once met him very briefly at the bookshop, so when the thought had occurred to him earlier, Michał Arct was only a hunch, as he knew very little about him.

"When you get to know him, Abram, you'll find Michał Arct is a delightful and caring man who is very well read, follows international affairs, and most importantly for us, is someone who understands business as well as he understands music. What's more, having three sons in their twenties, he also understands young people, which is well illustrated by his effective work with the students in this institution."

The discussion continued. As they parted with the warm embrace of friends of forty years, Stanisław said to Abram, "Michał is due in the conservatoire tomorrow. When I see him, if he is willing, shall I arrange a meeting between him and Aleksander?"

29

A few weeks later, when Aleksander was in Warsaw for a recital, the two met up.

In a letter written to Aleksander a fortnight before, Stanislaw had described Michał as an impressive looking man in his early seventies. "He has short, wavy grey hair and a chevron moustache and is always smartly dressed—usually in a perfectly tailored frock coat and white cravat. He looks like a prosperous businessman, but his success is wider. He is not just a capable publisher and bookseller, he is an author too, and prolific. He's edited dictionaries and encyclopaedias, written on modern science and scientific discoveries, and published works popularising scientific knowledge for the general public. You'll have a great chat."

And they did, although not altogether in the way Aleksander had expected.

Stanislaw's description of Michał turned out to be photographic, and when Michał arrived in the café near the conservatoire building, Aleksander recognised Michał Arct immediately.

"I am surprised and grateful you have time for me," Aleksander said as he rose from the table, offering a sincere and deferential bow.

Michał smiled warmly, "The boot is on the other foot, Aleksander. I am honoured to be of service to you. You know, in the early days, when I took over the bookshop from my uncle, while Abram and Anna were still domiciled in Warsaw, your father was a regular visitor. I only knew him a little but it was partly because of his excellent advice that we started to sell music scores, and also later through him that I connected with Stanislaw Barcewicz."

The two got on very well, swopped family stories, and Aleksander told Michał about the progress of his career to date, and about his need to find help with the management of his administrative load, especially where he felt he had no particular skills or abilities.

In short, the older man expressed his delight to be of assistance. As Aleksander wrote to his father that night: *"Michał Arct can read railway and shipping timetables like I can read a full score. He knows how to get to places and how to plan travel and recovery time. He has experience of what counts as expenses and how to record them. He understands contracts and their pitfalls. Really, Father, there isn't much on the whole subject of music administration that Michał Arct doesn't know."*

In their conversation, after Michał and Aleksander had spoken for almost two hours, Aleksander brought up the question of fees. "What should I expect to pay you, Michał?" In Aleksander's mind, with such expertise at hand, nothing would be too expensive. Michał Arct's reply was generous.

"Thank you. We should discuss that. But first, a number of matters occur to me. As I see things, you're young Aleksander, and just starting out. I'm retired. Through bookselling and music publishing I have had much success in my career. My banker will tell you I am in a fortunate position and that I don't need the money. But there's something of far greater importance than money to consider. It is that in these uncertain times, we, the Polish people need to support each other against expansionism and hatred, and especially to protect our Jewish friends and neighbours."

Michał Arct spoke with great passion and perception. Aleksander listened with growing attention.

"I ask you, Aleksander, what other group of people have made such an outstanding contribution? The debt our country owes to our Jewish community is immeasurable! Yet though their contributions—through the arts, philosophy, literature and music, through science, medicine and psychology—have changed this world, our world is now bent on changing *them*.

"The horrific intellectual and populist phenomenon of Anti-Semitism, as we now call it, for the nationalist movements in our country, has become something of a creed, and worse a rallying cry. We have all seen where that prejudice and hostility can lead. I'll never forget Warsaw on Christmas Day 1881. Many of us had just emerged from church, when those army thugs unleashed the Warsaw pogrom in all its murderous hatred.

"More recently we've had pogroms in Odessa, Kishiniev and Kiev. When we lived in Białystok, during the pogrom there six years ago, our family had to shelter our Jewish neighbours from the marauding Black Hundreds. The faces of our dear Jewish friends, the chiselled look of terror, until the pogrom had ceased and we were able deliver them to safety, was the stuff of nightmares. The instability in Białystok was the main reason we moved back to Warsaw. But as I said then, this is not the last persecution we're likely to see."

Michał placed a protective, fatherly hand on his new young friend's shoulder. "Who knows what will happen to Poland, even in my lifetime, and certainly in yours, Aleksander? Being conscious of the growing dark cloud on our horizons, I don't need any convincing that we must be fully active to help and support each other—and that, in whatever way and with whatever need comes before us. Sincerely, I thank you. But no, and respectfully, I don't need a fee."

30

Michał Arct had arranged everything for Aleksander's US trip. By the time the year had turned, the 1913 tour had been extended for Aleksander to play not only in New York but also in Boston. Personal recommendations from trustworthy sources were critical in these times. The US was a long way from Europe, and to send out a musical scout to hear the latest promising new virtuoso was expensive and impractical. Fortunately, there was a cache of well-established leading artists upon whose knowledge of rising talent and sound judgement American orchestras could readily rely.

Once again, Paderewski enters Aleksander's story. For it had been Paderewski, who was a regular soloist with the Boston Symphony Orchestra, who had suggested to Dr. Karl Muck, the orchestra's conductor, that he might ask Aleksander to play a concerto with the BSO.

Muck, who spoke American English with a strong German-Swiss accent, was described by Paderewski as the conductor who had transformed the BSO into a virtuoso orchestra. He spoke respectfully of Dr. Muck as "calm, undemonstrative, graceful, elegant, and aristocratic; a man of singularly commanding and magnetic personality." He also told Aleksander how quickly Karl Muck had made up his mind. "No sooner had I made my recommendation, than Muck, who had a passion to further the careers of brilliant young musicians, responded immediately, his accented words underlining his enthusiasm: 'I vant zer boy to comm. Vee most hav zer boy. Tell zer boy to comm, and comm qvuickly, Ignazy.'"

So it was, four weeks after the first invitation from New York, the postman arrived at No. 26 Arbat Street, Moscow. Resplendent in his usual black uniform, peaked cap, and handlebar moustache, Viktor Bogdanovich delivered not one, but two mystery envelopes to Apartment 5, each sporting the telltale George Washington stamp. Viktor was so excited to be the bearer of two missives from America, and on the same day! Of course, he would have loved to have known what secrets lay inside, but he knew the rules. A postman may only be privy to the origin of an envelope, not the contents.

Both letters were addressed to Aleksander. One was from the Boston Symphony Orchestra, the other, from Paderewski, to say "you can blame it all on me!"

When he had waived the postman away without a word, apart from "thank you," Aleksander took both envelopes upstairs to his music room to digest their contents. The Boston invitation, which did indeed owe its life to the calculated midwifery of Paderewski, was a suggestion for Aleksander to play two concertos (different from the ones chosen for New York) and two recitals (which could repeat the programmes already planned for New York city.)

Aleksander was certain as far as Ignacy was concerned, "blame" was entirely the wrong word. He was indebted to Paderewski and had been since he was 11, when Paderewski had so generously funded his Moscow training. Now that financial support was no longer required, Paderewski continued his mentorship with artistic advocacy. This letter was another example.

So everything for this trip was getting better by the day! What's more, in terms of getting him to these famous far-off places, Aleksander couldn't think of any requirement that Michał Arct had not already foreseen.

Some people have a gift for administration, just as much as others might have a musical gift. From Aleksander's viewpoint, it appeared that Michał was enjoying his new role and, ever efficient, had taken all the arrangements in his stride.

Once Michał had heard about the Boston invitation, he wrote to apprise Aleksander of the arrangements he'd been able to put in place. *"I've discovered a private service to collect and deliver letters between Warsaw and Moscow. It's quicker than the State Post, and among other benefits, will reduce the time between you sending me your US letters and my issuing replies to them. One immediate benefit is I have heard this morning that both Orchestras have agreed to one overall contract. This is encouraging as normally the orchestral managers appear to treat their orchestras like independent city-states. But their agreement will make life simpler for you."*

Michał had worked out the train times and reserved rail seats from Moscow to St. Petersburg, round trip. He'd also had a US colleague book the long-distance train out of New York to Boston and arranged personnel to meet Aleksander on his arrival and chaperone him during the entirety of his stay.

With all this welcome news, Aleksander felt he could sit back for a few moments, drink another coffee, and relax before his practice session. Four concertos and two recital programmes was going to be taxing! Unexpectedly, it was a second visit of the postman. Viktor apologised. Somehow another George Washington letter had slipped undelivered to the bottom of his postal satchel. It should have been delivered earlier this morning.

The letter was from Josef Hofmann, who was on tour in the US.

Dear Aleksander,

Greetings from this far-off but fascinating country! I hope you are surviving the rigours of professional work, particularly the touring involved. I trust your dear parents and siblings are all safe and well. We are hearing rumours of disturbing developments of the nationalist movement back home. I hope I'm wrong.

More positively, I am writing because I was delighted to hear from Ignacy that you have dates booked for New York and Boston. That is simply splendid. I have no doubt you will love these great orchestras and their fine conductors.

If you have a little time between engagements while you are here in New York, I was wondering if you would like to record some music for the new Duo-Art reproducing piano I told you about. Aeolian have a recording studio on 42nd Street, with a new concert grand Steinway. Their recording producers, W.Creary Woods and Arno Lachmund, are both well trained musicians and a delight to work with. I've already recorded with them, as have players of the calibre of Paderewski (who you know), Percy Grainger, Ignaz Friedman, and Josef Lhévinne.

It's a satisfying way to enable future generations to appreciate your artistry, as well as reaching an audience wider than the concert hall. I also thought, in addition to your solo recordings, you and I could perhaps re-form the Steinfeld-Hofmann duo. I'm sure your father would be pleased! We might record the Brahms Hungarian Dances. (I have never forgotten Behemoth and Leviathan! I'll be less distracting as I have rather smaller hands than Rachmaninoff!) Maybe we could also record the Schubert Fantasia in F minor. Anyway, you can play the top part—how about that!

31

he day before the first concert Aleksander was due to
play in New York, Aleksander arrived at 42nd Street to
record his solo items for Duo Art: the Liszt piano
sonata, and Beethoven's Hammerklavier Sonata. He liked the
idea of his recordings being like a gift to posterity. Though he
wondered how his performances now would compare with how
he might play these works in thirty years' time.

It was disappointing that as it worked out, Hofmann's schedule
meant he had to be away from New York when Aleksander was
in the city. They said they would certainly try to get together
next time.

At the studio, Aleksander discussed Hofmann's extraordinary
virtuoso pianism with the two producers. "Unlike
Rachmaninoff," he said, "Josef has the smallest hands in the
business." It wasn't gossip exactly, but Creary Woods and Arno
Lachmund told Aleksander that Steinway had just delivered the

piano with narrower keys. Hofmann could now stretch larger intervals with ease.

That was one pianist story worth the retelling. But here's another which from the moment the story occurred was destined to propel its subject into instant North American stardom. It was an event for which Aleksander received no warning.

On Saturday the 8th February at 8:15 p.m., the audience of Carnegie Hall, New York, politely though a little nervously, welcomed Aleksander Steinfeld to play Tchaikovsky's Piano Concerto No. 1.

Within the Orchestra's board, the booking of an unknown Polish pianist had caused more than a whiff of controversy. "Aleksander who?" some asked. Others were more forthright. "Unknowns don't fill concert halls. Who spends dollars on newbies!"

As it turned out, those predictions, even if a little dismissive, were well founded. Despite it being the opening concert of the season, which would normally be a sell-out, the hall was half empty. In fact, only 1,000 of the 2,800 available seats had been filled. As the audience assembled, there were a few cross "told-you-so" faces from the Board members present.

Nonetheless, despite the poor turnout, Josef Stránský was convinced about the rightness of the invitation and knew "zer boy" would do well. The rehearsal had been exciting and the orchestra were already full of admiration for Aleksander. With their comments, and the confidence generated by Paderewski's good report, Stránský was hopeful that a magnificent performance would boost the bookings the following Saturday.

The conductor was now waiting at the podium. And when the "unknown" had adjusted the piano stool, he gave the conductor the customary nod, and Josef Stránský began the first movement with its dramatic opening. The horn playing the brass motif was clear and definite, and Aleksander commanding a rich and powerful tone conveyed a confident authority with the rising piano chords and his exposition of the lyrical opening theme.

Everything had started well.

Nearly forty years before Aleksander's performance, when Tchaikovsky first wrote the concerto, the great composer had faced a torrent of criticism from his distinguished inner circle about the difficulty of the piano part. Tchaikovsky revised it three times. Finally, with the help of Alexander Siloti, Aleksander's teacher, who at that time was Tchaikovsky's friend and editor, effective changes were made. It was Siloti who had suggested the striking gesture of those famous rising chords in the opening piano part.

Despite the difficulties of its conception, and that the work is still monumentally demanding for the pianist, by 1913 it had become enormously popular with the public. For this reason the relatively small Carnegie Hall audience were aware of its demanding nature. They were willing "zer boy" on to produce a sparkling performance. This was, after all, what they had paid their money for.

As the work proceeded, with its soaring themes and intricate passage work, first impressions were good. Some of those board members and several audience members offered approving nods to each other. The performance was going better than they had expected. In fact, they had to admit, it was absolutely riveting.

So what happened next, without exception, took everyone by surprise, including Aleksander.

A fuse had blown and the lights went out. All of them. The audience was clearly shaken, and so was the orchestra. Some of them continued to play in the dark, as they could remember their parts. But even the few of them who did remember eventually had to stop.

The only one who continued playing was Aleksander.

Aleksander often played in the dark. He was used to it. When he practiced at home, he'd turn off the lights as it helped him to concentrate and listen better, to avoid watching his hands and to strengthen his memory. So, of course in the concert hall, unlike the orchestra who always play from the score, the soloist has the music in his head.

With head and hands perfectly synchronised, Aleksander played on. After their first few moments of disruption, the audience settled down and listened with even greater concentration.

Within a few minutes, there were some gasps around the auditorium. Discerning listeners had realised Aleksander was not just playing his own hugely demanding solo part. As he did so, he was completely rearranging it to add in the missing instrumental parts. The Carnegie Hall Steinway, like a full orchestra, thundered fortissimo with a thrilling and massive power. Then, in a hushed pianissimo, sang as sweetly as an a cappella choir. The concerto for piano and full symphony orchestra played on a single instrument by a single virtuoso! It was unforgettable.

The fuse mended and the lights came flickering on. Aleksander continued and Josef Stránský skilfully brought the orchestra back in at the beginning of the third movement. There was a ripple of applause over the music as he did, but nothing like the storm which would erupt with the final bar.

The audience realised what they had heard, though not seen, was a display of incredible virtuoso musicianship as well as extraordinary pianism. The concerto moved on towards its conclusion. For Aleksander, the last twenty minutes solo playing had been exhilarating but had felt like he had "diced with death." There was plenty that could have gone wrong. But "unknown" or not he was up to the challenge! His technique, nerves, musicality and creativity had all passed the test and served him brilliantly. Unexpectedly, Aleksander was thoroughly enjoying the whole experience.

So now, the endorphins flowing freely, all fired up, and only minutes to go, Aleksander felt he was up to any kind of challenge. That was how one of those rare, spur of the moment "now or never" decisions occurred to him.

The very fast two-handed octaves and octave jumps, which form a kind of bravura cadenza at the climax of this concerto, for the soloist are an extremely demanding technical challenge.

It's one of the passages which need constant practice and re-practice, and in performance you take extra care; "fast but not too fast, in case you smudge it."

In the matter of just a split second, Aleksander decided not to allow his usual margin for error. He'd throw caution to the wind and treat the audience to the fastest, most powerful, most accurate octaves they would ever hear in any concert anywhere. They would love it and so would he.

With any other pianist, it might have been reckless. With Aleksander, the result was spectacular. The audience looked on in awe. The Steinway roared like a pride of angry lions as Aleksander's hands raced up and down the keyboard, so fast the image blurred like a dust cloud. There was not a note out of place. Every person present—conductor, orchestra and audience alike were stunned in admiring disbelief that there could ever be such a display of completely fearless and perfect virtuosity.

Later, Stránský described the performance as superhuman. Many felt so moved they wanted to applaud before the end of the piece. Of course, they had to wait. But when the moment came, "Storm Aleksander" exploded with such joyous passion and delight, the ovation was louder and longer and more foot-stampingly enthusiastic than any applause heard, even from a capacity Carnegie audience for many a long day. It was one for the record books.

Overnight, Aleksander had become New York's "latest thing" and premier attraction! The following Saturday the word had gotten around. Predictably, the second concert was a sell out!

32

The reviews of the New York and Boston concerts had been unstinting in their praise.

"A magician of the keyboard."
"Stupendous technique."
"Inspiring musicality."
"Audience wild with enthusiasm."
"Virtuoso, virtuoso, virtuoso!"

Following the enormous success of Aleksander's first US tour, concerto and recital invitations poured in. The Americans, who seemed to have an orchestra in every city, were keen for their chance to hear "the young super-virtuoso whose octaves are faster than any pianist alive!" Promoters in Europe, especially Paris, Berlin, London and Rome were also keen for a taste of the action—and with the help of their best orchestras and conductors.

However, there were downsides to success. It was something Aleksander decided to discuss with Michał Arct, who had come to visit him in Moscow.

"Solitude doesn't really suit me, Michał. And there is plenty of that on the road. I miss my friends and hearing Polish spoken. What's more, living out of a suitcase is fine for a few days, but not for weeks on end. I'd also like to get married. I know there's not much you can do about that! But in this line of work, being on my own is not great, yet spending half your life on trains, the chances of meeting someone is miniscule. Overall though, the main disadvantage of being a travelling virtuoso is the months I spend away from my family."

It was clear that Aleksander's parents, his sister Gerda, and the twins Jakub and Syzmon, came a clear first in his affections. Above all, he loved to spend his birthday with them. Ever since he moved to Moscow, that week of the year was always a priority.

So as always, Aleksander had cleared a week in his diary to spend with his family. On the 14th April 1915 the day before his 24th birthday, Aleksander had travelled the 20-hour journey from his Moscow apartment to his parent's home in Lwów.

As usual, the welcome was wonderful. Aleksander always looked round to see if his parents had made any changes in the house. Once he came inside the biggest innovation was the new Steinway piano. Aleksander was aching to try it, but with a chuckle Abram shoved him aside and said, "We've been practising. Listen to this!" Then, the old master pianist sat down at the piano, and with notes flying everywhere, he broke into a Lisztian arrangement of "Happy Birthday To You" and with Anna, Gerda Jakub and Syzmon, their arms gesticulating wildly, singing the words in four parts, looking and sounding like a mock Wagnerian opera ensemble.

⊢——————⊣

The accident was a completely freak event. Aleksander, still tired from the journey, was just thinking he'd like a snooze and had gone into the quiet sitting room for forty winks. Unfortunately, not concentrating, he had wandered too close to the open fire.

There was a sudden snap and sparks landed, one on his starched collar, another on the sleeve of his right hand, and both immediately caught fire. Momentarily paralysed by the pain, he called out. His mother burst into the room. When Anna saw what was happening, without delay she seized a rug and swiftly wrapped it around him, smothering the flames.

If it had not been for her quick action, Aleksander's injuries might have been worse, if not fatal. In the event, he was burnt around his neck, and on his right hand. The scarring would endure throughout his life, especially the scarring to his neck, although over time the redness gradually faded. The irreversible and most distressing effect was on his piano playing. The outcome was catastrophic.

33

⊢————⊣

There was much toing and froing to the best doctors in Moscow and Warsaw. At first the specialists were optimistic. Napoleon Nikodem Cybulski, a leading Polish physiologist, was cautious. "Let it rest. Let it heal. Let's wait and see, and not jump to early conclusions," he said. "The body has remarkable ability to heal itself and recover."

But the body didn't heal.

Despite the many invitations, Michał had no choice but to put all Aleksander's concerts on hold. It was not until, following a year of regular consultations, reluctantly, the doctors were in agreement. After every medical effort and physical therapy of the highest standard available, although the scar on Aleksander's hand was healing, the fibrosis was not.

Dr. Cybulski gave the verdict. "We are very sorry Aleksander, but the damage is likely to be permanent."

It was an immense blow. Aleksander's brilliant career in which he had shone so brightly had come to an abrupt and devastating conclusion.

His grief and depression continued many months more.

34

During this time, Aleksander moved back to his flat in Moscow. But when he found it difficult to manage, both practically and emotionally, Alicja and Pyotr were there to help. They opened their home to him, and Aleksander moved in with them once more. He was grateful to receive many letters from friends, colleagues, and well-wishers, among them from Count Alfred Potocki, Stanisław Barcewicz, Emil Młynarski , Karl Muck, Josef Stránský, Siloti, Paderewski, Rachmaninoff, and Hofmann.

He was overwhelmed by their kindness and had intended to reply to each one. However, as soon as he tried writing, he realised the present state of his right hand made it difficult to write clearly. It was another major frustration as he had always been a keen correspondent with friends across Europe and America. Fortunately, his Aunt and Uncle jointly offered to be his amanuensis.

Throughout these early months, Pyotr spoke with Aleksander on a daily basis about his state of mind. He encouraged Aleksander to be realistic about his feelings and how he saw the immensity of his loss. He neither minimised the inner pain nor ignored the need to eventually move on and rebuild his life and skills. It was because of Pyotr's suggestions that sometime soon after one of these conversations Aleksander set about learning to write with his left hand.

Some friends asked Aleksander if they could come to Moscow and visit him. He tried to resist. He was scared of the power of his emotions, of being diminished in their eyes by the sight of his scars and what in consequence he had lost. He feared sympathy and how his friends and colleagues would feel sorry for him. He was worried that his feelings might get the better of him, and that he'd lose control. He'd said no to all.

Alicja and Pyotr missed their dog, Sasha, who they had owned since he was a puppy. To exercise a large dog in the middle of Moscow is a challenge, especially when the dog's off the lead. On a couple of occasions, Sasha, by now full grown, had jumped up and frightened some neighbours and their children. When this happened a third time, and because the children had been scared (Sasha was just being friendly) reluctantly, the Yermolovs decided to send their much-loved Caucasian Shepherd to live with Pyotr's cousin in the country. They'd miss him, but at least he'd have plenty of space to run around and other dogs to play with.

That was two years ago, and Alicja and Pyotr had had thought of finding another, smaller dog. Aleksander's needs brought the idea back again. "Even if Aleksander is with us only for a few months it will be worth the effort, especially if having a dog turns out to be a comfort to him."

Given the circumstances, the benefit turned out to be considerable.

Ilya was a Samoyed puppy—that fluffy white Russian breed with a permanent, rather endearing smile. Ilya was certainly smaller and not as strong as Sasha, but in every way he was just as delightful and playful. It is said the upturned corners of a Sammie's mouth keeps the dog from drooling. In the Russian winters this prevents icicles from forming on its face. Icicle prevention is hardly the main selling point! Most owners love their Sammies for their cheerful disposition. In any family that optimistic smile can be a power for good.

It certainly was for Aleksander. Being a puppy, Ilya loved to have his tummy rubbed and would fall asleep on Aleksander's lap. By night, he would often creep up to Aleksander's room and jump on the bed. Soothed by the company of his new-found friend's gentle snoring, he would immerse himself in the enhanced luxury of the soft covers and soon would join in the night-time song.

Then by day, when Aleksander was sitting in the smoking room speaking with Pyotr, there would be a rustling sound; pushed by Ilya's snout, the door would open. Taking up residence at Aleksander's feet, Ilya would rub his paw against Aleksander's leg to encourage him to stroke his fur. Then, when the moment seemed right, he'd jump on his lap for fuller cuddles.

If you want a name for it, I suppose you'd have to call it "stroking therapy," although that doesn't do justice to the deeper sense of connection and empathy it created. It's a mystery how it worked, but it did. Each time at the end of an hour's conversation between Ilya, Pyotr and Aleksander, Aleksander would say, "Thank you so much Pyotr. You have helped me so much!" Both knew that much of that credit was due to Ilya.

The postman, the one with the handlebar moustache, knew nothing of Aleksander's accident. Although he had wondered why the post from the US had multiplied so significantly! George Washington stamps were no longer quite the novelty they once had been. Nonetheless, curiosity being the powerful instinct it is, he would still speculate who might the writer be and what exciting message the envelope might contain.

He knocked at the door of the Yermalov house, and as he was about to say, "This is for Mr. Steinfeld," Aleksander opened the door. For the last few months, it was always Mrs. Yermalov or Yelena who would take in the post. So surprised, he handed the latest American letter direct to Aleksander. As he did so, he was shocked to notice the scars on Aleksander's neck and hands. Maybe he had stared. Whatever it was, he knew he shouldn't say anything. But Aleksander did.

"They are burn marks, Victor. A fire at my parents' house. I am lucky to be alive."

Victor was shocked, stunned even, and with a bowed head said, "I am so very sorry, Mr. Steinfeld."

"That's alright, my friend. I appreciate your concern. But, if I may say, and don't misunderstand me—I'm sure you'll realise why. Thank you for not asking."

35

|———————|•

That latest letter from the USA was one of several hundred that had arrived in the past year. The surge in Aleksander's international reputation following the two city concerts, and the burgeoning press interest, meant the volume was no great surprise.

Apart from those sent by friends, the greatest number came from strangers, shocked at what they had read about. All sent "Get well soon" cards or similar messages, but painfully the well-meaning sentiment didn't apply. For no amount of good wishes were going to restore Aleksander's playing career. It was gone forever. It was the hardest fact for him to face.

When the accident first happened, Aleksander had immediately heard from Alexander and Vera Siloti. It had been a long, sensitive letter expressing such wise thoughts, so kindly. As close as they were or had been, Aleksander hadn't expected to hear from them again. This was one of the conflicts he felt the most sharply. No longer being what he once was, he felt his friends would simply want to "let him go" and not continue to be interested in him.

In childhood as in adulthood, and now since his accident, Aleksander had wonderful parents who loved him with a love he could only describe as unconditional. In childhood and adolescence, insightfully, they had addressed the paradox of the exceptional child: to nurture his gifts, and in the same way to protect him from them. They both knew how performers can confuse their human value with their musical worth. How a poor performance can drag down the inner world with it, tumbling towards the abyss.

So it was neither from any deficiency—in the love of Aleksander's parents, nor the healthy esteem of his friends—that for whatever reasons Aleksander had unconsciously come to measure his personal value by the brilliance of his virtuosity. Especially since the accident, this way of accounting his value had become considerably more focussed. Now and in the days since he was a prodigy, it was his gifts, not his personhood, that had become the index of his worth.

Great performance inspires adulation, and most recently and so spectacularly, international acclaim. A single, random spark had destroyed all that. Until now, he'd not thought about his Grandmother's words, "Even the best gifts don't last forever."

36

Awaking from his daydream, and with Siloti's letter still in his hand, Aleksander read their words again. "We'd love to come and see you. We'll be in Moscow on May 16th. If it's not convenient, leave a message for us at the Hotel Metropol, otherwise, if we may, we'll be with you around 2:30 that Sunday."

Later, Aleksander was to describe the reunion as incredible. There were hugs, many tears on behalf of all three of them, but so much to smile about, so much laughter, so many memories, so much love and kindness. It was real friendship, strengthened and deepened by the passing of years, a recognition of the true value of Aleksander the person. He felt it.

In the afternoon and evening which followed, many topics were discussed, but none more important for Aleksander's next step than this.

"Be a teacher, like me, Aleksander. You have so much to offer. Who knows how many young musicians whose gifts will turn from good to great with the insights and guidance you uniquely can give! Think of Liszt, Leschetizky, Anton Rubenstein, even Dry Old Stick."

Aleksander laughed. "You mean Taneyev?"

"Yes, the one you beat at chess. All of these are my heroes, and to a man, great players who became great teachers. Each one has given so much to generations of pianists. I would say, ever since I taught my cousin, Rachmaninoff, I have realised this is how we preserve the tradition in which we ourselves have been taught. By passing that tradition on. It only happens when we allow teaching to become as high an art as playing. Those other greats who have gone before you, Aleksander—they have seen this as a duty. You might too. To pass on the rich value of our heritage, from one generation to the next. And of course, as always, I'll be glad to help you."

Aleksander realised that Siloti had come today as his dear friend but also as a man on a mission. Of course, he had planned to say all this. However, in no sense did the pre-meditation undermine his wisdom. For Aleksander, the perspective and thoughtfulness behind the words enhanced the significance of the message.

The Silotis stayed for supper as Alicja had hoped they would. Before they said their farewells that evening, Siloti asked if he could play the piano for them. He said, "I have something of a gift for us all. It's rather special, and I guarantee you won't have heard it before."

From his music case, Siloti produced a manuscript which he placed upon the music stand of the grand piano in the drawing room. "This is a new piece by Nicolai Medtner. You know him from the conservatoire, Aleksander. He's Rachmaninoff's great friend and another fine pianist. Most of all, though, he is a prolific composer for the piano. In years to come, we'll all hear a lot more from him.

"Anyway, Nikolai Karlovich has sent me this to try out. It arrived yesterday, so I've only looked it through, and not tried it at the piano. His letter says it's not finished yet, but even in this draft version he's encouraged me to play it to friends and give him some feedback. So I'd love to play this for all of us.

"Just a little explanation before I try it out. As we have said several times today and sometimes painfully—change and loss are fundamental to the nature of life. Indeed, with nations in conflict and talk of revolution, the entire world is implicated in the damage wrought by such loss. But the power of memory cannot easily be extinguished, and if we use it to celebrate the past and passing, such memories will remain forever within our reach.

"Medtner's called the piece *Sonata Reminiscenza*. As the title suggests, Reminiscenza means a recollection, a celebration of a vanished world; a way to honour and value its memory and discover a deeper meaning, while the world around us is subject to massive realignments. Given such changes, which, of course, affect you enormously Aleksander, but in different ways for all of us—who knows when or how—I'd suggest this music is timely.

"The way music expresses joy, sorrow, wistful recollection, even nostalgia, is to explore the world of the emotions. That's a unique gift the composer brings to a world of change. Think of the reminiscences we have expressed today, and the unexpressed reflections which live on inside of us. By the exploration of an exquisite and returning melody, Medtner transports us to an other-world of remembrance and emotion. This is not a world of pictures, but a world of feeling, where we can value again, embrace what is past and passing and allow ourselves to look positively to the future.

"I should add that Medtner has asked me to say, absolutely no one has heard this before!"

With that, Siloti opened the piano lid, checked the score and prepared to play. But there was a late arrival. A quiet rustling, and Ilya appeared from behind the door. Looking around the room, smiling as always, he immediately settled at Siloti's feet, ready to listen.

The audience, finally assembled, there in the drawing room of the Yermalov's Moscow home, Vera turned the pages. And Alexander Siloti played the first ever performance of Nicolai Medtner's Sonata Reminiscenza in A minor.

37

After several more months of recuperation, and with the continuing help of the Silotis, Aleksander prepared himself for a new future. By now, he could play a little with his right hand, enough to explore scores for himself, but not well enough to perform again. He was told not to expect any further improvement.

However, Siloti did encourage him to play with just one hand and to further develop his left-hand technique. He pointed to him a small but established repertoire of works by Reinecke, Saint-Saëns, Scriabin and others, all originally written for the left hand alone. But on his most recent visit, Siloti came on his own, bearing a gift. He had brought with him a work of double genius: a collaboration of Bach and Brahms across the centuries. It was Brahms' brilliant arrangement for the left hand of Bach's masterful Chaconne in D minor, originally written for solo violin.

"Did you know that Brahms made this arrangement for Clara Schumann in 1874 when she injured her right arm and could only play with one hand? I have here his letter that he sent with the score."

"In my opinion, Clara, Bach's Chaconne is like an ocean without a seabed—one of the most wonderful and unfathomable pieces of music ever written. The man creates a whole world of deepest thought and conveys the most powerful feelings of emotional excitement and tension, all with one small instrument. My dear Clara, in the absence of a great violinist, may I suggest the most exquisite joys are brought forth by the same effort of technique at the piano—when the Chaconne is played with the left hand alone. Its deep world of thought and feelings open a window into heaven itself."

Siloti was planning to play it to Aleksander. But inspired by Brahms words, Aleksander immediately stood up and walked towards Siloti.

"May I?" He took the score, sat, and played Bach's Chaconne in D minor with his left hand alone. It was the first time he had played a complete piece since the day of the accident. It was like a homecoming. At the end he was in tears.

"It is as Brahms says it is," he said to Siloti. "It's a window into heaven itself. Once I have practiced it more, I feel the window will open wider."

The gift was indeed a master stroke, as it enabled Aleksander to begin a new and continuing relationship with the instrument that had been part of his world for so long. Siloti, who himself was famous for many arrangements of Bach's music for two hands, promised to make more left-hand transcriptions. He also suggested Aleksander could try arranging music for one piano, three hands, to make duets possible again.

One comment Siloti had made to Aleksander which especially stayed with him was to do with the future. "I feel sure, Aleksander, there will come a time when composers of substance will not just write solo pieces for the left hand, but whole concertos. Why would they do that? Because what you see in Brahms' arrangement of the Bach Chaconne is big technique harnessed to rich musical expression. It's a kind of model that tells us it can be done. For the composer, it releases considerable creative and expressive possibilities."

Following that conversation, as he left the Yermalov's house that day, Siloti recapitulated his theme. "Playing with the left hand alone? So much has changed for you, dear friend. I know that. But in another sense so much hasn't. Strong fingers, strong emotions. It's still what counts. Make sure your left hand is ready for that day."

38

With his considerable reputation preceding him, when Aleksander decided to return to his hometown of Lwów, a new career was effectively set up and waiting for him. He had his own music room, complete with the Bösendorfer upright.

He had been home only a matter of weeks when he received an envelope with a logo he recognised immediately. It was from Steinway and Sons in New York.

Dear Mr. Steinfeld,

We have heard in the press and from your colleague, Mr. Siloti, about your dreadful accident. I and all the board of Steinway wish to express most sincerely our sorrow and condolences. This last two years must have been a harrowing time.

More happily, we have heard that you are exploring repertoire for the left hand, and also that you are to take up a new career in teaching. As a professor, you will be following in the footsteps of some of the greatest pianists of recent years. We have no doubt that you will not only have significant influence as a teacher but will pass on the valuable traditions you have received. With your reputation, it seems certain you will attract many of the best and emerging talents of our time.

To this end, our board would like to offer you a gift of a Steinway grand piano. We hope that this might assist you in your vocation as a teacher and additionally serve to showcase the Steinway reputation to your students.

If indeed this would be welcomed by your good self, then I will ask one of our staff from Steinway Hall in Hamburg to contact you to discuss which model from our range you would like to choose.

This letter, and with the gift that it promises, comes from the Board of Directors at Steinway, with the expression of our enormous respect and appreciation for your advocacy of our instruments, your many inspired performances, and the new opportunities teaching offers us all through you.

I remain, sir, your obedient servant.

Henry Ziegler
Vice Chairman
Steinway and Sons

Stunned, but very encouraged, Aleksander put the letter down, and called his father.

"Do you think the music room floor can take the weight of another piano, Papa?"

From order to delivery, it took about three months for Steinway to manufacture and deliver the new model B grand piano. When it arrived, it took five men to get it up the stairs, but it fitted perfectly in the window of the large music room.

That evening, Abram and Aleksander gave an inaugural concert for the whole family. On the Bösendorfer, Abram played the solo part of the Mozart concerto in F major K. 459, while Aleksander cleverly arranged the orchestral part for the left hand only and made the Steinway sing like a full orchestra. After that, Abram joined Aleksander at the new piano, and with Aleksander playing the top part, celebrated the rest of the evening with Schubert's Fantasy in F minor "in a new arrangement for three hands by Aleksander Steinfeld."

It was glorious music, wonderful playing and such unadulterated fun. Aleksander was beginning to forget his disability. Or, at least, he was finding effective ways to cope with it.

Teaching was also proving very rewarding. He began with children. He was able not only to offer piano lessons to the children of rich families, but also take on the especially gifted. Some of those could not afford to pay, but Aleksander was able to teach them pro bono.

With young people, Aleksander had a wonderful gift. He knew how to connect to their world. Just like Siloti and his father, he played games with the children, encouraged them, made them laugh, and brought out their very best. Inspired by Siloti all those years back, he even donned a clown's outfit!

One especially serious child, who played the piano well, but always solemnly, was struggling with Beethoven's tongue in cheek, "Rage over a lost penny." He made it sound so serious and completely missed the humour. After several failed attempts to get the boy to put some fun in it, Aleksander said, "Carry on playing." The boy continued the dirge, looking anxious as Aleksander left the room. Moments later, Aleksander returned wearing that clown's costume, and started to roam around the room, performing all kinds of antics.

The boy stopped playing, and laughing, said to Aleksander, "Is that how you want me to do it?"

"Exactly," said Aleksander.

And he did, fast and furious, catching every nuance of Beethoven's humour—causing Aleksander to comment, "Good job he didn't lose a dollar!" Beethoven would have laughed too.

As the months went on, it was clear that Aleksander was now well restored and flourishing. This was reflected in the number of outstanding young professional players who flocked to be taught by him, and who telegraphed their satisfaction across Europe and as far as the United States.

In view of Aleksander's growing and distinguished reputation as a teacher, his father—now Lwów's Principal and the Conservatoire's most senior professor—called a meeting of its directors. He wished to explore the possibility of an appointment for Aleksander. In recent years, the profile of the Lwów Conservatoire had grown significantly and had built a magnetic reputation, rivalling Moscow, Saint Petersburg, and

Warsaw for pedagogic excellence, distinguished faculty and its accomplished and famous graduates. The institution was offering courses for gifted children, and those preparing for professional careers.

Abram informed the board of his wish to remain a professor of piano, but to step back from the overall leadership of the Conservatoire. He said new leadership required a younger musician of high accomplishment, international recognition and wide experience of teaching and coaching. He did not need to say more, as the board immediately proposed Aleksander should take over from his father and become Principal and Music Director of the Lwów Conservatoire.

It took little time for Aleksander to gratefully accept the offer, and he took up the new post without delay. His new colleagues welcomed him with warmth and determination to build on the already strong foundations of the Institution. He was held in high esteem by students and faculty alike.

It marked a new era for the Conservatoire, for Aleksander, and the wellbeing of his whole family.

39

|————|

"On a crisp spring day, under the warmth of the
shining sun, where birds of richly patterned
splendour sing symphonies of song.
Where grass and trees, flowers, plants and all things
beautiful, speak of nature's re-awakening.
In this rich harmony, the music of the spheres declares
the world 'in bloom'. It's flourishing never to end.
"But the Idyl fades. The clouds darken, and a distant
rumbling crescendos into crashing thunder.
A lightning burst rips across the sky, and in an
instant the firmament fractures.
Nature awakes once more - and now with angry
voice bellows derision.
So the riven heavens release a pounding deluge, a
piteous ricochet, destroying everything beautiful
which once had bloomed."

In such manner came the persecutions.

The date is etched in the family's memory. Aleksander had been the Principal of the Lwów Conservatoire for just eleven months. On the morning of Thursday the 21st November 1918, he was teaching advanced analysis to a class of music students, when a colleague passed him a hastily written note. It said there had been attacks in the town's Jewish quarter.

With concern for his family's safety, Aleksander quickly closed the class and hurried home through the eerily silent streets. As he came into the Jewish quarter, he could feel the fear mounting. Shopkeepers were bringing down the shutters, the roads practically deserted. He began to hear the angry cries of a chaotic rabble approaching from less than a mile away.

By mid-morning Lwów was engulfed in a violent eruption of devastating, vicious assaults. Jews were the target. The violence, from Polish soldiers, civilians and criminals. The purpose, ethnic cleansing.

On that Thursday until the following Saturday, Jewish civilians were attacked, and many Jewish stores and homes were burned and looted. The atrocities were numerous, including horrific rapes. No pity was shown to anyone. A soldier's execution of an elderly Hasidic man was typical. The Hasid tried to protect his payos (side curls) from being ripped off. The soldier, who was drunk, shot him dead and ransacked the corpse for valuables.

The mob was out of control; their behaviour, brutal and rancorous. In ragged, drunken groups of thirty the soldiers went from house to house. Demanding entrance, they banged on doors, and where there was no reply they used grenades to force their way in. Every house in the quarter was vandalised and plundered, and its occupants beaten, arrested or shot on sight. Shops and businesses too were looted, and the stolen goods loaded onto army trucks and driven away.

By the afternoon, the whole area was ablaze. Fire officials deliberately allowed the conflagration to spread, and some firemen laughed in derision as three synagogues burned to the ground. In a three-day firestorm of bloodthirsty hatred, over 50 apartment buildings and 500 Jewish businesses were destroyed, and two thousand Jews were left homeless. Accounts vary but clearly there were many fatalities. Up to one hundred of the Steinfelds' Jewish neighbours were brutally murdered by Polish soldiers and civilians, with many more injured and arrested.

Abramczyk's family, Aleksander included, were among the first to be forced out of their home, arrested and interred in one of the secure makeshift compounds. It was not difficult for Abramczyk and Anna to foresee the family's coming fate.

Together, Aleksander's father and mother agreed on a "survival plan." In the past few hours they had seen the extent of the hatred and violence of the rioting forces. They knew there would be no justice, protection or hope for those who remained under arrest. They understood, reluctantly, the end for their family was inevitable.

The plan was not for themselves.

Some faced with such an alarming situation might be paralysed into inactivity. But all along, Abramczyk felt keenly his responsibility, not only to his own family, but to future generations; a commitment he had long maintained. The plan was to preserve the Steinfeld inheritance. It was a costly and perilous solution and was formed with the heaviest of hearts and many tears.

It worked in this way. With their extinction just hours away, Abram and Anna would designate their eldest son to be their chosen survivor. If Aleksander achieved his freedom, given time, he would become a bridge between the world that is rapidly passing, and a new more peaceful world. A world where eventually he would be able to pass on the Steinfeld inheritance and its unique teaching: how to bring to birth a virtuoso pianist, how to nurture musical excellence, and how to pass on the insights of generations past and convey its mysteries onwards to generations to come.

Their eyes connected and held the gaze. Abramczyk did not need to explain. For Aleksander understood. With unimaginable pain, their eyes spoke everything needing to be said.

So it was, late on that Thursday evening, the 21st November 1918, the first day of their incarceration, out of sight of the guards, and moving at a snail's pace on account of their newly acquired chains, the whole family shuffled the 80 yards towards the south wall of the compound.

When they arrived, with military precision, Abramczyk directed his wife and brothers to form a human tower—his father strong and muscular, like a foundation stone holding steady at the base. As soon as the escape tower was deemed stable, the word was given. Aleksander scrambled up upon their shoulders, and after a brief moment of unsteadiness, the manoeuvre was successful. Aleksander climbed over the south wall of the Lwów pogrom compound, stood tall, and jumped to life and freedom.

Farewells had been minimal; the parting, swift and heart breaking. There was neither time nor opportunity to look back. If the wall had been transparent he would have seen his parents, Abramczyk and Anna, twins Jakub and Syzmon, and his sister, Gerda, being angrily beaten by a guard.

Despite his best efforts, Aleksander never found out what happened to his family. He said Kaddish for them for the rest of his life.

40

Aleksander escaped with a bag containing a few photos and mementos, and the mezuzah from the front door of their home which Abram had placed into his hand just before the escape. He had nothing else. His clothes were dirty. He had no food. Where was he to go for help and safety? Moscow was too far; besides, on account of Pyotr's army work, his aunt and uncle had moved to the Russian Far East. But fortunately, Aleksander's family had relations a little closer in Łódź: his mother's parents, Karol and Zuzanna Rosenwasser.

The Rosenwassers were prosperous factory owners, producing decorative fabrics of silk, cotton wool, felt, knitting and hosiery. A couple of days before the pogrom, anticipating that something might happen, Anna had already sent word that the family might need temporary sanctuary in their home—"till everything blows over." She mentioned this to Aleksander; for this reason, his grandparents would not be surprised to see him.

When Aleksander breached the wall's defences he ran continuously for several miles. Fortunately the camp had only just been set up, so they didn't yet have a roll call of inmates, and no one came after him. Distressed and disorientated, Aleksander walked his way to Łódź. He was fit, but the journey took him six days. He managed to survive by night, sleeping under bushes, by day, eating whatever he could find or buy with the small amount of cash his mother had hurriedly sewn into the lining of his jacket.

A few hours before the eve of Shabbat, at his grandparent's comfortable home, No. 104 Piotrkowska Street, the house was already tidied and the food prepared. As his grandmother placed the two Shabbat candles on the table, she heard a commotion outside. As violence against Jews was increasing, she thought someone had been pushed off their bike. But it wasn't a bicycle. It was the exhausted Aleksander who had stumbled in the dark. From the light of the front door she immediately recognised his characteristic blond side curls, the payos, and beard. She called out, "Aleksander!" He didn't hear her at first, but when he did, his heart broke. Rushing towards her, Aleksander fell into his Grandmother's arms, sobbing deeply.

41

For several months, his grandparents nursed Aleksander back to emotional health. It was a hard road for all, but Karol and Zuzanna Rosenwasser were the epitome of kindness and tender care. However, there was one reason above all others that Aleksander re-discovered the will to live.

Aleksander's Uncle and Aunt, Aaron and Liliana Rosenwasser and their daughter Leah, also lived in Łódź. Aleksander hadn't seen his cousin Leah in years. But over the months they became wonderfully close. Leah had a beautiful, lyrical soprano voice. Aleksander would accompany her at the piano with just one hand. "You make the piano sound like a whole orchestra, Aleksander, but beautifully expressive too."

In just under a year, Aleksander proposed, and a few months later the couple were married. The service was beautiful, nostalgic and meaningful. Aleksander missed his parents and his siblings more than he could say. Leah squeezed Aleksander's hand when she sensed the bittersweetness of his daydreams. It was still an occasion of great happiness, and the couple were perfect for each other.

However, their life together in Łódź was to be short lived. Anti-Semitism was spreading across Eastern Europe like a deadly pandemic. In view of increasing persecution and threats to Jewish people, Leah's father, a senior diplomat, arranged safe passage to London for Leah and Aleksander, his own family, and Aleksander's beloved Grandparents.

3RD MOVEMENT

1

┥————┝

Through the generosity of Leah's father, Aleksander and Leah were able to find a small but comfortable house in Bolsover Street in the West End of London. It was well situated, near to the Middlesex hospital, and to Oxford Street.

Britain had just emerged from the Great War and change was in the air across the Capital. Oxford Street was no exception and by the turn of the century the now fashionable centre had changed in character from the dominance of residential property to commercial buildings. Drapers, cobblers and furniture stores began to open for business, and in time some became the first department stores.

John Lewis had started a small business at No. 132, and later Selfridges opened at No. 400. Oxford Street was rapidly becoming a premier centre for shopping—the prospect of which delighted Leah. It reminded her of a vastly expanded version of markets she knew back home in Łódź. But nowhere in the world had there ever been a market like this with such an array of goods, food, clothes and fashionable fabrics. In fact, in Oxford Street you could find practically anything you wanted, provided you could walk the 1.2 miles from Marble Arch to Tottenham Court Road!

The house was not just well situated, it was well equipped. It had three bedrooms, a substantial kitchen and bathroom; and the sitting room was easily large enough for a small grand or an upright piano. As Siloti had encouraged him, Aleksander was developing his left-hand technique and resolved to play, even in public performance, compositions and arrangements for the left hand alone.

So for teaching and practice it was clear to Aleksander and Leah that a decent instrument was a first requirement. But they realised the financial challenge, as a new piano might be prohibitively expensive. Nonetheless, they made tentative enquiries. Aleksander's grandparents were willing to help, as were his in-laws. But however willing and kind (and they had both already helped so much with their accommodation in Bolsover Street) neither Aleksander nor Leah wanted to put further strain on their families' generosity or resources.

Aleksander thought again and discussed it with Leah.

"Maybe as new arrivals in London, we should concentrate on getting ourselves established in our new home and city. Then we can wait two or three years before finding an instrument?"

They quickly decided this was both impractical and inconceivable. "If you are to teach as well as perform, Aleksander, you must have a quality instrument. For someone of your attainment, not to have a piano would be like losing your voice and the ability to speak and communicate."

Aleksander then thought of hiring a piano or finding a second-hand instrument. It could be a stop gap, although the quality would be nothing like the high-end instruments he had known since childhood. His mind flashed back to the piano in the music room at home, where, when he was three years old, he had first played the *sing me a song* game with his father. There was something sweetly visceral about the feel and response of a finely regulated keyboard. As he recalled that early life discovery, it gave him a warm and positive feeling. He remembered being told that Beethoven had owned a British piano. So he decided there must be a piano shop somewhere in London where he could go and find some advice.

He did not need to go far. Partly due to the renown of the Broadwood fortepiano, which was gifted to Beethoven in Vienna in 1817, the British piano industry was well established. Beethoven said the Broadwood was his favourite instrument. That well deserved accolade alone established Broadwood as Britain's leading piano manufacturer. But since that time the piano had undergone a massive increase in domestic popularity and had become the main form of entertainment in British homes.

Responding to this demand, by 1911, there were 136 piano manufacturers in Britain, mostly based in London. By the end of the war this figure had doubled and would peak at 300 by the early 1920s. With new developments, higher end names such as Broadwood, Welmar, Kemble and Knight took advantage of opportunities afforded by new engineering technologies. Features such as cross-stringing, under-damping, iron frames and the use of better manufacturing techniques swiftly improved their instruments.

As with any sales boom the products of these quality manufacturers were soon to be challenged by the production of cheap imitations. The lower middle classes wanted smart design and good prices but weren't prepared to pay for quality. Responding to this demand, by the early 1900's, many companies began to build cheap and less well functioning instruments. Their unique selling point was to ensure they looked good.

Looks, however, are not everything. In fact, in a piano good looks offer no musical value at all. Although these instruments, mainly uprights, had many ornate features, they were built of inferior parts, were ungratifying to play, and their sound bore no comparison to the more sophisticated instruments they aimed to imitate. They were, as widely advertised, much cheaper than the quality competition.

Aleksander knew nothing of this and thought all British pianos were likely to range from the ordinary to the good, though perhaps not great. He also didn't know the contemporary London saying: "You're never more than 10 minutes from a piano shop." Although ignorant of these insights, he was delighted to find there were two piano manufacturers practically on his doorstep: Edward Hale, in Percy Street, a small turning off Tottenham Court Road, and Charles Hammar, at 35 Charlotte Street, near Fitzroy Square.

2

Aleksander decided to visit Hales, not realising their pianos were in the *quickly-fall-apart* category. It was a warm day and an easy, pleasant walk. Invitingly, the showroom door was pinned wide open when he arrived. Aleksander went in and with a few glances left and right, slightly disappointed, he could not fail to notice the cheap finish of the instruments. All the pianos were uprights, and he was about to look at the action of the one nearest to him, when the proprietor appeared from a curtained off area at the back of the shop. Forcing a smile—it clearly was not his preferred demeanour—Mr. Hale managed to supress his usual greeting of, "don't touch till it's yours," and just managed a "Good morning," sotto voce.

Mr. Hale was a salesman, through and through. Like a blazing burst of fire from a Vickers machine gun, his questions were overwhelming.

"Looking for a piano, are we? What's your budget? Paying cash or instalments? Are you a beginner or can you play a bit? We can provide lessons for adults and children. And do you mind me asking about your accent, sir? Are you German by any chance? Or Jewish perhaps?"

Aleksander felt a freezing sensation in his spine. Given the war, he could understand the German question. But in the past, his experience of being asked if he was Jewish was almost always prejudicial. He didn't wish to jump to conclusions, but neither did he want to take risks. Mr. Hale could have been the world's greatest piano manufacturer, but he was not the most tactful person Aleksander had met in London.

Aleksander briefly thanked the proprietor for his trouble, and quickly returned to the front door of the shop. Mr. Hale, looking startled and not a little cross, watched Aleksander run off down Percy Street and into Tottenham Court Rd. He didn't look back.

When Mr. Hale went back into his showroom, he lit his pipe, puffed a while, and through the comfort of the billowing smoke remarked to himself, "Shame, I was sure I could have sold him an upright. Mind you, I think he was some kind of sportsman. Anyone who can sprint that fast must be a professional runner. Anyway, Jews don't make good pianists!"

The next day, Aleksander had more luck with Charles Hammar, whose showroom was in Charlotte Street near Fitzroy Square, again just a short stroll from Bolsover Street. Aleksander arrived at around 10:30 a.m. He found the showroom easily. It was brightly lit and generously adorned with yellow freesias, fragrant blue hyacinths, tulips and orange roses.

As he came through the front entrance, their sweet bouquet reminded him immediately of his family's garden at home. Aleksander thought of his mother's green fingers and the vases full of fresh cut flowers they would have throughout the house. For a moment, he stood lost in thought, especially as the sound of Paderewski's Minuet in G was coming from the back of the showroom.

The familiar music of his Polish mentor, and the sweet-scented flowers filling the air with their perfume, provided a kind of double counterpoint to the bittersweet memories they provoked in Aleksander's memory. But it was a good space to be in, and coming-to and looking around, Aleksander could see the long room was full of handsome looking uprights with a couple of small boudoir grands, all the pianos bearing the gold Charles Hammar insignia.

Mr. Hammar was immediately welcoming. He took Aleksander's coat and placed it carefully on a hanger. While he was doing so, Aleksander enquired, "Was that you, playing the Paderewski?"

"Yes, it was."

"You played it very nicely. It is good to hear some Polish music in London. Did you know Paderewski's Minuet is played so often that it has had vastly more concert performances than his Symphony, Piano Concerto and opera combined?"

"Yes I do. That's a shame, isn't it, because he is a fine composer. Some pieces especially catch the public's imagination. It's like Rachmaninoff says, he's asked to play his C sharp minor prelude wherever he goes."

While Aleksander was distracted by one of the pianos, Mr. Hammar could not help noticing something about Aleksander's neck and hand. It was of course the scars, healed well, but still telling their story.

When Aleksander looked up, Mr. Hammar said, "May I offer you coffee or sherry, sir?"

Aleksander, pleased at the friendly reception, gratefully accepted the sherry. His experience of the British and coffee was they served it, "not too hot and not too strong," rendering it not too palatable!

Charles Hammar took sherry also.

After he had poured two glasses of Amontillado, the piano maker invited Aleksander to take a seat so they could talk. Unintentionally, Aleksander had neglected to introduce himself, so he was surprised when the hospitable gentleman addressed him by name.

"Mr. Steinfeld, I must tell you I feel confident I know who you are. As soon as you entered our showroom, I recognised you as the Aleksander Steinfeld who played Rachmaninoff so wonderfully at the Proms in the Queen's Hall. I was there in the front row. It must be ten years ago now. It is you, isn't it, sir?"

Aleksander felt this was a far safer environment than Percy Street had been and was happy to identify himself. He smiled and nodded.

"Since your Prom appearance, I've followed your career closely, read reviews and listened to your Duo Art recordings."

Mr. Hammar could see from the scars around Aleksander's neck and on his right hand, the evidence for the fire at Aleksander's home, which had been reported in the Times newspaper. "If I may say sir, I've read about the accident, and about the recent devastating events in Lwów. Although I have only just met you, I hope you won't consider it forward of me to mention such personal matters, Mr. Steinfeld, but I would like to express my very sincere condolences."

Charles Hammar was a sympathetic and kindly man. Aleksander could feel his warm sincerity and was content to convey some aspects of his family's story.

"Leah and I have so much to be grateful for, not the least being the new start your government is allowing us to have with joint British-Polish citizenship. Although I cannot imagine if or when we would ever wish to go back to our country after what they did to us in 1918. But hearing you play the Paderewski minuet evoked such memories. It reminded me Poland is still my home, and I miss my homeland and my family more than I can say."

"And what about playing, sir? That also must be a terrible loss."

Aleksander looked at him, thinking before his reply. "Fortunately I still have one hand that works!"

Charles Hammar was navigating private waters and realised these were sensitive matters. He did not at all wish to cause offence and sought to change direction to a different subject. But before he could do so, Aleksander added, "I have been encouraged by various friends to explore repertoire for the left hand alone, and I have been making some left-hand piano arrangements of my own. Frankly, in terms of polyphony, velocity and expression I have been surprised how much can be achieved with just half the orchestra."

"Yes, indeed," said Hammar, who by now Aleksander had discovered had once been a piano student of Arabella Goddard at the Royal College of Music. She had been a Thalberg pupil, and back in 1853 had given the British premiere of Beethoven's "Hammerklavier" Sonata.

"Miss Goddard used to say the left hand has an advantage over the right, for it has the strongest fingers to carry the upper voice of chords and melody. Then, when you think of the lower parts of the keyboard, physically the left hand is perfectly placed to create rich sonority. So when the performer develops agility and tonal colour, and the composer creates imaginative harmony, polyphony and ingenious figuration, the virtuoso and expressive powers of the left hand alone are practically limitless."

Aleksander nodded. "And of course, the use of the sustaining pedal becomes even more important. But then the right pedal has always been a more subtle resource than many professional players realise."

The two men continued to speak as though they had been friends for years rather than hours. They discussed exile, music and post-war politics, before moving on to a potential piano purchase, which over two hours ago had been the main purpose of Aleksander's visit to Charlotte Street.

Aleksander went on to explain his needs. "What about renting a small grand or purchasing a second hand upright?" he asked.

Charles listened carefully, and clearly wished to help.

After some further discussion he said, "I am sorry to be disappointing, Aleksander, but I think you will have already realised our instruments are aimed at the domestic market and not at your level. If you are to play again, my advice is, tailor your dreams not to your budget, but to your vision. Ways can always be found for an artist of your standing. There is only one name in the whole piano world that can truly meet your needs, and that is Steinway."

Aleksander was quiet for a moment, before responding, "Hamburg is a long way away, Charles."

It was Charles Hammar's turn to pause. Then he smiled and said, "Have you not heard that in London you're never more than 10 minutes from a piano shop?"

Aleksander looked puzzled.

"Steinway Hall is at 44 Marylebone Lane. Out your front door, turn right, left and right again and you'll find it."

3

Charles Hammar was right on almost all counts. Located in London's West End, Steinway Hall had been opened in 1875, the first Steinway Hall in Europe. It was indeed right, left and right again from Bolsover Street, although at a comfortable pace it took Aleksander around fourteen minutes, not ten! It was still effectively on his doorstep and he was delighted to discover Steinway had a home in London. He had played many fine pianos in his time, Bechsteins, Bösendorfers and Érards, but to Aleksander, Steinway was more than a piano—Steinway was almost family.

The connection went right back to childhood and that entrancing day in Zachodnia Avenue, when he made the acquaintance of the mighty Model D concert grand. Apart from not being able to reach the pedals, from that moment Aleksander's early attachment was indissoluble. In any concert hall in which he played, he always felt at home when he saw a Steinway waiting for him.

There was no question, Steinway had been good to him. After his accident, the connection was firmly re-established by their unexpected and generous gift of a Model B grand. Once again it was a wonderful instrument—his father enjoyed playing it as much as he did. Tragically, like the rest of his world in Lwów— that piano must have ended up in ashes.

Aleksander would always love those instruments and even with his left hand alone would welcome the opportunity to renew their friendship. But he was realistic. He knew it was unlikely he would ever own one again. Yet even with that well understood, Aleksander found it strangely comforting—his world having changed so much—to discover that Steinway and Sons was just a short walk from his front door.

Later, Aleksander was eager to tell Leah about his sherry with Charles Hammar and the Steinway epiphany. They agreed he should definitely plan a visit and not for sentimental reasons alone. There was a slight possibility that they might remember him, although he did doubt whether anyone would be interested in a one-handed pianist. But depending on his reception (he hoped they would not throw him out), maybe they could offer some advice or perhaps a lead towards some solution to his need.

Although Leah knew already they were not in a position to purchase, she encouraged him to visit Steinway Hall before the end of the week.

The next morning Aleksander took his normal walk around the West End. He was a little later than usual; the two of them had stayed up late, as they often did, talking and putting the world to rights. By the time Aleksander left the house, it was getting near midday; but since Leah was off to see her parents, there wasn't any especial pressure on time.

Aleksander thought he would try out the walk to Steinway Hall, so he could be confident about directions for his planned visit tomorrow. The walk was refreshing. The route he'd worked out took him down Cavendish Square, an attractive open space just off Oxford Street, and into Wigmore Street.

If Steinway being in London was a total revelation, the Wigmore Hall was a case of amnesia. He'd forgotten its existence, probably because when he first played there in 1911 it was called by its original name, The Bechstein Hall. It had been changed to Wigmore Hall only recently in 1917.

It was and is a leading attraction for chamber music and world-famous players. It was opened on 31 May 1901. As the Bechstein Hall, the first concert featured pianist and composer, Ferruccio Busoni and violinist Eugène Ysaÿe. Since then it had become a hub for the world's greatest musicians including Artur Schnabel, Pablo Sarasate, Percy Grainger, Myra Hess, Camille Saint-Saëns, Jascha Spivakovsky and Max Reger.

Aleksander recalled that Siloti had played at the Bechstein Hall in its opening season. They had discussed its fine acoustic and of course its beautiful Steinway piano. As he stood opposite the entrance in Wigmore Street, he also remembered the concert he'd played there. He daydreamed the programme.

It had been all Schumann: The Davidsbündlertänze, the C major Fantasy, and the Symphonic Studies—some of the great peaks of romantic piano music. For a moment, the thought of these outstandingly great works rekindled his sense of loss. He'd never play them again. And then it occurred to him that Schumann, early in his playing career, had also lost the use of his right hand. It was poignant, and he tried to imagine the feelings of devastation Schumann must have felt. He wondered whether Clara had been as sensitive and kind to her husband as Leah had unwaveringly been to him.

A passing car hooted. Day dreaming, without looking, he had wandered into the road. But as he came to, he realised there had been a change. Not in that instant, but this was the first time he'd become aware of any progress in his feelings. Instead of waking every day to the familiar dark cloud—the loss of his family most of all, and the ending of his playing career—he realised the sky looked bright and the fresh air tasted sweet. He was moving on, not fighting his multiple bereavements as much as he had been. He felt he was becoming just a little more accepting of the past; not constantly looking back to what he'd lost, but beginning to set his sights on the future to what he might achieve.

Now fully aware the Wigmore Hall was his old concert venue and still a major performance centre, Aleksander noticed a big crowd of people queuing to get in. He enquired of an older gentleman to ask if there was a concert. "Yes," he said. "It starts in ten minutes. It's the Russian pianist, Ossip Gabrilowitsch."

Aleksander had a mild intake of breath. Surprised, he thanked the man and went straight into buy a ticket. "You're just in time," the young lady at the ticket booth said. "That's the last seat. You won't be able to see much, but you'll hear everything."

"That's alright," said Aleksander, smiling, and handing over the cost of the ticket, "I've only come to listen."

The reason for Aleksander's surprise (and delight) was he knew Ossip Gabrilowitsch to be a graduate of the Saint Petersburg Conservatoire, and as his father had done, had spent two years studying piano with Theodor Leschetizky in Vienna. Aleksander and Gabrilowitsch had never met, although he had heard his father speak of him with glowing praise.

Apart from a few fluffs in the Liszt, for even the greatest players aren't immune from small accidents, the recital was excellent. There were two Beethoven Sonatas in the first half, Liszt and Brahms in the second. Then three encores: The Chopin Minute Waltz, Liszt La Campanella, and coincidentally, the Paderewski Minuet that Charles Hammar had played in Charlotte Street yesterday. Hearing it again, it reminded Aleksander of the Polish master's enormous efforts to champion an Independent Poland. He was a man who never gave up, whatever the obstacles. When Aleksander contemplated the obstacles in his own situation, his old patron reignited in him something of that determined, tenacious inspiration.

Aleksander toyed with the idea of going to the Green Room to introduce himself and thank Gabrilowitsch for the recital. He wasn't shy. He never had been, but since the accident and particularly the pogrom, something had happened to his social confidence. He'd talked to Leah about it that evening when she returned from her parents.

Nonetheless, Wigmore Street's fresh air (figuratively speaking) had done him a power of good. He realised it wasn't just loss he'd been struggling with. It was to do with self-worth. He had gained the habit of looking back and forgotten the art of looking forward. He had been thinking of himself as a has-been, doomed by a couple of crackling sparks, never to play again.

Following the Gabrilowitsch recital, all that changed. Aleksander decided his playing career was not to be extinguished. Like Paderewski had recently shown the world, "Be determined, never give up." It would cost him a massive effort. But he was resolute. He would play again. And when he was ready for his new debut, he'd ensure his renewed, stunning virtuosity would outclass any pianist alive. Except, as he told Leah, "Aleksander Steinfeld will play with his left hand alone."

4

After that conversation, Aleksander's mood was buoyant. It was like a car wheel spinning in the mud, which suddenly gains traction. His mind was immediately engaged, and he was full of energy. Leah was so happy to hear him sound so positive.

Over breakfast, Aleksander told Leah about the recital and the Wigmore Hall. "Listening to Gabrilowitsch playing so well, I felt that burning energy to play. It's the music that counts, not the number of fingers you have. It won't be the same repertoire of course, but I'll work and practice so hard that I'll change the piano world. I'll blaze a trail for left-handed pianists to give them a chance to thrill, delight and soothe as much as any two-handed player. And I'll play a Wigmore to prove it."

Leah was delighted to hear Aleksander speak like this.

She didn't know what was in the letter that had just arrived in the morning post, but she hoped, seeing the insignia on the envelope, it would cheer him even more. After they had finished speaking she handed Aleksander the letter.

It was from Steinway's London Director.

Dear Mr. Steinfeld.

Permit me if I may to introduce myself. My name is James Painter-Reeves, and I am the Director of Steinway Hall in London. I have heard you play on several occasions. I have never forgotten your performance of the Rachmaninoff 2nd concerto at the Proms in 1911. I was also present in New York the night the lights went out and you played the Tchaikovsky first concerto so magnificently.

May I say I was so sad to learn both of your dreadful accident and the subsequent devastating loss of your family. This must have caused you pain without measure. On behalf of Steinway, and especially our staff in London, I want to express our most sincere and heartfelt condolences.

There is another reason for this letter. I have been instructed by Henry Ziegler, our Vice Chairman, to make contact with you. Mr. Ziegler is conscious that your previous Steinway Model B will have been destroyed in the fires in Lwów. As an artist of such international acclaim and your continued standing in the world of teaching and performance, we believe you should always have a fine instrument at your disposal. For this reason we offer you and Mrs. Steinfeld the deep respect and good wishes of Steinway and Sons as you settle into your new home in London, in the hope you may also accept from us the gift of a new Steinway piano of your choice.

I hope this letter finds you at least beginning to recover from your ordeal. Please contact me personally if I can be of any further help, and especially when you are ready to visit us at Steinway Hall.

I am, sir, Yours faithfully

James Painter-Reeves

Aleksander read the letter with emotion at the memories it evoked. But more than anything with joy at the kindness and compassion he had been shown by Steinway over so many years. To absorb what Steinway was offering, he read what James Painter-Reeves had written a second time over. He was so thrilled; he couldn't wait to show the letter to Leah.

"What do you think, Leah. Have we got room for a piano?"

"Of course we have!"

"Then can we have one?"

"If I can have a new frock from Oxford Street!"

It was an easy decision. The deal was done. She went this way, and he went that way. Aleksander to Marylebone Lane, and a happy looking Leah to Oxford Street.

Aleksander had a wonderful time. James Painter-Reeves reminded him so much of Mr. Lewandowski, the manager of Lew i Sala. He was well over six foot and clearly a good musician. Conscious of Aleksander's left-hand disability, he also kindly offered to demonstrate the instruments. Aleksander appreciated the kindness but explained using his left hand alone he could still play. "Just to make it sound good, I have to work a little harder."

Impressed, the manager pointed towards a brand-new concert grand. "This instrument has just arrived from Hamburg, sir. It has been tuned and regulated this morning. I would say it is ready and waiting for you."

5

In the history of piano virtuosity both Chopin and Liszt, two of the greatest composer-pianists of their time, were both inspired by the faultless technique of the violinist, Paganini. They consciously set out to achieve for the piano vastly enhanced levels of technique comparable with the achievements of the greatest violinist of their age, and perhaps of any age. Chopin and Liszt achieved their goal magnificently with great musical and technical mastery. Their twin technical peaks were Liszt's Grandes Études de Paganini and Chopin's two sets of Études, op 10 and op 25.

Year on year, the best of pianists would learn to scale those peaks magnificently, but would such heights ever be exceeded?

As the centuries turn, and one era of invention gives way to another, the world has witnessed many surpassing glories. For instance, over the centuries, the humble wheel has been elaborated from a cumbersome circular stone, to a wheel and axle cart. When chariots gained spokes, they drove to war at untold speeds; most recently, air pumped into rubber tyres has enabled a new generation of wheels to reach unparalleled velocity—on motorways, runways, and racetracks.

The piano, too, has undergone many transformations since around 1700, when Bartolomeo Cristofori first invented the instrument. But as far as playing is concerned, it was seriously considered that in Chopin and Liszt the ceiling of virtuosity had been reached. But it hadn't.

Leopold Godowsky, some twenty years older than Aleksander and a friend of Abramczyk, was a self-taught Jewish Polish American pianist whose name was and still is a byword for the ultimate in virtuoso pianism. He was a pianist's pianist and found a way to make demands of a pianist's hands which no one previously had the ingenuity or technical facility to achieve.

In the genre of composition he inherited from Chopin and Liszt, no one else even approached Godowsky's breath-taking extension of piano technique. His main technical work, which he intended for public performance, is the 53 Studies on Chopin's Études, written between 1894—1914. Based on Chopin's already demanding originals, twenty-two of them are for the left hand alone. One of these, the Revolutionary Study, Aleksander had worked on as an eleven-year-old student with his teacher, Alexander Siloti.

Godowsky had read in the American press something dreadful had happened in Lwów in 1918 but did not discover what had befallen the Steinfeld family till Aleksander and Leah had arrived in London. As soon as news reached him he sent

Aleksander a sensitive, moving letter of clearly heart-felt condolences, expressing his solidarity of feeling with his dear friend's son. Then, finally, in a cheerful PS he added, "Enclosed are a few pieces for the left hand, designed to make any virtuoso sweat. Although having heard from Siloti how you polished off the Revolutionary Study, Aleksander, you'll probably master the lot of them in no time at all."

Even Godowsky could exaggerate. The 53 studies are a marvel of invention and among the most difficult piano works ever written. But the most difficult of all? The 22 composed for the left hand alone. They are bruisers!

Years ago, Siloti had taught Aleksander to learn scores away from the piano. It redeemed the time on long journeys, but it encouraged attention to technical and musical detail and the sweep of the whole piece. So not having access to a piano, when Aleksander received the Godowsky left-hand piano studies, Aleksander decided to study No. 5 in D flat major, with a score but no keyboard. The study is based on the Chopin Étude in E major op 10 No. 3, which has a well-known and beautiful song-like melody. He felt sure if the audience shut their eyes they would think it was definitely a two hander.

Aleksander would have loved Siloti to have been present on this day and to experience the fruit of his wise teaching. Of course, neither of them ever imagined this is how Aleksander would commit Godowsky's magical D flat major study to memory and then play it unrehearsed before an audience. Let alone to the staff and customers at Steinway Hall.

As invited, Aleksander sat down at the Steinway Model D, and adjusted the stool. His eye caught James Painter-Reeves. Was there a hint of something? "I think he was worried what my playing would be like," he said to Leah later. "He needn't have. I know I lost one, but I kept a spare!"

Leah smiled, but look concerned. "It's okay my darling, I didn't say that—I just played."

And so he did.

Godowsky's arrangement was beyond perfection, and so was Aleksander's rendition. Like setting out on a summer's day, the skies blue, the birds singing, the best company—Aleksander transported himself and his listeners on a voyage to another world. Breathing every musical phrase, the melody sang out so clearly. The harmony, Chopin's own but elaborated a little and beautifully by Godowsky, was rich and perfectly balanced.

The left hand created a pianistic effect, so richly sonorous, warm and supremely passionate, that as the ship finally came into shore, Aleksander looked up, and found himself surrounded by the entire Steinway staff, and many professional pianists who were there in Steinway Hall that afternoon.

There was a moment of stunned silence, followed by a sustained round of applause. It brought tears to Aleksander's eyes.

He told Leah, "I didn't dare say, 'That's the first time I have played it!' Instead I said, as a joke, 'I'll take it.' And James Painter-Reeves looked so delighted I had to quickly say, 'No I couldn't possibly. I mean, we don't have room for it. It wouldn't go through the front door!'"

Leah laughed, as had his audience. After a few shared reminiscences from those who had heard him play in previous years, everyone returned to their activities, several gently touching his arm and thanking him for the moving, memorable performance.

James said to Aleksander. "I understand there are more Godowsky left hand studies."

"Yes," said Aleksander, "He sent me twenty-two."

"Twenty-two studies are more than enough for a recital, and as you know, there are plenty of other left-hand pieces to choose from. Is it too early to think about it, or would you ever consider playing repertoire of this kind? The obvious venue is the Wigmore, but you could try the programme here in one of our lunch time recitals. You know, Aleksander, London has not forgotten you."

leksander knew that even if he did start playing recitals, and even a concerto if there ever was to be one, he could never emulate his previous career. But as he remembered telling Michał Arct, he'd long moved on from the joys of living out of a suitcase. Now Leah and Aleksander were thinking of starting a family, even if he hadn't suffered a hand injury, those old aspirations belonged to a completed chapter. But to teach advanced students and pass on the Steinfeld traditions of virtuoso pianism, with occasional concert opportunities, that would open a new chapter with hopeful prospects.

Steinway had agreed that the 9-foot Model D wouldn't squeeze through the Steinfeld's front door. But somehow they had worked out how to successfully deliver a Model B instrument like he'd had in Lwów. And there it was, in pride of place in their front room, a miracle of design and manufacture. Aleksander was like a little boy with a new football. If he could have taken it to bed with him, he would have. But it gave him and all who heard it such joy. While he was playing and practising, he'd notice neighbours and passers-by standing outside the window of their ground floor, forming an impromptu audience.

One day a policeman knocked at the door. Aleksander thought he'd probably caused an illegal assembly and was about to be arrested under the Riot Act. The policeman took off his helmet and introduced himself as PC William Blandford and asked if he could have a minute of Aleksander's time.

It was understandable that Aleksander's experience of the police should be coloured by his more recent experience in Poland. But the British constabulary were different. He had already learnt that. One of the attractions of life in Britain was the British police had high professional standards and were nothing like those who had so criminally assisted the mob in Lwów.

PC Blandford explained that he had not come on police business. It was about music. William and his wife Celia were keen amateur musicians. They sang in the choir of Holy Trinity, Euston Road, and in addition were both instrumentalists: Mrs. Blandford, a fluent violinist, and her husband, a pianist of a good standard. As a child, William had an excellent teacher and spoke of learning the earlier Beethoven sonatas and some Chopin Nocturnes. It was about piano teaching he wished to enquire.

"We now have two children. Jeremy is eight and Martha is six. At the moment, Martha isn't particularly interested in learning an instrument. But Jeremy has taken to the piano like I did at his age. He is able to play some quite grown-up pieces, like the easier movements of some Mozart and Haydn sonatas, and with feeling. So the reason I've called is when I have been on the beat round here, I have often joined the crowd outside your house and listened to your marvellous playing.

"I was so impressed, I asked our sergeant if he knew anything about you. He just said he'd heard what I had, that you and your wife are from Poland, and that you are a world-famous pianist. So I expect you're too busy with your playing and that, but I still thought I'd ask you if you do take pupils; and, as you're local, if you would consider listening to Jeremy play and perhaps take him on for a few lessons?"

Jeremy turned out to be a gifted child and did very well with Aleksander's encouragement and teaching. He was the first from many families in the Fitzrovia neighbourhood who asked for lessons for their children. Aleksander's unintentional concertizing from their front room couldn't have been a more successful advertisement for his services.

In the West End the going rates for piano lessons were the highest in the country and substantial enough to ensure Aleksander and Leah were not only financially secure but would soon no longer need to rely on family subsidies. Although money wasn't Aleksander's first concern—he had no interest in amassing wealth—Aleksander had what he called "a fair rate of charges" based on a rough estimate of each family's situation.

So the poor, from the Cleveland Street area, of which there were many, paid next to nothing for their lessons; and the rich, from the area around Fitzroy Square, of which there were a good number, paid their dues in full. In less than a year, having arrived in London with practically nothing, Aleksander and Leah's finances were secured on a healthy footing. There was more than enough for their rent, their weekly shop in Berwick Street market, and other recurring expenses, plus more than a few pounds left over each month for new frocks and tickets for London's many concert venues.

8

In the 1920s, in their part of London it was quite usual for visitors to arrive unannounced. Bolsover Street was a safe area, and when the door knocked, in between checking through the curtains and opening the front door, Leah had come to enjoy speculating who it might be and why they were calling.

So when the door knocker, with a firm rat-a-tat-tat, announced his presence, through the net curtains Leah could see a tall military-looking English gentleman with a friendly face, red hair and a goatee beard. He was holding an attaché case under his arm. "Surely he must be an Insurance salesman? Or perhaps he's another one selling Encyclopaedias?" On this occasion, Leah's instincts turned out to be entirely wrong!

"Hello," she said as she opened the door. "How can I be of assistance?"

"You must be Mrs. Steinfeld. Forgive me for just turning up and not writing in advance. My name is Sir Gerald Williamson, and

I am chairman of the Board of Governors at The Guildhall School of Music in John Carpenter Street in Blackfriars."

With the mention of the Guildhall, London's newest conservatoire, his interest kindled, Aleksander appeared from behind the door. The two men shook hands, and Aleksander invited Sir Gerald into the sitting room.

As soon as the man from the Guildhall set eyes on Aleksander's new Steinway, he was clearly impressed. "That's a very fine instrument. The best, indeed. I heard you playing it while I was outside. Wonderful sound. The locals seem to enjoy it. I see people flocking here to stand and listen. And you teach Roderick, our neighbour's son."

"Yes," said Aleksander. "Young Roddy is doing very well."

"Mr. Steinfeld, my wife and I are your neighbours. We live in Clipstone Street, just up the road. So in one sense, this is a friendship visit, to say how good it is to have a musician of your calibre in our neighbourhood and to extend our welcome to you and your wife. On a typically grey English morning to walk past your house and hear you playing, as so many of us do, is a real fillip. But I am here not just because you have created a significant local following, but because of your enormous reputation internationally."

Aleksander continued to listen without interruption.

"As you know, sir, our British press reported the terrible fate of your family, and the devastation caused by your accident, for which it is only appropriate that I sincerely offer my true and heartfelt condolences. But my friend, James Painter-Reeves, with whom I understand you are acquainted, tells me after a period of mourning you appear to have new wind in your sails. In particular, he's mentioned you are working to recover your playing with your left hand alone."

Aleksander nodded.

"James said he was filled with joy and so moved when he heard you play a Godowsky-Chopin study. 'If ever a pianist had ever made the piano sound like a full orchestra, with such sensitivity and passion and phenomenal technique, it was that occasion,' he said. 'And with the left hand alone! I will never forget it.'"

"He's a very generous man."

"I'll come to the point, Mr. Steinfeld. For many years, you have played and it seems will play again at the highest level of musical and pianistic achievement. Your musicality and musicianship is an inspiration to audiences, whether in great numbers as we read about in New York, or in informal, intimate settings like Steinway Hall only a few weeks ago. I know you were taught by two of the greatest pianists and teachers of Eastern Europe: your father, Abramczyk Steinfeld, and Alexander Siloti. You yourself have taught pianists at the highest level at the Lwów conservatoire. To the world of music, and conservatoire training, the Steinfeld inheritance and tradition of playing and teaching you represent is priceless.

"May I also explain our situation at the Guildhall. We opened our doors to students in 1880, so we are London's newest leading Conservatoire. In the last forty years, we have trained many now famous musicians. The public's support for our work is so enthusiastic, for the first time this year we are introducing full time courses for advanced pianists preparing for a concert career. We are looking for someone to be a figurehead and lead professor for the Department of Piano Performance. Someone with international standing and experience as a performer, and someone who intimately understands the technical and musical needs in the professional development of young players.

"I was present when you played the Brahms 2nd concerto with Dr. Muck and the Boston Symphony. I know you are used to superlatives when people like me admiringly describe your playing, so I will just say it was indeed, glorious, utterly glorious! Added to that, many on our board were present at your Prom performance of the Rachmaninoff. We have no one else in mind; we are unanimous in our desire to ask you if you would be prepared to consider helping us in this way?"

Aleksander was quiet for a moment. He could sense Leah out of the corner of his eye nodding very gently encouraging him to say 'yes' right away. But he didn't.

Instead, he smiled at Sir Gerald Williamson, and said calmly, "Are you sure you want a man who is now only half a pianist?"

Sir Gerald thought about his reply, "I can hardly imagine the depth of loss and frustration you must experience every morning when you sit down to play your new Steinway. And of course we understand, alas, that your career cannot continue in the way it once did. But even now you can still play with one hand—and marvellously; you can still inspire—your profound sense of 'the music within the music' still reaches out to the heart with deep emotion; and of course, you can still teach.

"What you represent as an inheritor of the Steinfeld tradition of performance and teaching cannot be anything but of inestimable value to the contemporary world of music and piano performance. Your country has produced so many extraordinary virtuoso composer-teachers: Chopin, Tausig, Rubinstein, Godowsky, Hofmann, Leschetizky, Moskowski, Paderewski. The list goes on and on. May I say with all sensitivity I am terribly, deeply sorry for what that accident did to your hand. But even that does not detract in any way from the brilliant musician that you continue to be—and all you have still to offer the world."

9

By May 1921 Aleksander had completed his first two terms as Head of Piano Performance at the Guildhall. The school boasted such excellent facilities, and he felt his colleagues and students were beyond compare. It reminded him so positively of his experience at the Lwów Conservatoire, but without the tiresome administration!

At the time of Aleksander's appointment, Sir Gerald had also kindly promised Leah a part time role in the library. Leah was quite a linguist, and her knowledge of Russian, French, Polish and Italian would be very useful in cataloguing music books and scores. She was fluent in all four languages and could get by in German, Spanish and Portuguese.

When Sir Gerald heard that Leah needed to resign her position, he was quick to respond. "You have made such a contribution, Leah, and are so valuable to us, that if you wish we can keep the appointment open for you, so you can return to us at a suitable time after the baby is born."

Baby Steinfeld was not long off arriving. On Wednesday, the 11th May 1921, in the East Wing of the Middlesex Hospital on the corner of Cleveland Street and Mortimer Street, exactly two weeks earlier than his expected due date, Leah and Aleksander were delivered of a little boy. While he was not a large baby, for Leah, his mother, labour had been long and intense. After 18 hours of unassisted effort, the Obstetrician called time and ordered a Caesarean. So that evening, very shortly after 10:16 p.m., Daniyal Steinfeld made his debut upon on the world's stage, a little bloodied but otherwise unblemished.

Leah remembers delightedly checking his long fingers, as though other normalities hadn't mattered. "Big hands," commented the midwife. "He'll never regret those." When Leah relayed the comment back a few hours later, it made Aleksander smile. How could he forget Behemoth and Leviathan!

The midwife gave Daniyal a swift clean-up, weighed him and scribbled on his notes. Then she delivered her smiling verdict, "Baby is perfect, beautiful, adorable!" Thus after the combined and heroic efforts of mother, baby, and theatre staff, Daniyal was delivered in every sense, unmarked and unmarred by his experience. As he was placed in his cot, he looked as pretty and cheeky as any of Raphael's winged Cherubs; although at 5 lbs 7 ounces, not as chubby.

"Mazel Tov, Leah," said Aleksander, now husband and proud father, as he came through the door of her private room. They held hands for a moment while his eyes turned to Daniyal, who was sleeping contentedly and blowing little bubbles. Aleksander held on to Leah's right hand in his, and gazing devotedly at his son, with watering eyes and feeling rising emotion with every word, he prayed the ancient Hebrew Benediction:

Baruch Atah Adonai, Eloheinu Melech Ha'Olam, Sh'hecheyanu, V'Kiyemanu, V'Higianu LaZman HaZeh ("Blessed art Thou, O Lord our God, King of the Universe...")

The thanksgiving for the wonder of new life completed, Aleksander turned, beaming, towards Leah, reaching as he did for the bag of necessities pre-packed in readiness some 24 hours earlier. "Be prepared," had been the timely advice of their neighbours whose own new-born had raced well ahead of the arrival queue!

Aleksander drew out the bottle from the bottom of the bag, steadied it on the bedside table and peeled off the foil coiffe and undid the muselet. With the wire frame loosened, and then pulled off, with both thumbs he began to work the cork. The wine had warmed in the waiting and as though in protest, the cork put up some resistance. But the struggle was short. With a loud "pop" it flew out, ricocheting off the ceiling, and releasing a gushing deluge of foaming frothy fizz, the characteristic bouquet of vintage Dom Perignon, like sweet garlanded flowers, filling the room.

Their firstborn was safely delivered. Their joy was indescribable.

With his wine held in blessing high above the cot, *"L'chaim,"* said Aleksander in a loud voice, *"L'chaim v'l'vracha,"* replied Leah, tired but with equal enthusiasm. "To life, and to blessing."

In this fashion, with warm champagne served in small coffee cups with every sincerity, and minimum delay, Aleksander and Leah wetted the baby's head. A practice that Daniyal would gladly reprise (with a chilled bottle) throughout his adult life!

The Consultant had recommended at least four weeks further bed-rest postpartum. Since Dr. Frankel was Jewish, Leah put it to him, "What about the Bris (the circumcision) eight days after the birth?" Dr. Frankel was a gentle, kindly man. He looked at Leah like a father. He paused for a moment—he was always sympathetic—and then said, "Mrs. Steinfeld, sometimes we Jews have to choose. It's law or life. I can tell you about life and the best for you. If you want to talk about the law, you'll have to ask the Rabbi."

10

Bringing the baby home, especially the first born, is an important moment for any family. Leah had decided there was no need to consult further, and after a couple of days rest in the Middlesex, the three Steinfelds, Aleksander, Leah and Daniyal, returned to their Bolsover Street residence. As they entered the building, in remembrance, they touched the mezuzah on the door post—the same mezuzah that had come from Aleksander's home in Lwów. They kissed their fingers, and with the same that had touched the mezuzah, blessed their first-born child's blond haired sleeping head.

Mezuzahs, unlike Jews, don't come in all shapes and sizes; all mezuzah's contain the same extract from the Torah. The little mezuzah box, often at an angle, is attached to every door post in the home, and reminds Jews that we have a covenant with God. To everyone else it is a sign to declare this is a Jewish household, shaped by Jewish rules, rituals, and beliefs. "And you shall inscribe them on the doorposts (mezuzot) of your house and on your gates... the words that I shall tell you this day: that you shall love the Lord your God, believe only in Him, keep His commandments, and pass all of this on to your children."

This simple ritual of touching and blessing, the command to pass on the knowledge of the faith of their fathers to their sons and daughters was in the forefront of their minds as they brought Daniyal back to their home. Jews have observed the Torah command for centuries. By that simple act of touching the mezuzah, the Steinfelds expressed themselves one with their community, wherever that community might be dispersed.

So now the pressure was on. Since they first knew she was expecting, Aleksander and Leah had hoped for a boy, and his first name, Daniyal, had been warmly agreed between them weeks before his actual birth. The pressure arose from Jewish custom: they had eight days to decide Daniyal's second name, and 48 hours had already passed.

Ashkenazi Jews have a variety of customs for the choice of children's names. In Aleksander's tradition, the father chose the names for the first child, the mother for the second child; and for future children, they alternate the privilege. So it was simple, the choice was Aleksander's prerogative.

In practice, it is never quite as simple as that. In Jewish families, because there is such a sense of family solidarity, naming the new baby is definitely a big deal. And a shared deal at that. Father or Mother do have the final say, but there is never any shortage of contributions. Sisters, brothers, cousins, aunts and uncles, parents and grandparents queue up to make their suggestions—quite often this could be a memorial, a name linked to a long-passed family member. "The baby's got Uncle Solly's nose," or, "He's got rosy cheeks like my second cousin, Chaim," or, "He's boss—eyed like Asher," among many others.

Aleksander decided to give Leah, and Leah alone the chance to choose the second name for their son. It wasn't that he considered himself a particularly modern husband. Or that he didn't value the contributions of their families. It was instinctual. He had such an admiration for the way that Leah had managed the pregnancy, the demanding birth, and now beginning to look after the baby at home. Aleksander wanted to honour Leah for being the wonderful wife and mother she had proven herself to be.

Aleksander was gracious in his appreciation of the family's various suggestions and his defence of his wife's right to choose. "In any case," he said to Leah, "the boy can't have a dozen names, despite what our families might hope. Take your time and don't be rushed. A name not only identifies you. It's more than a label. It's like a container that holds in trust all that you are, inside and out. That's why I'd love you to feel you have made this important choice for Daniyal's life and future."

In the event, Leah's delivery of this responsibility for Daniyal's arrival was settled well in time for the eight-day deadline required by Jewish Law.

So, although permitting Leah little time for recovery from her surgery, but obedient to their tradition, Aleksander sent out invitations. At 11 am on Tuesday 24th May, 8 days following his birth (since the Jewish day begins the previous evening) Daniyal was to be named at his Bris ceremony at the Old Synagogue in Portland Place, London.

The day came and even though it was not far from their house in Bolsover Street, Leah still finding it too sore to walk, they placed Daniyal in his Moses basket and went the few streets by taxi.

Among other members of the two families gathered at the Synagogue were Aleksander's grandparents, Karol and Suzanna; his aunt and Uncle Pyotr and Alicja, who happily were on secondment in London; his mother's sister and husband and four grown up children; Leah's mother and father, Aaron and Liliana Rosenwasser (Aleksander's other Uncle and Aunt); Leah's sister and brother and three young children who had also recently come to make their home in England.

Aleksander and Leah were touched that Sir Gerald and Lady Williamson, twelve members of the teaching faculty at the Guildhall, and Aleksander's good friends, Charles Hammer and James Painter-Reeves, had all accepted their invitation. The whole group of family and friends were there at the entrance of the synagogue and eagerly awaited the first sight of the new baby and his parents.

As the taxi arrived, a roar of welcome greeted them. When the family of three alighted, there were bursts of flashlight from two waiting newspaper photographers, syndicated to run an update story on the world-famous pianist. "New birth and new beginning for Aleksander Steinfeld" was the headline next day in newspapers on both sides of the Atlantic. The happy news did not appear anywhere in Poland.

Aleksander helped Leah to the door, and the family of three were greeted by the Rabbi and were allowed to sit together.

In the short Bris ceremony, the Mohel performed the circumcision with solemn and careful expertise. He was in fact a Jewish doctor with a practice in nearby Fitzroy Square. But despite his professional skill, and in complete and inevitable accord with Steinfeld family tradition, Daniyal voiced his objection with the full force of an orchestral tutti, double fortissimo!

Fortunately, he calmed and recovered quickly, and was soon blowing his characteristic bubbles, enabling his new admirers, friends and family to cootchy-coo back, endorsing the midwife's verdict of "adorable, truly adorable."

At the formal meal afterwards, (the seudat mitzvah,) Aleksander and Leah again followed tradition and read out a letter specially composed for Daniyal. "Our son Daniyal. We are already so proud of you, and we know you will want to make us proud throughout your life. So we hope you will be proud of us this day, for we commit ourselves in love, care and well-being, to honour and protect you in every way—no matter what you should do, be or become in life. One day we hope you will read these words and be able to see then whether we have succeeded in our sincere aspirations for you. Most of all we pray for your happiness, that you will live your life fairly and justly, love and embrace mercy, and walk humbly with the God of our fathers, the God of Abraham, Isaac and Jacob."

There was applause. Then, a hushed silence followed as those assembled waited for the Jewish naming ceremony.

Leah had asked Aleksander if the choice of Daniyal's second name could come as a surprise and be revealed in the synagogue ceremony itself. To Aleksander it felt like a birthday present, which, of course it was. He certainly had no idea what was to come.

Mordecai, their delightful Rabbi, asked Leah to come to the Lectern with Daniyal, followed by Aleksander. Leah handed the baby to his father. With the two parents standing together, Mordecai said a prayer in Hebrew and then turned to Leah.

"Leah, will you please name your child?"

Leah beamed at Aleksander, then she turned towards the congregation; with a firm and joy-filled voice said, "Our child is to be called Daniyal Abramczyk Steinfeld."

An audible intake of breath was followed immediately with a huge burst of delighted applause. Leah handed baby Daniyal to Suzanna, his great grandmother, and turning again to Aleksander (careful of her surgery) gave her husband a warm, long hug.

Aleksander couldn't help it. He was so pleased, but his feelings welled up like an emotional avalanche. Tears gushed forth. He could think of no greater memorial for his father. But the sweetness was mixed with gall. In that moment he felt so much pain. Pain of loss, of anger, and unfulfilled longing. How he missed his mother and father, Jakub and Syzmon, Gerda, friends like Paweł and Mirtel, and others close in their family's circle who he believed had also perished in those three days of evil madness. He would have so loved for them all to be present for this occasion.

In one way of thinking, maybe they were. The finality of death being so awful, is it so surprising our minds attempt to duck the agony of loss? We hope against hope, and clutch at straws, especially in the early stages of grief. Yet the truth is, while we remain in this life, it's only in our dreams we encounter our loved ones again.

It's an observation I have made several times in therapy: that when someone close to us dies, in a sense, we don't lose them all at once, but gradually in pieces. It's a recognition that grief is a process, rather than an event lasting just days or weeks. Our sorrow so often expressed in tears actually needs those tears to accompany our loss on its journey; in some mysterious fashion, our grief is enriched and dignified by the rituals and remembrance which take place on its way.

Aleksander understood how and why the ritual of naming had kindled the strong feelings he had just experienced. So wonderfully but unexpectedly hearing his father's name brought a perspective not only of loss, but also of overwhelming gratitude. For all the loving, generous, faithful care of his parents. For the sheer delight of music and the piano. Anna's amazing cooking. So many birthdays and celebrations. All those many encouragements which made the children feel they were really valued. Yes, it was all so cruelly cut short, and yet paradoxically, in a strange way, it felt complete.

Everyone in the synagogue was chatting excitedly. At that point, most didn't notice Aleksander. While the tears flowed, Leah continued to hold him. Then when they stopped, Aleksander looked at her, his face lighting up like the morning sun. He said simply, with all the meaning he could envelop in a single phrase, "Thank you."

11

Memories fade, and with the passing years, most faces are forgotten. The advent of photography changed all that. Early in the nineteenth century the invention heralded a far-reaching revolution in the way memories can be preserved and passed on. Within a couple of decades, a new social phenomenon, the family photo album began to take its place in households throughout middle-class Europe and America. Its presence, soon to be ubiquitous, became a precious antidote to the fading past, and a cherished testimony for future generations.

The Steinfeld family album was typical of many. It was a large bound leather book with stiff, heavy leaves. With the turning of each page, history itself turned. The past awoken, ghost-like portraits emerged from their slumbers. Bearing little resemblance to their day-to-day get-up-and-go vivacity, they were now ever to be remembered as unsmiling, maybe severe, certainly self-conscious, and possibly none too happy to be disturbed.

Old photos are rarely cheerful or relaxed. It has something to do with the prevailing culture of formality, and quite frankly, the mechanics. "Stay still. Don't move, or you'll blur the exposure!" This is why Aleksander and his siblings used to like to play, "What did they say next?"

The oldest photo in the Steinfeld gallery was of Solomon Ebenezer Steinfeld, Aleksander's grandfather. There he was with his black Yarmulka, side curls and long beard. He was standing with his hand on the side of the piano, the first volume of his edition of the Beethoven Sonatas open on the stand. He is gazing straight at the camera, clearly unwilling to say 'cheese,' and looking as though he wishes he were somewhere else.

The flash bulb pops. What did he say next? The children dreamt up many answers.

"Do you really want to hear another sonata?"
"If you misbehave, I'll make you listen to all 32 of them."
"Time for another encore?"
"For goodness sake, I need to sit down."

The family had such fun, and the photos, even though mainly stiff backed, certainly kept alive the memories and the myths of the Steinfeld dynasty. It was their early introduction to the wise saying, "People will not look forward to posterity who never look back to their ancestors." That describes perfectly Abram's devotion to the Steinfeld forbears and traditions.

Abram's family were one of the first to benefit from this new invention. Photography came into vogue in Poland around the middle of the 1850s (which was roughly the time that photo of Solomon Ebenezer was taken.) Although photography and the new breed of professionals called photographers were at first an expensive luxury, improvements in technology and growing popularity soon made portrait photography accessible to all. As the teller of tales of family history, the photo album moved quickly to premier position, second to none in most family's annals.

In their family album, alongside framed prints, Abram and Anna had pictures not only of their parents and siblings, but also of their own childhoods. Bearing in mind Abram was born in 1850, it sheds light on what his age must have been in one of the family's favourite. It was a small carte de visite and unusual for the time for its informal pose. It was taken on the beach at Sopot in northern Poland. Abram was a picture of manliness, so smart in his wee short trousers, and appearing to suck his thumb. He can't have been more than 7 or 8. All his children loved that one.

Most of the more formally posed portraits in the family collection were early techniques of photography known as daguerreotypes or ambrotypes. Both were expensive and fragile, and protected under glass usually with a gilt surround. Aleksander remembers often being told, "Look, don't touch!" The photos were not only valuable objects and easily spoiled, they were heirlooms and as such were unrepeatable, effectively priceless.

In the flames which engulfed the Steinfeld's home on the 21st November 1918, every one of those old photographs, the complete and treasured family album, its recollections, its history and values—all were wickedly and viciously destroyed. Their memories, deleted and unrecoverable, were effectively lost for ever.

In his last hours, Abram knew this loss of memory would be part of the fate that was to engulf his family. He decided what he would do, and prepared what Aleksander would later describe as "our family's solemn commission."

As the family had prepared to catapult Aleksander over the wall of the arrest compound in Lwów, Abramczyk took Aleksander's right hand in his. He looked straight into Aleksander's eyes with the unwavering gaze so characteristic of his strength of mind and depth of heart.

The tears welled up as he spoke.

"Remember our faces, Aleksander, and never forget how much we love you. Remember the care with which you were raised, our family's values, our home and our homeland. Remember our music and our teaching. Share this precious legacy with generations to come. Aleksander, today we place these remembrances into your hands. Our family bequeaths to you the Steinfeld name and legacy—you are now our future. My dear firstborn son remember us wherever you go. Convey this inheritance to your children, and to your children's children—and pray for a kinder, better world than this."

Then he paused, and not able to hold his gaze any longer, he looked away. Nothing more was said. Aleksander never forgot a single word.

12

I t was said by Ralph Waldo Emerson that every man is a quotation from his ancient ancestors. It is an evocative thought, and an expression of the connectedness of life that for centuries philosophers observed but struggled to explain.

Today we call this connectedness *heredity*. The debate as to its nature and function stretches back to brave theories put forward in their turn by Greek thinkers such as Aristotle, Theophrastus, Hippocrates and Aeschylus. The precise truth, however, was elusive, and many centuries would pass until its unveiling. Finally in 1865, when Gregor Mendel published his pioneering work on pea plants, the essential connectedness of life moved from the realm of philosophy, and at last became the subject of scientific observation.

Mendel was an Augustinian monk who was a trained and skilled scientist. From his experiments he discovered that individual traits in plants were inheritable. This unlocking of heredity provided a key for future geneticists who eventually found that Mendel's laws applied to other living things, including humans.

Put simply, heredity is what we inherit from our ancestors, and genetics tells us how that happens. For this pioneering work, Mendel is popularly known as "the father of genetics." All kinds of benefits continue to come from his work, especially in the field of medicine. But it is one of those nonetheless complex scientific discoveries that, once established, seems so obvious we say, "why didn't we think of it before?" To which the answer is you might have done had you been a scientific genius like Gregor Mendel!

Fortunately, families required neither genius nor science to recognise family likenesses and characteristics in their photo albums. And when the pages of history turn to the present, and there's a new addition to the dynasty, heredity really comes into its own. "Oh, can't you see? Baby has her mother's jaw; his father's ears; her granny's eyes; grandpa's crooked middle finger! Looks like Uncle Jack to me, a bit of a hoodlum in his heyday." It's true. Or may be true. And if it is, it all goes back to pea pods.

Little Daniyal certainly wasn't a hoodlum, but he did share some traits of his ancestors. His hands, like his father and grandfather, were large, strong and with a long thumb and wide stretch. Yes, his eyes and nose too were characteristic of the male side of his family.

But there were aspects to Daniyal's inheritance which were subject to factors about which Mendel and Emerson would have never dreamed. The kind of inheritance, which is unseen by the eye, but like a storm will come to rage in the heart. For Daniyal not only inherited the Steinfeld name with its inspiring family characteristics; he inherited the Steinfeld history, with its mix of outstanding achievement and devastating trauma.

13

In Jewish families, in the choice of forenames it is customary to choose at least one of Hebrew origin. Daniyal Abramczyk Steinfeld was honoured with two.

The connection between the Hebrew Daniyal (the one who survived the fiery furnace) and Daniyal's father's escape from the flames of Lwów is evident. But Daniyal's second name, Abramczyk (a Polish spelling of Abraham,) was chosen for a different reason. Not because Abraham was the greatest of the Patriarchs, but because of the memory of Abramczyk, Daniyal's grandfather.

In years to come, wherever he went, he would carry his grandfather's memory like a pocket photo; Abram's image merging with Daniyal's in a living memorial. "Oh yes," he would say. "I was named after my grandfather, who was a great Polish pianist and teacher." And from the prompting, he would be able to share other reminiscences too.

Leah's choice was of course benevolent and generous. But maybe instinctively, the intake of breath at the naming ceremony warned of another dimension. In general, of course, the link of the family name to the dreadful events of the Lwów pogrom was inescapable. But for Daniyal's identity, forever to be wedded to the name of his dead grandfather ratcheted up future discourse. "Oh yes, I was named after my grandfather. He was murdered, with his family, because they were Jews."

Leah would have been appalled to think that the terrible events of 1918 might one day rage like a storm in Daniyal's heart. Or that the incessant questioning, at school ("Oi, Steinfeld, why yer called Abramczyk?") and similar interrogations in later life, might exacerbate such conflicts.

What neither Leah nor anyone of her time could yet grasp is the intergenerational consequences of extreme trauma. We now know that for survivors of persecution, internal pain often leapfrogs to the second generation. For many centuries of ongoing persecution this experience of re-traumatisation has been felt by Jews, but with analysis or explanation beyond reach. Guilt, depression and pain, and some more complex personality states were and still are the result of this intergenerational legacy.

In this way, to be a quotation of our recent ancestors, may be more to do with ghosts than genes. Like a continuous cymbal crash, its resonance lingers; and like the living dead haunts the corridors of our minds. As a quotation of our ancestors we may smile at baby's inheritance of sweet dainty feet, a long or short nose or even a gift for music. It's probably just as well we cannot see the flames of rage flickering in the soul, the echoes passed on from one generation to the next.

No one could predict how the events in Lwów and his link to them would affect the growing Daniyal. But what would Daniyal become in life? That is a question at some point every parent will discuss.

Back home from the ceremony at the synagogue, Leah didn't have an axe to grind, but she realised our inability to foretell events meant it was worth exploring the uncertainties and perhaps having other plans in reserve.

"What would it mean for us if Daniyal didn't become a pianist or any kind of musician? Or if he did, but wasn't that good?"

"And then," added Aleksander, "what if he were to become a scientist? Or not have any kind of academic or artistic prowess at all?"

"Yes, and where would that leave the Steinfeld Commission?" asked Leah.

It is hardly surprising that most parents exhibit an intense yet unanswerable curiosity of this order. Even if the jaw, eyes, nose or ears resemble Uncle Jack, truthfully, who looks at a baby and can see its future?

Of course, some parents use all their energies to fix that future—often with serious risk of damage. There are some famous musical examples.

Clara Schumann, married to the composer Robert Schumann, in her own right and time was a brilliant pianist and composer. But

Clara was a victim of her father Friedrich Wieck's thwarted ambitions to be a front-rank pianist. With the extreme discipline he exerted she must have had a dreadful childhood. Friedrich had economic as well as musical ambitions. He was determined that Clara would be both a child prodigy and with that an advertisement for his school of piano playing. Her father was unyielding in his negative moods and strict discipline, and from her earliest years planned Clara's career and life down to the smallest detail.

Friedrich Wieck was a good musician, but an obsessive, exploitative and in some ways detestable personality. Clara was a woman of outstanding strength. Her father could have ruined her. Instead, she became one of the greatest pianists of all time, but at considerable personal costs and family tragedy.

The example of Mozart is also well known. As a child prodigy, he also was tirelessly exploited by his father, Leopold. Of course, Mozart turned out to be a towering genius. But even an emerging genius deserves a proper childhood; to have friends, to play with his toys, ride his bike, and to be loved and liked by his family and friends for who he is, not just for what he does. Who knows? If Wolfgang had not been pushed so much by his father, and as a result hadn't faced so much emotional suffering, maybe he wouldn't have written such great music. But maybe he'd have had a happier life.

Both Clara and Wolfgang survived their parents' ambition. But mainly in a professional sense. The emotional toll was significant.

Fortunately for Daniyal, his parents had come from families where both of them knew from babyhood onwards what it means to be loved and cherished. Aleksander wasn't going to force his son into a mould.

As they concluded this first round of discussion on Daniyal's future, Aleksander said,

"If God has given us a musical son, Leah, so be it. But let him be our son first, before any decisions are made for his future. Whatever he does, the final choice should be his; our aim must be to promote his happiness."

Looking at Daniyal as he lay in his cot, still just a few weeks old, gurgling and blowing bubbles, who indeed could predict his future? One thing was certain. Daniyal didn't yet have hands big enough to play anything on the piano. For his parents. it was genuinely a matter of wait and see. They saw their role to love and nurture their son. It would not be Aleksander and Leah, but the flames of history that would haunt Daniyal Abramczyk's future.

14

It was Easter Saturday, the 7th April 1928. At 6 o'clock a queue was already forming. In the warm spring weather the atmosphere was relaxed and the chatter clearly excited about the prospects for the coming evening. The Wigmore Hall's celebrity recital was an annual event, where for the gala concert the management aimed to slate their most popular performers. Such was the anticipation, the Hall had been fully booked for weeks. Those who hadn't booked in advance were hoping for returns, "no shows" or the few seats reserved for on-the-day purchase. Like previous years, with standing room only, once again the Wigmore Hall would be packed to overflowing.

This was Aleksander Steinfeld's fifth Easter Saturday recital. As a personality and pianist, he was immensely popular. His first solo concert five years ago had been an outstanding success. One review had said, "The power of Steinfeld's left hand is unparalleled. By turns it sings as sweetly as a choir boy, and then turns the page to roar like an orchestra at full throttle."

The Wigmore management were delighted at the musical richness and the popularity of the man and his music. He was clearly a major draw for audiences, which is why they persuaded him to play for their annual gala each Easter Saturday. In practice, Aleksander did not need much persuading. At 37, and from getting on for ten years living and working in London, he had rediscovered his performing confidence and rebuilt his repertoire as a left-handed pianist.

Since his accident, Aleksander had often recalled Siloti's words. "Playing with the left hand alone? So much has changed for you dear friend. I know that. But in another sense, so much hasn't. Strong fingers, strong emotions. It's still what counts. Make sure your left hand is ready for that day."

Aleksander had taken those words to heart, sometimes through tears, sometimes seeing progress and then with massive encouragement. He had worked extremely hard on his left-hand technique. There was now nothing in the existing repertoire which proved too hard for him. The real challenge was either finding new left-hand pieces or arranging or sometimes composing new works himself. Overall, he had certainly learnt to do almost effortlessly with one hand what many professionals struggle to achieve with two. He joked to Leah that since practice makes perfect, after a little extra effort and encouragement, Behemoth and Leviathan have learnt to play as one.

At the first Wigmore Hall concert, he'd realised some of his audience would come out of simple curiosity. It reminded Aleksander when as a child he had played at the Potocki Palace, there was clearly some novelty in a near infant playing Chopin. That didn't matter; he gave them the best he could, and the big takeaway was the audience loved the music.

So about his first Easter recital, Aleksander had been similarly sober. The novelty value was inevitable. As he said to Leah, "It's a good job I am not in PT Barnum's freak show. 'Roll up, roll up for the world's most famous, death defying, left-handed piano player.' At least the audience is not expecting me to play Bach from a flying trapeze!" Aleksander's humour had seen him through many hurdles. It was a way to keep him sane. And it did.

By now as a left-handed pianist Aleksander had played many recitals, in London and around the UK, in Paris, Vienna, Berlin, and Rome. In every concert the curiosity value, and some of the scepticism which accompanies it, quickly wore off. An audience always needs music. That's what they come for, and with Aleksander it was the heart of music they received: beautiful, moving, sometimes fiery, always inspiring. As Aleksander played, some naturally would close their eyes, entranced by the song-like intimacy of his gentle touch; in the next moment, a firestorm from Aleksander's powerful left hand would explode in thunder and lightning which blew skywards everyone listening.

As was his practice these days, Aleksander had given the same recital divided into two parts at two separate lunchtime recitals at the Guildhall School of Music. It gave him a chance to give back to the staff and students a gift of music, and also the (usually) unspoken encouragement of "never give up even when the worst happens." It was a lesson he had learnt, and Aleksander was keen not only to model the value of perseverance, but to emphasise that great music making is not just technique and interpretation but draws on the whole of the artist's life. He wondered if one day he might give the students a lecture recital on this theme.

There was another dimension to these pre-recital events. They enabled him to be on the receiving end of critical input. Siloti had taught him all those years ago, "Because the aim of your performance is the ears of others, you need to listen to what their ears are hearing." Siloti had added, "If by chance you ever think you have arrived and don't need the ears of others, it's a clear indication you haven't!"

As a student, Myra Hess had been a gold medal winner at the Guildhall, and Aleksander had invited her back to give some masterclasses the same week as his recitals. She was a year older than Aleksander and was recognised as an outstanding pianist. She had toured widely in Europe and the United States, and in time would organise the never to be forgotten war-time concerts at the National Gallery in London. They lasted six-and-a-half years and she herself would play in 150 of them.

"Myra Hess playing through the air raids" is how's she is remembered today, but Aleksander knew an earlier dimension to her reputation. Like so many Jews, her family had faced the evils of antisemitism, and like him, she too had persevered and won through.

Myra Hess was also a fine interpreter of the classics. Aleksander had sat in on some of her student masterclasses. He was impressed with her insights and gracious manner and was delighted to see her at both his recitals, her warm smile radiating encouragement from the back row.

Aleksander had played some of his own transcriptions of Bach organ preludes and fugues. After the second recital, during drinks in the Principal's office, when they were out of earshot, Aleksander asked his colleague if she had any observations about his performances.

Myra was in awe of his ability to arrange and play these demanding pieces and was tremendously complementary. But she asked Aleksander a question which he realised later had been first put to him in Moscow by Sergei Ivanovich Taneyev, when he was twelve.

"Do you ever sing the parts of a Bach fugue away from the piano?"

It was such a valuable question, but Taneyev had left it hanging. By contrast, Myra Hess left nothing to chance. Straightening her back, she took in a full breath like an opera singer preparing for an aria. "Sing out loud," she exclaimed. "Sing with style, with vigour. Sing with sensitivity and grandeur. Fill your lungs with joy, my boy, and sing for all your worth. And when you've done all that, go back to the music, and tell each part how much it matters; tell them you love their voices, and each is absolutely indispensable. I promise you," she said with a twinkle, "if you do that, when you return to the piano, the music will sound even more wonderful."

"Thank you so much," Aleksander said sincerely, making a note. "My fingers need to hear my voice." It was the first singing lesson he'd had in years!

15

The staff had squeezed in everyone who queued, ticketholders and hopefuls alike. By the time the concert was ready to begin, the Wigmore Hall was full to bursting. Aleksander knew among the large audience there would be a few personal supporters, in particular some colleagues and students. In the event, he was delighted to learn the Guildhall piano faculty *en bloc* had turned up to support him. It was encouraging to see familiar faces.

At 7:25 p.m., while he was soaking his hands in warm water (a pre-performance tip he had picked up from Josef Hofmann) Aleksander was handed a small envelope. When he saw the embossed names, Alexander and Vera Siloti, his heart leapt. The card inside said, "In London for Easter. Looking forward to your recital! With our love, A+V."

Nothing could inspire him to play better!

By now Aleksander was an extremely popular artist, and the Gala audience was especially warm and enthusiastic, cheering their welcome. "But I haven't played anything yet!" he thought, as he bowed his appreciation.

In celebration mood, they continued applauding. As he took his second bow, he saw Leah in the front row with the children, Daniyal, almost 7 and Sara who had just turned 5. It was a special treat for them, and they had promised not to whisper to each other while Daddy was playing. Aleksander gave them a little wave.

Then, as the applause continued, like a curtain rising on a brightly lit stage, the next scene took his breath away. Sitting next to Aleksander's family were leading representatives of the world's piano aristocracy: a whole row-full of leading virtuosos. His teacher, Alexander Siloti and his wife, Vera. Next to them, Josef Hofmann, the great Polish virtuoso, and his father's former duet partner. Then, Leopold Godowsky, the Polish pianist with a truly astonishing technique, and the composer of the Studies based on Chopin Études. They were described in the Wigmore programme as "the most impossibly difficult piano music ever written."

Towards the end of the row, there were pianists Vladimir de Pachman and Benno Moiseiwitsch. And, an enormous honour, the former Polish prime minister, pianist and composer, Aleksander's benefactor, Ignacy Jan Paderewski and his wife Helena.

Aleksander leant down towards them, showing his obvious pleasure at their presence. He smiled broadly and said in a mock stage whisper, "I would have practiced, if I'd known you were coming!"

They laughed and applauded even more enthusiastically.

Aleksander went to the piano. The audience went quiet. When he was sure a pin drop could be heard, he began the recital.

Felix Blumenfeld's Étude for the Left-Hand, op 36 was first on the programme. It is one of the Russian composer's best known but technically most demanding works. With echoes of Chopin, Tchaikovsky and Rachmaninoff, it has more than enough notes for two hands, and for the left hand alone, it is a miracle of design.

The beautiful lilting phrase with which it begins is enclosed in a dizzying cascade of notes which spray out like water sparkling from a fountain. It is an amazing piece of piano writing, and even more remarkable to play it well. Some in the audience leaned forward to gain a closer view of Aleksander's left hand. He ascended and descended the keyboard with the speed of a harpist's glissando. There was drama and there was poetry. There was lightness and there was passion and power. Aleksander sent his fingers into song with the mellifluous vocal quality the music deserved. The audience were utterly charmed

Godowsky was especially pleased to hear Blumenfeld's étude so well played, as the composer had dedicated the piece to him the year it was written, in 1905. Godowsky pointed out to Aleksander afterwards, not only was the performance note perfect, but musically perfect too, especially that he had enabled the melody to sing so euphoniously by such skilful use of the sustaining pedal. "I was in awe," he said.

The recital continued with left hand works by Godowsky, Reinecke, Saint-Saëns, and Alkan. The final work was the Bach/Brahms Chaconne in D minor where the rich reminder to ensure all the voices in the counterpoint are allowed to sing came most into its own. It was a performance of engaging depth and spirituality. Aleksander reminded himself to make this a key point in his Guildhall teaching. "When the left-hand plays on its own, the challenge is not just to reach the notes, but to let them sing their hearts out in long, unbroken lines. You only achieve this by first using your voice, and then by slow practice."

The Chaconne clearly touched the hearts of the audience. They applauded loud and long, some with tears in their eyes. Aleksander gave only two encores. (The audience would have loved more!) He knew he mustn't over run, as some in the audience would have trains to catch, and the management had planned a reception for afterwards.

Conscious of the composer's presence, and his debt of encouragement to him, he chose two of the Godowsky left hand Chopin transcriptions, both in C sharp minor, Nos. 6 and 22. He played both of them so fast, so musically, so passionately, that at the end the entire audience, including the assembled pianists, let out an audible gasp at their amazement and pleasure. Then they clapped and on their feet clapped and clapped again.

Throughout the recital Daniyal and Sara had kept their concentration admirably. It was evident to everyone who could see the children that they were so proud of their father. They didn't need to be reminded not to whisper. Instead, they hung on every note he played; during the gaps between the items, with Leah keeping the peace, they played a game of "Who was the composer?" The question received some amusing answers!

But now the children had a chance to make some noise. Daniyal led the ovation with cheers, whistles and whoops, jumping up and down, shouting "more, more." Sara did pretty well too, but she was less noisy than Daniyal. Daniyal was growing up to be a performer—like his father.

Aleksander returned to the platform a further four times. Each time he placed his right hand on his chest and bowed respectfully. Finally, he turned towards the piano. "Thank you, dear friend," he said quietly. "I owe you so much." Daniyal bowed towards the magnificent Steinway piano, his co-artist of the evening.

16

While friends and family gathered in the Green Room, a long queue formed inside the hall. Like the one that had preceded the Gala, the chatter was full of excitement, but the anticipation was different. Now there was the prospect to actually meet the Wizard of the Keyboard, exchange a few appreciative words, and to request an autograph.

Aleksander so appreciated the kind comments and remarks. While he signed autographs and met members of the public the Green room was filling up. Champagne and canapés were being served, and he was looking forward to seeing his friends and family, including the cohort of distinguished pianists who had so honoured him by their presence.

As he was coming to the end of the waiting line, Aleksander was just preparing a sigh of relief when an elderly gentleman grabbed his left hand, and said in a strong Russian accent, "My dearest Aleksander, I thought if I could just tooch your hand, zee effect on my technique vould be magical."

It was the eighty-year-old Vladimir de Pachmann, a world-renowned pianist, famous both for his fine interpretations of Chopin, and for his sometimes-wild eccentricity. Pachmann's performances were excellent but unquestionably unconventional. In them he would mutter to himself and sometimes to his listeners, sometimes stopping the performance and speaking to the audience directly. He did this in his own Wigmore Hall concert: "You wonder how my legato is so smooth? I keep my fingers supple by milching cows!"

One critic called him "The Chopinzee." Another, reviewing that same Wigmore Hall concert wrote, "Mr. Pachmann gave his well-known pantomimic performance, with accompaniments by Chopin."

By this time, Leopold Godowsky had returned to the auditorium to see if he could help Aleksander get back to the Green Room. De Pachmann continued to hold on to Aleksander's hand. "Your left hand, my dear Aleksander, is von of zee vonders of zee vorld." Seeing Godowsky coming, he confided in Aleksander. "I vant you to know, dear boy, in those frantic Godowsky pieces I observed very carefully, and I've memorised your fingerings." And well within Godowsky's earshot, raising his voice he said, "Yours are such a great improvement on Leopold's originals!"

No one could ever be sure with de Pachmann. Was he teasing? Could he be serious? Or was it just a screw loose?

Godowsky marched Aleksander to the Green Room. On his arrival, there was a big round of applause. Everyone congratulated him, especially the children, who were busy helping the staff with fresh supplies of canapés. Aleksander was immediately handed champagne, which he quickly drank and his glass was refreshed. Leah had reserved a plate of canapés which she proceeded to feed him in between conversations.

Aleksander made a brief speech in which he thanked everyone for coming. He thanked the Wigmore Hall for their support and hospitality; Steinway Hall for their marvellous pianos; his Guildhall colleagues for giving up their Saturday. He singled out Siloti and Paderewski for their special contributions over the years. And finally, "Last, but certainly not least..."

"The most amazing left hand in the business!" interjected Vladimir de Pachmann. It wasn't quite what Aleksander was going to say, but everyone joined in the spirit of it and cheered their approval.

Aleksander held up his hand in a signal for the hagiography to cease, and keeping it raised, smiling with warmth and thoughtfulness, he said, "I've learnt in life you have to work with what you have, not with what you don't have. There's a lot less heartache that way, and far greater success." He put his left hand down again.

He could see more cheers coming, so before they did he added, "And I was about to say, last but certainly not least—Leah, Daniyal and Sara are my absolute joy, and my constant inspiration. In this wonderful country we now call home, it is Leah who has filled and sustained my heart with love. I would not have achieved any of this without her by my side." He caught Leah's eye, and she waved at him. "May I ask now if you could hold back the applause while I propose a toast: To Leah, and to our children, Daniyal and Sara."

"Leah, Daniyal and Sara," came the reply. Aleksander squeezed Leah's hand and hugged the children. More applause, and the party continued.

Aleksander was so glad to see his friends, James Painter-Reeves, Charles Hammer and Sir Gerald Williams, and his pianist friends; all were full of praise for the recital. Leah and Aleksander hadn't seen Charles since Sara was born. Aleksander and Vera had been to stay with them early in their time in Bolsover Street, but for the Easter holiday were staying for ten days at the Savoy in the Strand. They hadn't wanted to distract the family until after the recital.

Aleksander was also keen to get a word with Paderewski, who he hadn't seen for a number of years. There were many Polish people in the room and they thronged around the great pianist and statesman. Paderewski was nothing less than a superstar. The esteem in which he was widely held was a combination of magnetic personality, musical brilliance and Polish patriotism.

In the manner of the early audiences of Franz Liszt, Paderewski was feted in all his concerts; audiences went wild, women swooned. But at the height of his career, he was not only a very fine pianist, he worked passionately for Polish Independence.

It has been said that "Paderewski was a fund-raising institution, a Polish embassy abroad, and a living monument to the public image of Poland." More through his efforts than any other single figure, in 1918 Poland regained its independence. In January the next year, Paderewski became its prime minister.

After Aleksander had the opportunity to catch up with his old patron, exchange memories, and talk about their families, the Poles in the room gathered excitedly around the piano. The pianists present nominated Josef Hofmann, his Polish and pianistic credentials being impeccable, to be the accompanist for "Mazurek Dąbrowskiego," the Polish National Anthem.

Unsurprisingly, Hofmann supplied a super-virtuoso accompaniment in the style of a Lisztian paraphrase—octaves pounding, whizzing scales, with passage work in double thirds and sixths. And with Paderewski conducting, their fervour ennobled by champagne, the whole room joined in a passionate rendition of the patriotic marching song. Afterwards there were slaps on the back and hugs all round. It was a lovely atmosphere.

Alexander and Vera Siloti had been standing with Daniyal by the upright Steinway piano while Josef Hofmann played. When he'd finished, Daniyal said to him, "That was incredible. When you were playing that fast I thought you must have more fingers than I was born with." Hofmann held up his hands and grinned. "Same as you, Daniyal, except my hands are a lot smaller than most—and miniatures compared with that great bear Rachmaninoff. As your father said, you have to work with what you have, not with what you don't have. But I seem to get by." With that, he went off to get some more champagne. When he'd gone, Alexander and Vera chatted with Daniyal.

"How old are you now, Daniyal?" Alexander asked.

"I shall be seven next month. My birthday is the 11th May."

"And how tall are you?"

"I'm just over four foot." Daniyal was looking very smart in his St. Marks School blazer and tie. "Mother says I am tall for my age. She says I can wear long trousers when I am properly seven."

"Well, here's something grown up we can do now. I hear you play very well, Daniyal. If I can find some music, would you like to play something with me?"

"Yes please," Daniyal said immediately. "I know where there's some music. There's a pile of duets on the windowsill over there. Shall I get them?"

Without waiting for an answer Daniyal went off like a shot. He returned carrying a selection of what he had found. "This one looks fun," he said. "Do you know how to play these?"

"I can try my best," said Siloti. "What about you?"

"No, I don't know them, but they look quite fun."

"Well I expect the music's already stored in your genes.'"

Daniyal didn't know what Siloti meant by that. But while he was putting Brahms Hungarian Dances on the music stand, Siloti turned to Aleksander and gave him a wink.

The room saw what was going on, and everyone quietened. Daniyal announced in his clear, high voice: "Brahms' Hungarian Dances, Book 2." And with that, the distinguished piano duo of Daniyal Steinfeld and Alexander Siloti, like a couple of whirling dervishes, made their dizzying debut on the London stage. Or rather—the Green Room of the Wigmore Hall.

Because of the hour they just played a brief selection of the dances. But the brevity didn't stop all the pianists gathering round the piano with keen eyes and ears focussed on every note played by the seven-year-old wonder. There were knowing looks exchanged and looks back and forth to his father.

Daniyal played wonderfully. (So did Siloti, but at almost sixty years his senior he'd had plenty of practice.) When they finished, the pianists joked among themselves, and said, "Shall we sign him up now?"

Siloti turned to Daniyal. He shook his hand, and said, "Thank you, Maestro."

As he did so, there was a rustle through the crowd. Vladimir de Pachmann pushed his way to the front. Going down on one knee, and like a trophy, holding high a bar of Cadbury's chocolate, he exclaimed loudly, "Take zis, Daniyal. Ve all rejoice. For today, a star ist born."

4TH MOVEMENT

1

╟────────╢

The Blitz—the Luftwaffe's bombing campaign—began on the 7ᵗʰ September 1940. The assault on London and major cities across Britain continued for 57 days and nights. Never before had such a deluge of terror and destruction been experienced. Two million houses were damaged or destroyed, 43,000 civilians were killed, and 139,000 civilians were injured. The Blitzkreig—the Nazi's lightning war offensive, was Hitler's masterplan to batter and crush the British spirit and force the people into submission and surrender. The losses were shocking. The destruction, unparalleled.

Early in 1920 the Steinfelds had made their home in London and had lived in the same house in Bolsover Street for 21 years. They had put down roots, raised their children, and made many friends. Aleksander quickly became a local celebrity; the sound of his piano attracted many passers-by who would stand outside his window in spellbound concentration enjoying the music.

When walking tours of the West End became popular, guides would point to the house, "Over there you can see the home of Aleksander Steinfeld, the internationally acclaimed left-handed pianist."

From the sweet, civilising sound of Aleksander's piano to the screaming wail of sirens was a chilling transformation. The blazing searchlights and the nightly visits of hundreds of German bombers was an unprecedented terror, not just for Bolsover Street, but for London as a whole; especially at this time for Oxford Street, where Leah bought her frocks, and the whole family so often walked and shopped.

During the night and early hours of 17th-18th September 1940, the Luftwaffe repeatedly bombed Oxford Street from Tottenham Court Road down to Marble Arch. The fires raged out of control, acting as beacons for the Luftwaffe bombers to return and multiply their damage many merciless times over. By sunrise on the 18th September, the destruction was all-embracing and Oxford Street's four largest stores, John Lewis, Selfridges, Bourne & Hollingsworth and Peter Robinson, were all engulfed in flames.

These ravaging attacks, and their enormous toll in death and destruction, might have destroyed the very soul of the British people. That is, if it had not been for the emergence of an extraordinary resilience and determination to resist Hitler's plan. With each fresh onslaught this now legendary Blitz Spirit grew ever stronger. Throughout the attacks it wasn't that those in London and other cities weren't frightened of the bombs. It was a fearful time of near crippling uncertainty and much suffering.

However, looking back to Hitler's onslaught, the Blitz Spirit cannot really be explained away as nostalgia or propaganda; the evidence suggests the British countered his bullying intimidation with a dogged determination to "keep calm and carry on." Despite all the losses and pain, cheerfulness and defiance became growingly irrepressible.

A regular diet of comedy shows on the BBC helped to boost morale and kept the nation chuckling. Most popular of all their wartime shows was Ted Kavanagh's ITMA ("It's That Man Again"—a phrase used originally to lampoon Hitler.) The show was first aired in 1939 and ran throughout the war and beyond. It was classic BBC comedy, and starred the comedian, Tommy Handley, as the good-natured, fast-talking anchor-man. The cast of eccentrics, like Colonel Chinstrap and Mrs. Mopp soon became (fictitious) household names. Even their catch phrases like "Can I do yer now sir?" and "Ta-ta for now," from Mrs. Mopp; and "Don't mind if I do," (from Colonel Chinstrap, who saw every enquiry as a drink's invitation); "After you, Claude— no, after you Cecil"; and "D'oh!" (eventually taken up by Homer Simpson.) All these caught on as part of the national banter, and cheered the soul when times were hard.

There was no denying it. Yes, in London, life was incredibly hard. When the sirens blared, some 150,000 people a night took cover in London Underground stations, as did the Steinfelds, sleeping on the platforms and in tunnels. Others spent the nights in air-raid shelters and under railway arches. Families took refuge under the stairs in their homes, or even under the kitchen table. Despite the need for these precautions, the Blitz Spirit did not dim. During daylight hours a great number continued with their lives and work in as normal fashion as they could; and in addition to their daily work, some "doing their bit" by volunteering for "Dad's Army" as the Home Guard was nicknamed,.

More than any other, the main contributor to the country's growing resilience, this unique Blitz Spirit, was the wartime leadership of Winston Churchill. In the face of Hitler's vicious expansionism, the powerful oratory of the Prime Minister had a galvanising effect and united the country "never to give in or give up." On the 13th May 1940 in his first speech to Parliament as Prime Minister, his gritty, almost superhuman resolve set the scene for his morale-strengthening leadership for the rest of the war.

"I would say to the House as I said to those who have joined this government: 'I have nothing to offer but blood, toil, tears and sweat.' We have before us an ordeal of the most grievous kind. We have before us many, many long months of struggle and of suffering.

"You ask, what is our policy? I will say: it is to wage war, by sea, land and air, with all our might and with all the strength that God can give us; to wage war against a monstrous tyranny, never surpassed in the dark and lamentable catalogue of human crime. That is our policy. You ask, what is our aim? I can answer in one word: Victory. Victory at all costs—Victory in spite of all terror—Victory, however long and hard the road may be, for without victory there is no survival."

And to survive the Blitz—Londoners were determined. That first night of the Oxford Street Blitzkrieg, the 17th September 1940, when the four largest stores were hit by German bombers, John Lewis was destroyed and Bourne & Hollingsworth was also a main target. It was one of London's great department stores, built in 1894 and remodelled in art deco style in 1928. It was extremely popular with the public as a place to meet, stroll, shop and eat.

The effect of the high-explosive bombs and incendiary devices, which showered the building with a mixture of burning oil and petrol, was devastating. Most of the store was in flames. The missiles ripped the heart from the interior; they smashed their way through several floors, and in front of the store left behind a thick carpet of broken glass which stretched all the way round the corner into Berners Street. All four stores were ablaze and it took 30 fire engines to deal with the flames.

The public response was a powerful example of the "Blitz Spirit." The next day, carefully navigating the damaged structure, the staff returned in full number. They unfurled large Union Flags to cover bomb damage to the store front, and a week later they succeeded in reopening part of the eastern wing to the public, who were by no means backward in their support. Indeed, from the staff of all the stores that were so badly damaged that night, there was a similar, inspiring commitment to Churchill's "never give in."

A further element which contributed to encouraging the spirit of Londoners were a range of wartime chamber and orchestral concerts. At the National Gallery in Trafalgar Square, Myra Hess, whose advice following his Guildhall concerts Aleksander had so much valued, played a leading part in arranging almost 2,000 lunchtime recitals throughout the war. During the Blitz especially, they were a real morale booster; and in recognition of this contribution in 1941, King George VI made her a Dame Commander of the Order of the British Empire.

The other major venue for these kinds of wartime concerts was the Queen's Hall. It was built in 1893 in Langham Place, a small street just north of Oxford Circus, connecting the extensive Portland Place to the north with Regent Street to the south. The significance of Langham Place was out of all proportion to its size. No less than five buildings of iconic importance dominated the site.

Walking up from Oxford Circus, you came first to the Queen's Hall. Built on Crown land and dedicated to Queen Victoria, with its fine acoustic and seating for 2,500, it was London's premier concert venue. Next door was St. George's Hall, built in 1867— a popular theatre, vaudeville and lecture facility. Then came the famous All Souls Church with its pepper pot spire, built by John Nash in 1824. Continuing your stroll just two steps past All Souls brought you to BBC Broadcasting House, built by the corporation in 1928.

Finally, opposite all four of these venerable institutions loomed the vast Langham hotel, built in 1865, and when it was first opened, London's largest facility of its kind. Langham Place, once described as the best pitch in all England, for these five fine buildings, their pole position also made them vulnerable to the sights of the Luftwaffe.

It was for this reason during the Blitz the Queen's Hall struggled to provide a consistent programme of musical events. At the outbreak of war in September 1939, for safety's sake, the BBC moved its flagship BBC Symphony Orchestra from its Queen's Hall home to Bristol. In the process it had to withdraw its financial support for the Queen's Hall Promenade Concerts, which Sir Henry Wood had founded in 1895.

With the same Blitz Spirit, Sir Henry eventually found backing from the London Symphony Orchestra, the Royal Philharmonic society, and a private entrepreneur for an eight-week concert season. Although greeted with great jubilation, in the event only four weeks of concerts were completed. It was to do with an intensification of bombing in the area. Local attacks caused damage to doors and windows, and the hall had to be closed several times. However, after further damage on 6 April 1941, swift repairs were once again made. The management, believing that live music boosted the morale of Londoners, decided to re-open the hall for concerts.

2

The 11th May 1941 would mark not only the end of the Blitz, but also Daniyal Steinfeld's 20th birthday. From the age of ten onwards, Daniyal had played many acclaimed recitals and concerto performances throughout Europe and America. And since the beginning of the war, with his father, had taken part in National Gallery and other concerts, raising money for Red Cross ambulances and their wartime crews. Daniyal and Aleksander were also conscious of the morale raising value of live classical music, and Daniyal had an idea for his birthday.

"Could we give a two-piano concert?" he asked his father. "And where should it take place? Which would be more suitable? The Queen's Hall or the National Gallery?"

Aleksander was enthusiastic. "The Queen's Hall is a perfect setting in every respect. The brilliant acoustic, its capacity and accessibility. It's the ideal venue—and for a charity concert too. Just think of all those who'll be sleeping in the tube station. If we time it right, we can encourage lots of them to come. That on its own will practically guarantee a large crowd, and I am sure many others will want to join us. And yes, of course, playing together will be such a nice way for the two of us to celebrate your birthday."

"So how can we make it happen?"

"We need to practice," said Aleksander, slightly tongue in cheek. "And to keep to time, no encores, Daniyal."

"What?" Daniyal answered, amused that his father appeared to have found him out.

"I hear that you gave four encores at your recital at Carnegie Hall last year; including the Godowsky Passacaglia, which must take near 18 minutes."

"I can do it in 17! Anyway, the audience practically demanded them," said Daniyal. "And I wished you could have been there."

"Me too. I would have been very proud of you. But promise me you'll keep an eye on your thirst for 'more!' My father used to say, 'Acclaim is like strong drink. At first it refreshes but take too much and your thirst becomes unquenchable.' It's something a super virtuoso like you needs to keep an eye on."

"I have you, father, for that!" He paused to give Aleksander one of his youthful, knowing looks. "But seriously," he said.

"I was being serious!"

"Thank you," Daniyal conceded. "So what actually do we need to make this all happen?"

Daniyal and Aleksander split the duties for the concert between them. Daniyal contacted the Queen's Hall management for agreement, a date and time. Aleksander contacted Steinway for a two piano hire and rehearsal facilities.

"We will be delighted to help," said James Painter-Reeves, when Aleksander came to see him at Steinway Hall. "And I am looking forward to meeting Daniyal again. If his reviews are anything to go by, he has become an outstanding young artist."

"He is indeed," said Aleksander. "He's been well taught, following the best Steinfeld principles!"

"Which is what the *New York Times* music critic said. If I remember rightly, 'Daniyal Steinfeld brings alive the phenomenal virtuosity of the Steinfeld past—a worthy heir and successor to the Steinfeld tradition.'"

The irony was not lost on Aleksander. Amused, he said, "Fortunately, this old Steinfeld is still with us, despite attempts to achieve the contrary. You know, James, I have learnt over the years, virtuosity is one thing. Learning to handle your virtuosity is quite another. Don't you agree, the roar of the crowd is a drug of considerable potency? Look what it has done to dear Josef Hofmann. And there are many others."

"I do agree, Aleksander. Though it's hardly likely, if that-man-again tries to knock you off your perch, don't worry. I'll keep an eye on Daniyal's ego for you."

Aleksander grinned his appreciation.

So the concert was organised for 10th May 1941. Daniyal and Aleksander decided to cover all the costs themselves so that everything apart from the Hall fees could go to the Red Cross Ambulance fund. Steinway, with their usual generosity, were not charging for their two model D concert grands. The concert was timed for 4:00 p.m. That would allow for a complete rehearsal run through, and for the piano tuners to make their adjustments before and after.

Daniyal worked out a plan both for the concert on Saturday and for his birthday the next day.

Daniyal's fiancé, Mariah, had asked her parents if Daniyal, Aleksander, Leah and Sara could join them for Sunday lunch at their house in Church Row, Hampstead. John and Jennifer Headley had immediately agreed. Since Daniyal and Mariah announced their engagement three weeks prior, the parents had met just once over drinks at the Langham Hotel. They were, of course, entranced with Daniyal and looking forward very much to getting to know better the distinguished couple who were soon to become Mariah's parents in law.

The plan was that following the concert and meeting friends and members of the audience, Daniyal would travel with the Headleys up to Hampstead and stay the night. Then, on Sunday morning, Aleksander would drive the rest of the family in his 1.5 litre Jaguar to join everyone in Hampstead. There was agreement all round, and Jennifer started menu planning, checking if there were any kosher or other food requirements.

3

The afternoon of Saturday, 10 May 1941 arrived. Outside the Queen's Hall, the people queued in great numbers. As Aleksander predicted, those sleeping in Oxford Circus underground were delighted to have the prospect of a concert. There was also a big take up of advance bookings. In the end, all 2,500 seats were filled. Even though they had kept the prices low, it would mean a big contribution to the Red Cross funds.

Aleksander and Daniyal came on to the platform to tumultuous applause. Aleksander winked at Daniyal, and they both bowed low to acknowledge the acclaim.

Aleksander had arranged all the works for two pianos, three hands. The programme began with Brahms Hungarian Dances, the significance of which was not lost on either of them. The audience simply loved the fun of the music, and the way Aleksander and Daniyal were so in tune with each other, catching each other's eye, bobbing their heads in unison, and lifting up their arms triumphantly at the conclusion of each piece.

They played works by Mozart and Schubert with tremendous style and virtuosity, ending with the first performance of Aleksander's breath taking three handed arrangement and paraphrase of Liszt's Hungarian Rhapsody No. 2. As if Liszt hadn't put in enough notes already, Aleksander added quite a few more! The three handed cadenza was electric and the performance brought the house down. The audience roared and roared for more.

So despite "no encores" the audience got their way. In fact, Aleksander had prepared the encore intentionally, and he and Daniyal had rehearsed it that day! It was a beautiful winsome arrangement with enriched Jazz harmonies of Vera Lynn's most famous war-time song, "We'll Meet Again."

The audience simply loved it, joining in, as Aleksander conducted them. Aleksander and Daniyal continuing to play:

We'll meet again,
Don't know where, don't know when,
But I know we'll meet again
Some sunny day.
Keep smiling through,
Just like you always do,
'Till the blue skies drive the dark clouds far away.

It was a very popular ending to a wonderfully successful and enjoyable concert. Because of the blackout, concertgoers were encouraged to leave quickly. So Daniyal, Mariah and the

Headleys prepared themselves for their car journey to Hampstead. And Aleksander, Leah and Sara would walk back to Bolsover Street and join them in the morning.

As they walked over to the car for their farewells, Aleksander asked Leah, "Shall we sleep at home tonight? I think after all the exertion I'd appreciate a proper bed." Leah agreed.

"Well done, Daniyal. Great playing," they said. "And you got your encore!" said Aleksander, laughing.

"See you on your birthday, big brother," said Sara, kissing Daniyal on the cheek.

"You have a sack full of fan mail and birthday cards waiting for you at home," said Leah, straightening Daniyal's bow tie. "We'll bring them with us tomorrow."

"Daniyal Abramczyk Steinfeld. Twenty years old. Can you believe it!" said a proud and delighted Aleksander.

With that, they all hugged and went their separate ways.

It was to be the last night of the Blitz. With the moon bright and the skies clear, the Luftwaffe launched their seven-hour assault. Following the line of the Thames, in a massive crescendo of destructive force, 505 German bombers dropped more than 700 tons of high explosive and 86,000 incendiaries on homes and public buildings across London.

The House of Commons, the British Museum and Westminster Abbey sustained serious damage. Then, in the early hours of Sunday morning, the Queen's Hall was hit by a single incendiary bomb. The destruction was calamitous. It left the building a smouldering ruin—a pile of rubble beyond any hope of repair and restoration.

1,364 people died at the hands of the Luftwaffe that night, the largest single loss of the war. Among them the occupants of the house in Bolsover Street, a local attraction, where, for 21 years passers-by had stopped, listened and marvelled at the music of its famous pianist.

5TH MOVEMENT

1

I t was May 11, 1957. Mariah had prepared a special birthday dinner for Daniyal. The couple now lived in Weymouth Street, in the West End of London, where they were close to Marylebone High Street. For both, the location was convenient. For Mariah, it was just ten minutes' walk to All Souls School in Foley Street where she was a part-time teacher. For Daniyal, among other things, the house was very close to Steinway Hall in Marylebone Lane, where he often practiced and rehearsed.

Steinway especially valued their connection with the "Steinfeld Dynasty." Jeremy Woolfson, the new manager, was every bit as accommodating as his predecessor, and soon after the war, like they had for his father, Steinway offered Daniyal unlimited use of their practice facilities.

It was kind and of course worked both ways. In the piano world, the Steinfelds were legendary. So for the Steinway Hall staff it was quite a boost to morale to have regular contact with the charming international super virtuoso. For Daniyal, the support was admirably practical.

His father's grand piano—the one upon which he had practiced from childhood—had been destroyed in the Blitz, alongside his family and all their belongings. The bomb destroyed everything, even Aleksander's few precious photos of his parents and the collection of the children's youthful exploits. He found their album in the rubble with all its memories crumbled into ash.

The only memento Daniyal did recover from Bolsover Street was attached to their front door. Unlike everything else, which was crushed and blackened out of all recognition, the mezuzah was unblemished; it was the same mezuzah which Abram had pressed into Daniyal's father's hand as he escaped the pogrom in Lwów. This now was Daniyal's only tangible reminder of his family's past. Attached to the door post in Weymouth Street, in a simple but profound way, it connected that past to his present and future.

Daniyal spent a long time running away from the pain of all this. With some difficulty he later admitted to me that the un-faceable loss of his family was behind his drinking. The optimistic Blitz Spirit had been real, but equally, for those who sustained losses, was the trauma and near inconsolable emotional agony.

Over the years, I have observed how people agonize and grieve in a variety of ways. Bereavements come in different shapes and sizes. Emotionally, sometimes a lesser loss stands in for a greater, more complex loss, where the heart works its way through the pain from the lesser to the greater. That was the case with the Steinfeld's grand piano. After the loss of his family, Daniyal felt its destruction as his biggest heartbreak. It was a symbol of loss; like his family, it was irreplaceable.

So it was out of respect for his father's memory that Daniyal had bought a modest second-hand, make-do, Bechstein upright for his music room. It was adequate, but frankly without the response he needed for the bigger scale repertoire. So when Daniyal wanted thunder and lightning, off he went to Steinway Hall.

Normally, these days Daniyal preferred to spend his birthdays quietly with Mariah. They had been married for 14 years. They had no children, although they would have loved to have had a family; but they were devoted to each other and never stopped talking. They often discussed music, the arts and politics, particularly of Eastern Europe. Mariah used to say, "No one understands the world like Daniyal." And Daniyal used to reply, "No one understands Daniyal like Mariah."

May was a difficult month for Daniyal. To have the date of his birthday so indelibly associated with the bombing in Bolsover Street practically forced him to re-live the trauma. The loss of his parents and sister still stalked his mind like an unsleeping apparition. Sure, it was improving over time, and as his therapist friend, informally, I had helped him talk through these rumbling memories; but some demons remained unexorcised

In Daniyal's small intimate circle of family and friends, Mariah's parents continued to be an anchor for Daniyal. They were close by in Hampstead, still living in Church Row. Mariah's father, Robin Headley, who was the chairman of the National Provincial Bank, had told Daniyal that although he was no professional counsellor, his door was always open for Daniyal. Robin lacked nothing in terms of insight or compassion.

Daniyal found the openness and care of Robin and Sheila to be an immense strength, both at the time of the bombing, and subsequently as the years rolled on, when the pain stubbornly refused to budge. Robin and Sheila had come to mean much more to Daniyal than just being parents-in-law.

Daniyal had returned to London at 10 p.m. last night, following four concerts in a row, two in Paris and two in Rome. By the time he came in from the airport there had been little time for anything more than a welcome home kiss, and a brief chat before brandy and bed. So Daniyal was looking forward to a proper catchup over supper tonight. It was Saturday, and as it was his birthday, he was planning they might go out to eat.

Daniyal went upstairs to the kitchen, where he could smell Mariah was baking.

"My darling," said Mariah, holding a couple of eggs in her hand, "I thought I should ask you. I've invited some guests for supper. Will that be okay?"

Daniyal paused his answer, and Mariah could feel him freeze over.

"Depends who they are," he said, trying to smile.

"Mummy and Daddy?"

Daniyal immediately relaxed. "Thank you, my darling. It will be so lovely to see them."

"And there's another couple."

Daniyal looked straight at her, expecting disaster. Perhaps Mariah had invited some other pianist—or worse, some famous conductor, plus boring spouse!

"Don't worry, darling. It's James and Georgina Painter-Reeves. You probably remember James is due to retire as chairman of Steinway in a couple of months. Apparently James and Georgina are moving away from Manchester Square to a house in the country. I thought you'd like to see them before they move."

"I'd absolutely love to see them. Thank you so much, Mariah. I can't think of four nicer guests."

It was a long time since Mariah and Daniyal had seen the Painter-Reeves, mainly because James's role as Steinway chairman meant he often worked out of London, and Steinway Hall had a new manager. However, they had been dinner guests along with Robin and Sheila on several occasions. Both couples kept an eye on Daniyal's wellbeing, being aware of the multiple levels of emotional trauma that afflicted him. Although they had planned something special for his birthday, they had decided not to mention it till the last part of the evening.

After his initial trepidation, Daniyal began to look forward to an evening in such nice company.

"Now," he said, "What can I do?"

He had quickly switched into let-me-take-over mode, but his wife had already picked up the signal.

"No," said Mariah. "It is your birthday, so leave the kitchen to me. If you like, you can organise the wine. We will need an aperitif, white for the hors d'oeuvre, red for the beef, and a dessert wine to follow. I'll have cheese if anyone wants some, so you better have another red to hand. I don't know about Brandy and cigars—remember that Georgina coughed a lot when you men lit up last time the Painter-Reeves were here."

Daniyal agreed to give the Brandy and cigars a miss. After enquiring a little more about the menu, he set off to the wine shop. He wanted to make sure he had plentiful supplies of white, red and sparkling. Although he would tell you he didn't know much about wine, he certainly loved drinking it.

Half an hour later, Daniyal took a taxi to his favourite wine merchant, Justerini & Brooks in St. James's Street, off Piccadilly. Their knowledge and service are legendary, and they remembered him when he arrived.

"Good morning, Mr. Steinfeld. It's a pleasure to welcome you back, sir. What can we help you with today?"

Daniyal was pleased with the warm reception; it always made him feel good. He explained what he was looking for, and the manager asked him for more details. "If you are able to tell me exactly what Mrs. Steinfeld is planning to serve, that will help me assist you in making the perfect choices for your dinner party."

Perfect choices were made. The bill was settled, and a cheerful Daniyal was shown to the door by a happy manager who hailed a taxi for him to take three cases of red, white and sparkling home to Mrs. Steinfeld.

2

⊢————⊩

Mariah had made a wonderful meal, and everyone was relaxed and delighted to celebrate Daniyal's 36th birthday together. The company, food and wine were all, indeed, perfect choices.

The guests had arrived together. Unbeknown to Daniyal, James and Georgina had earlier invited Mariah's parents to come to their house in Manchester Square at 7 p.m. James had wanted to seek some more advice about the little birthday gift they'd planned for Daniyal. So they chatted for a while, drank an aperitif, and then walked round to Weymouth Street.

They arrived a minute or so after 8 p.m., and were warmly greeted by a cheerful Daniyal, who had already enjoyed an aperitif or two. Mariah will tell you, Daniyal always said that champagne was invented to get a party going. So, as soon as the guests were in the door, Daniyal invited everyone into their capacious drawing room (which was large enough for a modest sized orchestra) and beneath the sparkling Bohemian glass chandeliers, Daniyal served everyone with well chilled Bollinger champagne. Turning his party theory into practice, he managed to fill and refill his guests glasses (and his own) well before it was time to go upstairs to their dining room.

Chatting together, James said to Mariah, "I've always admired your two chandeliers. They seem very special to me. Are other houses around here lit in the same way?"

"No, I don't think so," answered Daniyal, "As you say, these two are particularly special. Actually, they are original to the house and were made for this room by Christoph Palme in Parchen, Bohemia—when Bohemia was part of Austria-Hungary. Each of them has 3,000 pieces of individually cut glass and weighs over quarter of a ton."

"And they are a nightmare to keep clean," added Mariah.

"Of course, that's my job," proclaimed Daniyal to howls of disbelief. "But seriously," he said, "have I ever told you about the Polish connection? When Poland gained its independence in 1919, the Polish government bought this house as its first London embassy. Paderewski visited many times, and played the piano in this very room, lit by these chandeliers."

"So you could do with a piano down here?" asked Sheila.

"Mmm. It's an expense, Sheila. But I have got my old Bechstein upstairs."

Changing the subject, Georgina asked Mariah about the neighbours. "Teaching at the school, you must have got to know lots of the mums. Do you get to meet up with any?"

"Well, I would like to, but most of the children at our school come from the area around Cleveland Street where the housing is quite poor. I would love to visit them, but when I have suggested it, I have felt a resistance which I think probably is an old class issue. Equally, I'd love to invite some around here, but in a reverse kind of way, I feel as embarrassed as I sense they are, as our house is such a palace."

"Yes," Robin said. "We need some levelling up in this country. Now Mr. Macmillan is leading us, hopefully once he's found his feet, we'll see some real change. But, Georgina, you mention women. At the bank we are conscious of the financial plight of the war widows. Their pensions are over-taxed, and they are largely ignored by the government and the rest of us."

"Yes," said Daniyal, "We honoured the men who died but forgot the widows and orphans they left behind. Our neighbour, Mrs. Segal, is a war widow. Her husband was Polish. He was a pilot and was shot down in 1945 the day after Emperor Hirohito's surrender announcement. In fact, she's one of the mums Mariah and I have got to know, as Jacob was at All Souls School. He's 11 now and will soon be off to Highgate Boys School."

"Is that the house with the mezuzah on the door?" Robin had noticed it on the way in.

"Yes it is." said Daniyal. "There are still some of us left."

Mariah took that as the moment to grandly announce, "Dinner is served!" Laughing and joking they climbed the narrow stairway to the dining room.

The menu was full of Daniyal's favourites. They started with Leek and Potato soup, which was his mother's special recipe made with fresh chicken stock, cream and unsalted butter, plus a few gentle shakes of Worcestershire sauce and enriched with a dash of vodka. The amount of vodka depended on the season and how cold it was. It was always added at the last moment.

Then, Mariah served her rabbit and beef pie. Daniyal had weened her off the British habit of potatoes with everything. So she served it with three salads. Endive, lemon and tarragon; Cream cheese and dandelion; Cauliflower and beetroot—the ingredients fresh from the greengrocers in the High Street. And from the Boulangerie next door, she'd also picked up some freshly baked French bread.

Finally, her planned two deserts expanded to three. Mariah had baked a Pineapple Upside-Down Cake, Daniyal's post-war favourite; and had produced a large bowl of hulled and halved strawberries; the addition was an enormous box of delicious handmade chocolates from Harrods that James and Georgina had brought. It would have been quite wrong not to enjoy them together!

For their gifts, Robin and Sheila brought bottles of Tia Maria and Drambuie, and a well-aged Rémy Martin.

"One for your cellar, Daniyal," Robin said when he arrived. Although there was little chance it would live down there for long.

The combination of chocolates, coffee, and liqueurs went beautifully together, and drew a fitting conclusion to a happy and convivial celebration.

When Georgina and Sheila noticed Daniyal stifle a yawn, they realised the time had come—not for them to return home—but to complete the business of the evening. They signalled to their husbands, and the chairman of Steinway put up his hand to calm the chatter.

"Daniyal," said James, waking up his admired and valued friend. Daniyal had been daydreaming, but now gave James his full attention. He did wonder what all this might be about. Hadn't they had a full round of toasts earlier on? Perhaps this was a farewell speech? Daniyal felt a knot in his stomach—saying goodbye always did that to him.

"My dear friend, what I have to say is on behalf of Robin and Sheila, and Georgina and myself. And of course, we have taken advice from Mariah."

Mariah smiled.

Daniyal had no idea what was coming next, so with an appropriate twinkle, asked if they were about to make an offer for the chandeliers.

"No, not exactly," James replied, "but you have chosen the right room."

If that was a clue, it was a bit cryptic. Daniyal made sure he listened carefully.

"This is a story you may not know. When your parents moved to London, they had no piano; but in the way he had been taught by Siloti, your father continued to learn new scores for the left hand alone, just by practising in his head. That's the background to the first time your father visited Steinway Hall. As you know, I was there; it was also the first time Aleksander and I had met. But I don't think I have ever told you what happened that day.

"After the accident, supremely great pianist as he was, how your father developed his left-hand technique with such effectiveness. How after arriving in London he had not touched a real piano in many months. How, on coming into our showroom, he had immediately sought out our best Model D Steinway. And how faultlessly and with wondrous singing phrases he played the most perfect rendition of Godowsky's left-hand version of Chopin's op 10, E major Étude. How he had managed to learn this new Godowsky arrangement away from the piano and commit it to memory, I have no idea. It was the first time he'd ever played it."

Daniyal said, "That's a terrific story, James. Thank you."

"There's a little more to add, Daniyal. Your father really loved that piano. In fact, after playing the Chopin he jokingly said, 'I'll take it.' When he saw I thought he was serious, he swiftly adjusted the volume and said, 'No I couldn't possibly. I mean, we don't have room for it. It wouldn't go through the front door!'

"Which brings me to what Robin and Sheila, Georgina and I have planned for your birthday, Daniyal. That Steinway is still too big to go through your front door, but my technicians are confident they can hoist it through the front windows. And Mariah agrees you have plenty of space in your sitting room. You know, Daniyal, I've always thought of it as your father's second piano, and what better new home could it have than in your home in Weymouth Street.

"But if you prefer something else, I am sure we can rustle up more chocolates and liqueurs."

Everyone laughed, and Daniyal, completely lost for words, immediately jumped up from the table. His heart pounding with emotion, he signalled his overwhelming delight with long appreciative hugs for everyone.

Later, when everyone had left and Mariah was finishing in the kitchen, unbidden, his tears flowed. The memories, the pain, and yet tremendous gratitude.

3

|—————|

The impact of the Blitz on the nation's capital was of such intensity it was described as "The Second Great Fire of London." However, once the Blitz had ended and Hitler had turned his attentions to Russia, it was clear he would be back; the war from the air would continue, no doubt with worse to come.

Throughout the Blitz, public spiritedness and mutual community support had been at a high point. But at this time , apart from the armed forces, no greater appreciation was heard for any public service than for the nation's fire fighters. Though the Luftwaffe's aerial bombing had stretched them to the limit, this large group of men and women, of which many were volunteers, earned unparalleled gratitude for their skills and bravery.

One of the first lessons to come from the Blitz was the need for a greater investment in firefighting, and the creation of one unified service for the whole nation.

Churchill's government moved quickly. In August 1941, the existing Auxiliary Fire Service (made up of over 200,000 volunteers) and the local authority fire brigades (about 1,600 of them) were amalgamated into a single rapid response team, the National Fire Service.

At a National Gallery lunchtime concert, Daniyal had been introduced to Sir Aylmer Firebrace, The Chief of the Fire Staff and the new head of the National Fire Service. It was about a year after the bomb had destroyed Daniyal's family home in Bolsover Street. He told Sir Aylmer about the valiant firefighters who had tried to rescue his family; though unsuccessful, he sincerely expressed how grateful he was for their efforts. He then added, without thinking what the response might be, "If you ever think of anything I might do to assist you in the war effort, do please be in touch."

Sir Aylmer Firebrace did get in touch. Or rather, it was his London Fire Brigade emissary from Substation Y13, Maresfield Gardens NW3 who turned up at Weymouth Street on the following Monday morning. The gentleman was dressed in his uniform: blue double-breasted serge tunic, waterproof trousers, rubber boots, his steel helmet tucked neatly under his arm.

Sitting down for a cup of coffee in the drawing room, the emissary explained: "Sir Aylmer says you would like to join us as a volunteer firefighter."

It wouldn't have taken any more for Daniyal to drop his coffee cup. But he kept a straight face, refrained from cracking jokes, and listened to what his polite visitor had to say. The more he heard, and the more he explained his own work, and what he could and could not do, the more it seemed there was something he could indeed offer the war effort. He hadn't exactly volunteered, but he was tall, fit and could ride a bicycle. More than that—he was motivated. He knew the devastation of fire. "If there is something I can contribute, then sign me up." Which is how the next week Daniyal found himself at his first training session, in Substation Y13 in Maresfield Gardens Hampstead.

Mariah had been a little surprised, to say the least. But she was supportive. She was aware of the need, and the need in Daniyal. "As long as you are careful with your hands," she said.

It was agreed that Daniyal would use the new fire-resistant gloves and the anti-flash gear developed by the Royal Navy. But as far as his hands were concerned, the training made quite a change from scales and arpeggios. His fellow volunteers were an agreeable group of men. They learnt everything together. How to pileup sandbags, and with a pickaxe how to demolish bomb damaged property. They practiced everything to do with water and water hoses; how to stay safe with a gas mask; how to rescue people safely through the flames. And a lot else besides.

As Mariah concurred, the need was considerable.

In November 1942, Winston Churchill had said, "Now this is not the end. It is not even the beginning of the end. But it is, perhaps, the end of the beginning." When the D-Day landings brought the end in sight, Hitler again proved Churchill's prescience correct. A few days after the launch of the Normandy landings, Hitler fought back.

On 13th June 1944, new unmanned Vengeance Weapons—Vergeltungswaffen—were deployed against London. Over 3,000 V1's, known by Londoners as "Doodlebugs," killed 9,000 people, and more than 24,000 others were seriously injured. Within weeks the V1's were superseded by the new improved V2's. These weapons carried a one-ton high explosive warhead, flew at 3,600 mph, and from Holland or Germany could hit the capital in five minutes. Unlike the buzzing Doodlebugs, Londoners did not even hear them coming.

With his team of colleagues, Daniyal fought fires across London: in Chiswick, in Duke Street (by Selfridges,) at Speakers' Corner, Hyde Park, and at New Cross SE14 where 160 were killed in one cruel attack. He rescued many from the flames, and when he retired his volunteer role at the end of the war, Daniyal was commended for his selfless bravery.

4

I n October 1957, Daniyal had agreed to a concerto marathon in Boston. The concerts were inspired by a 1939 series which had celebrated Rachmaninoff's US debut 30 years previously. This new Rachmaninoff Festival featured five US orchestras with close connections to the composer. The Boston Symphony played host to the New York Philharmonic, the Philadelphia Orchestra, the Cincinnati Symphony Orchestra and the Chicago Symphony Orchestra.

Daniyal was unusually thrilled at the prospect, especially as the concertos were scheduled with the Philadelphia Orchestra under Eugene Ormandy, who had recorded the concertos with Rachmaninoff himself as soloist. Daniyal was to play all four on succeeding nights, starting on the Wednesday evening, following on Sunday afternoon when he would play "the fifth concerto," the Paganini Variations. As the festival committee had planned, it could be a wonderful exposure to the composer's genius for audience and performers alike.

However, there are not many pianists who would consider or even be able to rise to such a monumental challenge. To prepare any single Rachmaninoff concerto is enough for most performers. But to practice, securely memorise and perform all five within a week would indeed be to turn a sprint into a marathon.

Of all the pianists who could take on such a contest, three great names had been considered. Josef Hofmann, Vladimir Horowitz and Daniyal Steinfeld. Sadly, Hofmann was not in good health and died at the beginning of 1957. Horowitz, despite his legendary brilliance, had unstable mental health and had been refusing engagements since 1953. Which left the considerably younger figure of Daniyal Steinfeld, about whom the un-minuted comment was made: "He'll play them brilliantly, passionately and like a technical marvel. He loves to be adored. He won't flag. He'll gain all his energy from the acclaim. You'll see it from how many encores he gives."

When Daniyal arrived at Boston's Logan International on the Monday evening before the first concert, at the queue for passport control, he looked around with slight nervousness for Big Ears. "As long as they don't think I am some escaping Nazi," he thought to himself.

"Passport please," the bright young lady said.

"So what next?" Daniyal thought, handing over his documents.

"Thank you, sir. Are you here for business?"

"No," said Daniyal. "I'm here for a marathon."

"Oh, that must be for Columbus Day." And with a minimum of protocol, she stamped his passport. "Welcome, Mr. Steinfeld. Welcome to the United States of America. And I hope to be with you for your concert on Wednesday night."

Daniyal beamed. From that point on, it was all refreshingly familiar. There was a kind reception in arrivals, and while he was signing autographs his agent, Andy Collinger, turned up. He was clearly pleased to see Daniyal. (Daniyal was the agency's star earner.) After a cheery welcome, Andy took his bags and placed them in the boot of the agency's VIP Cadillac Eldorado.

"You know where we're going, sir?" Daniyal nodded. He was tired after the journey. He had decided no alcohol on this trip. It had not served him well last time he arrived at Logan. And in any case he needed to keep a clear head for the five concerts. There was no free time to sleep off a hangover.

As Andy drove, Daniyal yawned and quickly dropped off. It was just 12 minutes to Dalton Street, where on arrival, his suite at the Old Boston was ready and waiting.

5

I had cancelled all my sessions for the week, so without Daniyal knowing I could sit at the back of the Hall and just close my eyes and listen. I must tell you what is already well known in modern performance history: the success of the five concerts was matchless. Ormandy was a great and sensitive accompanist. The Philadelphia Symphony Orchestra played with the greatest distinction. Needless to say, Daniyal's playing was incomparable—peerless and unsurpassed in brilliance, sensitivity and not a little showmanship. The showmanship turned up in full volume with the encores, which we should just say were plentiful.

On Sunday afternoon, the fifth concert, he decided to give full value, and as his first encore played his favourite Godowsky Passacaglia: 44 variations, cadenza and fugue on the opening theme of Schubert's "Unfinished" Symphony. As he told the audience, it was the 30th anniversary of its composition.

It was a stunning performance of a majorly inventive and super-virtuoso work. At the conclusion, the audience went wild. While they were applauding and stamping and shouting their appreciation, Daniyal bowed. He told me later, in the silence of his mind he was sure he heard his father's voice. "Acclaim is like strong drink. At first it refreshes but take too much and your thirst becomes unquenchable. Promise me, Daniyal, you'll keep an eye on your thirst for more!"

Daniyal decided that was enough. To the surprise of both audience and orchestra, there were no further encores.

"He was probably tired."

"What a marathon."

"After all, the Godowsky is equal to half a dozen encores."

The self-imposed limit didn't stop Daniyal soaking up the applause. The acclaim stoked his energy. He hadn't flagged. As I have said before, he loved to be adored.

Afterwards, as it had been in each of the concerts, there was a long queue for autographs. Daniyal always looked people in the eye and kept his gaze. He'd learnt it was the very least you could do to acknowledge another's personhood and worth.

"I realise now what you meant by 'I'm here for a marathon.'"

Daniyal laughed as he recognised the lady from passport control. "And this is my husband."

The man offered his hand. "Maestro Steinfeld," he said. He wasn't wearing his rumpled beige raincoat, but Daniyal just stopped himself from saying, "I'd recognise those big ears anywhere!"

"It was even more than we would expect from a Steinway!" said Big Ears. Columbo had a sense of humour after all.

Once the queue had come down to the final one, Daniyal realised that I had been waiting quietly all this time.

"I thought you were in New York, Michael."

"I was doing some supervisions last week, but it's only a short hop, Daniyal. But I would not have missed these concertos for the world. I've been at all five concerts, sitting at the back and taking it all in with especial pleasure. You played superbly throughout. They all went well. Did you have a favourite?"

"Yes, I think this afternoon was best of all. Not just because of the performance, because the orchestra and ensemble were excellent throughout. I think the 3ʳᵈ and the Rhapsody are my favourites of all the five works. They inhabit quite different emotional landscapes. But frankly, what brilliant orchestral playing in the Paganini Variations! I know lots of people fuss over the 18th variation, and it is supremely beautiful, of course. But in their different ways so are all the variations—wonderfully beautiful, inventive, expressive, and powerful."

"And in the way you played and shaped it. In fact, in the way that Rachmaninoff develops the material, the three sections did sound as though it had the depth and dignity of a 5ᵗʰ concerto."

"Yes, when it comes to it, they are all great works in their different ways. Oh, and by the way Michael, we sound like a couple of music critics."

"Well, there were plenty of them in the concerts. You can always recognise a critic—they scribble on their programmes during the quiet bits."

Before he went off to the airport, I joined Daniyal for breakfast at the Old Boston.

We had a quick look at the papers. The notices were very generous. Smiling, I said to Daniyal, "I see you still relish the applause—even in print."

Daniyal laughed. "That's an official secret, known only to you and my Dad. But I am managing it much better now than when we last touched on it."

This wasn't completely true, or indeed true at all. Over recent years, the thirst for acclaim had spread throughout Daniyal's inner world like fast growing ivy. The thirst had grown into a passion, prompting an aching and rarely satisfied need.

Daniyal realised this again as soon as he had spoken, and his father's words returned to him. "Strong drink... unquenchable." He was well aware of the symptoms, but not the cause. And the cure? Well, that would be a fine thing. The addiction wasn't a *wicked* secret. If anyone, it was Daniyal who was hurt by it, but no one else. Anyway, he wouldn't lie to me, but he did lie to himself. It was a kind of self-deception, like being in denial, a trick he'd learnt almost without thinking about it.

"Well," Daniyal reconsidered, "I admit I haven't altogether beaten it. But Michael, when you come to write my biography, at least it will give you something intriguing to explore. By the way, I don't know how far you have got with your research; but in view of all my dark secrets, I am coming to think it had better be a posthumous publication!"

At which we both roared with laughter.

Just before we parted, I said, "I have meant to ask you this for a while. Have you met Sasha Kuczynski? He lives near you in Devonshire Street. Sasha came to the UK from Poland in 1945. He's a rabbi who now teaches aesthetics and religion at King's College and has published a fascinating book on music and meaning."

"Jews who love music often make great company. No, I don't know him, but I'll see if I can make contact."

"If you like," I said, "I'll drop him a line and make an introduction. I think he could help you."

We chatted for another ten minutes and then it was time to leave.

"Give my love to Mariah, Daniyal. Practice well, and don't drink too much!"

"I thought you were my friend, Michael!" Daniyal said giving me a warm hug. "My love to Clara. You know Mariah and I would love to see you both in London. I want to show off my new Steinway. It's an even bigger beast than yours!"

In a few hours, I would be back in New York. And in a few more, Daniyal will have arrived in London.

6

As the taxi turned the corner from Marylebone High Street into Weymouth Street, Daniyal was so looking forward to seeing Mariah. He had phoned her from the airport but had only enough coins for a 3-minute chat. But it was mission accomplished. Brief though it was, Mariah knew Daniyal's flight hadn't be delayed and he was on his way. It was full speed ahead with supper. She had remembered to cool the champagne. And they would catch up shortly. Mariah was so looking forward to seeing him too.

Daniyal was horrified when he saw the flames billowing out of the top floor window. As the taxi drew nearer he was terrified it was their house on fire. The taxi drew up outside, not aware of what might be going on. Daniyal grabbed his case and the flowers he had bought for Mariah, thrust a note into the delighted drivers hand and looked up to what needed to be done.

The fire was actually next door at Mrs. Segal's house. There was no fire engine in sight and no time to call for help. Leaving his case and Mariah's flowers on the pavement, Daniyal knew exactly what to do—and the risk he was taking.

First he knocked loudly on the door, shouting urgently, "Mrs. Segal, Jacob, are you there?" With no reply, there was no other choice, he used his powerful right leg to batter the door open. Once, twice, and then it gave way.

He pushed himself through. Even by the front door, the smoke pouring down from upstairs was bitter, pungent and overpowering. Daniyal found Jacob first. He was lying on the front room sofa. Was he asleep or had the fumes already overwhelmed him? From the door, Daniyal called him, but Jacob didn't stir. Wasting not a moment, Daniyal went into the room, put his hand on his shoulder and called Jacob again. The boy opened his eyes. In a split second, his bewilderment turned to terror.

"What's happening?" Jacob asked groggily.

"Jacob, where is your mother?"

"She's upstairs, making supper."

"Jacob, listen to me. There's a fire in the house. I want you to go out onto the pavement right now, while I go and rescue your mother. Can you do that?"

The boy nodded.

Daniyal ran up three flights of stairs to the kitchen, from where he could feel the heat before he entered. The room was burning. Mrs. Segal was on the floor. He called her name. There was no response. Drawing on all his firefighting skills, Daniyal negotiated a path through the flames, scooped up Mrs. Segal in his arms, and brought her down the stairs and out of the house to safety.

An ambulance and fire engine had just arrived, called by Mariah who'd seen the flames after the taxi had driven away and Daniyal hadn't appeared. Coming downstairs, she had found Jacob distraught and helpless on the street.

The ambulance crew lifted Mrs. Segal onto to a stretcher.

"And what about you and the boy, sir?"

"I think Jacob may have inhaled some smoke, and I have too, but otherwise I'm unhurt. I'll be grateful if we can all come with you to Casualty. My wife too. She's Jacob's teacher."

The staff at the Middlesex Casualty Department could not have been kinder or tried harder.

Mrs. Segal recovered consciousness, just briefly, at the end. Jacob had held her hand and he saw her eyes flicker. Full of tears he said, "I love you, Mum." She held his hand all the stronger, and to Daniyal and Mariah, her voice failing, "Please look after Jacob." Jacob felt her grip loosen.

He had lost both his parents.

7

Daniyal's case and the flowers were still on the pavement when the ambulance brought them home to Weymouth Street. Jacob had been quiet and not said anything on the journey back. The only word he'd uttered was a silent nod when the social worker asked him if he wanted to go and stay with Daniyal and Mariah for a few days.

Emergency workmen had already been called to secure the front door of Mrs. Segal's house and would return tomorrow to begin to deal with the fire damage. Daniyal didn't know if there was insurance in place, but in any case, he intended to cover the work himself. He didn't know much about Jacob, except that he had no relatives to whom he could turn and was not of an age where he could be expected to handle any of these arrangements.

As Jacob came into the Steinfeld's house, it felt eerie. The layout of their home was identical to his, except for the fittings and decorations which were very artistic and luxurious by comparison with his own home. As he passed by the open door of the drawing room, Jacob stared at the big piano. He'd never seen such a huge instrument. It was three or four times the size of his piano next door. He wondered, if compared with his little upright, it produced three or four times the volume.

Once the funeral was over, and his mother was laid to rest in Willedesden Jewish Cemetery, Jacob returned to Highgate school where he had just started in the first year. Mariah drove him in every day, and another parent brought him home. For the first few months Jacob said almost nothing, ate only a little food, and seemed to be living in another world. The school was concerned about him and contacted Daniyal and Mariah who were now his legal guardians.

Daniyal and Mariah agreed with the school that they should try and get Jacob to talk, and Daniyal had a simple plan. He would offer to take Jacob out for walks in Regents Park and on Hampstead Heath to try and get to know him better. This was done with the hope that he might open up and express something of what is going on inside of him.

Their first walk was on a beautiful crisp Sunday morning in early December. Regents Park is not a long way from Weymouth Street, so they walked and talked. Or, rather, Jacob walked and Daniyal talked.

"I thought we could get to know each other a little more," Daniyal said. "I can tell you something about my background and my family. If you'd like that. Shall I go first?"

"No, can I go first?" Jacob asked, saying more than he had since his mother's death.

Daniyal, surprised, nodded. "Of course you can go first."

"It's just that you keep on calling me Jacob. That is my name, but I prefer to be called Kovi. That's what my mother always called me. I never knew my father, but I am sure he also would have called me Kovi. I know you're not my Dad, but I'd like it if you would call me Kovi too, please."

"It's a really nice name. Good to meet you, Kovi." Daniyal held out his hand and their eyes met with a smile.

The walks continued every Sunday, alternating the splendour of Regents Park with the more rugged scenery of Hampstead Heath. Even when it rained or snowed, Kovi was always game.

"We don't have to walk, Kovi."

"No, no, Mr. Steinfeld. I want to."

As time went on and slowly healed Kovi's wounds, he began to speak a little more. It helped when he understood the losses Daniyal had faced, and he'd felt the emotion in Daniyal's voice as he had told the story.

The second Sunday in early March 1958, there was a change of plan. Daniyal was booked to play the Piano Concerto No. 2 by Nicolai Medtner at the Royal Albert Hall. It was an afternoon concert at the time they would normally take their walk. Thinking Kovi would not be interested in a classical programme, instead of inviting him to the concert, Daniyal suggested when he came back home, that they would plan for an early evening stroll up to Fitzroy Square and back. Kovi liked the idea and told Daniyal he was glad they could still walk together.

When the Sunday came, as far as the audience was concerned the concert was a usual Steinfeld success. Most will not have noticed Daniyal's momentary memory lapse in one of the solo passages. No player, however brilliant can be perfect all of the time! He had quickly recovered but was still cross with himself. We had once discussed his fear of memory lapses, but in this case he said he been distracted by indigestion rather than tiredness. That however was not the reason why at the end of the concert Daniyal pulled himself away early. Despite the enthusiasm of the crowd, he had already decided on this occasion there would be no encores, a Daniyal Steinfeld first. He was keen to get back and keep his promise.

Their walks were fruitful and enjoyable. Daniyal felt they were doing him as much good as he hoped they were helping Kovi. Over the months, Daniyal and Mariah had learnt quite a lot about their young house guest, although they suspected there may be a few important parts of his story that at the moment he was not telling.

Daniyal came back by taxi. Mariah had the car and wouldn't be back till late. She often had a Mahjong game on Sunday evenings and loved meeting with her friends.

Getting out from the taxi, Daniyal was sure he could hear a piano being played. He decided it was probably from a radio coming through an open window. But when he opened their front door, it was clear that it was his own Steinway he could hear. Perhaps one of his pianist colleagues had visited, and Mariah was staying until Daniyal came home. Odd though, as the car wasn't in the street.

From outside the room, Daniyal listened to the beautiful, sensitive playing. He knew the music very well. Strangely, it was one of the Medtner pieces he might have played as an encore earlier: The Sonata Reminiscenza in A minor, op 38 No. 1. "I wonder who it is?" he thought. But to save disturbing the delicate, sensitive performance, he waited and listened.

The one movement sonata has a very expressive ending. It's a moment of great stillness. When he heard the final few notes, he respectfully lingered outside a further moment; and as the final chord died away, he opened the drawing room door and entered, clapping and shouting warmly, "Bravo, Bravo!"

Seated at the Steinway piano was Kovi Segal.

8

I had no idea. Why didn't you tell me? Who taught you? How long have you been playing? Were you sight reading? How is it you could live next door and none of us knew you could play, let alone like a true artist?

Daniyal's questions were as full of wonder as they were of consternation. He was baffled, if not stupefied, at the sudden revelation of Kovi's talent. But Daniyal was immediately and thoroughly delighted. It was like discovering the oil painting that's been in your family for donkeys years is in fact a previously unknown Rembrandt masterpiece.

"I'm sorry," Kovi said. "I should have asked you before trying out your piano. I shouldn't have touched it without your permission. Please don't be cross with me, Mr. Steinfeld. It won't happen again, I promise."

"And I promise you, Kovi, I am not cross at all. Not in any sense. I am just in awe of your talent. I also know from my own experience that having that kind of ability to explore the deep treasures offered by the world of music has such healing power for the soul."

And they went on talking till Mariah returned.

Kovi continued, "From what you were saying on our last walk, for both of us fire and destruction has claimed the lives of those we care about most. That's why I was pleased to have found your music for the Sonata Reminiscenza. It's like a memorial prayer, and so heartfelt. I was totally absorbed by it. Which is why I didn't stop."

"I am so glad you continued, Kovi. It was poetry. Like us, Medtner was Jewish—in his case from Russia. It could be that in 1920 when he wrote that piece, personal losses through pogroms, the war, or the revolution were what he had in mind. Who knows? But as you say in character, as in its title, it is a profound reminiscence, a memorial prayer."

In that moment, Daniyal realized that Kovi's journey with Daniyal and Mariah, young as he was, had taken on a new character. Unrecognized before, Daniyal could now see the boy had come of age. He was an artist with mature emotions and perceptions. "Kovi, we have so much to discuss."

"I want that, Mr. Steinfeld."

"You can call me Daniyal."

"I'd rather call you Father."

9

⊢————⊣

By March 1959 the arrangements for Kovi's adoption into the Steinfeld family were almost complete. Daniyal had assumed Kovi would keep Segal as his surname.

Over breakfast on Monday morning, before they drove to school, names were the main topic of discussion.

"Kovi, what would you like on your adoption papers. Am I correct in saying you would still prefer to be known as Kovi Segal?"

"Actually, I was hoping you would let me take your name. I'd like to be a Steinfeld."

Daniyal waited a few moments, composing his reply, and then said, "You know I'm really touched, Kovi. As you know, the Steinfeld name has a lot of history attached to it. Much that's good and inspiring, and some memories that are poignant and painful. I wouldn't wish you to become a Steinfeld, unless you understand our history, and are prepared to embrace the responsibilities that go with it."

Kovi also paused. "You mean 'The Solemn Commission'—to live the Steinfeld name for new generations? That's exactly what I want."

"The life of a concert pianist can be hard and demanding. Are you sure this is truly where your heart is?"

Kovi didn't hesitate. "I think you know my answer. I am absolutely certain. But only if you think I am capable of it and am worthy of the trust."

"You know Kovi," said Mariah, "Daniyal and I have already discussed this. For Daniyal, the Steinfeld commission is a solemn promise, and I know he believes you are worthy of it. Yes, and one day as a potentially great pianist. But worthy most of all because you are a person of immense value and quality who we both love and admire."

"But there's one more thing," said Daniyal. "Your professional name. Kovi Steinfeld is a great name, but some may think it's more suited for a sportsman than a pianist. Are you happy to be known by both names? Jacob for your engagements and Kovi for family and friends?

"I am already, Dad."

"Well, that is settled then. We will have to start working on your piano playing and turn you into a true Maestro."

10

The Queen of England has two birthdays, and so does Jacob Steinfeld.

Kovi celebrates his "second" birthday on the 11th May—the date in 1959 of his adoption ceremony and Bar Mitzvah. This second birthday marked three milestones: Kovi's new family, his new name, and his coming of age—in itself a memorial for his mother and all she continued to mean to him.

The choice of date was pure chance, but the significance was not lost on Daniyal. Ever since that final night of the Blitz in 1941, his birthday had never been the same. In Daniyal's heart the 11th May was blackened like soot.

The two little words, "if only" can generate powerful emotions out of all proportion to their simple meaning: often feelings of guilt or an unresolvable longing. Like, "If only I hadn't suggested that concert." "If only I'd stayed with them, and not gone off with the Headleys." "If only I had been there, we'd have stayed the night in the Tube station." And a dozen other *if onlys*. "...they'd still be alive."

Sixteen painful years of reflective introspection were coming if not to an end then certainly to a turning point. For both Daniyal and Mariah, Kovi's presence in their family had already brought comfort and encouragement, and for Daniyal considerable healing too. Kovi so welcomed the love he received from his new parents and felt so privileged to be taught and guided by the world's leading pianist. Daniyal's birthday and Kovi's spiritual birthday, as he called it, were blessed with transformation, thanksgiving and celebration—which was the theme of the address given by the Rabbi at the Synagogue that day.

At the reception afterwards, held at the Steinfeld's in Weymouth Street, there was music and musicians aplenty. Among the musicians were several composers and pianists and other friends from the neighbourhood and the Jewish and Polish communities. The locum Rabbi who had led the service, Sasha Kuczynski, also joined them.

Meeting Sasha reminded Daniyal of our brief conversation about him. "Sasha, thank you so much for the thoughtful way you conducted the service. One of these days, I'd love to talk to you about your book on music and meaning. I think we may have some ideas in common."

"Thank you, Mr. Steinfeld. I'd be delighted."

Such a discussion might have shone a search light into Daniyal's inner world, but that was where his feelings were most under guard, and probably unconsciously, it was the reason Daniyal forgot all about Sasha Kuczynski and never followed up the suggestion.

The party was getting under way. There were presents. Presents for Kovi, presents for Daniyal, and flowers in abundance for Mariah. On this occasion, because of the numbers involved, Mariah had asked the Polish delicatessen in the High Street to do the catering. They provided a glorious array of delicious kosher and non-kosher dishes, presented on beautiful hand-carved wooden platters, which Mariah served with the two helpers she had engaged.

Popping and pouring the chilled champagne was Head Sommelier Kovi, with two willing school friend assistants as wine waiters. Daniyal played the host throughout, speaking to everyone, introducing friends to new friends, and "Oh your glass is empty. Kovi, where are you—you're needed!"

Food, wine and presents. At a Bar Mitzvah, what more could anyone wish for? Speeches, of course. Whatever else might be said—Kovi's speech would be the traditional one.

In a Jewish family, a Bar Mitzvah is a recognition of a boy's coming-of-age. For several months in preparation, Kovi had studied Hebrew, Jewish customs and learnt the blessings for the Aliyah and how to lead the prayer services. Most important of all, he had learnt a Torah portion by heart, which he had the option to read or chant. Kovi chose the chant. It was the best choice, for in the ceremony his young tenor voice could easily have been mistaken for an experienced cantor. Everyone present was touched with his deep musical spirituality.

The Torah portion faultlessly accomplished, after the ceremony, Kovi would be able to commence his Bar Mitzvah speech with confidence. It was normal to use the traditional words, "Today I am a man."

The cry went up. "Speech, Kovi, speech!"

They were in the drawing room, the piano moved towards the window to make more space. Kovi passed the bottle of champagne he was holding to his assistant and walked calmly in the direction of the piano. In silence, like an actor preparing to deliver a soliloquy, slowly moving his eyes left to right, from person to person, he surveyed the assembled gathering. Finally, satisfied he had his audience's full attention, his demeanour serious, his words strong and forthright, Kovi began his Bar Mitzvah speech.

"Today I have come of age." He broke into a grin. "For today I am a Steinfeld!"

The grin turned into a delightful, wicked smile. And like the effect of a light switch on a darkened room, every face beamed in response.

Kovi added a few thank you's, to his short speech, which were heartfelt, and mainly directed to his parents. After which, it was Daniyal's turn to say a few words.

Daniyal began with sincere expressions of thanks for everyone's presence and for Mariah's part, plus a few jokes about Bar Mitzvahs and fountain pens and that sort of thing. Then, turning his head silently towards Kovi, he paused, gathering his thoughts for what he wished to say next.

"If I may be personal for a moment. I think you all know the history of our family and my part in it. We can hardly say we are the only ones who have found that life exists on a pivot. The pivot sometimes bending one way, at others tumbling right over in the other direction. In my family, both before and during my time, when the pivot has tumbled, I have felt its seismic waves resonate for years. Many of us have painful histories. But whatever a struggle it has been—though I have been close to it—long-term, though bruised, sometimes severely, I have never felt completely crushed or ruined.

"I've thought a lot about this and I put down this resilience, or whatever you might call it, to playing, listening and loving music. For me, music nourishes meaning and hope; the sense that despite appearances, we are sustained by the good; that evil, however strong its grip, will not finally prevail.

"For our family, like for others of us here, that conviction has been tested by trauma and appalling loss. Death is no friend, and we share our tears with many. But what I am building up to saying is to do with a mystery. That when darkness reigns, and circumstances are so dreadfully and devastatingly bad, it is not the end. The tide can still unexpectedly turn; the sun rises and dark clouds are banished.

"I say with sincerity, it has been like this with Kovi. Kovi's entrance into our lives is as precious as those welcome sustaining rays of sunshine; the joining of Kovi's life with ours has banished so much of what's hung over us since the dark days of the Blitz and in a sense the events of 23 years before that. And all I can say is we are so very, very grateful.

"I know these words by heart. They are what in our family we call the Steinfeld 'Solemn Commission.' My grandfather, whose name Abramczyk I share, felt keenly that as a family the Steinfelds have a legacy for future generations. He said these words to my father, Aleksander, just before he was catapulted over the wall from the pogrom in Lwów in 1918.

"'Remember our faces, and never forget how much we love you. Remember the care with which you were raised, our family's values, our home and our homeland. Remember our music and our teaching. Share this precious legacy with generations to come. Our family bequeaths to you the Steinfeld name; and you are now our future.'

"Mariah and I have not been able to have children of our own, but we are now blessed to know the Steinfeld legacy will see a new dawn. That is what is behind Kovi's words just now. Mariah and I love him and bless him for being one with us. And Kovi, we celebrate with you that today you are a man, indeed—a Steinfeld; you share our family's future, but most of all, you are our son."

There were murmurs of approval. Kovi looked moved, but clearly delighted by his father's words. Mariah could hardly hold back her tears. And the room as a whole exploded in joyful applause, eyes connecting, with "well said" and other expressions of appreciation.

"Music, we want music!" The cry reverberated around the room.

"More champagne first," Daniyal countered.

"No, we want music."

"Music now."

"More wine later."

Kovi took Daniyal's hand and led him to the piano. As he put the piano lid onto its long stick he announced, "This first piece needs four hands," A freshly written music manuscript awaited them on the stand, ready for Daniyal to play secondo, with Kovi sitting to his right to take the primo part.

When they were ready, Kovi announced to the assembled gathering, "This is the musical part of my Bar Mitvah speech. Father and I are to play you a Rhapsody on a Polish Jewish theme, composed specially for this occasion by Jacob Steinfeld."

There were murmurs of approval and anticipation.

Kovi nodded, and Daniyal began with a quiet, slow moving minor chord pattern, to which above Kovi added the gypsy-like Polish folk melody. As the piece progressed, the melody and its harmonic pattern were transformed into a series of variations— effectively short, interconnected movements. The music had an expressive logic about it, and in its quieter moments, an intense and haunting beauty.

In the last variation before the recapitulation of the theme, everyone agreed the exchange between the players was remarkable. The atmosphere was suddenly all drama and clashing swords. Daniyal thundered the harmonies in fast moving chords between the hands, while Kovi turned the melody into glistening cascades of fast-moving melodic patterns. Then the roles reversed. Kovi thundering the harmonies and Daniyal whizzing up and down in cascades faster than most would believe possible.

Suddenly the music stopped, the final notes of the variation sustained by the pedal and allowed to slowly die away. And when it was almost completely quiet again, the haunting, gypsy-like Polish folk melody returned, this time played by Daniyal, with Kovi decorating and enriching the minor chord pattern from above. A single statement of the whole Jewish theme brought the piece to a satisfying conclusion.

Quite clearly, the discerning audience for this first performance were more than satisfied. They clapped slowly at first, out of sheer respect for the music and the performance. Then, the clapping crescendoed into a mighty roar of approval, with Kovi's friends from Highgate cheering and whistling.

As the room-full of music lovers clearly wanted more. Daniyal said to Kovi, "Why don't you play them what we are studying at the moment?"

Kovi looked puzzled, "Do you mean the whole of it?"

"No just the second movement. The pianists here will be interested to see what you make of the skips."

11

Daniyal was referring to the Schumann Fantasie in C. Towards the end, the hands skip in opposite directions, in an exciting but pianistically demanding climax. Even Franz Liszt considered that passage too risky in performance and never played it in public. Today, when played well, it is a marvellous and exciting climactic moment. But performances can be "hit or miss."

Daniyal had been working on Kovi's technique using this piece as an exercise for a wider principle of the role of relaxation, a key element in the Steinfeld technical approach. Daniyal described a pianist he had once heard.

"The man was completely blind and had to be escorted to and from the piano. But that was all he needed. His actual playing was impeccable, musically and technically perfect. So when he came to this Schumann piece, as I expected, the playing was phenomenal; the speed and accuracy, note-perfect. Those famous jumps were as smooth as a five-finger exercise."

"So how do you achieve reliable accuracy, performance after performance?" asked Kovi.

"Here's what I said when I met him afterwards. I asked fairly bluntly how he did it. In reply, he didn't say anything, he just wiggled his elbows. They were so wobbly and relaxed, they looked like jelly. He said it's the same in the Schumann skips as for the octave trills in the Brahms D minor, or the octave jumps at the end of the Tchaikovsky B flat minor. Relaxation practice is as important as lifting weights is for an athlete.

"So Kovi, I am going to show you what it feels like. The aim is to keep your arms and shoulders very relaxed. Remember that tension is the enemy. It squeezes glue all over the keyboard and in all kinds of ways gums up your playing.

"You know what a suspension bridge is like? In one sense it is fixed, suspended solely from its outer points. Think of your arm like that—fixed at the shoulder and the fingertips only. Except in practice, we pianists allow the arm to get glued up with tension. So to get the feeling right, move the piano stool away and sit on the floor."

Kovi moved the stool and sat cross legged on the rug.

"Now, keeping your arm loose, feel what it's like to play like a suspension bridge. Using the weight of your fingers only, lift your fingers to the keyboard. Hold them there. Then play without tension."

Kovi played and experienced exactly what Daniyal had in mind. Although his playing was of a very high order, he had not received this kind of insight before. He was delighted.

Daniyal continued, "Of course, relaxation enables both musical and technical flow. My grandfather taught about the brain's remarkable capacity for micro travel. You know, I can touch my nose with my eyes shut; in complete darkness I can reach out for my water glass by my bed. In piano playing, technically speaking, sense is more important than sight. The legacy of Abramczyk's teaching is that strong fingers and strong emotions rely on relaxed weight and economy of motion, in the heart as well as in the body. Taken together, they are foundational for speed, accuracy, tone, and everything else in piano performance."

12

―――――――

Jacob Steinfeld sat alone at the keyboard of the 8 foot 11 3/4-inch model D Steinway in his parents' drawing room. He was surrounded by famous musicians, pianists, composers and conductors—the jury on this was still out. Could a boy of 13 really play like a Steinfeld? Did he possess those attributes of genius, those qualities of the super virtuoso, which in one family have been nurtured, taught and passed on through three generations? Is adoption into a musical family so powerful that a gifted child might absorb such star quality from his father and his teaching?

The verdict? Would it be, "That was the boy next door." Or "A fourth generation. A star is born!" With his parents close by, protective and keeping watch, the performance he was about to give felt far more than a debut; it was a test of his commission. Kovi was nervous.

The jury waited.

Kovi announced the work. "Schumann Fantasie in C, the second movement." Then he began to play, and as he did his nerves dissolved. His concentration was solely on the superbly beautiful music of Robert Schumann. As he approached the famous passage of hair-raising skips, he could recall Abramczyk's words, so often spoken by his father, "Stay relaxed, fingers close to the keyboard, no unnecessary movement."

Some always book their recital or concerto seats so they can see the pianists hands. If you weren't a pianist or didn't have your eyes glued to Kovi's hands, you might not have realised there was any kind of technical challenge in what you had just heard. Let alone a massive one.

As Kovi played the second movement of Schumann's intensely passionate fantasie, that day there was certainly no glue on the keyboard. Technically, the performance was marvellously accurate right to the last note. But that was completely secondary compared to the artistry, expression, and sheer joy of Kovi's recreation of Schumann's bright and unclouded music.

While everyone clapped, with whoops and whistles, and while Kovi was still seated, a delighted Daniyal placed his hand on Kovi's right shoulder. Clearly very happy, he bent over and whispered in Kovi's ear. "Well done my son and heir. Strong fingers. Strong emotions. Today you have come of age."

13

M onitor was a flagship and innovatory BBC television arts series, launched in February 1958. With Huw Wheldon as editor and principal interviewer, it ran until 1965. He always said that he would continue with the programmes "until I have interviewed everyone I am interested in interviewing." In 1964, Wheldon, ever on the lookout for stimulating arts subjects, began to investigate the possibility of some televised piano masterclasses. It had been put to him that great pianist-teachers like Liszt and Leschetizky had operated masterclasses for years, as had music colleges and conservatoires throughout Europe and the United States. But what about a series of televised masterclasses, where viewers could learn about the technicalities of playing and interpreting great music? He told his colleagues, "It won't be like a standard interview. But it could be extremely stimulating."

The concept was worked out at their planning meeting. The idea was to match one of the world's greatest players with three of today's most promising young pianists. It would not be a competition; there would be no winners, but they would prepare a concerto as though for an actual performance. The climax would be in a performance to be given by the masterclass leader himself. It would be timed for a televised concerto broadcast from the BBC Proms at the Royal Albert Hall. "Overall," said Wheldon, "if we can find that magic mix of four, we will create a fine and innovatory piece of arts broadcasting."

At first, this did not look a good fit for Daniyal Steinfeld. It was suggested to the Monitor team that if approached he would decline any offer made. But the researchers kept their ear to the ground. If Daniyal could be persuaded, he would be a great catch.

The fact was that Daniyal did not do much teaching; except for Kovi, who over the last four years he had taught intensively. The teaching had born much fruit since, in the last twenty months in particular, Kovi's debut recitals and concerto performances in Chicago, Warsaw, and London had attracted such attention and dizzyingly positive reviews, so polished was his playing you could be forgiven for thinking he would never need another lesson.

Since Kovi was Daniyal's only pupil, and that he routinely turned down every request for tuition, often with the offers of absurdly inflated fees, quite a number of Daniyal's friends had simply wondered why. They concluded either that Daniyal had an exaggerated sense of entitlement or that his bravado was a cover for something he was simply not good at. In fact, the latter was partly the case, but from his utterances you can be forgiven for thinking the former applied.

Usually it was after a glass or two of whisky, in private, Daniyal would make comments like he didn't suffer fools gladly, he had no interest in the kinderklavier and the young untalented. On one occasion Kovi was deeply shocked to hear him refer to beginners as the hoi polloi and challenged him for being so intolerant.

Daniyal tried to calm him down. "It's only the whisky, Kovi. Anyway it's not intolerant. It's Yiddish."

"It's not, dad, it's Greek. And in whatever language, it's always intolerant. If you say it outside this house people will think you're stuck up and ungenerous. Where will that get you? And worse, intolerance can be the breeding ground for persecution. If our family doesn't learn that lesson, who can?"

Daniyal felt cross, but probably more towards himself than Kovi. Daniyal shouldn't have said what he did. He thought he was being clever. He wasn't. But normally, no one challenged him. They didn't dare. But this was Kovi saying it. Daniyal knew it wasn't just intemperance, although it was and he should have known better. But it caused him to reflect that there are always reasons for the things we say and do. Even when we don't understand or have forgotten, our hidden history often holds the key. Daniyal had forgotten the connection, and the conversation brought it flooding back.

Kovi knew little of the history of his grandfather, Aleksander, apart from the broad brushstrokes. He knew of his international acclaim, the devastating accident to his right hand, the tragedy that befell his whole family in 1918, and of the bomb that destroyed Aleksander's home and family on the last night of the Blitz in 1941.

Daniyal decided to tell Kovi what lay behind what were his unguarded and yes, unnecessary and superior comments. He'd never told anyone about this childhood memory, not even Mariah. He had largely forgotten it, but recalling it now was unsettling.

The events weren't terrible or traumatic, but when, as a teenager, he had discovered what work his father had to do when he first came to London—how strongly the thought of it affected him!

Kovi will have known nothing about young Roddy, or Jeremy Blandford, or any of the many Fitzrovia kids his grandpa Aleksander had taken on as piano pupils. The fact is the income they brought in was welcome support for Aleksander and Leah for their early days in London, before Aleksander's Guildhall appointment brought them lasting financial stability.

"But think of the contrast, Kovi. And think of the pity," said Daniyal. "Before his accident, my father was a master pianist. In the age of the virtuoso, he was incomparable. At his Proms debut in 1911 he was 20, and even at that age was seriously compared with Godowsky, Hofmann, Rachmaninoff and Medtner—the world's leading pianists. Ernest Newman, Britain's greatest music critic, described him as 'the most outstanding virtuoso of his generation—bar none!'

"Now consider—he went from all that, to being hunted down as a Jew. In a freak accident, he loses the use of his precious right hand. He comes to London, and all that's left to him is to eke out a miserable living, teaching young kids to play five finger exercises. I am not saying anything about the children. Of course they have the right to learn and be taught well. It is just that my Dad, with all that he achieved, and the terror he went through, and all he lost in serial ways—it was shameful that teaching beginners was all that was left for him. When I found this out years later, it broke my heart.

"And yet. There are lots of and-yets. One is I have always marvelled at the Jewish spirit, and how Jews seem capable of bouncing back. Even with the evils of the Holocaust, though their hearts are scarred, you see Jewish survivors gradually come to life again with ingenuity, creativity and wonderful human spirit. We are an unusual race of people.

"That, too, was true of my father. He retrained his left hand for him to be the best left hand-only pianist and became a teacher and performer at the level for which he was properly suited."

Kovi realised this was why his father automatically turned down teaching opportunities. It was understandable without being rational. It was in this conversation he first came to see the inner burdens of memory his father carried.

At one time, the world's music conservatoires were lining up to offer him honorary professorships. They eventually got the message. Daniyal had not covered himself in glory when he replied to an understandably persistent approach from one of the London colleges, "Why should I waste my time with beginners when I can spend my hours with the great masters?"

It was an acerbic comment, and not at all characteristic of the great encourager he could be. Like the majority of his less worthy comments, it had something to do with the intergenerational consequences of extreme trauma, how internal pain often leapfrogs to the second generation. For all his bravado, Daniyal was an introvert. These comments connected there, and with the loosening effect of the alcohol Daniyal had imbibed. Some weeks a bottle of whisky wouldn't last more than two or three days!

Several of his friends had noticed the volume of his consumption. Mariah knew he used it to dampen down his inner pain but was concerned about the effect it was having on his health. Strangely, he never seemed drunk, and the whisky didn't seem to affect his performances; but neither had it solved anything. After all these years, Daniyal still had nightmares and sleep terrors.

Exaggerated by the fact he had been drinking, partly underlying Daniyal's comment about beginners, was really his discomfort with those whose musicianship and technique were not yet fully developed. He had the ability but lacked the patience. Masterclasses might be a different matter, and in these he could shine. Which was the vision put to Daniyal when Huw Wheldon walked round the corner from BBC Broadcasting House to Daniyal and Mariah's home in Weymouth Street.

14

Huw Wheldon had a memorable face. He was a picture of intelligence, with piercing eyes, thin lips which broke easily into a smile, a deep forehead, and large pointed ears shaped never to miss even the quietest word. Which they never did, for he had an especially concentrated and focused way of listening. Some said it was as though he was watching you on two screens at once. The one portraying the outside you and the other which played out the inner workings of your soul. If some felt they were being inwardly scrutinised, they probably were.

A man of considerable substance, Huw Wheldon was a Welshman and had been awarded the Military Cross for bravery in the D-Day landings. He had a searching mind, a tough resourceful character, very considerable ability and wide intellectual sympathies. He had strong and principled views about public service broadcasting. He saw the role of the BBC "to make the popular good and make the good popular." His belief in excellence characterised his reign as Managing Director of BBC Television. But before that, between 1958 and 1965, as editor and principal anchor of *Monitor*, he made his mark as a responsible innovative programme maker for the arts.

When the knocker sounded, Mr. Wheldon had arrived five minutes earlier than expected. Mariah put down her lesson preparation and came down to let him in.

"How do you do, Mrs. Steinfeld," he said, bowing deferentially.

"Do please come in, Mr. Wheldon. We are expecting you. May I take your coat?"

While Mariah was putting his coat on a hanger, the sound of the piano came from the drawing room.

"Is that your husband?"

"No, it's our son, Kovi. Daniyal is giving him a lesson."

"Oh, I hadn't realised Mr. Steinfeld is a piano teacher."

"He isn't normally. And he is certainly not drawn to work with beginners. But yes, he has taught Kovi ever since his adoption."

"From the sound of it, that's Beethoven, the Hammerklavier."

"You have a good ear. Yes, Kovi's just started learning it today."

"Either Kovi is an exceptionally quick learner or Daniyal is an exceptional teacher."

"I think both. Kovi's playing has come on by leaps and bounds since Daniyal has been teaching him. We're very proud of him."

"Mr. Huw Wheldon, welcome!" It was Daniyal, pounding down the stairs and keen to welcome his distinguished guest. Shaking his hand he said, "Why not come up to the drawing room. You can meet Kovi, and we can all have some coffee together. Unless I can offer you something different or stronger."

As they entered the room, Kovi came over to be introduced. "Kovi, this is Huw Wheldon, a leading producer and presenter for BBC television. Huw, this is my son Kovi. He is a fine pianist."

"Well, I know. I heard him just now. Exceptional, I would say. Kovi, I am delighted to meet you."

"And me you sir." If first impressions count for anything, and Mrs. Segal had always said they did, Kovi was struck by Mr. Wheldon's intelligent face and warm manner.

Mariah came in with a tray of coffee, and a selection of Fortnum and Mason's chocolate biscuits.

After they had chatted for a while, drained the coffee pot, and finished the biscuits, Huw said, "Why don't I tell you some more about the proposal I wrote to you about?"

They talked about the idea of masterclasses. Apart from the idea that it might appeal to Daniyal's ego—which it did; more importantly, it would give him an opportunity to teach and mentor outstanding young players. To do so as he had come to realise, through teaching Kovi, this was part of the Steinfeld commission, "to share this precious legacy with generations to come."

Also, he would like to find a way to put right the ungenerous things he had said about teaching youngsters. He would not have the patience to serve them well. But these would be highly talented, accomplished young artists of considerable maturity. He could help them, and it would show he had found the best focus for his teaching métier and not ignominiously turned his back on the noble profession altogether. If asked, he would say yes.

"I don't wish to take up too much of your time just now, and we can work out practical details later. But there are two things I want to ask you about. You will appreciate that I am not a musician and have never been anywhere near a piano masterclass. So my first question is, how does a masterclass actually work and how could we make it accessible for viewers?"

Daniyal thought for a moment, and then said, "Let me show you." Then he turned to Kovi. "Kovi, would you like to help us? I'll be the teacher and you can be the pupil."

"I am quite used to it that way round, Dad!"

Daniyal explained to Huw, "Viewers will need to understand that a true masterclass is for learners, but not beginners. This is a different take on the normal teacher-pupil relationship. It works when it is perceived as a relationship of equals. That nourishes rapport and respect both ways.

"Take Kovi as an example. If he were in a masterclass, I would be teaching him because he is already attaining the highest level of artistry and technique. The idea is to draw what is already there inside of him—the very best he can bring to the music—

technically, stylistically, expressively, with strong fingers and strong emotions. He is learning from someone of longer, more extensive musical experience than himself. Call him a master if you will, but I am not in essence better than him.

"Let's play Mr. Wheldon some of the Hammerklavier, Kovi."

Kovi began the first movement of Beethoven's twenty-ninth piano sonata. Composed in the years 1817-18, it is a work of colossal intellectual and emotional power, and unquestionably Beethoven's most demanding composition for the piano.

After four to five minutes, Daniyal put his hand on his shoulder. "Do you mind if we pause there, Kovi?"

Kovi stopped playing and looked up at his father.

"Thank you. That was fine playing. The music is new to you, I know. But I sense your heart is fully engaged, and you are doing well with the complex range of voices.

"So I just want to remind you of two things which I think will help the music breathe. The first affects your range of colour, the way you vary your tone. Remember this piece is more orchestral than any other of his solo works. By the time Beethoven writes this sonata, he has already composed eight of his nine symphonies, his violin concerto and all five piano concertos. It is as though in this sonata, Beethoven has a whole orchestra at his disposal. It's highly pianistic but uses lots of instrumental colour and texture too. Think of a phrase and what orchestral instrument he might choose, and it will all breathe more richly."

Kovi nodded his understanding.

"And then, Beethoven's personal life? What has he to deal with the moment he puts his pen down? He's in the middle of a massive family battle. Beethoven was struggling to gain custody of his nephew, Karl. Karl was the son of his dead brother, Kaspar. Beethoven had huge concern for Karl's wellbeing, yet every possible legal barrier was put in his way. Again remember what it must have been like to be deaf—the difficulties of explaining yourself, the frustration at being misunderstood, the sheer difficulty over practical issues. So managing the legal requirements and court cases was a major preoccupation. The relationship issues were even more bruising, and the whole episode caused him major heartache."

Huw Wheldon was hanging on his every word.

"It is hardly surprising Beethoven produced less music during this period than at any other time in his life. But he produced this sonata. Is it surprising it is the most demanding and defiant of all his works for the instrument? So frankly there's agony here, and in the piano he now has the colours of the whole orchestra with which to express it and help him overcome.

"Kovi, in the light of that, I want to ask you to play me the opening again. Think of it in two ways. As a fanfare. And as Beethoven's determination to overcome his agony of spirit."

Kovi played the opening and then Daniyal stopped him.

"Do you mind if I play the same music, and you tell me if you can hear any difference?"

Daniyal moved to the keyboard. He played the same opening, same pace, same dynamic. "So did you notice any difference between yours and mine? I mean, we both played what Beethoven has written as far as the notes are concerned."

"I think your way of playing it was more taught, more determined," Kovi said. "It's strange to say, but it seemed to have more character. Though I can't work out why."

"Remember again that when we describe meaning in music, the meaning lives in the abstract world of our hearts. This is not a sonata about Beethoven's nephew, but behind its composition we can certainly feel the emotional complexity of Beethoven's life.

"So think about the intention or intentionality of the music. And now, by contrast, let me play you an extract from a Czerny study. This is the last of the octave studies. No. 6 in B flat."

Daniyal played the short, demanding study, breathtakingly fast to make the point. When he'd finished, he asked Kovi, "What would you say is the essential difference between playing the Hammerklavier and the Czerny piano studies?"

Kovi didn't hesitate. "There is sweat in the studies, but no passion. In the Beethoven there is sweat *and* passion from the very first note."

"Exactly, Kovi. Now play me the beginning again."

Kovi played the fanfare opening once more. But clearly wasn't happy with the result. "Dad, you are going to have to help me with this. I can't play it like you and I want it."

"You just have to play the music as it is written on the page. I'm sure you noticed I did. Because I noticed you didn't! You have only just started learning it, and this is absolutely no rebuke. It's all to do with that massive two octave quaver leap from that bottom B flat to the B flat chord in the first and third bars. It's incredibly difficult.

"But I notice the Edition you are playing from actually recommends leaning over to play the arresting lower B flat with the right hand. Of course, that turns the incredibly difficult into the incredibly easy. It also risks destroying the passion Beethoven intended. Why else would he write that massive jump for the left hand alone? He may have been deaf for much of his life, but he had been a brilliant pianist too. He knew you don't normally write extra hard stuff right at the start and fill the performer with anxiety. But here he does. He builds in danger from the very first bar. He knows you could miss, but you must not. It is more about the passion than the dangers.

"So play it again, Kovi. This time exactly how Beethoven wrote it. Yes, feel the danger, the anger, feel the agony, the defiance, the passion of it."

And so Kovi, like an animal about to pounce on its prey, stared at the low B flat and held it in his unwavering gaze—and then began the fanfare opening all over again.

It was completely transformed. He played it like a master.

"Very well done, Kovi."

Kovi beamed.

Huw Wheldon was clearly moved. "I only wish the cameras had been here to capture that. If you are willing to accept, then we have our master pianist, and if you will agree, the first of our outstanding young masterclass players."

15

⊢————⊣

Huw Wheldon's legendary series of Steinfeld masterclasses, commissioned for the BBC's *Monitor* programme, began on Sunday 4th April 1965. The three weekly programmes were broadcast live direct from the Monitor Studio at BBC Television Centre in London's White City. I was able to see the whole programme on NBC at our other home in Boston, just a few days later. It was a thrilling experience.

At 8:00 p.m., Huw Wheldon introduced the programme. "Tonight, we begin the first of three masterclasses on Rachmaninoff's Piano Concerto No. 3. They are to be conducted by the internationally acclaimed British pianist, Daniyal Steinfeld. Before a small studio audience we will welcome three outstanding young pianists whose careers have already shown much early promise.

"Mr. Steinfeld has asked me to say this is not a competition. It is an occasion to showcase talent and a passing on of the baton.

A chance for these young players to receive first-hand from Mr. Steinfeld insights into the performance practice of the late romantic pianists. Names such as Rachmaninoff, Hofmann and Godowsky; and of course, the extraordinary Steinfeld dynasty, three generations of internationally acclaimed super virtuosi, Abramczyk Steinfeld, Aleksander Steinfeld and with us today, Daniyal Steinfeld. This is a rare opportunity for the British public, and the BBC is honoured Mr. Steinfeld has accepted our invitation."

He turned to the studio audience. "Will you please welcome our teacher and guide for these programmes, the internationally acclaimed and distinguished pianist, Daniyal Steinfeld."

The audience applauds as the camera captures a long shot of Daniyal, who is seated with Huw Wheldon. Behind them, we can see two concert grand pianos. And to the left of the pianos, the three young concert pianists seated together.

Huw Wheldon turns to Daniyal. "Daniyal Steinfeld, welcome indeed to *Monitor* and what I believe will be a special experience, not only for three highly accomplished young pianists, but for our audience at home. So before the first masterclass begins, I would like if I may, to ask you three questions. The first is about the music we shall hear. The second, about the student performers. The third, if you are willing, about yourself.

"So let's start with the music. Why did you choose the Rachmaninoff third Piano Concerto for these young players?"

"Mmm. Thank you Huw. I suppose there are lots of reasons. The first is I love the music and want others to love it too. It is so heartfelt, so lyrical and dramatic, so fearsomely difficult and gripping as well. But in that difficulty you hear the struggle of the man's heart.

"When he was writing this concerto, we know Rachmaninoff was thinking about the fragility of his homeland, and these concerns were partly the cause of his depression. He already knew if he needed to leave his beloved Russia he'd be unable to return. In fact, in the eight years that led up to the violence of the Revolution, all that Rachmaninoff most feared—inexorably came to pass. In particular, exile, the loss of family and friends, and the confiscation of his family estate.

"But Rachmaninoff's life was not all gloom, by any means. My father, Aleksander Steinfeld, knew him well, and there are all kinds of happy family stories of when Rachmaninoff came to my grandparents' house. He could be immensely humorous and enjoy practical jokes; but he also told me of the times when he would retire into his shell for long periods, gloomy and depressed.

"So I think the key to understanding Rachmaninoff's music is that he is a soul poet. He opens his heart to us, and in doing so, much of that inner angst gets resolved, gloriously so, as his inspirational voice is revealed. In short, the Great Russian Bear has a soaring spirit, so vital, so alive. In this beautiful and inspiring piece I gain the overwhelming impression that though the worst may come, it will not reign. And emotionally that struggle to overcome is reflected in the music. Put simply, along with the second Symphony, I think this is his very best work."

"Thank you. And what would you like to tell us about our three pianists, one of whom is your son, Jacob Steinfeld?"

"We asked a number of well know conservatoire professors to sponsor names for these masterclasses, but it was the BBC Music Department who kindly made the final choices. I think you'll see they have chosen well. If this were a competition, which of course it isn't, we'd probably find that all three would turn out to be joint first prize winners. So let me introduce them to you.

"The first to play tonight will be a young Russian, now living in London. He is Yuri Tomakov. Yuri is a fine and exciting player, trained in the Russian tradition, and a graduate of the Moscow Conservatoire. Yuri is continuing his studies in London with the eminent pianist and teacher, James Gibb.

"Second is Jane Waterman. Jane is a wonderful, expressive player with an outstanding technical ability. Jane is a gold medal winner of the Guildhall School of Music and for the last year has been attending postgraduate classes at the Paris Conservatoire. At present, Jane is studying with the great French pianist, Vlado Perlmeuter.

"The third pianist will be my son, Jacob Steinfeld, who started the piano when he was three. I have been Jacob's teacher since he was 11, although, as you'll hear, he hardly needs more teaching from me. But in the last couple of years, Jacob has benefitted enormously from being a visiting student of Nadia

Boulanger in Paris and Fontainebleau. Those are our three highly accomplished pianists."

The camera returned to Huw Wheldon. "Thank you. Now before we hear our three players, may I ask you about yourself?

"I noticed this in a review of your recent LP recordings of the late Beethoven piano sonatas. 'There is something interior about Steinfeld's music making, as though the music flows from deep within his soul. You get the sense that it is not a performer but the composer himself at the piano.' Is this a characteristic of the Steinfeld Legacy? Not just brilliantly agile fingers, but a quality of passion and intensity in performance?"

Daniyal paused for a moment, thinking through his reply. "As many families are able to testify, there are certain ideas and values that are passed down from generation to generation, and that has certainly been the case with our family. For the Steinfelds, it goes back to the teaching of my grandfather, Abramczyk. He was an outstanding pianist, but I think he will be mainly remembered as a remarkable teacher. He often used little aphorism-like phrases to glue a thought firmly in the heart. One of those phrases comes to mind. 'Strong fingers, strong emotions.' My father told me Abramczyk said this to all his pupils.

"What he meant by strong fingers and strong emotions is that the expressive power of a performance is only as strong as the technique which undergirds it. But that technique is never meant to take the lead. Where is the music to be found? Not in fast scales and thundering octaves, for music is a language of

425

the emotions. With all the technical command at his control, the pianist needs to enter the emotional world of the music; he is its servant, identifying with it, presenting it as though the composer himself is speaking. That is why I have come to believe the performer's role is to discover and portray the beating heart of the music.

"This is where the life of any great musical work and 'portrayal'—I prefer the word to 'performance'—is to be found. In fact, I would go further. To discover this life, if there should be no agony in your own heart, how will you recognise the composer's agony and portray it? And correspondingly, should there be no resonance of hope within you, how will you recognise the light for what it is and when it shines forth through the music? Strong fingers and strong emotions. That's what it means. And I can't think of anything that more faithfully describes the challenge of this enduringly great work of Sergei Rachmaninoff."

16

The public interest in the masterclasses had been considerable. Like the public reaction, Daniyal had been highly impressed with all three pianists. However, many of the reviews mentioned Kovi with special praise: "One to watch," and "A young player of astonishing virtuosity and insight."

During the preparation and run up to the *Monitor* programmes, Kovi had asked Daniyal about his view of international piano competitions. The subject came up at a special dinner to welcome Clara and I when we came from Boston for a few days as the Steinfelds' house guests.

At the beginning of the meal, just after the first course I put down my soup spoon, and Daniyal immediately chimed his wine glass, chanting "Speech, speech, Michael."

If it was a speech, it was from the heart. "Mariah, this is a wonderful meal, and your hospitality is as great as ever. You have been such magnificent friends to us over the years, and it is so good to have this reunion." Mariah and Daniyal caught each other's eyes and beamed with appreciation.

"But then Daniyal and Kovi, Clara and I also want to tell you we were enthralled by the *Monitor* programmes. We both said in your different roles you brought that concerto alive in a way that neither of us have ever before experienced it. It was like an Insider's Guide to the heart of Rachmaninoff."

Clara was nodding, "Yes, and if you are thinking about competitions, Kovi, this fan of yours says you're already the best of the bunch. I'd give you first prize any day."

Kovi enjoyed the praise from the one he called his American Aunt. "Thank you Aunty Clara. That's sweet of you."

Lots of different views were exchanged on the subject, and after they had all enjoyed going happily round in circles, Daniyal stood up to pour more wine. And then, was he being impish? It was difficult to tell. Maybe he'd drunk a lot?

"Of course, you know my grandfather frowned rather severely on piano competitions; in fact, he absolutely forbade my father to compete in one. He used to say a pianist is not a circus performer who can be judged by his prowess at juggling or the high wire, or even his ability with lions or elephants. And of course, he was right about that."

"So is that the Steinfeld tradition?" asked Clara equally impishly.

"Mmm," said Daniyal, "the Steinfeld tradition. It has served us very well so far. We don't want to change it do we?"

"But if great grandpa Abramczyk took that view, why then did Abramczyk and Josef Hofmann become patrons of the Liszt-Chopin competition?" said Kovi, with a hint of triumph.

"Good boy," I said. "Good question."

Daniyal paused and didn't say anything for a moment. "I think we have to allow Abramczyk the benefit of the doubt," Daniyal said, sipping his wine. "After all, no one is one hundred percent consistent. It's possible he changed his mind."

At which I joined in the roar of approval from around the table.

Daniyal ruminated again. "I suppose the world has changed since Abramczyk's time, especially the way the public gets to hear of you. You know Van Cliburn, the American pianist. He told me his career was supercharged by winning the Tchaikovsky competition. That was in Moscow in 1958. I think the piano world recognises that for a winner at either Warsaw or Moscow, international acclaim is pretty well guaranteed."

Trying not to sound too much like a therapist, I steadied my gaze inquiringly on our host. "Daniyal, tell us what lies behind your thinking. What's in your heart?"

Daniyal looked suddenly serious and professorial. If he had smoked a pipe he would have given it a couple of puffs before answering. "Mmm. Thank you," he said. "Kovi and I have discussed this," and he began to smile. "Kovi has been accepted to compete in the Liszt-Chopin Competition in Warsaw this September. An excellent idea, if you ask me!"

An even greater roar of approval filled the room.

17

Early on Wednesday 1st September 1965 Mariah drove Daniyal and Kovi to the airport. They were to fly British Airways direct to Warsaw. Daniyal would need to come back a couple of days earlier for his concert. But Kovi would stay the full eleven days. British Airways pulled out all the stops, treating them as VIP passengers, providing privacy and comfort, and had assured them they would do everything they could to avoid delay to their schedules.

It had turned out that both the Warsaw finals concert and Daniyal's concert were programmed for the same day, the 11th September. As agreed with Huw Wheldon, on the Saturday night at the Royal Albert Hall in London, Daniyal would play the Rachmaninoff 3rd piano concerto with the BBC Symphony Orchestra and Sir Malcolm Sargent as conductor. By contrast, Kovi had to have three concertos ready. The Liszt E flat, the Chopin F minor and the Rachmaninoff No. 3. The jury would

decide who of the three finalists would play which concerto—
and whether Kovi would be one of them.

"It's obvious who's drawn the short straw. And it's not you,
Dad!"

Daniyal laughed and then touched his chest.

"Are you in pain?"

"No, it is just a bit of indigestion I don't seem to be able to shift.
Your mother knows all about it."

"Oh well then, you mustn't drink too much on the plane!" Kovi
joked.

"Just try and stop me!"

Daniyal had been having minor chest pains for a couple of
weeks. He was no hypochondriac, but over the years I'd noticed
even minor concerns about his health seemed to trigger deeper
uncertainties. We had discussed how these feelings appeared to
have begun in childhood. In Daniyal's inner world, whispered
conversations and stories of his family's chequered history had
slow-grown an approaching sense of dark clouds and rumbling
thunder drawing close from a far off place.

Childhood recollections of trauma superglue themselves to our
hidden memory bank. They are never forgotten, although for
years their voice may remain muffled and unprocessed. In
adulthood if the sense of dread should increase, this may
indicate such unfinished emotional business, stalking and
unresolved, somewhere in our early memories. It would prove to
be so for Daniyal when he would come to retrace the agonizing

history of his family's life in Lwów. The booming storm would move overhead, with the resulting trauma, no longer muffled, but deafeningly unveiled.

Conscious of all this, when Daniyal mentioned his concern to me, I was keen to reassure him. "It's probably too much of your favourite spicy food, Daniyal. Plus red wine and whisky in the amount you get through could also be the culprit. But I'm no doctor. As you have the best doctors in the world on your doorstep, why don't you treat yourself to a consultation and put your heart at rest?"

It was indeed his heart that Daniyal was worried about, so a few days later at the end of August, Daniyal took the short walk to Harley Street for a consultation he had booked with Dr. Benjamin Isaacs, a prominent heart specialist.

The famous consulting rooms in Harley Street were not built as private clinics. They were converted from large and lofty houses with several floors similar to those in Weymouth Street. Daniyal found himself a little out of puff by the time he reached the top floor of No. 72, but there with a welcoming smile was Mrs. Parkes, the secretary he had spoken to when he had booked the appointment yesterday. "Hello Mr. Steinfeld. I hope you had a good journey. If you remove your coat, I'll hang it up for you. Take a seat in the waiting room. Doctor won't keep you long."

The waiting room was a comfortable area, with three big sofas and a large table in the centre of the room. The table was piled high with back copies of *Home and Garden*, *The Economist* and *Good Housekeeping* magazine, plus the last two days' editions of

The Times and *The Daily Telegraph.* No one else was waiting to be seen. Daniyal rather enjoyed the time to browse. But as Mrs. Parkes had said, Doctor didn't keep him long.

Dr. Isaacs was tall, with dark hair, a pleasant man in his fifties. He wore a crisply ironed Savile Row Suit with what looked like an Oxford College tie. After initial introductions, Dr. Isaacs took a medical history and carefully examined Daniyal's chest, and afterwards sat down with Daniyal at his desk.

"I have to say we don't have much in the way of tests that we can run for this, but my stethoscope tells me a certain amount. Experience is really our guide in these things. So I can give you an opinion. I think your symptoms could be more than the dyspepsia or heartburn you have described. What I hear through the stethoscope is the sound of the blood as it flows through the heart, and the heart valves, opening and closing. Now I did hear a murmur. And that is an extra or unusual sound which is sometimes caused by a related heart problem. Although quite often, it's not an indicator of anything wrong at all.

"Now I stress I cannot be certain that there is nothing wrong. So my advice is conservative. I suggest you take it easy for four to six weeks. Keep off the alcohol if you can. Do a little gentle gardening, read a few novels, and come back and see me at the end of September or beginning of October. And of course, contact me if you're worried in the meantime.

"By the way, Mr. Steinfeld, what do you do for a living?"

"I am a pianist," Daniyal said, a little irritated that he had not been recognised.

"Well, I do not know whether you ever play concerts, but for the time being I would suggest you stick to playing at home or try piano duets with friends."

Looking through the window, for a moment Daniyal didn't say anything.

"Mmm. Thank you. Thank you, doctor. Thank you very much."

The famous pianist and the famous doctor shook hands. Dr. Isaacs went off to his next patient and Daniyal went home to Mariah.

As he came in the door at Weymouth Street, Mariah called down the stairs, "What did he say?"

"All fine," called back Daniyal. "Just indigestion."

18

Warsaw stands on the Vistula River in east-central Poland. It is the country's capital and Poland's most extensive and populous city. The capital's premier concert hall is The National Philharmonic at 5 Jasna Street. It was built between 1900 and 1901 and reconstructed in 1955. Ten years later, all its facilities still fresh and up to date, it was ready once again to host the five yearly Liszt-Chopin International Piano Competition.

Daniyal and Kovi had arrived in Warsaw on Wednesday afternoon. Daniyal had been amused and not a little flattered by the reception at border control. Handing back their passports, the young official said innocently, "Thank you Mr. Steinfeld, and Mr. Steinfeld." Like an afterthought, he added, "Did you know that Steinfeld is an honoured name in our country?"

"Really?" said Daniyal.

"Yes," said the official. "The Steinfelds are a musical family of several generations. Solomon Ebenezer was a great scholar; Abramczyk was a great pianist and teacher; and many have said that Aleksander was the greatest pianist of his time."

On this occasion, there was no-one waiting behind them. "You seem to know a lot about the Steinfeld family. May I ask you what you do?" asked Daniyal. "I mean, apart from here at the airport?"

"Oh, I want to be a pianist. I am studying with Professor Paweł Bohdanowicz. He's 75 and an inspiration to me. They call him the unashamed accompanist, like your Gerald Moore. The connection is when Paweł was a teenager, he was taught by Abramczyk Steinfeld."

"Well that is remarkable," said Daniyal. "As I know for a fact that my father Aleksander Steinfeld used to play for Paweł. They were close friends for a long time."

"Are you both pianists, Messrs Steinfeld?" said the young man, whose complexion like a boiled beetroot had now turned crimson.

"We are," said Daniyal and Kovi in unison.

Daniyal smiled warmly, and said sincerely, "It's good to be welcomed back to my family's homeland, and to know that despite everything, their memory lives on."

Kovi and Daniyal held out their hands, and Kovi said, "May we ask your name?"

The complexion was returning to normal. "Actually, I am Paweł Bohdanowicz too. Professor Bohdanowicz is my grandfather."

Daniyal was moved. But it was time to go to the hotel.

"Thank you, Paweł. Thank you so very much."

"Thank you Messrs Steinfeld. Welcome to Warsaw and have a nice day."

19

After check-in at The Polonia Palace Hotel on Jerusalem Street, Daniyal and Kovi had a late supper together. From the excellent Polonia menu, they chose Żurek soup made from soured rye flour and meat, and an enormous dish of Sauerkraut and Mushroom Pierogi, washed down with several bottles of Grodziskie beer.

The Polonia Palace Staff had been exemplary in the warmth of their welcome. Daniyal had requested a practice piano for Kovi, and when they were shown into the Presidential suite, there was a Model A Steinway awaiting them. Everything had been provided just as requested.

From the Polonia's staff point of view, they were excited to have Mr. Steinfeld and his son as guests. The competition was famous, and any winner was bound to be a future star. And to think, Mr. Steinfeld senior is a world-famous pianist too! Meeting such people was one of the big benefits of hospitality work!

The manager and his deputy stood to attention as the bags were brought in. They remained when the bell boy left. For a moment they did not say anything , and Daniyal looked at them quizzically. They were not waiting for a tip, they wanted to hear the piano!

"Would you like to check that the piano is to your liking, Mr. Steinfeld?"

"Thank you. It is really for his benefit, not mine. So go on Kovi. Why don't you try it out?"

Which Kovi did, running up and down the keys, like dazzling confetti showering dozens of notes all over the room.

After a couple of minutes, he stopped and declared himself well pleased with "the fine instrument." Whereupon the two managers looking delighted, bade their farewells, bowing and walking backwards at the same time.

"Is it okay?" asked Daniyal.

"Yes, it's just the job. Thank you."

Daniyal looked at his watch. "Long day tomorrow. I guess it is time for bed?"

It was, so they gave each other a hug and went to their ensuites to sleep. Daniyal didn't fall asleep immediately as he had some more indigestion. "It must have been the sauerkraut," he said to himself. He took a tablet his GP had given him, and soon he was snoring contentedly.

The sun rose at 6:30 a.m., which was when Daniyal awoke, not having closed the curtains. Because the car and driver were due at 8:00 a.m., the timing was perfect. That is, if he could get Kovi up in time.

Daniyal knocked. No reply. Kovi was fast asleep. Daniyal quietly entered Kovi's room so as not to wake him abruptly. Seeing Kovi lying there motionless took Daniyal back to the terrible fire which had killed his mother and left Kovi an orphan. How grateful he was for that fire service training. Without it, he would have been powerless, especially as there was no time to spare. If there had been any further delay to the rescue, Kovi also would have been overcome by the fumes and flames. And yet he was spared.

Daniyal was so grateful for the deep privilege—that his mother had committed Kovi into their care, and that Kovi freely chose them as his new parents. "How wonderful that we were able to be that for him and what a truly great son he has become to us," he thought.

All his professional insight and experience convinced Daniyal that Kovi would win this competition. He had not a scintilla of doubt. Kovi was certainly born with this talent, and Mrs. Segal had clearly given him a first quality start as a pianist. But one thing Daniyal had learnt from what his grandfather had taught about the shaping of a concert pianist, the magic is in the training.

That's why there is so often an unbroken line from the great players of the past to the great players of the present. That's how those great gifts turn into great performers. That's how the unique Steinfeld vision, the training and inspiration, has been handed on from one generation to another, from Abramczyk to Aleksander, from Aleksander to Daniyal, and now from Daniyal to Kovi. Daniyal's heart was full of thanksgiving, and he prayed an old synagogue prayer which he had known since childhood.

"Come on Kovi, wake up. Or you'll miss your entry!"

Kovi awoke with a start. "That's funny, I was just dreaming of you. You were carrying me in your arms after the fire next door."

20

The plan for their day off together was for some sightseeing. Daniyal was keen for Kovi to see Lwów, the city where the Steinfelds had lived for so many generations. As Daniyal had said to Mariah, "Steinfeld is not only Kovi's adopted name, he has taken on so much of the Steinfeld inheritance and commission. It will be a great opportunity for him to connect to his Steinfeld forbears."

Lwów is now no longer universally known by its Polish name, but as Lviv, as the city is now part of the Ukraine. Lviv became part of the Soviet Union after the German-Soviet invasion of Poland in 1939 and then part of Soviet Ukraine.

In the years before World War 2, Lviv had the third-largest Jewish population in Poland. This was increased to over 200,000 when war refugees fled to the city. The advancing German army took Lviv in 1941. Such was the intensity of the persecutions, pogroms, and murderous killings of those transported to the Belzec concentration camp, three years later when the liberating Soviet forces reached the town in 1944, only 200—300 Jews remained.

It was a grim story painted on a larger canvas of callous violence. In earlier times, the persecutions experienced by the Steinfelds and other Jewish families were on nothing like the scale which was eventually to engulf the whole city. But the mad intentions and terrifying brutality were the same; the loss and trauma were so profoundly experienced that for many, intergenerationally, its bewildering pain lives on.

Kovi was really keen to visit Lviv. He had heard so much about it from his father. It would be a long day, five hours each way to and from Warsaw, but it would certainly be worth it.

The driver was waiting for them when they came outside after breakfast. His name was Jonas, and he spoke good English. Jonas had grown up in Lviv, so was an ideal guide. The office had briefed him on the Steinfelds' connection with the city and what they wished to see. He was told they were VIP's and he should take especially good care of them.

As they began the drive, Daniyal and Kovi agreed it was a far better idea than driving themselves, map in hand, getting lost and getting cross! Jonas knew all the possible routes and the best way to avoid congestion. He decided to take the Korczowa-Krakovets border crossing, and his instinct was rewarded. Happily, there was no delay.

Though they stopped briefly on the way, their arrival in central Lviv was in good time for lunch. They would have liked to have tried a kosher restaurant—at one time the city would have been full of them—but they couldn't find a single one. However Jonas recommended the long established Szkocka in Shevchenka Avenue. Daniyal and Kovi agreed and invited Jonas to join them. He politely declined. He had planned to visit his cousin, but agreed he would return at 2:00 p.m.

After a beautifully prepared light salad with peppers, ham and sausage, Daniyal was still feeling some indigestion. It came and went, and after another tablet, normal service was quickly restored. As they emerged from the restaurant, Jonas was waiting and sped them away for their requested sight-seeing tour.

While he drove, Jonas explained the long and turbulent history of Lviv.

"If you look up you'll see Castle Hill, and the ruins of our Lviv High Castle. From the 13th to the late 19th century it was one of the city's main defensive forts. And how our city needed defence! Over the centuries, Lviv has faced multiple invaders, among them the Tartars, the Turks, Swedes, and Cossacks and ultimately the Nazis in 1941. I don't need to remind you the Nazi occupation was the most brutal and deadly of all. These days we use the term ethnic cleansing. And it was. My parents weren't Jews, otherwise I wouldn't be here. But they lived through it and witnessed the systematic destruction of Jewish life, culture and the extermination of the city's majority Jewish population."

Jonas paused while they waited at the traffic lights.

"Keep that in mind as we pass some of the city's best landmarks. Lviv has many historic churches, many painstakingly restored.

So there, just coming round the corner, you can see the Boim Chapel. Then we'll come to the Church of Saints Olha and Elizabeth, and shortly the Armenian Cathedral of Lviv. Reflect that before the war, Lviv had no less than 45 synagogues—all of them reduced to rubble by order of the Führer."

They arrived at the Krakivsky Market, one of the largest, but not the oldest in the city. "Would you like to stop here so you can buy some fruit and souvenirs?" asked Jonas.

"No, let's go straight on," said Kovi. Neither of them were in the mood for souvenir hunting.

"No problem. However, can I point out that before World War 2, Lviv's oldest Jewish cemetery was located here on the site of this market. The cemetery was founded in the 14th-15th centuries in the reign of King Jagiello. Many rabbis and leaders of Lviv's Jewish community, including prominent musicians, were buried here. Up to August 1855 when the cemetery was closed during the epidemic, this would have been the resting place of early members of your Steinfeld family. Today, the reason you see a market and not a burial place is the Nazis destroyed the cemetery and used the memorials as paving stones."

"I am not sure I can take much more of this," Daniyal whispered to Kovi. "He is doing a great job and I really appreciate it, but it is tough to hear."

Kovi spoke from the back seat, "Jonas, can we make our ways to Słoneczna Street?"

"Yes, of course." Jonas checked on his map which had the old street names. "I should tell you that Słoneczna Street is now called Kulisha Street. So don't be confused if you don't see Słoneczna on the street name. Kulisha is definitely the street where your grandfather and his family lived."

He drove through the afternoon traffic and in minutes they had arrived. Jonas parked the car, and they were about to set out on foot, when Daniyal said, "This part of our trip is quite personal, Jonas. Would you mind if Kovi and I walk this part alone?

"Of course. I'll look after the car and see you when you come back."

"We won't be that long."

Kulisha street is in the heart of Lviv. Today, there are many apartment buildings. But Daniyal knew from what his father had told him that the old house was on the corner of Kulisha and Vahova Streets. He wasn't expecting the old house still to be standing, as it was burned by the rioters during the 1918 pogrom. With so much reconstruction having taken place since then, and since the Second World War, what they found was a considerable surprise.

As they came round the corner, there was a space between the other buildings with room for twelve cars. Daniyal was genuinely shocked. "Well I never. It's a car park, at least, a sort of car park." He had not known what to expect, but still, they had found it—the ruins of the old Steinfeld family home. Two outer walls were standing, and the rest was rubble, ground down by many years of cars coming and going and parking there.

"So here it is, Kovi. It is all that is left, I'm afraid. It's scarcely believable that so much life and creativity should come to this. A car park—built on a pile of rubble!"

Kovi stood, lost in thought. But something had caught his attention. A car had just left the car park. Its spinning back wheels had dislodged some pieces of stone from the ground at the back of the house, exposing the hardened earth underneath. The sun was bright and looking in the direction of the now vacant car parking space, Kovi thought he saw a glint of light from where the earth had been dislodged. Craning his neck forwards, Kovi looked again and walked in that direction. Using his penknife to dislodge whatever it was from the mud and prise it out, he brought over his find to show Daniyal.

Daniyal shuddered. He stared at the intricately designed oblong cylinder with a cone at each end. "That's a mezuzah, Kovi. A silver mezuzah." He held it in his hand and polished it with his handkerchief. "Of course, I can't be sure it is the same one, but my father was given a silver mezuzah for the door post of his bedroom at his Bar Mitzvah."

Daniyal closed his hand over it and stood in silence. After a few moments tears began to roll down his cheeks. He stared at Kovi, distraught. He was choking his words. "All that goodness and worth and creativity ends up in ruins. Why do they hate us so much? My father lived in this house. He named me after my grandfather. The whole family was murdered because they were Jews. What have we done to deserve all this?"

And with those words the repressed pain of persecution and loss leap-frogged the generations and returned to the place where Daniyal and Kovi were standing. To the rubble—all that remained of Abramczyk Steinfeld and his family and their precious Lwów home.

Then came the crash. The pain hit Daniyal like a Panzer tank. The flood gates opened, everything around appeared to be spinning out of control, and Daniyal began to sob in an agony from deep within, a distress that appeared inconsolable.

Two women and a child passed close by. They looked concerned and appeared to offer help. Kovi gave them an appreciative hand wave to signify, "Thanks and we're okay actually."

And they were okay. After some minutes, Daniyal was feeling calmer. "I'm really so sorry Kovi. I had no idea it would affect me like this. I think this has waited years to come out."

Kovi smiled and gave his father a long hug.

21

The journey back to Warsaw was long and uneventful. Daniyal slept most of the way. Kovi catnapped, but while it was light he enjoyed the changing scenery. Jonas had done a wonderful job, and the car arrived back at the Polonia Palace by 11:30 p.m. Alighting, they both thanked their driver warmly and Daniyal pressed a large tip into his hand. Jonas was appreciative, if perhaps a little embarrassed, as he had sensed something of the pain they had experienced on their visit.

There was nothing else planned for the evening, so with the competition beginning tomorrow, it was straight to bed.

They both slept well. Daniyal especially. He didn't always dream sweetly, but this was an exception. He was playing piano duets with his father at the Queen's Hall in London. What year was this? There was no Blitz and no war. It was a beautiful sunny evening, and as they chatted about everything good in life, in family and in music, they could hear the birds singing in full voice as they walked up Langham Place towards the hall.

When they arrived they found the audience to be full of friends and family. Daniyal's grandparents, Abramczyk and Anna had come from Lwów, along with his aunt Gerda and Uncles Jakub and Syzmon. They were joined by Alexander and Vera Siloti, as kind and considerate as ever. Alexander was wearing his clown's outfit; and like a warmup artist was performing handstands, backflips and magic tricks with flower posies, much to the audience's delight, and Leah's amusement.

First on the programme was the second book of Brahms Hungarian Dances. The music is so carefree, and the audience clapped along, enjoying every moment. Most of all, it was such fun playing with his Dad again, especially since Aleksander's right hand was as good as new, and he was able to play with both hands. Then onto the stage, who should appear, but Kovi, beaming but looking so smart and debonair, twenty years older than Daniyal remembered him. Kovi played a lovely expressive "Ballade for the left hand"—his own composition, and exquisite in every sense. Mariah looked on with such pride.

Then the finale. From his place in the front row, Abramczyk joined them. Anna and the children beamed at him as he walked round to climb the few steps to the stage. Abramczyk seemed overjoyed to be with his Steinfeld family. Smiling broadly as he joined the others, the audience had reserved for him the most enthusiastic welcome of all. And so four generations of pianists gathered to make music together. Aleksander, Daniyal and Kovi taking the lower parts, with Abramczyk on top. One piano, eight hands.

The next morning, Kovi and Daniyal washed and dressed, Kovi making sure he looked extra smart. After breakfast, feeling upbeat and in far stronger spirits than yesterday, Kovi and Daniyal took a cab to 5 Jasna Street, The National Philharmonic Concert Hall.

On the way in, while Kovi completed the registration, Daniyal had noticed with pleasure on the Information Board that Nadia Boulanger was to be the chair of the jury. And there she was, making her way coming towards him. Her eyesight was not good, and he could see her peering in his direction through her thick, grey tinted lenses. Then, when she was close enough to make him out, in her heavily French accented English she uttered a joyful cry of recognition, "But you are I am sure, Daniyal Steinfeld, and I am so pleased to see you."

There were kisses on both cheeks and one more for luck, and the two figures began to reminisce about the coaching that, as a teenager, Daniyal had received from Mademoiselle. (Mademoiselle was Boulanger's preferred mode of address. Only Aaron Copland called her Nadia, and we always gained the impression that she would have preferred him not to!)

Most of her pupils linked this formality to Boulanger's family. She was the daughter of the Russian princess, Raissa Myshetskaya, and there was a Royal correctness in her demeanour and expectations of others. One of her pupils called her "the tender tyrant," for she was a woman of enormous passion and the highest musical standards.

It's true Boulanger could be strong, even strident at times, but so many pupils knew her to be the kindest and most compassionate of women. During the short time when Kovi took consultation lessons with her, he had strained a muscle in his back. Boulanger immediately contacted her own physician and made every effort to personally supervise his care.

It was no exaggeration when a musicologist described Nadia Boulanger as "the most influential teacher since Socrates." The list of those she taught and mentored is breath-taking. It includes Igor Stravinsky, Dinu Lipatti, Clifford Curzon, Leonard Bernstein, Aaron Copland, Quincy Jones, George Gershwin, Astor Piazzolla, Philip Glass and many others. Given the range, ability and attainment of her students, Nadia Boulanger certainly justifies her reputation as the most influential, advanced teacher of music of the 20th century, and probably of all time.

Before entering the National Philharmonic Hall, Daniyal had not realised Mlle Boulanger was to chair the jury. So he was delighted, not only to see Mademoiselle again, but also to know that her presence would ensure the members would make a well-informed decision in the choice of the prize winners.

Daniyal was disappointed he could not stay for the finals gala concert on Saturday, as he was due to play the Rach 3 at the Last Night of the Proms. However, there was time for him to attend some of the preliminary sessions, and to hear Kovi rehearse his three concertos and play his recitals, as well as to explore some of the culinary attractions of this lovely city.

22

├────────┤

Thursday 9th September came, and it was time for Daniyal to return to London. Through the competition thus far, Kovi had played with exemplary style and expression, and with his usual super virtuosity. Boulanger had remarked quietly to Daniyal, "Kovi plays like a muse inspired. His keyboard skills are unparalleled. Such spontaneity of heart! It's as though the music is composed for us as we listen. He is a true Steinfeld." And smiling warmly, she pressed Daniyal's hand in her own.

Kovi had nothing apart from practice on his agenda that morning, so he planned to spend part of the time travelling to the airport with his Dad. Before he did, he asked his father for some help with the three concertos he had to have ready for the final—if he made it that far.

"Of course you will make it that far Kovi. But I am glad to see your modesty. As I think you will know, modesty has never come easily to me. Difficult though that visit to Lviv was, I can see more clearly now than ever, where the need for esteem and acclaim has come from. It's complex. But life is, isn't it, especially if you are a Jew. Let's just say I am so glad you have inherited the best parts of the Steinfeld Commission, and not the part that at times has almost crushed me."

Daniyal put his hand on Kovi's shoulder. "You are a great son, Kovi."

"And you're a great father. And you'll be even greater if you can help me figure out this passage in the Rachmaninoff first movement cadenza."

So Kovi played for Daniyal what is sometimes called the Ossia, which is in fact the cadenza as Rachmaninoff originally conceived it. It is virtuosity, invention, agony and joy all rolled into one. Even Rachmaninoff found it demanding. But Kovi played it like he'd known it since he was in nappies. His playing was fluent and commanding in every way.

Daniyal said to Kovi, "You remember what I said in the *Monitor* Masterclasses? 'If there should be no agony in your heart, how will you recognise the composer's agony and portray it? And without hope living deep within you how will you recognise the light when it shines forth through the music?'

"That's all I'd say to you. If they ask you to play the Rachmaninoff, make sure you feel every moment, the agony and the hope. Let your own experience of agony inform the way you play it. And let your hope and faith shine forth as light when the light appears. So play it to me again."

Kovi played the cadenza a second time.

"Exactly. Truly beautiful. Bravo. Bravissimo, Kovi."

23

As promised, British Airways took great care of their VIP passenger, and Daniyal's flight landed just after 4:30 p.m. Mariah was there to meet him, and she drove them back through the late afternoon traffic to the West End and to Weymouth Street. Daniyal was feeling cheerful and energized. He was pleased the indigestion had gone away. "Must have been all that beer and sauerkraut that did the trick. They should turn them into tablets!"

Daniyal told Mariah about his chance encounter with Mademoiselle, and how affirming she had been about Kovi's playing in the competition.

"Did you tell Kovi?"

"Of course I did."

"You'll make his head grow as big as yours if you're not careful!"

"I think that's unlikely. I have a special line in pride, from which I think he is pretty well immune. But I did suggest that he didn't brag about it."

"And I must tell you about our day trip to Lviv. It was 5 hours each way. Honestly, Mariah, the story is harrowing, to put it mildly. But overall I am glad we did it. It is a city that silently portrays the worst horrors of the Shoah and all the Nazis' devastation. Once the streets teemed with Jewish people. So it's a silent witness: the Jews aren't there anymore. Nor are the synagogues, nor any Jewish hospital, school, shop or cemetery, or any other connection. The Nazis attempted to wipe out every Jewish memory.

"But the main thing is—we found the house on Słoneczna Street. It was on the corner with Vahova Street as my father remembered. I say 'the house'—all that remained was two damaged walls and a pile of rubble roughly converted into a car park. I don't know what I expected to see, but that was a shock. And then Kovi found something special in the dried mud.

"A parked car that had just left the car parking space dislodged some rubble, revealing some dry earth beneath. Kovi saw something glinting in the sun, dislodged it with his penknife and I could not believe my eyes. It was an intricately carved silver mezuzah case, just like the one my father was given at his Bar Mitzvah. He had it on the door post to his bedroom.

"I can't be sure, of course. But I think it is very likely to be the actual one. Even if we can't prove it, I still felt the similarity of the engraved antique silver case and its chance discovery among the ruins of Aleksander's childhood home was so significant. I tell you, Mariah, it had quite an effect on me."

"Did you dissolve, my darling?"

"Yes my sweetheart, and how!"

"So where is the mezuzah?"

"It was sort of finders keepers. Lwów and Słoneczna Street meant a great deal to Kovi, and he asked if he could keep it in his pocket for the competition. 'It will remind me of the rock from which I have been hewn.' I am sure now he understands what that rock represents: so much of great worth, but memories of such great loss and sometimes crushing expectation. I said to him, 'It's a rock with jagged edges.' He knows that, but he is a fortunate young man. He has all the gifts, but none of the neuroses. And this is Kovi's week. Mark my words, Mariah, come Saturday, our son Kovi will show the world he is a true Steinfeld."

24

‖————‖

It was Saturday 11th September, Daniyal was to play at the Proms, and Kovi was expected to reach the final in the Warsaw piano competition. Daniyal had already rehearsed with the BBC Symphony Orchestra and Flash Harry, the promenaders' affectionate nickname for Sir Malcolm Sargent, their conductor.

Since he returned from Warsaw on Thursday, Daniyal had been practising the Rachmaninoff third Piano Concerto with his customary attention to detail and an eye to what Boulanger had taught him: la grande ligne, the big sweep of the music. Daniyal always said, no matter how many times you have played a piece you should take nothing for granted. It was the way Siloti had taught both his father and Rachmaninoff. For each performance, work as though you were learning the piece afresh. And in the demanding passages, "Very slow practice, increasing the speed by one metronome notch at a time at each play through. Any mistakes—practice that passage in isolation, then go back a notch and start again."

Daniyal gave special attention to the cadenza, Rachmaninoff's original, as it is the emotional hub not only of the opening movement, but in a sense—of the whole concerto. The orchestra comes to a pause, and the focus is entirely on the pianist and the composer's most inner thoughts and feelings. It is a masterpiece within a masterpiece, where agony and light are revealed in fullest measure. The virtuosity required is supremely demanding. It was so for its composer, and equally even for Daniyal Steinfeld.

Daniyal loved the challenge of this piece, its beauty and powerful emotional world. When he left the house he was looking forward to the concert with an enthusiasm he hadn't felt for quite a time. As they got into the car, he noticed the neighbours from next door where the Segals once lived, walking with their teenage son. He thought of Kovi, with deep gratitude for all the joy the three of them had so unexpectedly shared in life. As Mariah drove Daniyal back to the Royal Albert Hall, he said a silent prayer for Kovi for his important Saturday in Warsaw.

With Mariah's expert driving (Daniyal always preferred to be the passenger) they arrived as planned on the dot of 6:30 p.m. and Jimmy on the stage door recognised him immediately. Daniyal liked to be recognised. They walked to the Green Room, where one of the doors had his name on it. He put down his case. After a moment or two, there was a quiet knock. It was Sir Malcolm

Sargent who had come to welcome them. It was kisses for Mariah and a gentle handshake for Daniyal.

"Well it has been a wonderful Proms season, Daniyal. I am sure your Rachmaninoff is going to be a real highlight too. I've marked the score with all those tempo points we rehearsed so I won't forget. Oh, and we have arranged for a microphone so you can announce a couple of encores. I'm sure the promenaders will want more, but for the sake of the broadcast, could we stick to two please?"

"No problem," said Daniyal smiling, and not a little amused.

"The telephone in here works for incoming and outgoing calls. I've told the switchboard that you might receive a call from Warsaw, and if it comes in the next hour to patch it through. It's a joy to see you both, and such a privilege to have you play for us. Such a great work too."

Just after Sir Malcolm left, the telephone rang. The operator said, "Is that Mr. Steinfeld? I have a call for you from a Mr. Steinfeld. Do you wish to take the call?"

Daniyal could feel his heart beating. "Yes, of course, thank you," he said. Then after a few crackles, he heard Kovi's voice bursting with enthusiasm. "Hello Dad, it's your son and heir."

"That must mean it's you, Kovi." Daniyal was full of smiles. "How have you got on?"

"I've got to the final, Dad. There are three of us, and the concert has already started. Guess what? They have asked me to play the Rachmaninoff. So I'll be on at 8:30 p.m., after the interval."

"That's wonderful Kovi. Your time has come—you deserve to win it. By the way, if you get a chance, do tell Mademoiselle I am also playing the Rachmaninoff at the Proms while you're playing in Warsaw. It will make her smile. Look, I must go. Enjoy this wonderful music and feel it with every sinew of your soul. Strong fingers, strong emotions. I'll be with you every note of the way. Much love, Kovi, very much love. I'll pass the phone to your mother."

25

"This is the BBC Home Service. Welcome to this last night of the Proms brought to you direct from the Royal Albert Hall in London. This 49th concert in this 1965 series promises some outstanding music making and the usual last night party atmosphere. We are joined once more by the BBC Symphony Orchestra and the conductor, Sir Malcolm Sargent. In the first part of the programme we are to hear one of the most powerful and attractive works of the Piano Concerto repertoire. The Piano Concerto No. 3 in D minor, op 30 by Sergei Rachmaninoff.

"Rachmaninoff composed his concerto in the summer of 1909, and dedicated it to Josef Hofmann, like Rachmaninoff, one of the truly great pianists of the time. It is a work of intense beauty and feeling and reflects the master pianism of its composer. The work requires the highest level of technical and interpretive skill, and we are privileged tonight to welcome a master pianist of this generation, one of the world's greatest and most internationally acclaimed super virtuoso pianists, Daniyal Steinfeld.

"I was speaking to Mr. Steinfeld earlier, and he told me of 'a first for the record books.' That as Daniyal Steinfeld brings us Rachmaninoff's concerto here at the Royal Albert Hall, his son Jacob will play the same concerto in Warsaw as a finalist in the International Liszt-Chopin Piano Competition.

"Now I saw the leader come in just a moment ago, and we are waiting for Sir Malcolm Sargent and tonight's soloist, Daniyal Steinfeld.

"Here they come. They bow. It seems the party has already begun. Promenaders will hardly let him sit down. They are cheering him without a note yet played. What a welcome for Daniyal Steinfeld!

"Sir Malcolm has tapped his baton and our soloist is seated now. So we await a treat of music making.

"Rachmaninoff's Piano Concerto No. 3 in D minor."

26

At the National Philharmonic Hall in Warsaw, the last competitor in the gala final round had just taken the stage. He was warmly welcomed by the discerning audience, knowing his roots and treating him as one of their own.

Everyone was smartly dressed, including Kovi, who was in tails. There was a great sense of expectation in the hall. The magic of the Steinfeld name and reputation had somehow survived the persecution, rubble and passing years.

That afternoon Kovi had met a woman of 75 who had asked to see him. As a child prodigy, she had taken lessons from Abramczyk and knew Aleksander too. She squeezed Kovi's hand and said in Polish, "Cieszymy się, że możemy powitać naszego chłopca w domu." (We are so glad to welcome our boy home.)

Some had queued for over twelve hours for seats, and the organisers had decided in the afternoon that they would have to provide a sound relay for outside the hall, so as not to disappoint those they could not accommodate.

As Kovi came on to the platform to join the Warsaw National Philharmonic Orchestra he was greeted with much applause from everyone present, including the players. Kovi looked relaxed and controlled. He shook the conductor's hand and then the leader's. He had so enjoyed his week: the special time with Daniyal, getting to know the other competitors, and the initial rounds, as well as becoming reacquainted with Mlle Boulanger, the teacher from whom he and his father had both learnt so much.

Daniyal was right, when Kovi told her about the Proms performance, her face lit up with delight. "But now you should play duets," she joked.

Before Kovi signalled to the conductor to begin, he touched the mezuzah in his pocket and then kissed his finger. Then he nodded.

27

The applause was thunderous. The whole audience, all 5,000 of them, led by the Promenaders were on their feet cheering, stamping, and shouting 'Bravo.' It had been one of those performances where the wind had been in Daniyal's sails from the first note to the last. It was quite exceptional even by his standards. Sargent had set the tempi exactly right, and the orchestra's ensemble had been exemplary. The music, with its irresistible mix of glorious melody and high drama emerged in one long, unbroken line. It was, in short, a triumph for all.

The BBC announcer described the scene. "The Promenaders are stamping their feet, calling out 'Steinfeld, Steinfeld.' I hope he will respond and give us an encore or even two. Yes, for the fourth time, Mr. Steinfeld is returning to the platform. The audience are wild with enthusiasm. He bows once and sits at the piano."

Daniyal spoke through the microphone. "I noticed the programme mentions that my father Aleksander made his

Proms debut 54 years ago, in the old Queen's Hall, under Sir Henry Wood." (More cheering.)

"After he lost the use of his right hand, Aleksander gave several Proms performances with his left hand alone. As a tribute to him, I am going to play you the Revolutionary study of Chopin in the extraordinary left-hand arrangement by the Polish piano virtuoso, Leopold Godowsky.

"The city of Warsaw is behind this piece. Invaded by the Russians in 1831, it's said that as soon as Chopin heard of the invasion he ran straight to the piano and in passionate defiance improvised this remarkable Revolutionary Study. And tonight, Warsaw is in my thoughts too. For tonight is the final of the Warsaw International Piano Competition. As we speak, my son Jacob is playing the same Rachmaninoff concerto we've heard portrayed this evening. I am so proud of him, as I am of my father. I dedicate this performance to them both."

In the National Philharmonic Hall, in a sudden, thrilling extra burst of energy and passion, Kovi thundered the final octave passage, while the orchestra blazed the triumphant closing chords.

And what a triumph it was! Like the roar for a winning goal the audience exploded with joy. Kovi hugged the conductor, shook hands with the orchestra's leader, and then bowed, his right hand to his chest. Then came the bouquets of flowers. Four to start with. With a brief word of Polish, Kovi received each in turn. More and more arrived, and while the applause continued unabated, he left and returned to the platform four times.

Kovi wondered if his father would be playing his customary encores by now, and what he would play. But of course, no encores for Kovi. He could see the members of the jury getting up to leave.

It wouldn't be long.

There was more enthusiastic applause at the Royal Albert Hall. Daniyal left the platform. Of course it was a bit of a game. He loved the adulation. The audience cheered. The Promenaders began to stamp and continued their chant of "Steinfeld. Steinfeld." Sir Malcolm Sargent gave him a gentle push. "Go put them out of their misery, Daniyal." So Daniyal reappeared to hoots of approval and went straight to the piano.

"Thank you so much for your appreciation. It means a great deal to me, more than I can say. I am going to play for you a most exquisite piece by the friend and contemporary of Rachmaninoff, Nikolai Medtner. It's his Sonata Reminiscenza. Reminiscenza means more than its English equivalent, reminiscence. It means deep, sometimes painful memories. Emotion recollected in tranquillity. Like we might sometimes share a toast to absent friends. For Medtner, the reminiscence was to do with the world and the people that perished with the Russian revolution.

"For me, it's to celebrate what is now four generations of our Steinfeld family. Abramczyk, Aleksander, myself, and now a new beginning in our son Jacob, Kovi as we call him. Not least because we are Jews, in each generation our family has faced persecution. The miracle is that my grandfather's Steinfeld

Commission, which is for the benefit of the whole musical world, has not perished. The magic of it is in the teaching, which most certainly lives on, and which I'm sure you'll soon hear and enjoy in the playing of Jacob Steinfeld.

"So as I play this to you, I am thinking of my family. You may wish to bring your own memories of family, friends, or places you once knew which are no more. It is a Sonata Reminiscenza, after all. May I ask at the end, to respect the silence, and that you don't applaud until I lift my hands from the keyboard?

"Raise a glass to absent friends."

The hall hushed as Daniyal began to play.

In Warsaw, the Jury had finished their deliberations. The audience had taken their places. The three finalists were brought onto the stage by Nadia Boulanger. There was an excited buzz inside the hall. All the finalists had played well. Some said it was the highest standard of playing that could be remembered in any piano competition for many years. Boulanger tapped the microphone and spoke in English.

"First, we congratulate and thank you, the audience, for listening so attentively tonight and throughout the competition. Your warmth and enthusiasm has meant so much to our competitors."

There was some brief applause.

"Second, we thank all those who have competed so bravely over the last nine days. We understand the stresses of performance generally, but it is made all the harder by the competitive atmosphere. We have heard some wonderful playing.

"Third, we should remind ourselves this event is not really about the musicians but the music. All of us are servants. One composes, one plays, and one listens. 'We are the music makers, we are the dreamers of dreams.'

"The jury awards just the one prize in this five yearly Liszt-Chopin International Piano Competition. It is for the pianist who the jury believe gave us the greatest insight into the mystery of the music they presented to us, delivered with outstanding pianism.

"The jury were unanimous, and we believe you will be too. The first prize for Warsaw's 1965 Liszt-Chopin International Piano Competition goes to Jacob Steinfeld."

It was like a new Warsaw uprising. Inside and outside the hall the joy, clapping and applause were deafening. Kovi bowed and bowed. He could hardly believe all this enthusiasm was for him. In this way, Kovi was rather unlike his father. But Kovi knew that, and why. He also was under no illusion how very much he was indebted to Daniyal Steinfeld. "I can't wait to tell him, 'Dad I've won.'"

Daniyal played the Sonata Reminiscenza with a focused purity of line, and an intimacy which touched so many present in the hall and those listening at home. It is indeed music of deep mystery, pathos, and as Daniyal had described it, of exquisite beauty.

With unparalleled sensitivity and concentration as he came towards its quietly tapering ending, as many said afterwards, Daniyal looked as though he were in another world of memories and deepest thought.

And so Daniyal played the last soft notes of Medtner's piece, his thoughts dancing between Kovi and Warsaw, his father and the Queen's Hall concert, the bombing of Bolsover Street and the rubble of Słoneczna Street. At the final bar, he held his hands on the keys to allow the sound to fade naturally away.

And there he stayed, without moving.

After a minute's silence had past, Sir Malcolm, who had stood throughout listening from the podium, turned to look at Daniyal. "Daniyal," he whispered, "are you alright?"

When he received no reply, he went over to the piano, and gently put his hand on Daniyal's shoulder. The leader of the orchestra had also stood up to help.

But there was no waking him, for Daniyal Steinfeld had been gathered to his fathers.

28

OBITUARY

———

The New York Gazette
12 September 1965

The music world mourns the passing of the uniquely talented and great pianist, Daniyal Steinfeld, who died suddenly last night at the conclusion of a concert at the Royal Albert Hall in London. By all accounts, Steinfeld had played an astonishingly powerful rendition of the Rachmaninoff Piano Concerto No. 3; some say as luminous and moving as any in his career.

Daniyal Steinfeld was the third generation of Polish Jewish concert pianists, whose virtuosity and high achievements were marred by antisemitism, accident, and war-time tragedy. Daniyal, being born in London soon after his parents fled from the persecutions in Lwów in 1918, learnt the Steinfeld piano method. This followed the now legendary Steinfeld Commission instituted by his grandfather while with his family he was held captive in a pogrom in Lwów. All his life, Daniyal struggled with the memory of the traumatic events which befell his father's and grandfather's generation; but he loved the life of a concert pianist which was the gift bequeathed to him by his remarkable family.

Daniyal Steinfeld was a player in whom there was a perfect match of the most robust technique and deeply felt musicianship. Although he made no secret of his supreme technical facility, the music and its meaning always came first.

In a recently televised series of masterclasses for the BBC, Steinfeld said, "I have come to believe the performer's role is to portray the beating heart of the music... To discover this life, if there should be no agony in your own heart, how will you recognise the composer's agony and portray it? And correspondingly, should there be no resonance of hope within you, how will you recognise the light for what it is, and when it shines forth through the music?"

This great master pianist always said the magic which belongs to the Steinfeld Commission is uniquely found in the Steinfeld teaching. That was clearly recognised last night while Daniyal played Rachmaninoff in London, his son, Jacob, was declared winner of the five yearly Liszt-Chopin International Piano Competition in Warsaw. Jacob has proved himself a fine artist, a fourth generation and true Steinfeld heir—and for the world of music, a new star is born.

Michael Kowalski.

A biography of Daniyal Steinfeld by Michael Kowalski, *A Pianist's Legacy* will be published next year.

CHARACTER LIST

¦————————¦

(in order of appearance; historical figures listed in bold)

Daniyal Steinfeld, pianist

Passport official, aka Big Ears, Columbo

Michael (and Clara) Kowalski, psychotherapist

Sir Adrian Boult, conductor

Leonard Bernstein, composer

Andy Collinger, Daniyal's US agent

Aleksander and Leah Steinfeld, Daniyal's parents

Alexander (and Vera) Siloti, pianist and Aleksander's teacher

Josef Hoffman, Polish pianist

Abramczyk and Anna Steinfeld, Aleksander's parents

Mr Lewandowski, manager of Lew i Sala

Maciej Kremblewski, auctioneer

Sergei Rachmaninoff, Russian composer and pianist

Theodor Leschetizky, Abramczyk's teacher

Alfred Józef Potocki, former Minister-President of Austria and owner of the Potocki Palace

Edvard Grieg, Norwegian composer and pianist

Stefan Rosenwasser, Anna Steinfeld's brother
Gerda, Jakob and Syzmom Steinfeld, Aleksander's siblings
Grandma Elsa Steinfeld, Abramczyk's mother
Solomon Ebenezer Steinfeld, Abramczyk's father
Karol and Suzanna Rosenwasser, Anna's parents
Aaron and Liliana Rosenwasser, Leah's parents,
and Aleksander's uncle and aunt
Paweł Bohdanowicz, Aleksander's schoolfriend
Mirtel Grzelak, Aleksander's schoolfriend
Ignacy Jan Paderewski, Polish pianist, composer and politician
Vasily Safonov, Director of the Moscow Conservatoire
Sergei Taneyev, Moscow Conservatoire teacher, pianist and composer
Alicja and Pyotr Yermalov, Aleksander's aunt and uncle
Sasha, Caucasian Shepherd dog
Kyriena Siloti, daughter of Alexander and Vera Siloti
Ernest Newman, music critic
Josef Stránský, Conductor, New York Philharmonic Orchestra
Felix Weingartner, Conductor Vienna Philharmonic Orchestra
Victor Bogdanovich, Postman
Michał Arct, bookseller and Aleksander's 'agent'
Dr. Karl Muck, Conductor Boston Symphony Orchestra
Arabella Goddard, pianist and teacher
Ossip Gabrilowitsch Russian pianist
James (and Georgina) Painter-Reeves, Director, Steinway and Sons

Leopold Godowsky, Polish American pianist and composer
PC William Blandford, community policeman
Jeremy Blandford, Aleksander's pupil
Sir Gerald Williamson, Chairman of the Board of Governors, Guildhall School of Music
Sir Henry Wood, Conductor and founder of 'The Proms'
Robin and Sheila Headley, Mariah Steinfeld's parents
Jeremy Woolfson, Manager, Steinway and Sons
Sir Aylmer Firebrace, Head of the National Fire Service
Sasha Kuczynski, Rabbi and author of 'Music and Meaning'
Jacob Steinfeld (Kovi) pianist and adopted son of Daniyal and Mariah
Huw Wheldon, BBC 'Monitor' presenter
Yuri Tomakov, masterclass participant
James Gibb, British pianist and teacher
Jane Waterman, masterclass participant
Vlado Perlmeuter, French pianist and teacher
Nadia Boulanger, Celebrated French teacher and chair of the Warsaw competition jury
Van Cliburn, American pianist
Mrs Parkes, Harley Street receptionist
Dr. Benjamin Isaacs, Consultant physician
Jonas, Lviv driver
Jimmy, Stage door manager Royal Albert Hall
Sir Malcolm Sargent, Principal conductor BBC Proms

MUSIC PLAYED BY THE STEINFELDS

(in order of performance)

Liszt, Sonata in B minor

Liszt, Grand Galop Chromatique

Berlioz Symphonie Fantastique arr Franz Liszt

Vaughan Williams, Piano Concerto

J S Bach Prelude and Fugue in C minor Book 2, 48 Preludes and Fugues

Chopin, Nocturne in C minor op 48

Tchaikovsky, Pas de deux, The Nutcracker, arr Siloti

Chopin, Winter Wind Étude, No. 11 op 25

Brahms, Hungarian dances, for piano duet

Chopin, Fantaisie Impromptu op 66

Beethoven, Pathétique Sonata

Schubert, Wanderer Fantasy

Schubert, Die Wintereisse, song cycle

Schumann, Dichterliebe, song cycle

Gabriel Fauré, Aprés un rêve; Claire de lune

Alkan, Symphony for Solo Piano

Edvard Grieg, Piano concerto

Chopin, Prelude in E minor op 28 No. 4

Chopin, Revolutionary Study arr Godowsky for left hand

Beethoven, Hammerklavier Sonata op 106

Tchaikovsky, Piano concerto No. 1

Nikolai Medtner, Sonata Reminiscenza in A minor, op 38 No. 1

Bach, Chaconne in D minor arr Brahms for left hand

Mozart, Piano Concerto No 19 in F major K. 459

Beethoven, Rage over a Lost Penny, op 129

Paderewski, Minuet in G

Schumann, The Davidsbündlertänze op 6

Schumann, C major Fantasy op 17

Schumann, Symphonic Studies

Godowsky left-hand study No. 5 in D flat major

Brahms, Piano concerto No. 2

Felix Blumenfeld, Étude for the Left-Hand op 36

Godowsky, left hand Chopin transcriptions in C sharp minor,
Nos. 6 and 22

Godowsky, Passacaglia in B minor

Liszt, Hungarian Rhapsody No. 2

Vera Lynn, 'We'll meet again'

Rachmaninoff, Rhapsody on a theme of Paganini

Jacob Steinfeld, Rhapsody on a Polish Jewish theme (unpublished!)

Chopin, Revolutionary study arr Godowsky for the left hand

Rachmaninoff, Piano Concerto No 3 in D minor op 30

THE STEINFELD

FAMILY TREE

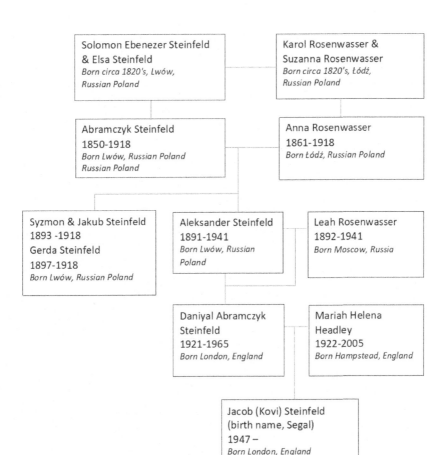

Solomon Ebenezer Steinfeld
& Elsa Steinfeld
Born circa 1820's, Lwów,
Russian Poland

Karol Rosenwasser &
Suzanna Rosenwasser
Born circa 1820's, Łódź,
Russian Poland

Abramczyk Steinfeld
1850-1918
Born Lwów, Russian Poland
Russian Poland

Anna Rosenwasser
1861-1918
Born Łódź, Russian Poland

Syzmon & Jakub Steinfeld
1893 -1918
Gerda Steinfeld
1897-1918
Born Lwów, Russian Poland

Aleksander Steinfeld
1891-1941
Born Lwów, Russian
Poland

Leah Rosenwasser
1892-1941
Born Moscow, Russia

Daniyal Abramczyk
Steinfeld
1921-1965
Born London, England

Mariah Helena
Headley
1922-2005
Born Hampstead, England

Jacob (Kovi) Steinfeld
(birth name, Segal)
1947 –
Born London, England

AUTHOR'S NOTE

International Acclaim is a work of fiction. Although the main Steinfeld characters interact with many historical figures, all the conversations and situations are imagined. Throughout the narrative I have drawn considerably upon my own professional experience as a composer, pianist and psychotherapist and my upbringing in a Jewish home. Apart from a few of my Polish family names, literary investigators will not unearth my veiled presence in the novel—as the story is neither autobiographical nor an exercise in wish fulfilment!

Authors often gain insight into their characters through the lens of their own experience, and there are a few general connections here. In the late 1970's, I was a composition and piano student of Nadia Boulanger, whose role figures prominently in aspects of the Steinfeld story. Through an accident, I lost the full facility of my right hand and can no longer play the piano as I once did. That gave me insight into Aleksander's disability. From early life, I was also affected by some aspects of the intergenerational pain suffered by Daniyal Steinfeld.

As a psychotherapist I have worked with several former child prodigies, some of whom, like Daniyal, struggle with issues of esteem arising from an excess of early life acclaim. I have drawn on such insights, but again, I am not Michael Kowalski and the account is not autobiographical.

However, one element here which is definitely me is the exploration of the passion that lies behind the music. That's how I chose to write a novel about four generations of Polish Jewish concert pianists, and to journey with the Steinfelds from 1850 to 1965. Their situations and musical achievements are of course exceptional, but their life-themes are common to us all: attachments, aspirations, attainments, losses, joys and sorrows. It's in that sense their emotional world touches my world with deeper meaning—and I hope, your world too.

Printed in Great Britain
by Amazon